In Praise of The Adventures of Telemachus

"... There is an agreeableness in the Odyssey that I strongly approve."

—Boileau, French poet, critic, 1699

~

"The [Adventures of] Telemachus is a unique book that is at the same time a novel and a poem. It seems that the author wanted to treat the novel as Bossuet treated history, in giving it a dignity and unknown charms, and above all in drawing from these fictions a moral useful to humankind."

—Voltaire, French writer, historian, and philosopher, 1731

~

"Speaking to the heart and mind, his work is able to achieve the beautiful, the noble, the grave, the sweet and the tender, for which it is worthy of admiration and eternal gratitude."

—Montesquieu, French philosopher, author, circa 1750

~

"Recommending several French books to Peter Carr, who was just starting to study the language, Jefferson placed [Les Aventures de] Télémaque first. The work, too, may have exerted an influence on Jefferson's nascent political thought. It not only emphasized the responsibilities rulers have to their subjects, but also affirmed the congruence between the government of man and the harmony of nature."

—Kevin J. Hayes, The Road to Monticello, The Life and Mind of Thomas Jefferson, 2008

"Mentor spoke truth: for three centuries, Fénelonian wisdom, struck with this intonation, did not cease being heard by men who write and think. And the unity of Fénelon's style—this style one recognizes among all others—has done much to prolong the signs of wisdom on earth. It is there the prestige of ideas takes shape: the style sustains them and their beauty is inscribed into memory. A sentence well done does not allow itself to be either corrupted or twisted, and a book well done, like *Telemachus* or the *Maxims of the Saints*, is the last thing one could tear apart."

—MARCEL ARLAND, French novelist, literary critic, 1951

~

"Fénelon may be the most neglected of the major moral and political thinkers of early modernity. His political masterwork [*The Adventures of Telemachus*] was the most-read book in eighteenth-century France after the Bible. Enlightenment philosophers from Leibniz to Bentham testified to his genius."

—RYAN PATRICK HANLEY, *Fénelon* (p. iii).
Oxford University Press. Kindle Edition. 2020

The Adventures of Telemachus

Fénelon

TRANSLATED FROM THE FRENCH BY N. HEWITT

2025

Fenelon Classics

Copyrighted Material

The Adventures of Telemachus

English translation and notes copyright © 2025 by Fenelon Classics LLC.

All rights reserved no part of this publication may be reproduced or transmitted in any form or by any means, electronic or mechanical, including photocopy, recording, or any information storage and retrieval system, without permission in writing from the publisher.

For information about permission to reproduce selections from this book, please write to Fenelon Classics LLC, PO Box 22041, Houston, Texas 77227 or info@fenelonclassics.com.

www.fenelonclassics.com

ISBNs:
979-8-9913959-0-8 (paperback)

Printed in the United States of America

Interior Design by 1106 Design.
Cover Design by Paraclete Design.

aux philosophes

to lovers of wisdom

TABLE OF CONTENTS

Foreword	ix
Prologue	xi
Book I	1
Book II	17
Book III	37
Book IV	59
Book V	77
Book VI	109
Book VII	133
Book VIII	159
Book IX	179
Book X	209
Book XI	243
Book XII	279
Book XIII	299
Book XIV	335
Book XV	371
Book XVI	397
Book XVII	415
Book XVIII	447

Afterword	471
Acknowledgments	475
Illustrations	477
Notes on Translation	483
Selected Bibliography	487
Provenances of Names	493
About the Author	503

FOREWORD

The Adventures of Telemachus (te-lem'-a-kus) is the story of a prince, written for a prince. It is an epic prose poem composed more than three centuries ago at the peak of the age of French classicism. Inspired by ancient Greek myths, this seventeenth-century masterpiece represents many aspects of modernity: it is the first "poëme en prose", as well as the first novel written for a young adult; it develops Homer's Mentor into the archetype of "mentorship"; it is thought by many to represent a new genre of the time—the roman à clef, that is to say, a thinly veiled portrayal of contemporaries and events; and lastly, it introduces the rise of the "honnête-homme"—one who is not necessarily noble, but is cultivated and knows the rules of *politesse*. Under the reign of Louis XIV, nobility was no longer understood to be a question of birth, but of merit.

Emulating classical Greece, the cultural elite of the seventeenth century privileged order and sobriety over the previous baroque era of flourishes and eccentricity. As the celebrated French poet and critic Boileau wrote in 1674, "Whatever is well conceived is clearly said, and the words to say it flow with ease." Theatrical, literary and musical works inspired by antiquity addressed a restricted audience, composed of the high society that gravitated to the court of Versailles. The chateau and its surroundings were adorned with classical Greco-Roman heroes, gods and deeds. Thus, mythological characters were not only familiar to, but popular with the prince, for whom this book was conceived.

Toward the end of his ten-year preceptorship to the royal princes of France, François Fénelon hurriedly pieced together *The Adventures of Telemachus* to amuse the young prince, while instilling lessons of wisdom and leadership befitting a future king of France. Many of these lessons were gleaned from earlier writings of Fénelon for his charges in the form of Fables and Dialogues of the Dead. It is written as an imaginative tale of young prince Telemachus, the son of Odysseus, and his coming of age while searching for a father he has never known. Throughout his adventures, he is accompanied by the goddess of wisdom, Athena, disguised as his guardian, Mentor. The events that unfold have Telemachus facing perils and hardships in the brutal world of ancient Greece. During the course of his journeys, he endures suffering and heartache, encounters heroes and villains, experiences love, lust and betrayals, wages war, fosters peace, all leading to hard-won lessons in the formation of a king who fosters good mores and the pursuit of happiness for his peoples.

PROLOGUE

The *prologue* and epilogue of *Telemachus* must begin, and end, with the epic poem from which it is spun, *The Odyssey*. Like the Greek poet Homer, Fénelon begins in medias res—jumping right into the action, before weaving in the backstory. He picks up the thread of the story where Homer leaves off, when Telemachus sets sail in search of his father. Therefore, some acquaintance with the first four books of *The Odyssey*, known as the Telemacheia, will establish the opening scene.

In the first few lines of Homer's Book 1 of *The Odyssey*, the audience is reintroduced to a hero of *The Iliad*, King Odysseus of Ithaca. Having angered Poseidon, the god of the sea, Odysseus has not been allowed to return home after the toppling of Troy. He has been held captive on the island of the nymph-goddess Calypso for seven years. At an assembly of the gods, from which Poseidon is absent, Athena, the goddess and protector of Odysseus, appeals to Zeus, to allow him to return home. Zeus assents.

Indulged by the father of the gods, Athena descends from Mount Olympus to the island of Ithaca, taking on the shape of a neighboring chieftain. Welcomed with princely hospitality by Odysseus' son, Telemachus, she listens to his woes caused by Odysseus' absence and witnesses the many suitors mocking the prince, exploiting the palace, and pursuing Queen Penelope. The chieftain (Athena in disguise) advises Telemachus to fit out a ship and set sail in search of his father.

With this encouragement, Telemachus confronts the brash suitors in an assembly. He is supported by old Mentor, to whom Odysseus had entrusted the care of his household. Mocked yet again by the suitors, Telemachus leaves the assembly to walk the beach and calls on the goddess Athena. He prays to her about the advice he had received from the neighboring chieftain and bemoans the perfidy of the suitors. In the shape of Mentor, Athena appears before him, urging him to follow the chieftain's advice and set sail. Without informing the queen, Telemachus and Mentor embark.

Meanwhile, on her remote island, the nymph-goddess Calypso has been commanded by Zeus, through his messenger Hermes, to allow Odysseus to return home. Piqued that Odysseus would choose Ithaca and Queen Penelope over her offer of immortality on a happy island, she bids him farewell and warns of the pains in store for him.

Odysseus departs on his vessel and thus this tale begins...

THE ADVENTURES OF
TELEMACHUS
SON OF ODYSSEUS

BOOK I

Calypso could not console herself after the departure of Odysseus. In her pain, she found herself unhappy being immortal. Her grotto no longer resounded with her song. The nymphs who served her dared not speak to her. She often strolled alone on the flowery turf that bordered her island in an everlasting springtime. But these beautiful places, far from moderating her pain, only served to remind her of the sad memory of Odysseus, whom she had seen alongside her so many times. Often, she remained motionless on the shore of the sea, watering it with her tears and incessantly turning toward the side where Odysseus' vessel, plowing the waters, had disappeared before her eyes.

Suddenly, she caught sight of debris from a ship that had just wrecked: shattered rowing benches, oars scattered hither and yon on the sand, a rudder, a mast, cordage floating along the coast. Then she spied from afar two men, one of whom appeared old; the other, though young, resembled Odysseus. He had his gentleness and pride, along with his build and majestic gait. The goddess realized that it was Telemachus, son of this hero, but, although the gods surpass by far all men in knowledge, she could not tell who the venerable man accompanying Telemachus was; for the superior gods hide whatever they please from those inferior, and Athena, who was accompanying Telemachus in the figure of Mentor, did not wish to be known to Calypso.

All the same, Calypso rejoiced at a shipwreck that put on her island the son of Odysseus, so like his father. She advances toward him, and pretending not to know who he is, asks, "Where does this temerity to land on my island come from? Know, young stranger, that one does not come into my empire with impunity."

She tried to cover under these menacing words the joy in her heart, which glowed on her face in spite of herself.

Telemachus answered, "O you, whomever you may be, mortal or goddess (though to see you, one could only take you for a deity), would you be insensitive to the misfortune of a son, who, seeking his father at the mercy of the winds and the waves, saw his ship break apart against your rocks?"

"Who is, then, your father that you seek?" resumed the goddess.

"His name is Odysseus," said Telemachus. "He is one of the kings who, after a ten-year siege, overthrew the famous Troy. His name was celebrated throughout Greece and throughout Asia for his valor in combat and even more for his wisdom in council.

Now, roaming the whole stretch of the seas, he crosses all the most terrifying reefs. His homeland seems to flee before him. Penelope, his wife, and I, his son, we have lost hope of seeing him again. I race on, with the same dangers as him, to learn where he is. But, what am I saying, perhaps he is now buried in the deep abysses of the sea. Take pity on our misfortunes, and, if you know, O goddess, what the destinies have done to save or to destroy Odysseus, deign to inform his son Telemachus."

Calypso, stunned and touched to see in one so young so much wisdom and eloquence, could not sate her eyes in gazing at him, and she remained silent. Finally, she said to him, "Telemachus, we will apprise you of what befell your father, but the story is long. It is time for you to unwind from all your travails. Come into my dwelling, where I will receive you as my son. Come, you will be my consolation in this solitude, and I will make your happiness, provided you know how to enjoy it."

~

Telemachus followed the goddess, surrounded by a throng of young nymphs, above which she rose a full head, the way a great oak in a forest raises its thick branches above all the trees surrounding it. He marveled at the radiance of her beauty, the rich purple of her long and flowing robe, her hair casually, yet charmingly, knotted behind, the fire that leapt from her eyes, and the sweetness that tempered this vivacity. Mentor, eyes downcast, keeping a restrained silence, followed Telemachus.

They arrived at the entrance to Calypso's grotto, where Telemachus was surprised to see, with an appearance of rustic simplicity, all that can enchant the eyes. One saw neither gold, nor silver, nor marble, nor columns, nor paintings, nor statues there. This grotto was carved into the rock, in vaulted ceilings filled with rockery and shells. It was tapestried with a young vine that stretched its supple branches equally on all sides. Gentle zephyrs preserved in this place, despite the blazing heat of the sun, a delightful coolness. Springs, flowing with a gentle murmur over fields sprinkled with amaranths and violets, formed in several spots baths as pure and clear as crystal. A thousand budding flowers enameled the green carpet that surrounded the grotto. There, one found a wood of those leafy trees that bear golden apples, the flower of which, blooming again in all seasons, spreads the sweetest of all perfumes. This wood seemed to crown those beautiful meadows and formed a night that the rays of the sun could not pierce. There, one only ever heard the singing of birds or the noise of a stream that, rushing from the top of a rock, tumbled in a great gush full of foam and fled across the meadow.

 The grotto of the goddess was on the slope of a hill. From there one beheld the sea, sometimes as clear and smooth as glass, sometimes madly angry with the rocks on which it shattered, groaning and billowing its waves like mountains. On another side, one saw a river where islands formed, bordered with blossoming linden trees and tall poplars that held their lofty heads in the clouds. Several canals that formed islands appeared to play in the countryside; some were rapidly rolling their clear waters, others had a peaceful and sleeping water, others, through long winding turns, were retracing their steps, as if ascending back toward their source and seemed unable to quit those enchanted banks. One spied in the distance hills and mountains that lost themselves in the clouds and whose bizarre shape formed a horizon to delight the eyes. The neighboring mountains were covered with verdant vines that hung in festoons. The grape, more brilliant than royal purple, could not hide under the leaves, and the vine was bowed by its fruit. The fig, olive, pomegranate, and all the other trees covered the countryside, making a great garden of it.

Calypso, having shown Telemachus all these beauties of nature, said, "Rest. Your garments are wet. It is time you changed out of them. Afterward, we will see each other again, and I will recount stories to you that will touch your heart."

At the same time, the goddess had him enter with Mentor into the most secret and remote part of a grotto neighboring the one where she dwelt. The nymphs had taken care to light a great fire of cedar wood in this place, the good scent of which wafted to all sides, and they had left garments for the new guests. Telemachus, seeing that a tunic of a fine wool, the whiteness of which surpassed that of snow, was intended for him, and a purple robe with gold embroidery, took the pleasure that is natural to a young man in considering this magnificence.

Mentor said in a grave tone, "Are these, O Telemachus, the thoughts that should occupy the heart of the son of Odysseus? Think instead of sustaining the reputation of your father and vanquishing Fortune who persecutes you. A young man who loves to vainly attire himself like a woman is unworthy of wisdom and glory. Glory is only due a heart that knows how to suffer difficulty and trample pleasure underfoot."

Telemachus answered, sighing, "May the gods destroy me rather than suffer that softness and voluptuousness capture my heart. No, indeed, the son of Odysseus will never be vanquished by the charms of a cowardly and effeminate life. But what favor from heaven caused us to find, after our shipwreck, this goddess, or this mortal, who showers us with goods?"

"Fear," Mentor rejoined, "that she does not laden you with evils. Fear her deceitful sweetness more than the reefs that broke apart our ship—shipwreck and death are less dreadful than the pleasures that attack virtue. Be very wary of believing what she will tell you. Youth is presumptuous. It expects everything of itself alone; though fragile, it believes it can do everything and never have anything to fear; it confides lightly and without precaution. Be wary of listening to the flattering sweet speech of Calypso, which will slither like a serpent beneath the flowers. Fear the hidden poison. Distrust yourself and always wait for my counsel."

Then they returned alongside Calypso, who was awaiting them. The nymphs, with their braided hair and white robes, first served a meal, simple, yet exquisite in taste and elegant in presentation. No meat was seen other than that of birds they had caught in their nets, or animals they had pierced with their hunting arrows. A wine sweeter than nectar flowed from great silver vessels into golden cups rimmed with flowers. Baskets were brought in filled with all the fruits that spring promises and autumn spreads over the land. At the same time, four young nymphs began to sing.

First, they sang of the combats of the gods against the giants, then the amours of Zeus and Semele, the birth of Dionysus and his education guided by old Silenus, the race of Atalanta and Hippomenes, who was victor by means of golden apples picked from the garden of Hesperides; lastly, the Trojan war was also sung, the combats of Odysseus and his wisdom were raised to the heavens. The head nymph, who was called Leucothea, joined the chords of her lyre to those sweet voices. When Telemachus heard the name of his father, the tears that streamed down his cheeks gave a new luster to his beauty. But as Calypso perceived that he could not eat and that he was seized with pain, she motioned to the nymphs. Instantly, they sang of the combat of the Centaurs with the Lapiths, and the descent of Orpheus to the Underworld to retrieve Eurydice.

When the meal was ended, the goddess took Telemachus aside and spoke to him, "You see, son of the great Odysseus, with what favor I receive you. I am immortal. No mortal can enter into this island without being punished for his temerity, and even your shipwreck would not save you from my indignation if I did not otherwise love you. Your father had the same good fortune as you, but, alas, he did not know how to profit from it. I kept him on this island for a long time. He had only to live here with me as an immortal, but blind passion to see his miserable homeland again made him reject all these advantages. You see all that he lost in order to see Ithaca again, which he was not able to see again. He wanted to forsake me; he departed, and I was avenged by the tempest. His vessel, after having been the toy of the winds, was buried in the swells. Profit from so sad an example. Since his wreck, you no longer have anything to hope for, neither to see him again, nor to ever reign on the island of Ithaca after him. Console yourself in having lost him since you find here a deity ready to make you happy, and a kingdom that she offers you."

The goddess added a lengthy speech to these words to show how happy Odysseus had been alongside her. She recounted his adventures in the cavern of the Cyclops Polyphemus and at the house of Antiphates, king of the Laestrygonians. She forgot nothing of what had befallen him on the island of Circe, daughter of the Sun, nor the dangers he had run between Scylla and Charybdis. She described the last tempest that Poseidon had unleashed against him when he left her. She wanted it understood that he had perished in this wreck, and she suppressed telling of his arrival on the island of the Phaeacians.

Telemachus, who had at first abandoned himself too promptly to the joy of being treated so well by Calypso, finally recognized her artifice and the wisdom of the counsel that Mentor had just given him. He responded in few words. "O goddess. Forgive my pain, now I can only grieve. Perhaps afterward I will have more strength to enjoy the fortune you are offering me. Allow me in this moment to mourn my father. You know better than I how much he merits being mourned."

Calypso dared not, at first, to press him further; she even feigned to enter into his pain and to soften toward Odysseus. But, to better know the means of touching his heart, she asked him how he had shipwrecked and by what adventures he was on these coasts.

"The story of my misfortunes," he said, "would be too long."

"No, indeed," she said, "I long to know them. Hasten to recount them to me."

She pressed him for a long time. In the end, he could not resist her, and he spoke thus:

"I had left Ithaca to go and ask the other kings returned from the siege of Troy for news of my father. The suitors of my mother, Penelope, were surprised by my departure—I had taken care to hide it from them, knowing their perfidy. Neither Nestor, whom I saw at Pylos, nor Menelaus, who received me with friendship in Lacedaemon, were able to inform me whether my father was still alive. Weary of always living in suspense and uncertainty, I resolved to go into Sicily, where I had heard it said that my father had been tossed by the winds. But wise Mentor, who you see present here, opposed this rash scheme. He represented to me on the one hand the Cyclops, monstrous giants that devour men, and on the other the fleet of Aeneas and the Trojans who were on those coasts:

"'Those Trojans,' he said, 'are animated against all Greeks, but particularly they will gladly shed the blood of the son of Odysseus.'"

"'Return to Ithaca,' he continued. 'Perhaps your father, loved by the gods, will be there as soon as you. But, if the gods have resolved his loss, if he should never see his homeland again, at the least you must go avenge him, deliver your mother, demonstrate your wisdom to all the peoples, and cause all Greece to see in you a king as worthy of reigning as Odysseus ever was himself.'

"These words were salutary, but I did not have enough prudence to listen to them. I only listened to my passion. Wise Mentor loved me so much as to follow me into a rash voyage that I undertook against his counsel, and the gods permitted me to commit an error, which ought serve to correct me of my presumptuousness."

While he was speaking, Calypso was looking at Mentor. She was stunned. She believed to sense in him something divine, but she could not untangle her confused thoughts; so, she remained filled with fear and distrust at the sight of this stranger. Then she became apprehensive lest Mentor should see her distress.

"Continue," she said to Telemachus, "and satisfy my curiosity."

Telemachus resumed, "We had for some time a favorable wind for going to Sicily. But then a dark tempest stole the sky from our eyes, and we were wrapped in a deep night. By flashes of lightning, we caught sight of other vessels exposed to the same peril, and we soon recognized that they were Aeneas' vessels. They were to be feared no less than the rocks. Then I understood, but too late, what the ardor of an imprudent youth had kept me from considering attentively.

"In this danger, Mentor appeared not only firm and intrepid but even more cheerful than usual; it was he who encouraged me. I felt that he inspired an invincible strength in me. He was tranquilly giving every order while the pilot was distressed. I said to him, 'My dear Mentor, why did I refuse to follow your counsel? Was I not unfortunate in having wanted to believe myself, at an age when one has neither foresight of the future, nor experience of the past, nor restraint to manage the present. O! If we ever escape this tempest, I will distrust myself like my most dangerous enemy. It is you, Mentor, whom I will always believe.'

"Mentor, smiling, responded, 'I am far from wanting to reproach you for the error you made. It suffices that you sense it and that it will serve to make you more moderate in your desires another time. But, when the peril is passed, the presumptuousness will perhaps return. For now, we must support each other through courage. Before plunging into peril, it must be anticipated and feared, but, when it is here, it only remains to scorn it. Be then the worthy son of Odysseus. Show a heart greater than all the evils that threaten you.'

"The gentleness and courage of wise Mentor entranced me, but I was even more surprised when I saw with what address he delivered us from the Trojans. At the moment when the sky was beginning to clear, and when all the Trojans, seeing us up close, would not have failed to recognize us, he noticed one of their vessels that the tempest had separated, almost identical to ours, and whose stern was wreathed with certain flowers. He hastened to put similar flowers on our own stern. He attached them himself with small bands of the same color as those of the Trojans. He ordered all our oarsmen to crouch as low as they could over their rowing benches to avoid being recognized by the enemy. In this state, we passed through the middle of their fleet. Seeing us, they loosed cries of joy, as if seeing companions they had thought lost. We were even compelled, by the violence of the sea, to go along with them for some time. Finally, we remained a little behind and, while the impetuous winds pushed them toward Africa, we made the final effort, by dint of rowing, to land on the neighboring coast of Sicily.

"We arrived there indeed. But what we sought was hardly less calamitous than the fleet we were fleeing. We found on this Sicilian coast other Trojan enemies of the Greeks. It was there that old Acestes out of Troy reigned. Barely had we arrived on this shore when the inhabitants believed we were either other peoples of the island armed to overtake them, or foreigners who were coming to capture their lands. In their first frenzy, they burned our vessel and slit the throats of all our comrades. They only spared Mentor and me to present us to Acestes so that he could learn from us what our designs were and where we came from. We entered the city with our hands tied behind our backs, and our death was only delayed to use us as spectacle for a cruel people when they learned that we were Greek.

"Straightaway, they presented us to Acestes who, holding his golden scepter in hand, was judging the peoples and preparing for a great sacrifice. He asked us, in a severe tone, for our country and the purpose of our voyage.

"Mentor hastened to answer, and said to him, 'We come from the coasts of the great Hesperia, and our homeland is not far from there.'

"In this way, he avoided saying that we were Greek. But Acestes, without listening further, and taking us for foreigners who were hiding their plan, ordered we be sent into a neighboring forest, where we would serve as slaves under those who govern his flocks. This condition seemed harsher to me than death. I cried out,

'O King! Execute us rather than treat us so unworthily. Know that I am Telemachus, son of the wise Odysseus, king of the Ithacans. I am seeking my father throughout the seas; if I can neither find him, nor return to my homeland, nor avoid servitude, take from me the life that I would not know how to bear.'

"No sooner had I pronounced these words than all the people, stirred up, cried out that the son of that cruel Odysseus, whose artifices had overthrown the city of Troy, must perish.

'O son of Odysseus,' Acestes said, 'I cannot refuse your blood to the mānes of so many Trojans that your father hurled onto the banks of the black Cocytus. You and the one who guides you, you will perish.'

"At the same time, an old man of the troop proposed to the king to sacrifice us on the tomb of Anchises. 'Their blood,' he said, 'will be agreeable to the shade of this hero. Aeneas himself, when he learns of such a sacrifice, will be touched to see how much you love what he cherished most in the world.'

"All the people applauded this proposition and only thought thereafter of sacrificing us. Already, they led us on to the tomb of Anchises; two altars had been erected there, where the sacred fire was lit. The glaive that should impale us lay before our eyes. They had crowned us with flowers, and no compassion could save our lives. We were done for when Mentor tranquilly asked to speak to the king. He said to him, 'O, Acestes! If the misfortune of young Telemachus, who has never borne arms against the Trojans, cannot touch you, at least may your own interest touch you. The science that I have acquired of presages and of the will of the gods causes me to know that before three days have elapsed, you will be attacked by barbarous peoples, coming like a torrent from the top of the mountains to flood your city and ravage all your country. Hasten to prevent them. Arm your peoples and waste not a moment to bring the abundant flocks you have in the countryside within your walls. If my prediction is false, you will be free to sacrifice us in three days. If, on the contrary, it is true, remember that one must not take the life of those to whom one owes it.'

"Acestes was stunned by these words that Mentor said to him with such assurance that he had never found in any man.

"'I see well,' he responded, 'O foreigner, that the gods, who have so poorly shared with you all the gifts of fortune, have granted you a wisdom that is more estimable than all prosperity.'

"At the same time, he delayed the sacrifice and diligently gave the orders necessary to prevent the attack with which Mentor had threatened him. From all sides, one only saw trembling women, stooped old men, little children with tears in their eyes, who were withdrawing into the city. The bellowing oxen and bleating ewes came in droves, quitting the rich pastures and unable to find enough stables for shelter. There were, from every direction, confused cries of people pushing one another, unable to hear each other, who, in the midst of this trouble, took a stranger for their friend, and who were running without knowing where to set their feet. But the principals of the city, believing themselves wiser than the others, thought that Mentor was an impostor who had made a false prediction to save his life.

"Before the end of the third day, while they were filled with these thoughts, they saw on the slope of the neighboring mountains a whirlwind of dust. Then they spotted a countless troop of armed barbarians—it was the Himerans, ferocious peoples, along with the nations that live on the Nebrodes Mountains and on the summit of Acragas, where a winter reigns that the zephyrs never ease. Those who had scorned Mentor's wise prediction lost their slaves and their flocks.

"The king said to Mentor, 'I forget that you are Greeks. Our enemies become our loyal friends. The gods have sent you to save us! I expect no less of your valor than of the wisdom of your counsel. Hasten to rescue us.'

"Mentor shows in his eyes an audacity that stuns the proudest fighters. He takes a shield, a helmet, a sword, a lance; he ranks Acestes' soldiers; he marches at their head and advances in good order toward the enemy. Acestes, though full of courage, can only, in his old age, follow him from afar. I follow him more closely, but I cannot equal his valor. His cuirass resembled, in combat, the immortal aegis. Death raced everywhere from rank to rank under his strikes. Resembling a Numidian lion that cruel hunger devours, and that enters upon a flock of weak ewes—he rends, he slaughters, he swims in blood, and the shepherds, far from rescuing the flock, flee trembling to get away from his fury.

"Those barbarians, who were hoping to take the city by surprise, were themselves surprised and disconcerted. Acestes' subjects, animated by the example and orders of Mentor, had a vigor they did not believe themselves capable of. With my lance I knocked the son of the king of this enemy people to the ground. He was my age, but he was much taller than me, for this people came from a race of giants who were of the same origin as the Cyclops. He scorned an enemy as weak as me. But, undaunted by his prodigious strength or his savage and brutal air, I thrust my lance against his chest and made him vomit, in dying, torrents of a black blood. He thought to crush me. In his fall, the noise of his armament reverberated to the mountains. I took his spoils, and I returned to Acestes with the armor of the dead that I had removed. Mentor, having put the enemy into disarray, carved them to pieces and pushed the deserters into the forests.

"An outcome so unexpected caused Mentor to be regarded as a man cherished and inspired by the gods. Acestes, touched with gratitude, warned us that he feared everything for us should Aeneas' vessels return to Sicily. He gave us one to return to our own country, showered us with presents, and pressed us to depart to prevent all the misfortunes that he foresaw. But he did not want to give us either a pilot or any oarsmen of his own nation for fear they would be too exposed along the coasts of Greece. He gave us Phoenician merchants, who, being in commerce with all the peoples of the world, had nothing to fear, and who must bring the vessel back to Acestes when they had left us in Ithaca. But the gods, who play with the designs of men, reserved other dangers for us."

END OF BOOK I

THE ADVENTURES OF
TELEMACHUS
SON OF ODYSSEUS

BOOK II

"The Tyrians, through their pride, had provoked the great King Sesostris, who reigned in Egypt and who had conquered so many kingdoms. The riches they had acquired through commerce and the strength of the impregnable city of Tyre, situated in the sea, had swelled the hearts of these peoples. They had refused to pay Sesostris the tribute that he had imposed on them upon returning from his conquests, and they had supplied troops to his brother, who had wanted, upon his return, to massacre him amidst the rejoicing at a great feast.

"Sesostris had resolved, in order to put down their pridefulness, to disrupt their commerce throughout the seas. His vessels were going in all directions, seeking Phoenicians. An Egyptian fleet encountered us as we were beginning to lose sight of the mountains of Sicily. The harbor and the land seemed to flee behind us and lose themselves in the clouds. At the same time, we see Egyptian ships approaching like a floating city. The Phoenicians recognized them and wanted to distance themselves, but there was no longer time. Their sails were better than ours. The wind favored them. Their oarsmen were in greater numbers—they come alongside us, seize us, and take us as prisoners to Egypt.

"In vain I represented to them that I was not Phoenician; they barely deigned to listen to me. They regarded us as slaves in which the Phoenicians trafficked, and they only thought of the profit from such a prize.

"We already notice the waters of the sea whiten through mixing with that of the Nile, and we see the Egyptian coast, almost as low as the sea. Then we arrive at the island of Pharos, neighboring the city of No; from there we proceed up the Nile to Memphis.

"If the pain of our captivity had not rendered us numb to every pleasure, our eyes would have been enchanted to see that fertile land of Egypt, resembling a delightful garden watered by an infinite number of canals. We could not cast our eyes on the two banks without seeing opulent cities, country homes agreeably situated, lands that are covered every year with a golden harvest, never resting, meadows full of flocks, plowmen who were bowed under the weight of the produce that the earth poured forth from her womb, shepherds making the sweet sounds of their flutes and chalumeaux echo all around them.

"'Happy,' Mentor said, 'are the people who are led by a wise king. They are in abundance; they live happily and love the one

BOOK II

to whom they owe all their happiness. It is in this way,' he added, 'O Telemachus, that you must reign and make the joy of your peoples, should the gods ever grant you possession of the kingdom of your father. Love your peoples as your children; enjoy the pleasure of being loved by them and make it so that they can never feel peace and joy without being reminded that it is a good king who brought them those rich presents. Kings who only think of making themselves feared and crushing their subjects in order to render them more submissive are the scourges of humankind. They are feared as they wish to be, but they are hated, detested, and have even more to fear from their subjects than their subjects have to fear from them.'

"I responded to Mentor, 'Alas! It is not a question of thinking of maxims by which one must reign. There is no longer any Ithaca for us. We will never see either our homeland or Penelope again, and, even if Odysseus returns full of glory to his kingdom, he will never have the joy of seeing me there; never will I ever have that of obeying him in order to learn how to command. We are dying, my dear Mentor. No other thought is permitted us any longer. Let us die, for the gods have no mercy on us.'

"While I was speaking so, deep sighs cut off my words. But Mentor, who feared evils before they arrive, no longer knew what it was to fear them as soon as they arrived.

'Unworthy son of the wise Odysseus," he exclaimed, "what then, you allow yourself to be vanquished by your misfortune! Know that you will one day see the island of Ithaca and Penelope again. You will even see in his former glory the one you have not known—the invincible Odysseus whom Fortune cannot beat down and who, in his misfortunes even greater than yours, teaches you to never be discouraged. O! If he should learn in the distant lands where the tempests have cast him that his son knows neither how to imitate his patience nor his courage, this news would crush him with shame and would be rougher on him than all the misfortunes he has so long suffered.'

"Then Mentor pointed out to me the joy and abundance spread throughout the Egyptian countryside, where one counted up to twenty-two thousand cities. He was admiring the good policies of those cities: the justice exercised in favor of the poor against the rich; the good education of the children, who are accustomed to obedience, work, sobriety; love of the manual arts and scholarship; exactness in all religious ceremonies; selflessness, the desire for honor, the fidelity to men, and the reverential awe of the gods that each father inspired in his children. He never wearied of admiring that beautiful orderliness.

'Happy,' he told me incessantly, 'are the people that a wise king leads in this way. But even happier the king who makes the happiness of so many peoples and who finds his own in his virtue. He is more than feared, for he is loved. Not only do they obey him, but more—he is even king of every heart; each, far from wanting to be rid of him, fears losing him and would give their life for him.'

"I noted what Mentor said and I felt courage born again deep in my heart as this wise friend was speaking to me.

"As soon as we had arrived in the opulent and magnificent city of Memphis, the governor ordered we go on to Thebes to

BOOK II

be presented to King Sesostris, who wanted to examine things himself and was extremely animated against the Tyrians. So we continued up the length of the Nile to that famous Thebes of a hundred gates where that great king lived. This city looked to be of an immense expanse to us and more populated than the most flourishing cities of Greece. The policies there are perfect for the cleanliness of the streets, the waterworks, the convenience of the baths, the cultivation of the arts, and public safety. The plazas are ornamented with fountains and obelisks. The temples are of marble and a simple, yet majestic architecture. The palace of the prince is like a great city to him alone. Only there does one see marble columns, pyramids and obelisks, colossal statues, furniture of gold and solid silver.

"Those who had taken us told the king that we had been found on a Phoenician ship. He listened each day at certain set hours, to all those of his subjects who had either complaints to make or advice to give him. He neither scorned nor rebuked anyone and believed himself king only in order to do good for all of his subjects, whom he loved as his children. As for foreigners, he received them with goodwill and wanted to see them because he believed that one always learned something useful in informing oneself of the mores and manners of distant peoples.

"This curiosity of the king caused us to be presented before him. He was on a throne of ivory, holding in hand a golden scepter. He was already old, yet agreeable, full of gentleness and majesty. Every day he judged the peoples with a patience and a wisdom that was sincerely admired. After having worked all day long to regulate affairs and to render an exact justice, he unwound in the evening by listening to learned men or conversing with the most upright people, whom he knew well how to choose for admittance into his inner circle. One could only reproach him throughout his life for having triumphed with too much pageantry over the kings he had vanquished, and of having trusted in one of his subjects, whom I will describe to you presently.

"When he saw me, he was touched by my youth and my pain. He asked me for my homeland and my name. We were astonished by the wisdom coming out of his mouth. I answered him, 'O great king, you are not ignorant of the siege of Troy, which lasted ten years, and her ruin, which cost so much bloodshed to all Greece. Odysseus, my father, was one of the principal kings who ruined that city. He roves over all the seas, unable to find the island of Ithaca again, which is his kingdom. I am seeking him, and a misfortune like his caused me to be taken. Restore me to my father and my homeland. Thus may the gods preserve you for your children, and have them feel the joy of living under so good a father.'

"Sesostris continued to regard me with an eye of compassion, but, wanting to know if what I said was true, he sent us back to one of his officers, who was charged with determining from those who had taken our vessel if we were actually Greeks or Phoenicians.

"'If they are Phoenicians,' said the king, 'they must be doubly punished for being our enemies, and even more for wanting to deceive us with a cowardly lie. If, on the contrary, they are Greek, I want them treated favorably and sent back to their country on one of my vessels, for I love Greece—many Egyptians have given laws to them. I am familiar with the virtue of Heracles, the glory of Achilles has reached us, and I admire what has been told me of the wisdom of the unfortunate Odysseus. It is my pleasure to come to the aid of hapless virtue.'

"The officer with whom the king charged the examination of our affair had a soul as corrupt and artful as the soul of Sesostris was sincere and generous. This officer was named Metophis. He interrogated us by attempting to entrap us, and as he saw that Mentor answered with more wisdom than me, he regarded him with aversion and distrust—for the wicked are irritated by the good. He separated us, and from that moment on, I did not know what became of Mentor.

"This separation hit me like a thunderbolt. Metophis was still hoping that, in questioning us separately, he would be able to make us say contradictory things. Above all, he thought to dazzle me with his flattering promises and make me confess what Mentor had hidden from him. In the end, he was not seeking the truth in good faith, but wanted to find some pretext to tell the king that we were Phoenicians in order to make us his slaves. Indeed, despite our innocence and despite the king's wisdom, he found the means to deceive him.

"Alas, what kings are exposed to. Even the wisest are often taken in. Artful and self-serving men surround them. The good withdraw because they are neither eager to please nor flatterers. The good wait until they are sought, and princes hardly know how to seek them. In contrast, the wicked are bold, deceitful, eager to insinuate themselves and to please, adept at dissimulation, ready to do anything against honor and conscience to satisfy the passions of the one who reigns. O how unfortunate a king is to be exposed to the artifices of the wicked! He is lost if he does not repulse flattery and if he does not love those who boldly tell the truth. Voila. Those were my reflections during my misfortune, and I recalled everything that I had heard Mentor say.

"Meanwhile, Metophis sent me to those mountains of the Oasis desert with his slaves so that I might serve with them in driving his great flocks."

At this spot, Calypso interrupted Telemachus, saying, "Well! What did you do then, you, who had preferred in Sicily death to servitude?"

Telemachus answered, "My misfortune was ever-increasing. I no longer had the miserable consolation of choosing between servitude and death. It was necessary to be a slave and exhaust, so to speak, all the rigors of fortune. There no longer remained any hope in me, and I could not even say a single word to strive to free myself. Mentor has since told me that he had been sold to Ethiopians and followed them into Ethiopia.

"As for me, I arrived in the dreadful deserts. There one finds scorching sands in the middle of the plains; snows that never melt, causing a perpetual winter on the summits of the mountains, and, for feeding the flocks, one only finds pastures among the rocks toward the middle of the slope of those craggy mountains. The valleys are so deep there that the sun can barely light them with her rays.

"I found no other men in this country than shepherds as wild as the country itself. There, I spent the nights deploring my misfortune and the days following a flock to avoid the brutal fury of a head slave, who, hoping to procure his freedom, incessantly accused the others in order to highlight his zeal and devotion to his master's interests. This slave was named Butis.

~

"I was bound to succumb in these circumstances. Pain pressing down on me, I forgot about my flock one day, and I stretched out on the grass alongside a cavern where I awaited death, no longer able to bear my sorrows.

"At that moment, I noticed the entire mountain quaked; the oaks and firs seemed to bow down from the summit of the mountain; the winds held their breath; a bellowing voice came out of the cavern, and caused me to hear these words:

'Son of the wise Odysseus, you must become, like him, great through patience. Princes who have always been happy are hardly worthy of being so—softness corrupts them, pridefulness intoxicates them. How happy you will be if you overcome your misfortunes and if you never forget them. You will see Ithaca again, and your glory will ascend to the heavens. When you are the master of other men, remember that you have been weak, poor, and suffering like them. Take pleasure in comforting them, love your people, detest flattery, and know that you will only be great to the extent you are restrained and courageous in vanquishing your passions.'

"These divine words penetrated to the bottom of my heart. They caused joy and courage to be reborn. I did not feel that blood-curdling terror that makes the hair stand on end when the gods communicate with mortals. I sat up tranquilly. Kneeling, hands raised toward heaven, I venerated Athena, to whom I believed I owed this oracle. At the same time, I found myself a new man. Wisdom enlightened my mind; I felt a gentle strength to moderate all my passions and arrest the impetuosity of my youth. I made myself loved by all the shepherds of the desert. In the end, my meekness, my patience, my exactitude appeased the cruel Butis, who was in authority over the other slaves and who had wanted, in the beginning, to torment me.

"To better endure the tedium of captivity and solitude, I sought books, for I was overwhelmed with boredom for want of some instruction that could feed my mind and sustain it. *Fortunate, I was saying, are those who are disgusted by violent pleasures and who know how to be satisfied with the sweetness of an innocent life. Fortunate are those who amuse themselves in learning and who find pleasure in cultivating their minds through the sciences. Wherever hostile Fortune casts them, they always carry with them something to amuse themselves, and boredom, which devours other men even in the midst of delights, is unknown to those who know how to occupy themselves through some reading. Fortunate are those who love to read and are not, like me, deprived of reading.*' While these thoughts were wheeling in my mind, I entered deep into a somber forest, where I suddenly spied an old man, who was holding a book in his hand.

"This old man had a large forehead, bald and a little wrinkled. A white beard hung down to his belt. His build was tall and majestic. His complexion was still fresh and ruddy, his eyes bright and piercing, his voice soft, his words plain and friendly. Never had I seen so venerable an old man. His name was Termosiris, and he was a priest of Apollo, whom he served in a marble temple that the Egyptian kings had consecrated to that god in this forest. The book that he held was a collection of hymns in honor of the gods. He came up to me in a friendly way. We talked together. He recounted things of the past so well that you believed you saw them, yet he told them with brevity, and his stories never wearied me. He foresaw the future through the profound wisdom that caused him to know men and the schemes of which they are capable. Along with so much prudence, he was cheerful, obliging, and the most playful youth does not have as much charm as this man had in his advanced old age. He enjoyed young people as well, when they were docile and had a taste for virtue.

"Soon he loved me tenderly and gave me books to console me. He called me 'my son.' I often said to him, 'My father, the gods, who have taken Mentor from me, have had mercy on me. They have given me another support in you.'

"This man, resembling Orpheus or Linus, was undoubtedly inspired by the gods; he recited verses to me that he had made and gave me those of several excellent poets favored by the Muses. When he was dressed in his long robe of a brilliant whiteness and took in hand his ivory lyre, tigers, lions, and bears came to nuzzle him and lick his feet. The Satyrs came out of the forests to dance round him. Even the trees appeared moved, and you would have thought that the boulders, touched with tenderness, were going to descend from the tops of the mountains under the spell of his sweet chords. He only sang of the greatness of the gods, the virtue of the heroes, and the wisdom of the men who prefer glory to pleasures.

"He often said to me that I should be courageous and that the gods would not abandon either Odysseus or his son. Lastly, he assured me that I should teach the shepherds to cultivate the Muses, following the example of Apollo:

'Apollo,' he said, 'indignant that Zeus, with his thunderbolts, troubled the skies on the most beautiful days, wanted to take vengeance on the Cyclops, who forged the thunderbolts, and he pierced them with his arrows. Immediately, Mount Etna ceased to vomit swirls of flames. One no longer heard the blows of the terrifying hammers, that, striking the anvil, made the deepest caverns of the earth and the abysses of the seas groan. The iron and brass, no longer being polished by the Cyclops, began to rust. Hephaestus, furious, comes out of his blazing furnace. Though lame, he hurriedly ascends toward Olympus, he arrives sweating and covered with black dust in the assembly of the gods. He makes bitter complaints. Zeus, angry with Apollo, chases him out of the sky and hurls him to the earth. His empty chariot makes its usual course on its own in order to give men the days and the nights with the regular changing of the seasons. Apollo, stripped of all his rays, was compelled to be a shepherd and guard the flocks of King Admetus. He played the flute, and all the other shepherds came to the shade of the young elms, along the banks of a clear spring, to listen to his songs. Up until then, they had led a wild and brutal life. They only knew how to drive their ewes, shear them, milk them, and make cheeses. The entire countryside was like a frightful desert.

'Soon, Apollo demonstrated to all those shepherds the arts

that can render their life agreeable. He sang of the flowers with which springtime crowns itself, the perfumes that it spreads, and the verdure that sprouts underfoot. Then he sang of the delightful summer nights, when zephyrs refresh men and dew quenches the land. He also mixed into his songs the golden fruits with which autumn rewards the labors of plowmen, and of winter repose, during which coltish youth dance alongside the fire. Lastly, he represented the somber forests that cover the mountains and deep vales, where rivers, by a thousand turns, seem to play together in the middle of laughing meadows. In this way, he taught the shepherds about the charms of the country life when one knows how to enjoy what simple nature has of the marvelous. Soon the shepherds, with their flutes, found themselves happier than kings, and their huts attracted in droves the pure pleasures that flee gilded palaces. Games, Laughter, and the Graces followed the innocent shepherds everywhere. Every day was festival day. One only ever heard the chirping of birds, or the gentle breath of zephyrs that played in the branches of the trees, or the murmur of a clear water that tumbled from some rock, or the songs that the Muses inspired in the shepherds who followed Apollo. This god taught them to bring home the prize from the race and to shoot the fallow deer and stags with arrows. The gods themselves became jealous of the shepherds; this life appeared sweeter to them than all their glory, and they called Apollo back to Olympus.

'‛My son, this story should instruct you, since you are in the same state as Apollo was. Clear this savage land; make the desert flourish like him; teach all these shepherds about the enchantments of harmony; soften fierce hearts; show them lovable virtue; make them feel how sweet it is to enjoy, in solitude, innocent pleasures that nothing can take away from them. One day, my son, one day the troubles and cruel worries that surround kings will cause you to lament from the throne the pastoral life.'

"Having spoken so, Termosiris gave me a flute so sweet that the echoes of those mountains, which caused it to be heard from all sides, soon attracted all the neighboring shepherds around us. My voice had a divine harmony; I felt moved and beside myself to sing of the charms with which nature adorned the countryside. We spent entire days and part of the nights singing together. All the shepherds, forgetting their huts and their flocks, were entranced and motionless around me while I gave them lessons. It seemed that those deserts no longer had anything of wildness, all had become gentle and laughing there. The politesse of the inhabitants seemed to soften the land.

"We often gathered together to offer sacrifices in the temple of Apollo where Termosiris was priest. The shepherds came crowned with laurels in honor of the god. The shepherdesses also came dancing with crowns of flowers and bearing on their heads baskets filled with sacred gifts. After the sacrifice, we had a country feast. Our sweetest dishes were the milk of our goats and our ewes that we took care to milk ourselves, along with fruits freshly picked with our own hands, such as dates, figs, and grapes. Our seats were the green lawns. Leafy trees gave us a shade more agreeable than the gilded paneling of the palaces of the kings.

~

BOOK II

"But what ended up making me famous among our shepherds is that one day a famished lion came to pounce upon our flock. He had already begun a dreadful carnage. I only had my shepherd's crook in hand. I advance boldly. The lion bristles his mane, bares his teeth and claws, opens a dry and inflamed maw; his eyes appear filled with blood and fire. He bats his flanks with his long tail. I throw him to the ground. The small coat of mail I had donned, according to the custom of Egyptian shepherds, keeps him from ripping me apart. Three times he rises again. He heaves roars that reverberate throughout the forests. Three times I beat him down. Finally, I choke him in my arms, and the shepherds, witnesses to my victory, want me to don the skin of that terrifying lion.

"The rumors of this deed, and that of the beautiful change in all our shepherds, spread throughout Egypt. It even reached the ears of Sesostris. He knew that one of those two captives, who had been taken as Phoenicians, had brought back the golden age in those almost uninhabitable deserts. He wanted to see me, for he loved the Muses, and all that can instruct men touched his great heart. He saw me, he listened to me with pleasure, he discovered that Metophis had deceived him through avarice, he condemned him to life imprisonment and took away all the riches that he unjustly possessed.

"'O, how unfortunate one is,' he said, 'when he is above the rest of men! Often, he cannot see the truth with his own eyes. He is surrounded by people who keep it from reaching the one who commands. Each is interested in deceiving him. Each, beneath an appearance of zeal, hides his ambition. They pretend to love the king, and they love only the riches that he gives. They love him so little that, in order to obtain his favors, they flatter and betray him.'

"Afterward, Sesostris treated me with a tender friendship and resolved to send me back to Ithaca along with vessels and troops to deliver Penelope from all her suitors. The fleet was already prepared, and we thought only to embark. I marveled at the strikes of Fortune, which suddenly lift up those that she has lowered the most. This experience caused me to hope that Odysseus might indeed return, after such long suffering, to his kingdom at last. I was also thinking to myself that I could yet see Mentor again, though he had been taken to the most unknown regions of Ethiopia. While I delayed my departure a bit, attempting to learn news of Odysseus and Mentor, Sesostris, who was very old, died suddenly and his death plunged me back into new misfortunes.

"All Egypt seemed inconsolable at this loss. Each family believed they had lost their best friend, their protector, their father. The old men, raising their hands to the skies, cried out, 'Never has Egypt had so good a king. Never will she have another like him. O gods! You should either not have revealed him to men or never have taken him from them. Why must we survive the great Sesostris?'

"The young people were saying, 'The hope of Egypt is destroyed. Our fathers were fortunate to spend their life under so good a king. As for us, we only saw enough of him to feel his loss.'

"His attendants were crying day and night. When the funeral rites of the king were held for forty days, all the most distant peoples came running in droves. Each wanted to see the body of

BOOK II

Sesostris once more. Each wanted to preserve the image of him. Several wanted to be placed in the tomb along with him.

"What increased the pain of his loss even more, it was that his son Bocchoris had neither humaneness toward foreigners, nor curiosity for the sciences, nor esteem for virtuous men, nor love of glory. The greatness of his father had contributed to rendering him so unworthy of reigning. He had been nurtured in a softness and a brutal pride. He counted men for nothing, believing they were only created for him and that he was of another nature than them. He only thought of satisfying his passions, dissipating the immense treasures his father had managed with so much care, tormenting the peoples and sucking the blood of unfortunate wretches, and, finally, following the flattering counsel of the senseless youth who surrounded him while he scornfully distanced all the wise old men who had had the confidence of his father. He was a monster and not a king. All Egypt groaned, and, although the name of Sesostris, so dear to the Egyptians, made them bear the craven and cruel conduct of his son, the son was racing to his ruin, and a prince so unworthy of the throne could not reign for long.

"I was no longer permitted to hope for my return to Ithaca. I remained in a tower on the edge of the sea near Pelusium, where our departure should have been, had Sesostris not died. Metophis had had the address to get out of prison and to re-establish himself alongside the new king. He had me shut up in this tower in order to avenge the disgrace that I had caused him. I spent the days and nights in a profound sadness. All that Termosiris had foretold and all that I had heard in the cavern seemed no more than a dream.

I was lost in the most bitter pain. I watched the surf that came to pound the foot of that tower where I was a prisoner. Often, I occupied myself in considering the vessels agitated by the tempest, which were in danger of breaking apart against the rocks on which the tower was built. Far from pitying those men threatened with wreck, I envied their lot. Soon, I said to myself, *they will end the misfortunes of their lives, or they will arrive in their country.* Alas, here, I can neither hope for one nor the other.

"While I was thus consumed in useless regrets, I spied a forest of ships' masts. The sea was covered with sails swollen by the winds. The water was spuming under the strikes of countless oars. I heard confused cries from every direction. On the shore I made out a group of frightened Egyptians who were running to arms and others who seemed to be going out to meet this fleet that was seen arriving. Immediately, I recognized that some of those foreign vessels were from Phoenicia, and others from the island of Cyprus, for my misfortunes were beginning to make me experienced with regard to navigation. The Egyptians seemed to be divided among themselves.

"I had no difficulty believing that the senseless King Bocchoris had, through his violences, caused a revolt of his subjects and ignited a civil war. From the top of this tower, I was spectator to a bloody combat. Egyptians who had called foreigners to succor them, after having favored their invasion, were attacking other Egyptians who had the king at their head. I saw this king who animated his men through his example; he looked like the god Ares. Streams of blood flowed round him. The wheels of his chariot

BOOK II

were stained with a black blood, thick and foaming. Barely could they roll over the heaps of crushed corpses. This young king, well built, vigorous, of a proud and haughty mien, had fury and despair in his eyes. He was like a beautiful horse, unbroken. His courage was pushing him haphazardly, and wisdom did not moderate his valor. He knew neither how to mend his errors, nor to give precise orders, nor to anticipate the evils that were threatening him, nor to manage the people of whom he had the greatest need. It was not that he lacked genius. His intelligence equaled his courage, but he had never been instructed by bad fortune. His masters had poisoned, through flattery, his beautiful nature. He was intoxicated with his power and his good fortune. He believed that all should cede to his fiery desires. The least resistance inflamed his anger—then, he no longer reasoned; he was beside himself; his furious pridefulness transformed him into a ferocious beast; his natural goodness and right reasoning abandoned him in an instant. His most loyal servants were reduced to flight. He only liked those who flattered his passions. So, he always took extreme sides against his true interests, and he forced all the good people to detest his mad conduct.

"For a long time his valor sustained him against the multitude of his enemies, but in the end he was overwhelmed. I saw him perish. The spear of a Phoenician pierced his chest. He tumbled from his chariot as the horses still dragged on and, no longer able to hold the reins, he fell under the horses' feet. A soldier from the island of Cyprus struck off his head, and holding it by the hair, he displayed it as if in triumph to all the victorious army.

"I will remember all my life having seen that head swimming in blood, his eyes closed and the light put out, that face pale and disfigured, that mouth gaping, which seemed to still want to finish the words begun, that superb and menacing air that even death could not blot out. All my life, it will be painted before my eyes, and, should the gods ever cause me to reign, I will never forget, after so gruesome an example, that a king is only worthy of commanding, and is only happy in his power, to the extent he submits it to reason. O what unhappiness for a man destined to make the happiness of the public, to be the master of so many men only to render them unhappy!"

End of Book II

THE ADVENTURES OF TELEMACHUS
SON OF ODYSSEUS

BOOK III

Calypso listened with astonishment to such wise words. What enchanted her the most was seeing how young Telemachus ingenuously recounted the errors he had made through precipitation and in lacking docility with regard to wise Mentor. She found a nobility and a stunning grandeur in this young prince who faulted himself and seemed to have profited so well from his imprudence so as to become wise, foresighted, and restrained.

"Continue," she said, "my dear Telemachus. I long to know how you got out of Egypt and where you found wise Mentor again, whose loss you so rightly felt."

Telemachus resumed his discourse:

"The Egyptians who were the most virtuous and loyal to the king, being the weakest and seeing the king dead, were compelled to cede to the others. They established another king named Termutis. The Phoenicians, along with the troops from the island of Cyprus, withdrew after having made an alliance with the new king. He returned all the Phoenician prisoners; I was counted as being among this number. They had me released from the tower. I embarked with the others, and hope began to shine again in the depths of my heart. A favorable wind already filled our sails, the oarsmen plowed the foaming waters, the vast sea was covered with ships, the sailors loosed cries of joy. The Egyptian shores fled far from us. The hills and mountains were flattening little by little. We were beginning to see nothing but sky and sea while the sun, which was rising, appeared to release her sparkling fires from the sea. Her rays gilded the summits of the mountains, which we were still barely finding on the horizon, and the whole sky, painted a somber azure, promised us a happy voyage.

"Although they had sent me back as being Phoenician, none of the Phoenicians I was with knew me. Narbal, who captained the vessel on which they had put me, asked me for my name and homeland.

"'Which Phoenician city are you from?' he asked me.

"'I am not from Phoenicia,' I told him. 'But the Egyptians had taken me at sea on board a Phoenician vessel. I remained captive in Egypt for a long time as a Phoenician. It is under this name that I suffered for a long time; it is under this name that they freed me.'

"'What country are you from, then?' resumed Narbal.

"Then, I said to him:

BOOK III

'I am Telemachus, son of Odysseus, king of Ithaca, in Greece. My father made himself famous among all the kings who besieged the city of Troy. But the gods have not granted that he see his homeland again. I have sought him in several countries. Fortune persecutes me like him. You see a poor wretch who only yearns for the happiness of returning among his own and finding his father.'

"Narbal was looking at me with astonishment and he believed to perceive in me a certain something, a favor that comes from the gifts of heaven and that is not in common man. He was naturally sincere and generous. He was touched by my misfortune and spoke to me with a trust that the gods inspired in him to save me from a great peril.

"'Telemachus, I do not doubt,' he said to me, 'what you tell me, and I would not know how to doubt it. The pain and virtue painted on your face do not permit me to distrust you. I even sense that the gods, whom I have always served, love you and desire that I love you too, as if you were my son. I will give you a salutary counsel, and in return I ask only for secrecy.'

"'Do not fear,' I said, 'that I would have any difficulty keeping quiet about the things you wish to confide in me. Though I may be very young, I have already aged in the habit of never telling my secrets and even more in never betraying, under any pretext, the secrets of others.'

"'How have you,' he said to me, 'been able to accustom yourself to secrecy at such a young age? I would be delighted to learn by what means you have acquired this quality, which is the foundation of the wisest conduct and without which all talents are useless.'

"'When Odysseus,' I said to him, 'set out for the siege of Troy, he took me on his knees and in his arms (that is what was recounted to me). After kissing me tenderly, he said these words to me, though I could not understand them: 'O my son, may the gods preserve me from ever seeing you again; may rather the scissors of the Spinner cut the thread of your days when it is barely formed, just as the reaper cuts with his scythe a tender flower which is beginning to open up; may my enemies crush you before your mother's eyes and mine should you one day become corrupt and abandon virtue. O my friends,' he continued, 'I am leaving you this son who is so dear to me; attend to his childhood. If you love me, distance from him pernicious flattery. Teach him self-control. May he be like a young sapling, still tender, that one bends in order to straighten it out. Above all, do your utmost to render him just, beneficent, sincere, and loyal in keeping a secret. Whoever is capable of lying is unworthy of being counted among men, and whoever does not know how to keep silent is unworthy of governing.'

"'I relate these words to you because they took care to repeat them to me often and they have penetrated to the bottom of my heart. I also repeated them to myself often. My father's friends took care to train me early in secrecy. I was still in tender boyhood, and they already confided in me about all the pain they were feeling at seeing my mother exposed to a great number of brazen suitors who wanted to marry her. Consequently, they have treated me since then as a reasonable and sure man. They secretly discussed the greatest affairs with me; they informed me of everything they had resolved in order to scatter those pretenders. I was delighted that they had this confidence in me, by which I believed myself already a sure man. Never have I abused this trust; never has there escaped from me a single word that could reveal the least secret. Often, the pretenders tried to make me speak, hoping that a child, who could have seen or heard something important, would not know how to keep it to himself, but I knew well how to answer them without lying and without informing them of what I should not say.'

"Then Narbal said to me, 'You see, Telemachus, the might of the Phoenicians. They are formidable to all neighboring nations through their countless ships. The commerce they conduct as far as the Pillars of Heracles gives them riches that surpass those of the most flourishing peoples. The great King Sesostris, who would never have been able to vanquish them by sea, had much difficulty vanquishing them by land with his armies, which had conquered all the East. He imposed a tribute on us that we did not pay for long. The Phoenicians found themselves too rich and too mighty to patiently bear the yoke of servitude. We took back our liberty. Death did not allow Sesostris time to finish the war against us. It is true that we had everything to fear from his wisdom, even more than from his might. But, with his might passing into the hands of his son, who was deprived of all wisdom, we concluded that we no longer had anything to fear. Indeed, the Egyptians, far from returning to our country, arms in hand, to subjugate us again, have been compelled to call on us for succor to deliver them from this impious and furious king. We have been their liberators. What glory is added to the liberty and opulence of the Phoenicians! But, while we deliver others, we are slaves ourselves.

'O Telemachus, fear falling into the cruel hands of Pygmalion, our king. He dipped them, those cruel hands, into the blood of Sychaeus, husband of Dido, his sister. Dido, filled with horror and vengeance, escaped from Tyre along with several vessels. Most of those who love virtue and liberty followed her. She founded on the coast of Africa a superb city named Carthage. Pygmalion, tormented by an insatiable thirst for riches, makes himself more and more miserable and odious to his subjects. It is a crime in Tyre to have great possessions. Avarice renders him distrustful, suspicious, cruel. He persecutes the rich, and he fears the poor. It is an even greater crime in Tyre to have virtue, for Pygmalion assumes that the good cannot tolerate his injustices and his infamies. Virtue condemns him, he is embittered and irritated by it. Everything agitates him, disquiets him, gnaws at him. He is afraid of his own shadow. He sleeps neither day nor night. The gods, to confound him, laden him with treasures that he dare not enjoy. What he seeks in order to be happy is precisely what prevents him from being so. He regrets everything he hands out, he always fears losing. He torments himself in order to win.

'"One almost never sees him. He is alone, sad, beaten-down in the depths of his palace. Even his friends dare not go up to him for fear of becoming suspect to him. A terrifying guard always keeps swords drawn and pikes raised all around his house. Thirty rooms connected one to another, each having an iron door with six huge bolts, are where he confines himself. One never knows in which of these rooms he sleeps, and it is assured that he never sleeps two consecutive nights in the same for fear of having his throat slit. He knows neither sweet pleasures nor friendship, sweeter still. If one speaks to him of seeking joy, he feels that it flees far from him and refuses to enter into his heart. His hollow eyes are filled with a harsh and fierce fire. They are incessantly roving in all directions. He lends an ear to the slightest rumor and is very upset. He is pale, haggard, and dark worries are painted on his ever-wrinkled face. He is silent, he sighs, he heaves groans from deep within his heart; he cannot hide the remorse that is ripping his entrails apart. The most exquisite dishes disgust him. His children, far from being his hope, are the subject of his terror. He has made of them his most dangerous enemies. He has never in his entire life had a moment of assurance. He only survives by dint of shedding the blood of all those he fears. Fool, who does not see that his cruelty, to which he entrusts himself, will destroy him! One of his attendants, as distrustful as he, will hasten to deliver the world from this monster. As for me, I revere the gods. Whatever it may cost me, I will be loyal to the king they have given me. I would prefer he have me put to death than to take his life or even fail to defend it. As for you, O Telemachus, be very careful of telling him that you are the son of Odysseus. He would hope that Odysseus, returning to Ithaca, would pay him some great sum to ransom you, and he would hold you in prison.'"

~

"When we arrived in Tyre, I followed Narbal's counsel, and I recognized the truth of everything he had recounted to me. I could not understand how a man could render himself as miserable as Pygmalion seemed to me. Startled by a spectacle so dreadful and so new to me, I said to myself: *Here you have a man who only sought to make himself happy. He believed to come by it through riches and through an absolute authority. He possesses all that he can desire and yet he is miserable through his riches and even through his authority. If he were a shepherd, as I was not so long ago, he would be as happy as I was. He would enjoy the innocent pleasures of the countryside and enjoy them without remorse. He would fear neither the sword, nor poison. He would love men; he would be loved by them. He would not have these great riches, which are as useless to him as sand since he dares not touch them. But he would freely enjoy the fruits of the land and suffer no true need. This man seems to do all that he wants, but that is not necessarily so—he does all that his fierce passions want. He is always swept along by his avarice, his fear, his suspicions. He seems to be master of all other men, but he is not master of himself—for he has as many masters and executioners as he has violent desires.*

"I reasoned thus of Pygmalion without seeing him, for one did not see him, and only gazed with fear upon those tall towers, which were surrounded night and day by guards, into which he had practically imprisoned himself, locked up with his treasures. I compared this invisible king with Sesostris, so gentle, so accessible, so affable, so curious to see foreigners, so attentive in listening to everyone and drawing from the hearts of men the truth that is hidden from kings. Sesostris, I said, *feared nothing and had nothing to fear; he showed himself to all his subjects as to his own children. This one here fears all and has all to fear. This wicked king is always* exposed to a gruesome death, even in his inaccessible palace in the middle of all his guards; on the contrary, the good King Sesostris was safe in the middle of a crowd of peoples, like a good father in his house, surrounded by his family.

"Pygmalion gave the order to send back the troops from the island of Cyprus, who had come to succor his own under an alliance between the two peoples. Narbal took this opportunity to set me free. He had me pass review among the Cypriot soldiers, for the king took umbrage at the least things. The flaw of princes too easygoing and distracted is to deliver themselves over with a blind confidence to artful and corrupt favorites. The flaw of this one was, on the contrary, that of distrusting the most upright men. He did not know how to discern straightforward and natural men, who act without disguise; indeed, he had never seen good people, for such people do not go seeking a king so corrupt. Besides, he had seen, since he had been on the throne, in the men who he made use of, so much dissimulation, perfidy, and dreadful vices disguised under the appearances of virtue, that he regarded all men without exception as if they were masked. He assumed there was no sincere virtue on earth. So, he regarded all men as more or less equal. When he found a false and corrupt man, he did not go to the trouble of seeking another, figuring that another would not be better. The good seemed worse to him than the most overtly wicked because he believed them just as wicked, and more deceptive.

"Coming back to me, I blended in with the Cypriots, and I escaped the penetrating distrust of the king. Narbal was trembling for fear that I might be discovered. It would have cost him his life, and mine too. His impatience to see us leave was incredible, but the headwinds detained us for some time in Tyre.

"I took advantage of this stay to get acquainted with the mores of the Phoenicians, so famous in all the known nations. I was marveling at the fortunate site of this great city, which is on an island in the middle of the sea. The nearby coast is delightful through its fertility, the exquisite fruits it bears, the number of towns and villages that almost touch each other, lastly, through the mildness of its climate: for the mountains shelter this coast from the scorching Southwinds; it is cooled by the Northwind that blows in from the side of the sea. This country is at the foot of Mount Lebanon, whose summit splits the clouds and goes on to touch the heavens. Eternal ice covers its brow. Rivers full of snow tumble like torrents from the peaks of the rocks that surround its head. Below, one sees a vast forest of ancient cedars that looked as old as the land where they are planted and that carry their thick branches up to the clouds. This forest has under its feet rich grazing lands on the slope of the mountain. It is there that one sees roaming the bellowing bulls, the bleating ewes along with their tender lambs that bound over the fresh grass. There flow a thousand different clear streams, distributing water everywhere. Lastly, one sees below those pastures the foot of the mountain, which is like a garden. Spring and autumn reign together there to join the flowers with the fruits. Never has either the pestilential Southwind that dries and scorches everything, nor the rigorous Northwind ever dared to fade the bright colors that adorn this garden. It is along this beautiful coast of the island, rising from the sea, that the city of

BOOK III

Tyre is built. This great city seems to swim on top of the water and to be queen of all the sea. Merchants flock there from all parts of the world, and her inhabitants are themselves the most famous merchants there are in the universe. When you enter this city, you believe at first that it is not a city that belongs to one particular people, but that it is the city common to all peoples and the center of their commerce. It has two long moles resembling two arms that jut out into the sea and embrace a vast harbor where the winds cannot enter. In this harbor, you see a forest of ship's masts, and these ships are so numerous that you can barely make out the sea that bears them. All the citizens apply themselves to commerce, and their great riches never put them off from the work necessary to increase them. There, in every direction, one finds fine Egyptian linen and twice-dyed Tyrian purple of a marvelous sheen. This double dyeing is so vivid that time cannot fade it. It is used for fine wools that they enhance with gold and silver embroidery. The Phoenicians trade with all the peoples as far as the Strait of Gibraltar, and they have even penetrated into the vast ocean that surrounds the entire earth. They have also made long voyages on the Red Sea, and it is by this route that they search unknown islands for gold, perfumes, and various animals that are not found anywhere else.

"I could not sate my eyes with the magnificent spectacle of this great city where all was in motion. There, I did not see, as in the cities of Greece, idle and curious men who go to seek news in the public square or to watch foreigners arriving in the port. In Tyre, the men are busy unloading their vessels, transporting their merchandise or selling it, arranging their warehouses, and keeping an exact account of what is owed them by foreign traders. The women never cease either spinning wool, or making embroidery designs, or folding the rich fabrics.

"'How does it come about,' I said to Narbal, 'that the Phoenicians have become masters of commerce over all the earth, and that they enrich themselves so at the expense of all other peoples?'

"'You see it,' he answered. 'The situation of Tyre is favorable for navigation. It is our homeland that has the glory of having invented navigation. The Tyrians were the first (if we must believe what is recounted of the most obscure antiquity) to subdue the tides, long before the age of Tiphys and the Argonauts, so vaunted in Greece; they were, I say, the first who dared put themselves in a frail vessel at the mercy of the billowing waves and tempests, who plumbed the depths of the sea, who observed the heavens far from earth following the science of the Egyptians and the Babylonians, lastly, who reunited so many peoples that the sea had separated. The Tyrians are clever, patient, hard-working, neat, sober, and frugal. They have exact policies. They are in perfect accord with one another. Never has a people been more constant, more sincere, more loyal, more sure, more accommodating to all foreigners. There you have it, without looking for other causes, that is what gives them the empire of the sea and what causes such useful commerce to flourish in their ports. If division and jealousy came between them, if they began to soften in delights and idleness, if the leaders of the nation scorned work and economy, if the industrial arts ceased being honored in their city, if they lacked good faith toward foreigners, if they altered even a little the rules of free commerce, if they neglected their manufacturers, and if they ceased making the great advances that are necessary to render their merchandise perfect, each in its way, you would soon see this might that you admire tumble.'

"'But explain to me,' I said to him, 'the true means of establishing one day such a commerce in Ithaca.'

"'Do,' he responded, 'as we do here: receive all foreigners well and readily. Have them find in your ports safety, convenience, complete freedom. Never allow yourself to be swept up by either avarice or pridefulness. The true means of winning a lot is in never wanting to win too much and knowing how to lose as need be. Make yourself loved by all foreigners. Even tolerate something from them; fear exciting their jealousy through your haughtiness. Be consistent in the rules of commerce; may they be straightforward and simple. Accustom your peoples to follow them inviolably, severely punish fraud, and even the negligence or flamboyance of merchants that ruin commerce in ruining the men who do it.

"'Above all, never undertake to interfere with commerce in order to make it accord with your own views. The prince must not meddle in it for fear of interfering with it, and he must leave all the profit from it to his subjects, who have the trouble of it. Otherwise he will discourage them. He will derive enough advantages from it through the great riches that will enter into his states. Commerce is like certain springs—if you want to divert their course, you cause them to dry up. There is only profit and convenience that attract foreigners to you. If you render commerce less convenient and less useful to them, they withdraw imperceptibly, and no longer return, because other peoples, profiting from your imprudence, attract them there and accustom them to passing you by.

"'I must even confess to you that, for some time, the glory of Tyre has indeed dimmed. O, if you had seen it, my dear Telemachus, before Pygmalion's reign, you would have been even more amazed. Now, you find here only the sad remains of a grandeur that threatens ruin. O unfortunate Tyre, in what hands you have fallen! Once the sea brought you the tribute of all the peoples of the earth! Pygmalion fears all, not only foreigners, but even his subjects. Instead of opening, according to our ancient custom, his ports to all the most distant nations in complete freedom, he wants to know the number of ships that arrive, their country, the names of the men on them, their type of commerce, the price of their merchandise, and the length of time they must stay here. He does even worse, for he uses chicanery to entrap the merchants and confiscate their merchandise. He worries the merchants whom he believes the most opulent. He establishes, under various pretexts, new taxes. He wants to enter into commerce himself, and everyone fears having any business with him; so, commerce languishes. Foreigners forget, little by little, the route to Tyre that was once so sweet to them, and if Pygmalion does not change his conduct, our glory and our might will soon be transported to some other people better governed than us.'

"Then I asked Narbal how the Tyrians had become so powerful on the sea, for I wanted to be ignorant of nothing that could serve in the governance of a kingdom.

"'We have the forests of Lebanon,' he answered, 'which supply the wood for the vessels, and we carefully reserve them for that use. They are only ever felled for public needs. As for the construction of vessels, we have the advantage of having able workers.'

"'How were you able to find those workers?' I said to him.

"He answered, 'They are trained little by little in the country. When those who excel in the industrial arts are well rewarded, you are sure to soon have men who lead them to their ultimate perfection. For men who have the most wisdom and talent do not fail to devote themselves to the arts to which great rewards are attached. Here, all those who succeed in the arts and the sciences useful to navigation are treated with honor. We respect a good surveyor, we highly esteem a good astronomer, we shower goods on a helmsman who surpasses others in his function. We do not scorn a good carpenter. On the contrary, he is well paid and well treated. Even the good oarsmen have rewards sure and proportionate to their service: we feed them well; we attend them when they are sick; in their absence, we attend to their wives and children; if they perish in a shipwreck, we indemnify their families; we send home those who have served for a certain time. In this way, we have as many of them as we want. The father is delighted to raise his son in so good a profession, and, from his earliest childhood, he hastens to teach him how to handle the oar, tend the ropes and scorn the tempests. This is how one leads men without coercion, through reward, and through orderliness. Authority alone never does well; the submission of inferiors is not sufficient; we must win hearts and cause men to see their advantage with regard to the things where we want to make use of their skill.'

"After this discourse, Narbal led me to visit all the warehouses, the arsenals, and all the professions that serve in the construction of ships. I asked for detail of the least things, and wrote down all that I had learned for fear of forgetting some useful particularity.

"Meanwhile, Narbal, who knew Pygmalion and loved me, impatiently awaited my departure, fearful lest I be discovered by the king's spies, who were going day and night throughout the city, but the winds did not yet permit us to embark. While we were busy curiously visiting the port and interrogating various merchants, we saw coming toward us an officer of Pygmalion, who said to Narbal: 'The king just learned from one of the ship captains who returned from Egypt with you that you brought a foreigner who passes for a Cypriot. The king wants him arrested and to know for certain which country he is from. You will answer with your head.'

"At that moment, I had stepped away to look more closely at the proportions which the Tyrians had used in the construction of an almost new vessel, which was, they were saying, due to the exact proportions of all its parts, the best sailing ship that had ever been seen in the port, and I was interrogating the workman who had set those proportions.

"Narbal, startled and frightened, answered, 'I am seeking this foreigner who is from the island of Cyprus.' When he had lost sight of this officer, he ran toward me to warn me of the danger I was in.

"'I had foreseen it only too well, my dear Telemachus. We are lost,' he said. 'The king, whose distrust torments him night and day, suspects you are not from the island of Cyprus. He orders you be arrested. He wants to have me killed if I do not put you into his hands. What will we do? O gods, give us the wisdom to pull ourselves out of this peril! I must, Telemachus, lead you to the king's palace. You will maintain that you are a Cypriot from the city of Amathus, son of a sculptor of Aphrodite. I will declare that I once knew your father, and perhaps the king, without delving further, will allow you to depart. I no longer see any other means of saving your life and mine.'

"I responded to Narbal, 'Allow to perish a poor wretch whom destiny wants to destroy. I know how to die, Narbal, and I owe you too much to want to drag you into my misfortune. I cannot resolve myself to lie. I am not a Cypriot, and I would only know how to say what I am. The gods see my sincerity. It is up to them to preserve my life through their might, if they desire it. But I do not want to save it through a lie.'

"Narbal responded, 'This lie, Telemachus, has nothing about it that is not innocent. The gods themselves cannot condemn it. It does no harm to anyone. It saves the lives of two innocents. It only deceives the king in order to keep him from committing a great crime. You push the love of virtue and the fear of wounding religion too far.'

"'It suffices,' I told him, 'that the lie is a lie to not be worthy of a man who speaks in the presence of gods and who owes everything to the truth. He who wounds the truth offends the gods and wounds himself, for he speaks against his conscience. Cease, Narbal, proposing to me that which is unworthy of you and of me—if the gods have mercy on us, they will indeed know how to deliver us. If they want to allow us to perish, we will be, in dying, victims of the truth, and we will leave to mankind the example of preferring unstained virtue to a long life. Mine is already only too long, being so unhappy. It is you alone, O my dear Narbal, for whom my heart is touched. Must your friendship for an unhappy foreigner be so ill-fated to you?'

"We remained in this type of conflict for a long time, but at last we saw a man arriving who was running out of breath. It was another officer of the king who came on behalf of Astarbe. This woman was beautiful like a goddess. She joined all the charms of the body with those of the mind. She was playful, flattering, insinuating. Along with so many deceiving charms, she had, like the Sirens, a cruel heart filled with malignity. But she knew how to hide her corrupt feelings through a profound artifice. She had known how to win the heart of Pygmalion through her beauty, her wit, her sweet voice, and the harmony of her lyre. Pygmalion, blinded by a violent love for her, had abandoned Queen Topha, his wife. He thought only of satisfying every passion of the ambitious Astarbe. Love for this woman was hardly less ill-fated to him than his infamous avarice. But though he had so much passion for her, she had for him only scorn and disgust. She hid her true feelings and pretended she only wanted to live for him at the same time that she could not bear him.

"There was, in Tyre, a young Lydian named Malachon, of a marvelous beauty, yet soft, effeminate, drowned in pleasures. He only thought of preserving the delicateness of his complexion, combing his blond hair that flowed over his shoulders, perfuming himself, giving a gracious turn to the folds of his robe, finally, singing of his amours on his lyre. Astarbe saw him; she loved him and became infatuated. He scorned her because he was passionate for another woman; besides, he feared exposing himself to the cruel jealousy of the king. Astarbe, feeling scorned, abandoned herself to her resentment. In her despair, she thought that she could pass Malachon off for the foreigner whom the king was seeking, and who was said to have come with Narbal. Indeed, she persuaded Pygmalion of it and corrupted all those who could have set him straight. As he did not like virtuous men and did not know how to discern them, he was only surrounded by self-interested, artful men, ready to execute his unjust and bloody orders. Such people feared Astarbe's authority, and they helped her to deceive the king for fear of displeasing this haughty woman, who had his complete confidence. Thus Malachon, though known as Lydian throughout the city, passed for the young foreigner Narbal had brought from Egypt. He was imprisoned.

"Astarbe, who feared that Narbal might go speak to the king and reveal her impostor, hurriedly sent this officer to Narbal, who said these words to him: 'Astarbe forbids you to reveal to the king which is your foreigner. She only asks for your silence, and she knows well how to arrange things in such a way that the king will be satisfied with you. Meanwhile, hasten to have the young foreigner that you brought from Egypt embark with the Cypriots so that he will no longer be seen in the city.' Narbal, delighted to be able to save his life and mine in this way, promised to keep quiet, and the officer, satisfied with having obtained what he asked for, returned to render an account of his commission to Astarbe."

"Narbal and I, we marveled at the goodness of the gods who rewarded our sincerity and who take such touching care of those who risk everything for virtue. We regarded with horror a king delivered over to avarice and voluptuousness. The one who has such excessive fear of being deceived, we told ourselves, merits being so and he is almost always grossly deceived. He distrusts good people and abandons himself to scoundrels. He is the only one who is ignorant of what is happening. Witness Pygmalion; he is the toy of an indecent woman. Meanwhile, the gods make use of the lies of the wicked in order to save the good, who prefer to lose their life than to lie. At the same time, we perceived that the winds were changing and becoming favorable to the Cyprian vessels.

"'The gods declare themselves!' exclaimed Narbal. 'They desire, my dear Telemachus, to keep you safe. Flee this cruel and accursed land! Happy the one who could follow you to the most unknown shores! Happy the one who could live and die with you! But a severe destiny attaches me to this unhappy motherland. I must suffer with her. Perhaps I must be buried in her ruins. What does it matter, provided that I always speak the truth and my heart only loves justice? As for you, O my dear Telemachus, I pray to the gods who lead you by the hand to grant you the most precious of all their gifts, which is pure and unstained virtue, until death. Live, return to Ithaca, console Penelope, deliver her from her brazen suitors; may your eyes be able to see, may your hands be able to embrace the wise Odysseus, and may he find in you a son who equals his wisdom. But, in your happiness, remember the unhappy Narbal and never cease loving me.'

"When he had finished this speech, I soaked him with my tears without responding, for heavy sighs kept me from speaking. We embraced each other in silence. He led me to the vessel, and he remained on the shore. When the vessel had departed, we did not cease looking at each other for as long as we could see."

END OF BOOK III

THE ADVENTURES OF
TELEMACHUS
SON OF ODYSSEUS

BOOK IV

Calypso, *who had been until that moment* motionless and transported with pleasure in listening to the adventures of Telemachus, interrupted him to have him rest. "It is time," she said, "that you enjoy the sweetness of sleep after so many travails. You have nothing to fear here; everything is favorable to you. Abandon yourself to joy then, enjoy peace and all the other gifts of the gods with which you will be filled.

"Tomorrow, when Dawn with her rose-red fingers cracks open the golden doors of the East and the horses of the Sun, emerging from the bitter waves, spread the flames of day to chase before them all the stars of heaven, we will take up again, my dear Telemachus, the story of your misfortunes. Never did your father equal your wisdom and your courage. Neither Achilles, victor over Hector, nor Theseus, returned from the Underworld, nor even the great Alcides, who purged the land of so many monsters, showed as much strength and virtue as you.

"I wish for a deep sleep to render this night short for you. But alas, how long it will be for me. How it will delay me seeing you again, hearing you, having you retell what I already know and asking you what I do not yet know. Go, my dear Telemachus, with wise Mentor, whom the gods have restored to you, go into this secluded grotto, where all is prepared for your rest. I pray for Morpheus to spread his sweetest spells over your heavy eyelids, to have a divine vapor flow through all your tired limbs, and send you light Dreams that, flitting round you, flatter your senses through the most pleasant images and repel far from you all that could wake you too quickly."

The goddess herself led Telemachus into this grotto separate from her own. It was neither less rustic nor less agreeable. A spring flowing in a corner made a gentle murmur that was calling Sleep. There, the nymphs had prepared two beds of a soft verdure on which they had laid out two large hides, one of lion for Telemachus, and the other of bear for Mentor.

Before allowing him to close his eyes in sleep, Mentor spoke in this way to Telemachus:

"The pleasure of recounting your stories swept you away. You have enchanted the goddess in explaining to her the dangers from which your courage and cleverness pulled you. By doing so, you have only inflamed her heart further and prepared a more dangerous captivity for yourself. How can you hope that she will allow you to get off her island now, you who enchanted her through the tale of your adventures? The love of vainglory made you speak imprudently. She had promised to recount stories and to inform you of the destiny of Odysseus, she found a way of speaking for a long time without saying anything, and she got you to promise to explain to her everything that she desires to know. Such is the art of flattering and passionate women. When is it, O Telemachus, that you will be wise enough to never speak out of vanity and will know how to keep quiet about all that is advantageous to you, when it is not useful to tell? Others admire your wisdom at such an age when it is forgivable to lack it. As for me, I can forgive you nothing. I am the only one who knows you and who loves you enough to warn you of all your errors. How distant you still are from the wisdom of your father!"

"What then," responded Telemachus. "Could I refuse recounting my misfortunes to Calypso?"

"No," resumed Mentor, "you had to recount them to her, but you should have done it by telling her only what could make her compassionate. You could say that you had been sometimes wandering, sometimes captive in Sicily and then in Egypt. That would have been enough, and all the rest only served to increase the poison that already burns her heart. Would to the gods that your own may be preserved from it."

"But what will I do then?" continued Telemachus in a restrained and meek tone.

"There is no longer time," Mentor rejoined, "to hide from her what remains of your adventures. She knows enough about them not to be deceived about what she does not yet know. Your reserve would only serve to irritate her. Finish, then, tomorrow by recounting to her all the gods have done in your favor, and learn another time to speak more soberly of all that can attract some praise for you." Telemachus received such good counsel with goodwill, and they slept.

As soon as Phoebus had spread his first rays over the land, Mentor, hearing the voice of the goddess who was calling her nymphs into the woods, awakened Telemachus.

"It is time," he said to him, "to vanquish Sleep. Let us go find Calypso. But distrust her sweet words—never open your heart to her; fear the flattering poison of her praises. Yesterday, she elevated you above your wise father, the invincible Achilles, the famous Theseus, Heracles, who became immortal. Did you not sense how excessive this praise was? Did you believe what she said? Know that she does not believe it herself. She only praises you because she believes you weak and vain enough to allow yourself to be deceived by praises disproportionate to your deeds."

After these words, they went to the spot where the goddess was awaiting them. She smiled at seeing them and hid under an appearance of joy the fear and unease that troubled her heart, for she foresaw that Telemachus, led by Mentor, would escape her the same as Odysseus.

"Hasten," she said, "my dear Telemachus, to satisfy my curiosity. I imagined throughout the night to see you departing Phoenicia and seeking a new destiny on the island of Cyprus. Tell us then what this journey was and let us not waste a moment." Then they sat on the grass sprinkled with violets in the shade of a thick grove. Calypso could not keep from incessantly casting tender and passionate looks at Telemachus and seeing with indignation that Mentor was observing even the slightest movement of her eyes. Meanwhile, all the nymphs were leaning forward in silence to lend an ear and forming a kind of semi-circle to better listen and see. The eyes of all assembled were fixed on and attached to this young man. Telemachus, lowering his eyes and blushing charmingly, thus resumed the rest of his story:

"No sooner had the gentle breath of a favorable wind filled our sails than the land of Phoenicia disappeared to our eyes. As I was with the Cypriots, of whose mores I was ignorant, I resolved to keep quiet, notice everything, and observe all the rules of discretion so as to gain their esteem. But during my silence, a sweet and powerful sleep gripped me. My senses were tied and suspended. I tasted a peace and a profound joy that intoxicated my heart. Suddenly, I believed to see Aphrodite, who split the clouds in her flying chariot drawn by two doves. She had that brilliant beauty, that vibrant youthfulness, those tender charms that appear in her when she emerges from the foam of the Ocean, and that dazzle the eyes of Zeus himself. She suddenly descended from a rapid flight just alongside me. Smiling, she placed her hand on my shoulder and, calling me by name, uttered these words:

"'Young Greek, you are going to enter into my empire. You will soon arrive on this happy island where pleasures, laughter, and coltish games sprout under my footsteps. There, you will burn perfumes on my altars. There, I will plunge you into a river of delights. Open your heart to the sweetest expectations, and be very careful of resisting the most mighty of all the goddesses, who desires to make you happy.'

"At the same time, I spied the infant Eros, who, with his tiny fluttering wings, was flying round his mother. Though he had on his face the tenderness, charms, and playfulness of childhood, he had a certain something in his piercing eyes that frightened me. He laughed while looking at me, and his laugh was malignant, mocking, and cruel. He drew from his golden quiver the sharpest of his arrows; he flexed his bow and was going to pierce me when Athena suddenly appeared to cover me with her aegis. The face of this goddess did not have that soft beauty and passionate languor that I had noticed in the face and the posture of Aphrodite. It was, on the contrary, a natural, unaffected, modest beauty. All was grave, vigorous, noble, full of strength and majesty. Eros' arrow, unable to pierce the aegis, tumbled to the ground. Eros, indignant, sighed bitterly about it. He was ashamed to find himself defeated. 'Away from here!' Athena cried out. 'Away from here, brash child! You will only ever defeat cowardly souls who prefer your shameful pleasures to wisdom, virtue, and glory.' At these words, frustrated Love flitted away, and I watched for a long time as Aphrodite in her chariot with its two doves ascended back to Olympus in a cloud of gold and azure. Then she disappeared.

"Lowering my eyes to earth, I no longer found Athena. It seemed to me that I was transported into a delightful garden such as the Elysian Fields are depicted. In this place, I recognized Mentor, who said to me, 'Flee this cruel land, this pestilent island, where one only breathes voluptuousness. The most courageous virtue must tremble here and can only save itself in fleeing.' As soon as I saw him, I wanted to throw myself at his neck to embrace him, but I felt that my feet were unable to move, my knees were buckling under me, and my hands, striving to grasp Mentor, were seeking a vain shade that always escaped me. In that effort, I awoke, and I felt that this mysterious dream was a divine warning. I felt filled with courage against pleasures and with distrust of myself so as to detest the soft life of the Cypriots. But what pierced my heart was that I believed Mentor had lost his life and, having passed over the waters of the Styx, was dwelling in the happy resting place of just souls.

"This thought caused me to shed a torrent of tears. They asked me why I was crying. 'The tears,' I answered, 'suit only too well an unhappy foreigner who wanders without hope of seeing his homeland again.' Meanwhile, all those Cypriots who were on the vessel abandoned themselves to a delirious glee. The oarsmen, hostile to work, were sleeping on their oars. The helmsman, wreathed with flowers, left the helm and was holding in his hand a large jug of wine which he had almost emptied; he and all the others, troubled by the fury of Dionysus, were singing—in honor of Aphrodite and Eros— verses that should horrify all those who love virtue.

"While they were forgetting so the dangers of the sea, a sudden tempest troubled the sky and sea. Unleashed winds bellowed furiously into the sails. Black surges were beating the flanks of the ship, which groaned under their blows. At times we rode the backs of billowing waves. At times the sea seemed to give way beneath the ship and fling us into the abyss. We saw alongside us rocks against which the angry waves were breaking with a terrifying noise. Then I understood through experience what I had often heard said by Mentor, that men, effete and abandoned to pleasure, lack courage in danger. All our despondent Cypriots were crying like women. I only heard pitiful cries, laments about the delights of life, vain promises to the gods to make sacrifices to them if they could arrive in the port.

"No one preserved enough presence of mind either to order maneuvers or to do them. It seemed to me that I must, in saving my life, save those of the others. I took the helm in hand because the pilot, troubled by the wine like a maenad, was not in a state to recognize the danger to the vessel. I encouraged the frightened sailors. I had them lower the sails. They rowed vigorously; we passed through the reefs, and we saw up close all the horrors of death. This adventure seemed like a dream to all those who owed me for the preservation of their life. They were looking at me with astonishment.

"We arrived on the island of Cyprus in the month of spring which is consecrated to Aphrodite.

"'This season,' said the Cypriots, 'suits this goddess, for she seems to bring all nature back to life and to make pleasures sprout like flowers.'

"Arriving on the island, I felt a gentle air that rendered the body loose and lazy, yet inspired a playful and coltish humor. I noticed that the countryside, naturally fertile and agreeable, was almost uncultivated—as so many inhabitants are hostile to work.

I saw, in every direction, women and young girls vainly attired, who were going, while singing the praises of Aphrodite, to consecrate themselves at her temple; beauty, charms, joy, pleasures glowed equally on their faces. But these charms were affected: you did not see a noble simplicity and a lovable modesty, which make up the greatest enchantments of beauty. The effete air, the art of composing their faces, their vain jewelry, their languishing walk, their gaze that seemed to seek that of men, their zeal for igniting great passions—in a word, all that I saw in those women seemed vile and contemptible to me. By dint of wanting to please, they disgusted me.

"They led me to the temple of the goddess; she has several of them on this island, for she is particularly adored in Cythera, Idalium, and Paphos. It is to Cythera that I was led. The temple is all marble. It is a perfect peristyle: the columns are of a thickness and height that render this edifice very majestic. Above the architrave and the frieze are, on each side, great pediments, where one sees in bas relief all the most pleasing adventures of the goddess.

"At the door of the temple is an incessant crowd of peoples who come to make their offerings. They never slaughter any victim within the interior of the sacred place. They do not burn there, as elsewhere, the fat of the heifers and bulls. They never spill their blood. They only present the beasts they offer before the altar, and none can be offered up that is not young, white, without defect and spotless. They cover them with streamers of purple embroidered with gold; their horns are gilded and adorned with bouquets of the most fragrant flowers. After they have been presented before the altar, they are sent to a place well away, where they are slain for the feasts of the priests of the goddess. They also offer all kinds of perfumed liquors and wine sweeter than nectar. The priests are dressed in long white robes, with bands of the same gold, and fringe down to the bottom of their robes. They burn day and night on the altars the most exquisite perfumes of the East, and they form a kind of cloud that mounts to the sky. All the columns of the temple are adorned with hanging festoons. All the vessels that are used for sacrifices are of gold. A sacred wood of myrtles surrounds the building. There are only young boys and girls of a rare beauty, who may present the victims to the priests and who dare to light the fire of the altars. But impudence and dissoluteness dishonor a temple so magnificent.

"At first, I was horrified by all that I saw. But imperceptibly I began to become accustomed to it. Vice no longer frightened me. All the gatherings inspired an inexplicable inclination for disorder in me. They mocked my innocence. My restraint and my modesty served as a plaything for those shameless peoples. They spared no effort to excite all my passions, to set traps for me, and to awaken in me a taste for pleasure. I felt myself weakening every day. The good education I had received almost no longer sustained me. All my good resolutions were vanishing. I no longer felt the strength to resist the evil that was pressing down from all sides. I even had a false modesty about virtue.

"I was like a man who swims in a deep and rapid river. At first, he slices through the water and swims against the strong current. But if the banks are steep, and if he cannot rest on the shore, he finally wearies little by little. His strength abandons him, his exhausted limbs go numb, and the river's current sweeps him away. Like so, my eyes were beginning to dim, my heart was failing, I could no longer recall either my reason or the memory of the virtues of my father. The dream where I believed I had seen wise Mentor descend to the Elysian Fields completed my discouragement. A secret and sweet languor was taking hold of me; I already loved the flattering poison that slipped from vein to vein and penetrated to the marrow of my bones. I still heaved, however, deep sighs. I shed bitter tears. I roared like a lion in my fury. 'O unhappy youth!' I said, 'O gods, who cruelly toy with men, why do you make them pass through this age, which is a time of madness and blazing fever? O may I be covered with white hair, stooped and near the grave, like Laertes my grandfather. Death would be sweeter to me than the shameful weakness where I find myself.' Barely had I spoken so when my pain eased and my heart, drunk with a mad passion, shook off almost all modesty. Then I found myself plunged into an abyss of remorse again. During this distress, I ran roving hither and yon in the sacred grove, akin to a doe that a hunter has wounded. She runs through vast forests to relieve her pain, but the arrow that pierced her in the flank follows her everywhere. She carries the murderous shaft everywhere. Like so, I ran in vain to forget myself, and nothing eased the cut in my heart.

"At that moment, I spied somewhat far from me in the thick shade of this wood the figure of wise Mentor, but his face looked so pale, so sad, and so austere to me that I could feel no joy in it.

"'Is it you, then,' I cried out, 'O my dear friend, my only hope, is it you? What then? Is it really you? Does a deceiving image come to trick my eyes? Is it you, Mentor? Is it not your shade, still sensitive to my woes? Are you not among the ranks of happy souls who possess their virtue, and to whom the gods give pure pleasures in an eternal peace in the Elysian Fields? Speak, Mentor, are you still alive? Am I fortuitous enough to possess you? Or rather is it only a shade of my friend?' Saying these words, I ran toward him, frenzied, until I was out of breath. He waited for me tranquilly, without taking a step toward me. O gods, you know what was my joy when I felt my arms touching him. *No, it is not a vain shade. I am holding him, I am embracing my dear Mentor.* That is what I cried inside. I drenched his face with a torrent of tears. I clung to his neck, unable to speak. He regarded me sadly, eyes filled with a tender compassion.

"Finally, I said to him, 'Alas! Where do you come from? In what dangers have you not left me during your absence, and what would I do now without you?'

"But, without answering my questions, 'Flee!' he said in a terrifying tone. 'Flee, hasten to flee! Here, the land only bears poison as fruit. The air one breathes is pestilent. The contagious men only speak to each other in order to spread a mortal venom. Craven and infamous voluptuousness, which is the most horrible of the evils released from Pandora's box, softens all hearts and tolerates no virtue here. Flee. What delays you? Do not even look behind you in fleeing. Blot out even the least memory of this execrable island.'

"He spoke, and immediately I felt as if a thick cloud dissipated before my eyes and allowed me to see pure light. A joy sweet and filled with a steadfast courage was reborn in my heart. This joy was very different from that other soft and coltish joy with which my senses had been poisoned at first: one is a drunken and troubled joy, which is interspersed with furious passions and stinging remorse; the other is a joy of reason, which has something of blissfulness and heaven. It is always pure and balanced; nothing can drain it; the more one plunges in, the sweeter it is; it delights the soul without troubling it. Then I shed tears of joy, and I found that nothing was so sweet as to cry so.

"'O happy the men to whom virtue reveals itself in all its beauty!' I said, 'Can one see it without loving it? Can one love it without being happy?'

"Mentor said to me, 'I must leave you. I am departing as we speak. It is not permitted for me to stay.'

"'Where are you going, then?' I responded to him. 'In what uninhabitable land would I not follow you? Do not think of being able to escape me. I would rather die in your footsteps.' Saying these words, I held him tightly with all my strength.

"'It is in vain,' he said to me, 'that you hope to detain me. Cruel Metophis sold me to Ethiopians or Arabs. They, being allied with Damascus in Syria for their commerce, wanted to rid themselves of me, believing to draw in a great sum from someone named Hazael, who was seeking a Greek slave in order to get acquainted with the mores of Greece and to learn about our sciences. Indeed, Hazael paid dearly for me. What I have taught him about our mores gave him the curiosity to spend time on the island of Crete to study the wise laws of Minos. During our voyage, the winds compelled us to put in on the island of Cyprus. While waiting for a favorable wind, he came to make his offerings at the temple. There he is coming out. The winds are calling us; already our sails swell. Farewell, dear Telemachus; a slave who reveres the gods must faithfully follow his master. The gods no longer permit me to be my own. If I were my own, the gods know, I would only be yours alone. Farewell! Remember the travails of Odysseus and the tears of Penelope. Remember the just gods. O gods, protectors of innocence, in what land am I compelled to leave Telemachus.'

"'No, no,' I told him, 'my dear Mentor, it will not be up to you to leave me here—I would rather die than see you depart without me. This Syrian master, is he merciless? Was it a tigress whose teats he suckled in his infancy? Would he want to snatch you from my arms? He must give me death or suffer me to follow you. You yourself exhort me to flee, yet you do not wish that I flee following your footsteps. I am going to speak to Hazael; he will perhaps have pity on my youth and my tears. Since he loves wisdom and he goes so far seeking it, he cannot have a ferocious and insensitive heart. I will fling myself at his feet. I will embrace his knees. I will not let him go unless he agrees to let me follow you. My dear Mentor, I will make myself a slave along with you; I will offer to give myself to him. If he refuses me, I am done for. I will deliver myself from life.'

"At that moment, Hazael called Mentor. I bowed down before him. He was surprised to see a stranger in this posture.

"'What do you want?' he said to me.

"'Life,' I answered. 'For I cannot live if you do not suffer that I follow Mentor, who is yours. I am the son of the great Odysseus, the wisest of the Greek kings who overthrew the superb city of Troy, famous throughout Asia. I do not tell you of my birth to boast, but only to inspire in you some pity for my misfortunes. I have sought my father by all the seas, having with me this man, who was for me another father. Fortune, to top off my woes, took him from me. She made him your slave. Suffer that I be one too. If it is true that you love justice, and that you are going to Crete in order to learn the laws of the good King Minos, do not harden your heart to my sighs and to my tears. You see the son of a king who is reduced to asking for servitude as his only recourse. Another time, I wanted to die in Sicily to avoid slavery. But my former woes were only weak attempts by the outrages of Fortune. Now I fear being unable to be received among your slaves. O gods, see my woes. O Hazael, remember Minos, whose wisdom you admire, and who will judge us both in the kingdom of Hades.'

"Hazael, looking at me with a kind and humane face, held out his hand and lifted me up. 'I am not ignorant,' he said to me 'of the wisdom and virtue of Odysseus. Mentor often recounted to me what glory he acquired among the Greeks and, besides, winged Rumor made his name heard by all the peoples of the East. Follow me, son of Odysseus. I will be your father until you find the one who gave life to you. Even if I were not touched by the glory of your father, by his misfortunes, and by yours, the friendship I have for Mentor would commit me to take care of you. It is true that I purchased him as a slave, but I keep him as a faithful friend. The silver he cost me acquired for me the dearest and most precious friend that I have on earth. I found wisdom in him. I owe him all that I have of love for virtue. From this moment, he is free; you will be also. I only ask each of you for your heart.'

"In an instant, I passed from the most bitter pain to the most vibrant joy mortals can feel—I found myself saved from a horrible danger; I was approaching my country, I found help to return there; I enjoyed the consolation of being alongside a man who already loved me through the pure love of virtue; lastly, I found everything again in finding Mentor, to part from him no more.

"Hazael advances along the sand of the shore. We follow him, we board the vessel, the oarsmen plow the peaceful waters. A light zephyr plays with our sails, animating the entire vessel and giving it a gentle motion. The island of Cyprus soon disappears.

"Hazael, who was impatient to know my sentiments, asked me what I thought of the mores of that island. I told him ingenuously to what danger my youth had been exposed and the struggle I had suffered within me. He was touched by my horror for vice, and spoke these words, 'O Aphrodite, I recognize your might and that of your son. I burned incense on your altars, but suffer that I detest the infamous effeteness of the inhabitants of your island and the brutal impudence with which they celebrate your festivals.'

"Then he conversed with Mentor about that first might that formed heaven and earth, that unique light, infinite and immutable, that gives to all without dividing, that sovereign and universal truth that illuminates all minds, as the sun illuminates all bodies. 'The one,' he added, 'who has never seen this pure light is blind, as if born blind. He spends his life in a profound night, like the peoples that the sun does not shine on for several months of the year; he believes himself wise, and he is foolish. He believes he sees all, and he sees nothing. He dies having never seen anything: at most, he glimpses somber and false glimmers, vain shades, phantoms that have nothing real. Like so are all men swept away by sensual pleasure and by the enchantment of the unreal. There are not on earth any true men, except for those who consult, who love, who follow this eternal reasoning; it is reason that inspires us when we think well; it is reason that corrects us when we think poorly. We do not hold reason less valuable than life. Reason is like a great ocean of light. Our minds are like streams that leave it and return in order to lose themselves in it.'

"Although I did not yet perfectly understand the profound wisdom of these discourses, I did not fail to appreciate a certain something of pureness and sublimity. My heart was warmed by it, and truth seemed to me to shine in all those words. They continued to talk of the origin of the gods, the heroes, the poets, the golden age, the flood, the first stories of humankind, the river of forgetfulness into which the souls of the dead plunge, the endless pains prepared for the impious ones in the gloomy pit of Tartarus, and of that happy peace which the just enjoy in the Elysian Fields, without fear of losing it.

"While Hazael and Mentor were talking, we caught sight of dolphins covered with scales that appeared to be of gold and azure. Playing together, they whipped the swells into lots of spume. After them came Tritons, who were trumpeting with their curved conch shells; they surrounded Amphitrite's chariot pulled by seahorses, whiter than snow who, plowing the salty waters, left far behind them a vast furrow in the sea. Their eyes were ablaze and their mouths steaming. The goddess' chariot was a conch shell of a marvelous shape. It was of a whiteness more brilliant than ivory, and the wheels were of gold. This chariot seemed to fly over the surface of the peaceful water. A throng of nymphs wreathed with flowers were swimming in droves behind the chariot, their beautiful hair hanging to their shoulders and flowing with the wind. The goddess held in one hand a golden scepter to command the waves, and in the other she carried on her knees the little god Palaemon, her son, nursing at her breast. She had a serene expression and a gentle majesty that made the seditious winds and all the black tempests flee. The Tritons drove the horses and held the golden reins. A great purple sail floated in the air above the chariot. It was half-filled by the puffs of a multitude of tiny zephyrs striving to push it with their breath. In midair, Aeolus could be seen, driven, restless, and ardent. His wrinkled and sorrowful face, his menacing voice, his thick and hanging eyebrows, his eyes filled with a somber and austere fire held the proud Northwind in silence and pushed back all the clouds. The immense whales and all the monsters of the sea, making the bitter water ebb and flow with their spouts, hastily came out of their deep grottos to see the goddess."

End of Book IV

THE ADVENTURES OF
TELEMACHUS
SON OF ODYSSEUS

BOOK V

"*After we had marveled at this spectacle*, we began to behold the mountains of Crete, which we still had some difficulty distinguishing from the clouds in the sky and the swells of the sea. Soon we saw the summit of Mount Ida that rises above the other mountains of the island, just as an old stag in a forest bears his branchy antlers above the heads of the young fawns who follow him. Little by little we saw more distinctly the coasts of this island that presented themselves before our eyes like an amphitheater. As much as the land of Cyprus had appeared neglected and uncultivated to us, so that of Crete revealed itself fertile and adorned with every fruit through the labor of its inhabitants.

"On all sides we noticed well-built villages, burgs that rivaled cities, as well as superb cities. We found no field where the hand of the diligent plowman was not impressed. Everywhere the plow had left deep furrows. Brambles, thorns, and all the plants that uselessly occupy the land are unknown in this country. We considered with pleasure the deep vales where herds of oxen bellowed in the rich grasses along the streams, the grazing sheep on the hillside, the vast countryside covered with yellow ears of grain, rich gifts of fruitful Demeter; lastly, mountains adorned with vines and clusters of a grape, already colorful, that promised winemakers the sweet presents of Dionysus to enchant the worries of men.

"Mentor told us that he had once been to Crete and explained what he knew of it. 'This island,' he said, 'admired by all foreigners, and famous for its hundred cities, effortlessly feeds all its inhabitants, though they are countless; for the Earth never tires of spreading her bounty on those who cultivate her, and her fruitful womb cannot be exhausted. The more men there are in a country, provided they are hard-working, the more they enjoy abundance. They never need be jealous of each other. Earth, this good mother, multiplies her gifts according to the number of her children, who merit her fruits through their work. The ambition and avarice of men are the only sources of their unhappiness. Men want to have it all, and they make themselves unhappy through the desire for superfluities. If they wanted to live simply and be content in satisfying true needs, one would see abundance, joy, peace, and unity everywhere.

'That is what Minos, the wisest and the best of all kings, had understood. All that which you will see of the most marvelous on this island is the fruit of his laws. The education he had given to the children renders healthy and robust bodies. They are accustomed from the beginning to a simple, frugal, and hard-working life. They assume that all voluptuousness softens the body and mind. They never propose any other pleasure to them than that of being invincible through virtue and of acquiring much glory—not only the glory that comes from the courage to scorn death in the dangers of war, but even that which comes from trampling underfoot excessive riches and shameful pleasures. Here, they punish three vices that are unpunished by other peoples: ingratitude, dissimulation, and avarice. As for flamboyance and softness, they never need to repress them, for they are unknown in Crete. Everyone works here and no one dreams of enriching himself. Each believes himself paid enough for his work to lead a gentle and orderly life, where he enjoys in peace and with abundance all that is truly necessary in life.

'Here, they tolerate neither precious furnishings, nor magnificent garments, nor delicious feasts, nor gilded palaces. The garments are of fine wool and beautiful colors, yet completely plain and unembroidered. The meals here are sober. They drink little wine, and good bread makes up the main part, along with the fruits that the trees offer, as if of their own accord, and milk from the flocks. At most, they eat a little plain meat, without rich sauces. Even so, they attend to reserve what there is of the best in the great cattle herds in order to make agriculture flourish.

'The houses here are clean, comfortable, pleasant, yet without ornamentation. Superb architecture is not ignored; however, it is reserved for the temples of the gods, and men would not dare have houses resembling those of immortals. The great possessions of the Cretans are health, strength, courage, peace and family unity, liberty of all citizens, abundance of necessary things, scorn for superfluities, the habit of work and horror of idleness, emulation of virtue, submission to the laws, and reverential awe of the just gods.'

"I asked him what the authority of the king consisted of and he answered, 'He has complete authority over the peoples, but the laws have complete authority over him. He has an absolute power to do good, but his hands are tied as soon as he wants to do evil. The laws entrust to him the peoples, as the most precious of all trusts, on condition that he will be the father of his subjects.

'They desire that a single man serve, through his wisdom and his restraint, the felicity of so many men, and not that so many men serve, through their destitution and through their craven servitude, to flatter the effete pridefulness of a single man. The king must have nothing above others except what is necessary either to relieve them in their arduous duties or to impress upon the people respect for the one who must sustain the laws.

'Furthermore, the king must be more sober, more hostile to softness, more exempt from flamboyance and haughtiness than any other. He must not have more riches and pleasures, but more wisdom, virtue, and glory than the rest of men. He must be the defender of the homeland without, in commanding armies, and the judge of the peoples within, so as to render them good, wise, and happy. It is not for himself that the gods have made him king. He is only king in order to be the man of the peoples. It is to the peoples that he owes all his time, all his attentions, all his affection, and he is only worthy of kingship to the extent that he forgets himself in order to sacrifice himself for the public good.

'Minos only wanted his children to reign after him on condition that they reign following these maxims. He loved his people even more than his family. It is through such wisdom that he rendered Crete so mighty and so happy; it is through that restraint that he eclipsed the glory of all the conquerors who want to make use of the peoples for their own grandeur, that is to say for their vanity; lastly, it is through his justice that he merited being in the Underworld the sovereign judge of the dead.'

"While Mentor was making this speech, we landed on the island. We saw the famous labyrinth, a work from the hands of the ingenious Daedalus, and which was an imitation of the great labyrinth that we had seen in Egypt. While we were considering this curious edifice, we saw people covering the shore and running in droves to a spot near the edge of the sea. We asked the cause of their eagerness, and this is what a Cretan named Nausicrates recounted to us:

"'Idomeneus, son of Deucalion and grandson of Minos,' he said, 'had gone like the other Greek kings to the siege of Troy. After the ruin of that city, he set sail to return to Crete. But a tempest was so violent that the pilot of his vessel and all the others who were experienced in navigation believed their wreck was inevitable. Each had Death before his eyes. Each saw the abysses opening up to engulf him. Each deplored his misfortune, not even hoping for the sad repose of the shades that traverse the Styx after having received sepulcher.

"'Idomeneus, raising his eyes and hands toward the sky, invoked Poseidon: "O mighty god," he cried out, "you who hold the empire of the waters, deign to listen to a poor wretch. If you cause me to see the island of Crete again, despite the furor of the winds, I will sacrifice to you the first head that presents itself to my eyes."

"'Meanwhile, his son, impatient to see his father again, was hastening to go out to meet and embrace him, poor unfortunate who did not know that he was running to his doom. The father, escaped from the tempest, arrived in the desired port. He was thanking Poseidon for having listened to his vows, but soon he sensed how ill-fated his vows were to him; a presentiment of his misfortune gave him a burning repentance for his indiscreet vow. He feared arriving among his own, and he was apprehensive about seeing again what he held most dear in the world. But cruel Nemesis, merciless goddess who keeps vigil in order to punish men, particularly prideful kings, was pushing Idomeneus with a fatal and invisible hand. He arrives. Barely does he dare to raise his eyes; he sees his son; he recoils, seized with horror. His eyes search, but in vain, for some other head less dear that might serve him as victim.

"'At the same time the son flings himself at his neck and is completely stunned that his father responds so poorly to his affection. He sees him melting in tears. "O my father," he said, "where does this sadness come from? After so long an absence, are you irritated finding yourself in your kingdom again and making the joy of your son? What have I done? You turn your eyes away for fear of seeing me?"

BOOK V

"'The father, crushed with pain, said nothing. Finally, after deep sighs, he said, "O Poseidon, what have I promised you? At what price have you saved me from shipwreck? Render me to the waves and rocks, which should, in breaking me apart, end my sad life. Allow my son to live. O cruel god! Here! Here is my blood, spare his." Speaking so, he drew his sword to impale himself. But those around him arrested his hand.'

"'The elder Sophronymus, interpreter of the will of the gods, assured him that he could satisfy Poseidon without giving death to his son. "Your promise," he said, "was imprudent. The gods do not want to be honored through cruelty; be very careful of adding to the error of your promise that of fulfilling it against the laws of nature. Offer one hundred bulls whiter than snow to Poseidon. Have their blood stream around his altar wreathed with flowers. Have a sweet incense burned in honor of this god."

"'Idomeneus was listening to this discourse, head lowered, without responding. Fury was alight in his eyes. His face, pale and disfigured, changed color every second. They saw his limbs trembling. Meanwhile, his son was saying to him, "Here I am, my father. Your son is ready to die to appease the god. Do not draw his anger to you. I die content, since my death will have saved you from yours. Strike, my father. Do not fear finding in me a son unworthy of you, who fears to die."

"'At that moment, Idomeneus, completely beside himself, as if ripped apart by the infernal Furies, shocks all those who are observing him closely. He sinks his sword into the heart of this child. He withdraws it all steaming and bloody to plunge it into his own entrails. He is once again restrained by those surrounding him. The child falls in his own blood. His eyes cloud over with the shadows of death. He half-opens them to the light, but no sooner has he found it than he can no longer bear it. Just as a beautiful lily in the middle of the fields, cut at its root by the blade of the plow, languishes, and no longer sustains itself; it has not yet lost that vibrant white and that brilliance that charms the eyes, but the earth no longer nourishes it, and its life is put out. So the son of Idomeneus, like a young and tender flower, is cruelly reaped in his earliest boyhood. The father, in the excess of his pain, goes insane. He does not know where he is, nor what he did, nor what he should do. He staggers toward the city and asks for his son.

"'The people, however, touched with compassion for the child and horror at the barbaric action of the father, cry out that the just gods have delivered him over to the Furies. Fury provides them with arms. They take up sticks and stones. Discord blows into every heart a deadly venom. The Cretans, the wise Cretans, forget the wisdom they had so loved. They no longer recognize the grandson of wise Minos. Idomeneus' friends no longer find any salvation for him other than taking him back to his vessels. They embark with him, they flee at the mercy of the waves; Idomeneus, returning to himself, thanks them for having snatched him from a land he had soaked with the blood of his son and where he would no longer know how to live. The winds drive them toward Hesperia, and they go seeking a new kingdom in the country of the Salentines.

~

BOOK V

"'Meanwhile, the Cretans, no longer having a king to govern them, resolved to choose one who preserves, in their purity, the established laws. Here are the measures they have taken to make this choice. All the principal citizens from a hundred cities are assembled here. They have already begun with sacrifices. They have assembled all the most famous wise men from neighboring countries to examine the wisdom of those who would appear worthy of commanding. They have prepared public games, where all the pretenders to the throne fight, for they want to give the kingship as a prize to the one who they judge victor over all the others, not only in mind but also in body. They want a king whose body is strong and able, and whose soul is adorned with wisdom and virtue. They summon here all foreigners.

"After recounting this astonishing story to us, Nausicrates says to us: 'Hasten, then, O foreigners, to come into our assembly. You will fight with the others and, if the gods destine victory to either of you, you will reign in this country.' We followed him, without any desire for victory but merely out of curiosity to see a thing so extraordinary.

"We arrived at a type of vast stadium surrounded by a thick forest. The middle of the stadium was an arena prepared for the fighters. It was bordered by a great amphitheater of a fresh lawn on which were seated and arranged a countless number of people. When we arrived, they received us with honor, for the Cretans are the peoples of the world who practice hospitality the most nobly and the most scrupulously. They had us seated and invited us to fight. Mentor excused himself based on his age, and Hazael on his weak health. My youth and my vigor denied me every excuse. I nevertheless cast a glance at Mentor to discern his thoughts, and I perceived that he wished for me to fight. So, I accepted the offer they made me.

"I stripped off my garments, they streamed sweet and glistening oil over all the limbs of my body, and I mingled among the fighters. From every direction, they were saying that it was the son of Odysseus who had come to try and take home the prize, and several Cretans, who had been in Ithaca during my childhood, recognized me. The first fight was that of wrestling.

"A Rhodian around thirty-five years old overcame all the others who dared stand before him. He was still in the full vigor of youth. His arms were sinewy and fit. With the slightest movement, one saw all his muscles. He was equally supple and strong. I did not look worthy to him of being vanquished and, regarding my tender youth with pity, he wanted to withdraw. But I stood before him. Then we seized each another. We squeezed each other breathless. We were shoulder to shoulder, foot to foot, every muscle stretched, and arms intertwined, like serpents, each striving to lift his enemy off the ground. At times he tried to overtake me by pushing me from the right side. At times he strove to lean on me from the left. While he was groping me so, I pushed him so violently that his back gave way. He fell on the sand and dragged me on top of him. In vain, he tried to put me under him. I held him fast under me. All the people shouted, 'Victory to the son of Odysseus!' And I helped the confused Rhodian to get up.

BOOK V

"The boxing match was more difficult. The son of a rich citizen of Samos had acquired a high reputation in this type of fighting. All the others ceded to him. I alone hoped for victory. At first, he beat me on the head, and then in the stomach with blows that made me vomit blood and spread a thick cloud over my eyes. I staggered, he squeezed me, and I could no longer breathe. But I was reanimated by the voice of Mentor, shouting out, 'O son of Odysseus, will you be vanquished?' Anger gave me new strength. I evaded several blows, which would have overwhelmed me. As soon as the Samian had swung and missed, and his arms were stretched out in vain, I surprised him in this forward posture. He was already recoiling when I raised my glove to fall upon him with more force. He wanted to dodge and, losing balance, he gave me the means of knocking him to the ground. No sooner was he stretched out on the ground than I held out my hand to help him up. He got up on his own, covered with dust and blood. His shame was extreme, but he dared not renew the fight.

"Straightaway they began the chariot races, distributing the chariots by lot. Mine found itself the least when it came to the lightness of the wheels and the vigor of the horses. We took off. A cloud of dust flew up and covered the sky. At the start, I let the others pass ahead of me. A young Lacedaemonian named Crantor immediately left all the others behind. A Cretan named Polycletes followed him closely. Hippomachus, Idomeneus' relative, who aspired to succeed him, loosening the reins of his horses that were steaming with sweat, was leaning far out over their flowing manes, and the motion of his chariot's wheels was so rapid that they looked motionless, like the wings of an eagle that slices through the air. My horses came alive and, little by little, putting themselves to work, I left far behind me almost all those who had taken off with such ardor.

"Hippomachus pushed his horses too hard. The most vigorous suddenly collapsed, and by its fall, denied its master the hope of reigning. Polycletes, leaning too far over his horses, could not hold firm over a jolt. He fell. The reins escaped him, and he was only too happy to be able to avoid death. Crantor, seeing with eyes full of indignation that I was right alongside him, redoubled his ardor. At times he invoked the gods and promised them rich offerings, at times he spoke to his horses to animate them. He feared my passing between the boundary and him, for my horses, better handled than his, were in position to pull ahead of him. There no longer remained to him any other recourse than that of closing off the passage to me. To succeed at it, he risked breaking apart against the boundary. Indeed, he broke his wheel on it. I only thought to make the turn quickly so as not to be embroiled in his disorder, and he saw me a moment after at the end of the course.

"The people cried out once more, 'Victory to the son of Odysseus. It is he whom the gods destine to reign over us.' Meanwhile, the most illustrious and the wisest among the Cretans led us into an ancient and sacred wood, secluded from the view of profane men, where the elders, whom Minos had established as judges of the people and guardians of the laws, assembled us. We were the same ones who had fought in the games. No others were admitted.

BOOK V

"The wise men opened the book where all the laws of Minos are collected. I felt seized with respect and shame when I approached those elders, whom age rendered venerable without taking away the vigor of the mind. They were seated with order and fixed in their places. Their hair was white. Several of them had hardly any. One saw shining on their grave faces a gentle and tranquil wisdom. They did not rush to speak. They only said what they had resolved to say. When they were of different views, they were so restrained in sustaining what they thought, on both sides, that one would have believed they all held the same opinion. Long experience of things past and the habit of work gave them great views on all things. But what perfected their reasoning the most was the calmness of their minds, which were delivered from mad passions and the whims of youth. Wisdom alone acted in them, and the fruit of their long virtue was to have so well tamed their humors that they effortlessly enjoyed the sweet and noble pleasure of listening to reason. Admiring them, I wished that my life could leap ahead to suddenly arrive at such an estimable old age. I found unhappy youth to be so impetuous and distant from that virtue so enlightened and tranquil.

"The first among these elders opened the book of the laws of Minos. It was a large book that was ordinarily kept encased in a golden coffer along with perfumes. All these elders kissed it respectfully, for they say that after the gods from whom the good laws come, nothing should be so sacred to man as the laws intended to render them good, wise, and happy. Those who have in their hands the laws to govern the peoples must always let themselves be governed by the laws. It is the law, and not man, which must reign. Such is the discourse of these wise men. Then, the one who was presiding proposed three questions, which should be decided according to the maxims of Minos. The first question is to know, who is the most free of all men?

"Some answered that it was a king who had over his people an absolute empire and who was victorious over all his enemies; others maintained that it was a man so rich that he could satisfy all his desires; others said that it was a man who did not marry, and who traveled throughout his entire life in various countries, without ever being subjugated to the laws of any nation; others imagined that it was a barbarian who, living off his hunt in the middle of the woods, was independent of all government policies and every need; others believed that it was a man newly set free, because in getting out of the rigors of servitude, he enjoyed more than any other the sweetness of liberty; lastly, others dared to say that it was a dying man, because death delivered him from everything, and all men together no longer had any power over him.

"When my turn came, I had no difficulty answering because I had not forgotten what Mentor had often said to me. 'The freest of all men,' I answered, 'is the one who can be free even in slavery. In whatever country and in whatever station he may be, he is very free, provided he reveres the gods and he reveres only them—in a word, the man truly free is the one who, released from all fear and all desire, only bows to the gods and to his reason.' The elders looked at each other, smiling, and were surprised to see that my answer was precisely that of Minos.

BOOK V

"Then they proposed the second question in these terms: 'Who is the most unhappy of all men?' Each said what came to his mind. One said, 'It is a man who has neither possessions, nor health, nor honor.' Another said, 'It is a man who has not one friend.' Others maintained that it is a man who has children, ungrateful and unworthy of him. Coming to a wise man from the island of Lesbos, he said, 'The most unhappy of all men is the one who believes himself to be, for unhappiness depends less on the things that one suffers than the impatience with which one increases his unhappiness.'

"At those words, all assembled cried out again. They applauded, and each believed this wise Lesbian would bring home the prize on this question. But they asked me my thought, and I responded according to the maxims of Mentor. 'The most unhappy of all men is a king who believes himself to be happy in rendering other men miserable. He is doubly unhappy through his blindness, not recognizing his unhappiness, he cannot heal himself of it; he even fears recognizing it; truth cannot pierce the crowd of flatterers to reach him; he is tyrannized by his passions; he does not recognize his duties. He has never tasted the pleasure of doing good, nor felt the enchantment of pure virtue. He is unhappy and worthy of being so. His unhappiness increases every day. He races to his ruin, and the gods prepare to confound him through an eternal punishment.'

"All assembled avowed that I had defeated the wise Lesbian, and the elders declared that I had met the true sense of Minos.

"As for the third question, they asked: 'Which of the two is preferable: on the one hand, a king conquering and invincible in war; on the other, a king inexperienced in war, yet suitable to wisely establish policies for the peoples in peacetime?' Most answered that the king invincible in war was preferable. 'What does it serve,' they said, 'to have a king who knows how to govern well in peace if he does not know how to defend the country when war comes? The enemies will vanquish him and reduce his people to servitude.' Others maintained on the contrary that the peace-loving king would be better because he would fear war and would avoid it through his attentions. Others were saying that a conquering king would strive for the glory of his people as well as his own and would render his subjects masters over other nations, whereas a peace-loving king would hold them in a shameful cowardice.

"They wanted to know my sentiment. I answered, 'A king who only knows how to govern in peace or in war and who is not capable of leading his people under both these conditions is only half a king. But if you compare a king who only knows warfare to a wise king who, without knowing warfare, is capable of sustaining it when necessary through his generals, I find him preferable to the other. A king entirely turned toward war would always want to wage it in order to extend his dominion and his own glory—he would ruin his peoples; what does it serve a people that their king subjugates other nations if they are unhappy under his reign?

"'Besides, long wars always drag after them much disorder. The victors themselves are out of kilter during those times of confusion. See what it cost them in Greece in order to triumph over Troy. She was deprived of her kings for more than ten years. While everything is on fire for war, the laws, the agriculture, the industrial arts languish. Even the best princes, while they have a war to sustain, are compelled to do the greatest of evils, which is to tolerate licentiousness and to make use of the wicked. How many scoundrels there are who would be punished during peace, and whose audacity must be rewarded in the disorder of war.

"'Never has any people had a conquering king without having suffered much from his ambition. A conqueror, drunk on his glory, ruins his victorious nation almost as much as the vanquished nation. A prince who does not have the qualities necessary for peace cannot have his subjects enjoy the fruits of a war happily ended. He is like a man who would defend his field against his neighbor, and would even usurp that of his neighbor, yet does not know how to plow or to sow in order to reap any harvest. Such a man seems born to destroy, ravage, and overthrow the world and not to render a people happy through a wise government.

"'Now we come to the peace-loving king. It is true that he is not suitable for great conquests; that is to say, he was not born to trouble the happiness of his people in wanting to vanquish other peoples that justice has not subjugated to him. But if he is truly suitable to govern in peace, he has all the qualities necessary to keep his people safe against his enemies. This is how: he is just, restrained, and accommodating with regard to his neighbors. He never undertakes against them any scheme that might disturb his peace. He is loyal in his alliances. His allies love him, do not fear him, and have a complete confidence in him. If there is some restless neighbor, haughty and ambitious, all the other neighboring kings, who fear that restless neighbor and who have no jealousy toward the peace-loving king, join up with this good king in order to keep him from being oppressed. His probity, his good faith, his moderation render him the arbiter of all the states that surround his. While the enterprising king is odious to all the others and incessantly exposed to their leagues, this one has the glory of being like a father and tutor to all the other kings. There, those are the advantages that he has without. Those which he possesses within are even more solid.

"'Since he is suitable for governing in peace, I must assume that he governs by the wisest laws. He curtails flamboyance, softness, and all the arts that only serve to indulge vices. He causes the other arts useful to the true necessities of life to flourish. Above all, he applies his subjects to agriculture. In doing so, he puts them in abundance of necessary things. This hard-working people, simple in their mores, accustomed to living on little, easily earning their living through the cultivation of their lands, multiplies to infinity. There are in this kingdom a countless number of people, yet a healthy, vigorous, robust, people who are not softened through voluptuousness, who are trained in virtue, who are not attached to the sweetness of a craven and indulgent life, who know how to scorn death, who would rather die than lose that liberty they enjoy under a wise king who applies himself to reign only in order to make reason reign.

"'Should a conquering neighbor attack this people, he will perhaps not find them so accustomed to encampments, to battle formations, or to erecting machinery to besiege a city, but he will find them invincible through their multitude, their courage, their

BOOK V

patience in struggles, their habit of enduring poverty, their vigor in combat, and a virtue that even setbacks cannot beat down. Besides, if the king is not experienced enough to command his armies himself, he will have them commanded by people who are capable of it, and he will know how to make use of them without losing his authority. Meanwhile, he will draw succor from his allies. His subjects will prefer to die rather than to pass under the dominion of another king, violent and unjust. The gods themselves will fight for him. You see what resources he will have amidst the greatest perils.

"'I conclude, therefore, that the peace-loving king who is ignorant of warfare is a very imperfect king since he does not know how to fulfill one of his greatest functions, which is to vanquish his enemies; but I add that he is nevertheless infinitely superior to the conquering king who lacks the necessary qualities in peacetime and who is only suited to war.'

"I perceived in the assembly many people who were unable to appreciate this opinion, for most men, dazzled by brilliant things, like victories and conquests, prefer them to what is natural, tranquil, and solid, like peace and good policies for the peoples. But all the elders declared that I had spoken like Minos.

"The head of these elders exclaimed: 'I see the fulfillment of an oracle of Apollo, known throughout our island. Minos had consulted the god in order to know how much time his race would reign, following the laws that he had just established. The god answered him, "Your race will cease to reign when a foreigner enters into your island in order to make your laws reign there."

"'We had feared that some foreigner would come to conquer the island of Crete. But the misfortune of Idomeneus and the wisdom of the son of Odysseus, who understands better than any other mortal the laws of Minos, show us the meaning of the oracle. What delays us in crowning the one whom the destinies give us as king?'

"Immediately, the elders leave the interior of the sacred wood, and the first elder, taking me by the hand, announces to the people, already impatient in awaiting a decision, that I had won the prize. Barely had he finished speaking when we hear a confused noise from the entire assembly. All loose cries of joy. The entire seashore and all the neighboring mountains reverberate with this cry, 'May the son of Odysseus, like Minos, reign over the Cretans!'

"I waited a moment, and I motioned with my hand for them to listen to me. At the same time, Mentor said in my ear, 'Are you renouncing your homeland? The ambition to reign, will it make you forget Penelope, who is waiting for you as her last hope, and the great Odysseus, whom the gods have resolved to return to you?' These words pierced my heart and sustained me against the vain desire to reign.

"Meanwhile, a profound silence from this entire tumultuous assembly gave me the means of speaking thus: 'O illustrious Cretans, I do not merit commanding you. The oracle that was just related shows indeed that the race of Minos will cease to reign when a foreigner enters into this island and causes the laws of this wise king to reign here. But it is not said that this foreigner will reign. I want to believe that I am this foreigner decreed by the oracle. I have fulfilled the prediction. I came onto this island. I revealed the true sense of the laws, and I hope that my explication serves to make them reign with the man whom you will choose. As for me, I prefer my homeland, the poor, small island of Ithaca, to the hundred cities of Crete, to the glory and to the opulence of this beautiful kingdom.

'Suffer that I follow what the destinies have decreed. If I fought in your games, it was not in the hope of reigning here. It was to merit your esteem and your compassion; it was so that you would give me the means of swiftly returning to the place of my birth. I prefer to obey my father Odysseus and to console my mother Penelope than to reign over all the peoples of the universe. O Cretans, you see the depths of my heart. I must part from you, but death alone will be able to end my gratitude. Yes, until my last breath, Telemachus will love the Cretans and will be as interested in their glory as his very own.'

"No sooner had I spoken than there arose a deafening sound, like that of ocean waves crashing together in a tempest. Some were saying, 'Is this some deity beneath a human figure?' Others maintained that they had seen me in other countries, and that they recognized me. Others cried out, 'We must compel him to reign here.'

"Finally, I spoke again, and each hastened to be silent, not knowing if I was going to accept what I had at first refused. Here are the words that I said to them: 'Suffer, O Cretans, that I say to you what I think. You are the wisest of all the peoples. But wisdom demands, it seems to me, a precaution that escapes you. You should choose not the man who reasons the best about the laws but the one who practices them with the most constant virtue. For me, I am young, consequently inexperienced, exposed to the violence of passions, and more at the stage of educating myself in obeying so as to command one day rather than to command now. Do not seek a man, therefore, who has vanquished others in these games of mind and body, but one who can vanquish himself; seek a man who has your laws written deep in his heart and whose entire life has been the practice of these laws. May his actions, rather than his words, cause you to choose him.'

"All the elders, entranced by this speech, and seeing the assembly's applause still rising, said to me, 'Since the gods deny us the hope of seeing you reign among us, at least help us to find a king who would cause our laws to reign. Do you know of someone who might command with this restraint?'

"'I know,' I told them, 'of a man for whom I hold all that you have esteemed in me. It is his wisdom and not mine that just spoke and he inspired in me all the answers that you just heard.'

"At the same time the entire assembly cast their eyes on Mentor whom I was indicating, holding him by the hand. I recounted the cares he had taken of my childhood, the perils from which he had delivered me, the misfortunes that had melted down on me as soon as I ceased following his counsel. At first, they had not looked at him because of his simple and scruffy garments, his modest countenance, his almost continual silence, his cold and reserved air. But, when they made the effort to look at him, they discovered in his face a certain something of firmness and elevation; they noticed the vivacity of his eyes and the vigor with which he did even the least deeds.

"They questioned him. He was admired. They resolved to make him king. He declined unemotionally. He said that he preferred the sweetness of a private life to the brilliance of kingship, as the best kings were unhappy in that they almost never did the good that they wanted to do, and they often did, through enterprising flatterers, the evils they did not want to do. He added that, if servitude is miserable, kingship is no less so, since it is servitude in disguise. 'When one is king,' he said, 'he depends on all those he needs in order to be obeyed. Happy the one who is not obliged to command! We only owe to our motherland alone, when she entrusts the authority to us, the sacrifice of our liberty in order to strive for the public good.'

"Then the Cretans, unable to get over their surprise, asked him which man they should choose. 'A man,' he answered, 'whom you know well, since he must govern you, and who fears governing you. The one who desires kingship does not know it, and how will he fulfill the obligations of it, not knowing them? He seeks it for himself, and you must desire a man who only accepts it for the love of you.'

"All the Cretans were in a strange astonishment to see two foreigners refusing the kingship sought by so many others. They wanted to know with whom they had come. Nausicrates, who had led us from the port to the stadium where they celebrated the games, pointed out Hazael, with whom Mentor and I had come from the island of Cyprus. But their astonishment was even much greater when they learned that Mentor had been the slave of Hazael, that Hazael, touched by the wisdom and virtue of his slave, had made him his counselor and best friend, that this freed slave was the same who had just refused to be king, and that Hazael had come from Damascus in Syria, to learn from the laws of Minos, so much had the love of wisdom filled his heart.

"The elders said to Hazael, 'We do not dare pray for you to govern us, for we judge that you have the same thoughts as Mentor. You scorn men too much to want to be burdened with leading them. Besides, you are too detached from riches and the brilliance of kingship to want to attain that brilliance through the difficulties attached to the governance of the peoples.'

"Hazael responded, 'Do not believe, O Cretans, that I scorn men. No, indeed, I know how grand it is to work to render them good and happy, but this work is full of difficulties and dangers. The brilliance that is attached to it is false and can only dazzle vain souls. Life is short, and grandeurs irritate passions more than they can satisfy them. It is in order to learn to do without those false possessions, and not in order to come by them, that I have come so far. Farewell. I only dream of returning to a peaceful and secluded life where wisdom nourishes my heart and where the hopes that one draws from virtue for another better life after death consoles me in the griefs of old age. If I had something to wish for, it would not be to be king; it would be to never separate from these two men whom you see.'

"Finally, the Cretans cried out, speaking to Mentor, 'Tell us, O wisest and greatest of all mortals, tell us then, who is it that we can choose for our king? We will only let you go when you have informed us of the choice that we must make.'

BOOK V

"He answered, 'While I was in the crowd of spectators, I noticed a man who demonstrated no eagerness; he is an old man, yet vigorous enough. I asked who this man was. They answered that he was called Aristodemus. Then I heard that someone told him his two children were in the number of those who fought. He seemed to take no joy in it. He said that as for the one, he would not wish the perils of kingship on him, and that he loved his homeland too much to consent the other ever reigned; by that, I realized this father loved with a reasonable love one of his children, who has virtue, and he did not indulge the other in his unruliness.

"'My curiosity rising, I asked what the life of this old man had been. One of your citizens answered me, "He bore arms for a long time, and he is covered with scars, but his sincere virtue and hostility to flattery rendered him inconvenient to Idomeneus; it is what kept the king from making use of him in the siege of Troy. He feared a man who would give him wise counsel that he could not resolve himself to follow. He was even jealous of the glory that this man would not fail to soon acquire. He forgot all his military service. He left him here poor, scorned by uncouth and cowardly men who only esteem riches, yet content in his poverty. He lives cheerfully in a place set apart on the island where he cultivates his field with his own hands. One of his sons works with him. They love each other tenderly. They are happy. Through their frugality and work, they have an abundance of the things necessary for a simple life. The wise old man gives to the poor and sick of his neighborhood all that remains to him beyond his needs and those of his son. He makes all the young people work; he exhorts them, he instructs them, he judges all the disagreements of his neighborhood. He is the father of all the families. His misfortune is in having a second son who does not want to follow any of his counsel. The father, after having tolerated him for a long time to try to correct him of his vices, finally ran him off. The son abandoned himself to a mad ambition and to every pleasure."

"'There you have it, O Cretans; this is what I was told. You must know if this story is true. But if this man is as they depict him, why do these games? Why assemble so many strangers? You have amidst you a man who knows you and whom you know, who knows warfare, who has shown his courage, not only against arrows and spears, but against frightful poverty, who has scorned riches acquired through flattery, who loves work, who knows how useful agriculture is to a people, who detests flamboyance, who does not allow himself to be softened by a blind love of his children, who loves the virtue of the one and condemns the vice of the other—in a word, a man who is already the father of the people. There is your king, if it is true that you desire to make the laws of the wise Minos reign here.'

"All the people cried out, 'It is true, Aristodemus is just as you say. It is he who is worthy of reigning.' The elders had him called up. They searched for him in the crowd where he was blended in with the people farthest away. He looked tranquil. They declared to him that they wanted to make him king. He responded, 'I could only consent under three conditions: first, that I will quit the kingship in two years if I do not render you better off than you are, and if you are resistant to the laws; second, that I will be free to continue a simple and frugal life; third, that my children will have no rank, and after my death they will be treated without distinction, according to their merit, like the rest of the citizens.'

"At these words, there arose in the air a thousand cries of joy. The diadem was placed onto Aristodemus' head by the chief of the elders, guardians of the laws. They made sacrifices to Zeus and the other great gods. Aristodemus made gifts to us, not with the magnificence usual with kings, but with a noble simplicity. He gave to Hazael the laws of Minos, handwritten by Minos himself. He also gave him a collection of the complete history of Crete since the reign of Saturn and the golden age. He had a vessel loaded with good fruits of every kind from Crete and unknown in Syria, and he offered him all the assistance he could need. As we were hurrying our departure, he had a vessel with a great number of good oarsmen and men at arms readied for us. He had clothing and provisions put on board for us. At that instant, there arose a favorable wind for going to Ithaca. This wind, which was not favorable for Hazael, compelled him to wait. He saw us departing; he embraced us like friends who he should never see again.

"'The gods are just,' Hazael said. 'They see a friendship that is based only on virtue. One day they will reunite us, and those fortunate fields, where they say the just enjoy an eternal peace after death, will see our souls meet, never to separate again. O if my ashes could also be gathered with yours . . . !'

"In pronouncing these words, he shed torrents of tears, and sighs choked off his voice. We cried no less than he, and he led us to the vessel.

"As for Aristodemus, he told us, 'It is you who just made me king. Remember the dangers where you have put me. Ask that the gods inspire true wisdom in me, and may I surpass other men in restraint as much as I surpass them in authority. As for me, I pray for the gods to guide you happily to your homeland, to confound the insolence of your enemies there, and to have you see Odysseus reigning with his dear Penelope in peace there. Telemachus, I give you a good vessel full of oarsmen and armed men; they will be able to serve you against those unjust men who persecute your mother. O Mentor, your wisdom, which has need of nothing, leaves me nothing to desire for you. Go, both of you. Live happily together. Remember Aristodemus, and if ever the Ithacans have need of the Cretans, count on me until the last breath of my life.' He embraced us, and we could not, in thanking him, hold back our tears.

~

"Meanwhile, the wind that swelled our sails promised us a gentle voyage. Already, Mount Ida was no more than a hill to our eyes; all the shorelines disappeared. The coasts of the Peloponnese seem to advance into the sea to welcome us. Suddenly, a black tempest enveloped the sky and stirred up all the waves of the sea. Day turned into night, and Death presented itself before us. O Poseidon, it is you who excited, with your superb trident, all the waters of your empire! Aphrodite, in order to take vengeance for our having scorned her even in her temple of Cythera, went to find this god. She spoke to him in pain; her beautiful eyes were bathed in tears. At least, that is what Mentor, learned in divine things, assured me of.

"'Do you suffer, Poseidon,' she said, 'that those impious men make light of my might with impunity? Even the gods sense it, and those brash mortals have dared to condemn all that I have done on my island. They pride themselves on unfailing wisdom, and they treated love as folly. Have you forgotten that I was born in your empire? Why do you delay burying in your deep abysses those two men who I cannot suffer?'

"Barely had she spoken when Poseidon heaved the swells to the sky, and Aphrodite laughed, believing our wreck inevitable; our pilot, distressed, cried out that he could no longer fight the winds that were violently pushing us toward the rocks. A gale broke our mast, and a moment after we heard the peaks of the rocks breaking open the hull of the ship, water enters from all sides. The ship sinks, all our oarsmen loose lamentable cries to the sky. I embrace Mentor and say to him, 'Here is Death; we must receive it courageously; the gods have only delivered us from so many perils to have us perish today. We are dying, Mentor, let us die. It is a consolation for me to die with you. It would be useless to fight for our life against this tempest.'

"Mentor responded, 'True courage always finds some resource. It is not enough to be ready to tranquilly receive Death. One must, without fearing it, make every effort to repulse it. Let us take, you and me, one of these large rowing benches. While this multitude of timid and distressed men lament life without seeking the means of preserving it, let's not waste a moment to save ours.'

"Quickly, he takes a hatchet. He successfully cuts the mast that was already broken and leaning into the sea, putting the vessel on its side. He throws the mast out of the vessel and launches himself on top amidst the furious waves. He calls me by name and encourages me to follow him. Just as a great tree that all the conjured winds attack, yet remains unmoved on its deep roots, such that the tempest can only agitate its leaves, so did Mentor, not only firm and courageous, but gentle and tranquil, seemed to command the winds and the sea. I follow him—and who would have been able not to follow him, being encouraged by him?

"We drove ourselves onto the top of that floating mast. It was a great help to us, for we could seat ourselves on top, and, had it been necessary to swim without resting, our forces would have soon been drained. But the tempest overturned that great shaft of wood often, and we found ourselves plunged into the sea. Then we drank bitter water, which flowed from our mouth, nostrils, and ears, and we were compelled to fight against the waves to get back on top of that mast. Sometimes a tall cresting wave like a mountain came passing over us, and we held ourselves firm for fear that, in this violent jolt, the mast, which was our only hope, would escape us.

"While we were in this dreadful state, Mentor, as peaceful as he is now seated on this turf, said to me, 'Do you believe, Telemachus, that your life could be abandoned to the winds and the waves? Do you believe that they could destroy you without the command of the gods? No, indeed, the gods decide everything. It is the gods then and not the sea that must be feared. Were you at the bottom of the abyss, the hand of Zeus could pull you out. Were you on Olympus, seeing the heavens under your feet, Zeus could plunge you into the depths of the abyss or hurl you into the flames of gloomy Tartarus.'

"I listened and pondered this discourse, which consoled me a bit, but I did not have a clear enough mind to respond. He did not see me; I could not see him. We spent the entire night, shivering from cold and half-dead without knowing where the tempest had cast us. Finally, the winds began to be appeased, and the bellowing sea resembled a person who, having been angry for a long time, no longer has but a remnant of distress and emotion left, being weary from having been put into a fury. She grumbled dully, and her waves were hardly more than the furrows that one finds in a plowed field.

"Meanwhile, Dawn opened to the Sun the doors of the sky and announced a beautiful day to us; the East was all afire, and the stars, which had been hidden for so long, reappeared and fled upon the arrival of Phoebus. We caught sight of land in the distance, and the wind was bringing it to us. Then I felt hope reborn in my heart. But we saw none of our comrades. By appearances, they had lost courage, and the tempest had submerged them all with the vessel. When we neared land, the sea was pushing us against the peaks of the rocks that had broken us apart, but we attempted to present the end of our mast to them, and Mentor did with that mast what a wise helmsman does with the best rudder. In this way, we avoided those dreadful rocks, and we finally found a gentle and uniform coast where, swimming effortlessly, we landed on the sand. It is there that you saw us, O great goddess who inhabits this island. It is there that you deigned to receive us."

End of Book V

THE ADVENTURES OF
TELEMACHUS
SON OF ODYSSEUS

BOOK VI

When *Telemachus had finished this discourse*, all the nymphs, who had been motionless, eyes fixed on him, looked at one another. They were saying with amazement,

"Who are then these two men so cherished by the gods?"

"Have you ever heard told such marvelous adventures?"

"The son of Odysseus already surpasses him in eloquence, in wisdom, and in valor."

"What mien, what beauty!"

"What sweetness, what modesty!"

"Yet what nobility, and what grandeur!"

"If we did not know that he was the son of a mortal, we would easily take him for Dionysus, for Hermes, or even for the great Apollo."

"But what is this Mentor, who appears to be a simple man, obscure and of a common class? When one looks at him closely, one finds something about him that is beyond man."

Calypso was listening to these discourses with a distress that she could not hide. Her roving eyes were incessantly going from Mentor to Telemachus, and from Telemachus to Mentor. Sometimes she wanted Telemachus to start that long tale of his adventures over again. Then, suddenly, she stopped herself. Finally, rising brusquely, she led Telemachus into a myrtle grove alone where she spared no effort to learn from him whether or not Mentor was a deity hidden beneath the shape of a man. Telemachus could not tell her, for Athena, accompanying him beneath the figure of Mentor, had not revealed herself to him due to his youth—she did not yet trust him enough with her secret to confide her designs to him. Besides, she wanted to test him through the greatest dangers, and if he had known that Athena was with him, such an aid would have been too supportive. He would have had no difficulty scorning the most dreadful accidents. So, he took Athena for Mentor, and all of Calypso's artifices were useless in uncovering what she desired to know.

Meanwhile, all the nymphs assembled around Mentor took pleasure in questioning him. One asked him the circumstances of his Ethiopian trek. Another wanted to know what he had seen in Damascus. Another one asked him if he had once known Odysseus before the siege of Troy. He answered all of them with gentleness, and his words, though simple, were full of charm.

Calypso did not leave them in this conversation for long. She returned, and as her nymphs set about picking flowers while singing to amuse Telemachus, she took Mentor aside in order to draw him out. The sweet vapor of sleep does not flow more sweetly into heavy eyelids and into all the weary limbs of a beaten-down man than did the flattering words of the goddess that were creeping in to bewitch the heart of Mentor. But she always felt a certain something that repelled all of her efforts and mocked her spells.

Like a steep cliff that hides its brow in the clouds and mocks the rage of the winds, Mentor, immovable in his wise designs, allowed himself to be pressed by Calypso. Sometimes, he even allowed her to hope that she would rattle him with her questions and draw the truth from the depths of his heart. But, just when she believed she was about to satisfy her curiosity, her hopes vanished—all she thought in her grasp escaped her in an instant, and a curt response from Mentor plunged her into her uncertainties again. She passed the days in this way, at times flattering Telemachus, at times seeking a way to detach him from Mentor, whom she no longer hoped to draw out. She used her most beautiful nymphs to light the fires of love in the heart of young Telemachus, and a deity more mighty than she came to help her succeed.

~

Aphrodite, still filled with resentment for the scorn that Mentor and Telemachus had shown for the worship that was rendered her on the island of Cyprus, could not console herself upon seeing that these two brazen mortals had escaped the winds and the sea in the tempest excited by Poseidon. She made bitter complaints about it to Zeus, but the father of the gods, smiling, without wanting to reveal to her that Athena, beneath the figure of Mentor, had saved the son of Odysseus, permits Aphrodite to seek the means of taking revenge on these two men. She quits Olympus, she forgets about the sweet perfumes they burn on her altars in Paphos, Cythera, and Idalium. She flies in her chariot hitched to doves. She calls to her son and, pain spreading new charms on her face, she spoke,

"Do you see, my son, those two men who scorn your might and mine? Who will want to venerate us after this? Go, pierce with your arrows those two unfeeling hearts. Descend with me onto that island. I will speak to Calypso."

She spoke and, slicing through the air in a golden cloud, she presents herself to Calypso, who at this moment was alone on the bank of a spring somewhat far from her grotto.

"Unhappy goddess," she said to her. "The ungrateful Odysseus scorned you. His son, even more harsh than he, prepares a similar scorn for you. But Love himself comes to avenge you. I am leaving him with you. He will dwell among your nymphs, just as the infant Dionysus was once raised by the nymphs of the island of Naxos. Telemachus will see him as an ordinary infant. He will be unable to distrust him, and he will soon feel his power." She spoke and, ascending again in that golden cloud from which she had come, left after her an ambrosial fragrance with which all of Calypso's woods were perfumed.

Love stayed in Calypso's arms. Even though a goddess, she felt the flame that already flowed in her breast. To assuage it, she quickly gave him to the nymph who was alongside her named Eucharis—but alas, afterward, how many times did she repent having done it! At first, nothing seemed more innocent, more gentle, more lovable, more ingenuous, and more charming than this infant. To see him playful, cuddly, always laughing, one would have believed that he could give only pleasure. But barely had one trusted his caresses when they felt somehow poisoned. The malignant and deceptive infant only caressed in order to betray, and he only ever laughed from the cruel evils that he had done, or that he wanted to do. He dared not approach Mentor, whose severe air terrified him, and he sensed that this stranger was invulnerable such that none of his arrows would be able to pierce him. As for the nymphs, they soon felt the fires that this deceitful infant lights. But they carefully hid the deep cut that festered in their hearts.

~

Meanwhile, Telemachus, seeing this infant who was playing with the nymphs, was taken in by his sweetness and his beauty. He embraces him, he takes him at times in his lap, at times in his arms, he feels an uneasiness inside for which he cannot find the cause. The more he seeks to play innocently, the more he is flustered and weakened.

"Do you see these nymphs?" he said to Mentor. "How different they are from those women on the island of Cyprus, whose beauty was shocking due to their immodesty! These immortal beauties display an innocence, a modesty, a simplicity that enchants." Speaking so, he blushed without knowing why. He could not stop himself from talking, but barely had he started when he could not continue. His words were cut off, unintelligible, and sometimes nonsensical.

Mentor said to him, "O Telemachus, the dangers of the island of Cyprus were nothing if they are compared to those of which you are now unsuspecting. Crude vice horrifies; brutal impudence yields indignation, but modest beauty is much more dangerous. In loving it, one believes to love only virtue and, imperceptibly, indulges in the deceptive allure of a passion that is only perceived when there is almost no time left to put it out. Flee, O my dear Telemachus, flee these nymphs, who are only so discrete in order to better deceive you. Flee the dangers of your youthfulness. But above all, flee this infant whom you do not know. It is Love whom Aphrodite, his mother, brought onto this island to avenge the scorn you showed for the worship they render her in Cythera. He wounded the heart of the goddess Calypso. She is passionate for you. He burned all the nymphs who surround him. You are burning yourself, O wretched young man, almost without knowing it."

Telemachus interrupted Mentor often, saying to him, "Why would we not stay on this island? Odysseus no longer lives. He had to have been buried in the ocean waves a long time ago. Penelope, seeing neither him nor me return, will not have been able to resist so many pretenders. Her father, Icarius, will have compelled her to accept a new spouse. Shall I return to Ithaca to see her committed to new bloodlines and failing to keep the faith that she had given my father? The Ithacans have forgotten Odysseus. We could only return there to seek an assured death since Penelope's suitors have occupied all the avenues of the port to better assure our death upon our return."

Mentor answered, "There, that is the effect of a blind passion. One subtly searches for all the reasons that favor it and turns away

BOOK VI

for fear of seeing all those that condemn it. One is only ingenious in deceiving himself and smothering his remorse. Have you forgotten all the gods have done to bring you back to your homeland? How you got out of Sicily? The misfortunes that tested you in Egypt—were they not suddenly turned into prosperity? What unknown hand snatched you from every danger that threatened your head in the city of Tyre? After so many miracles, are you still ignorant of what the destinies have prepared for you? But what am I saying? You are unworthy of it. As for me, I am leaving, and I know well how to get off this island. Craven son of a father so wise and so generous, lead an effete and dishonorable life here amidst women. Do, despite the gods, what your father believed unworthy of him."

These scornful words pierced Telemachus to the bottom of his heart. He was touched with tenderness for Mentor. His pain was mixed with shame. He feared the indignation and the departure of this man, so wise, to whom he owed so much. But a nascent passion, which he did not recognize in himself, caused him to no longer be the same man.

"What then," he said to Mentor, tears in his eyes, "you count for nothing the immortality offered to me by the goddess?"

"I count for nothing," answered Mentor, "all that which is against virtue and against the commands of the gods. Virtue calls you back to your homeland to see Odysseus and Penelope again. Virtue forbids you to abandon yourself to a mad passion. The gods, who have delivered you from so many perils to prepare for you a glory equal to that of your father, command you to quit this island. Love alone, that shameful tyrant, can detain you here. Ho!

what will you do with an immortal life without liberty, without virtue, and without glory? That life would be even more unhappy in that it could not end."

Telemachus only responded to this discourse with sighs. Sometimes, he wished that Mentor would have snatched him, in spite of himself, off the island. Sometimes he longed that Mentor would depart so as to no longer have before his eyes this severe friend who reproached him for his weakness. All these contrary thoughts agitated his heart in turn, and nothing about them was constant. His heart was like the sea, which is the toy of all the contrary winds. He often remained stretched out and motionless on the shores of the sea, often deep in some gloomy wood, shedding bitter tears and heaving cries like the roars of a lion. He had become thin. His hollow eyes were filled with a devouring fire. To see him pale, beaten-down, and disfigured, one would have thought that it was not Telemachus—his beauty, his cheerfulness, his noble pride fled far from him; he was perishing. Like a flower which, having bloomed in the morning, spreads her sweet perfumes in the countryside and wilts little by little toward dusk. Its vibrant colors fade away, it languishes, it dries up, and its beautiful head droops, no longer able to support itself. Thus was the son of Odysseus at the Gates of Death.

~

Mentor, seeing that Telemachus was unable to resist the violence of his passion, conceived a plan full of deftness to deliver him from so great a danger. He had noticed that Calypso madly loved Telemachus, and that Telemachus loved, no less, the nymph

BOOK VI

Eucharis; for cruel Love, in order to torment mortals, makes it so that one hardly ever loves the person who loves them. Mentor resolved to excite Calypso's jealousy. Eucharis was supposed to take Telemachus on a hunt.

Mentor said to Calypso, "I have noticed in Telemachus a passion for hunting that I have never seen in him. This pleasure is beginning to disgust him with every other. He no longer likes anything but the forests and the wildest mountains. Is it you, O goddess, who inspires this great ardor in him?"

Calypso felt a cruel spite listening to these words and was unable to hold back. "This Telemachus," she answered, "who scorned all the pleasures on the island of Cyprus, cannot resist the mediocre beauty of one of my nymphs. How dare he boast of having done so many marvelous deeds, he whose heart cravenly melts for voluptuousness and who seems only born to spend an obscure life amid women?" Mentor, noting with pleasure how much jealousy troubled Calypso's heart, said nothing more about it for fear of making her distrust him; he only displayed a sad and beaten-down face.

The goddess revealed to him her pains over all the things she was seeing and she incessantly made new complaints. This hunt, of which Mentor had advised her, tipped her into a fury. She knew that Telemachus was only seeking to rid himself of the other nymphs in order to speak with Eucharis. They had even proposed a second hunt already, where she foresaw that he would do as in the first. To frustrate Telemachus' plans, she declared that she wanted to be in the hunt. Then, suddenly, no longer able to hold back her resentment, she spoke to Telemachus in this way:

"Is it like this, then, O young brazen one, that you came onto my island to escape the just shipwreck that Poseidon prepared for you as vengeance from the gods? Did you enter onto this island, which is open to no mortal, only to scorn my might and the love that I have shown you? O divinities of Olympus and of the Styx, listen to an unhappy goddess. Hasten to confound this perfidious man, this ingrate, this impious one. Since you are even more harsh and more unjust than your father, may you suffer evils even longer and more cruel than his! No, indeed, may you never see your homeland again, that poor and miserable Ithaca, that you have been shameless in preferring to immortality. Or rather may you perish seeing it from a distance, in the middle of the sea, and may your body, becoming the toy of the waves, be rejected without hope of sepulcher on the sands of this shore; may my eyes see it eaten by vultures! She whom you love will see it too. She will see it. She will have her heart broken apart by it, and her despair will make my happiness."

As she was speaking so, Calypso's eyes were red and inflamed; her gaze never stayed on any spot. They had an indescribable gloom and fierceness. Her trembling cheeks were covered with dark and livid stains. She changed color every moment; often, a mortal pallor spread over her entire face. Her tears no longer flowed with abundance as they once did—rage and despair seemed to have dried them up at the source and barely did a single tear stream down her cheek. Her voice was hoarse, trembling, and choked up.

Mentor observed all her movements and no longer spoke to

Telemachus. He treated him like a hopeless invalid whom one abandons. He often cast looks of compassion at him. Telemachus felt how culpable he was and unworthy of Mentor's friendship. He dared not lift his eyes for fear of encountering those of his friend, whose very silence condemned him. Sometimes, he wanted to throw his arms around his neck and show him how much he was affected by his error, but he held back—at times by a feigned modesty, and at times by the fear of going further than he wanted to pull himself out of peril; for the peril seemed sweet to him, and he could not yet resolve himself to vanquish his mad passion.

The gods and goddesses of Olympus, assembled in a profound silence, had their eyes fixed on the island of Calypso to see who would be victorious, Athena or Love. Love, playing with the nymphs, had set everything ablaze on the island. Athena, beneath the figure of Mentor, was making use of jealousy, inseparable from love, against Love himself. Zeus had resolved to be the spectator to this fight and to remain neutral.

~

Meanwhile, Eucharis, who feared that Telemachus would escape her, was using a thousand artifices to keep him in his chains. She was already leaving with him for the second hunt and was dressed as Artemis. Aphrodite and Eros had spread new spells over her, of the sort that, this day, her beauty eclipsed that of the goddess Calypso herself. Calypso, regarding Eucharis from a distance, regarded herself at the same moment in the clearest of her springs and was ashamed at the sight. So she hid deep in her grotto and spoke all alone:

"It serves me nothing, then, to have wanted to trouble these two lovers in declaring that I want to be in this hunt! Will I be in it? Will I go to make her triumph, and to use my beauty to enhance hers? Must Telemachus, in seeing me, be even more passionate for his Eucharis? O wretch, what have I done? No, I will not go. They will not go themselves. I know well how to keep them from it. I am going to find Mentor. I will urge him to take Telemachus away. He will take him back to Ithaca. But what am I saying, and what will become of me when Telemachus departs? Where am I? What remains to be done? O cruel Aphrodite, you deceived me. O perfidious present that you gave me! Pernicious child, pestilent Love, I only opened my heart to you in the hope of living happily with Telemachus, and you have brought into this heart only distress and despair. My nymphs are rebellious against me. My divinity only serves to render my unhappiness eternal. O, if I were free to give myself death to end my pains.

"Telemachus, you must die since I cannot die. I will avenge your ingratitudes. Your nymph will witness it, I will pierce you before her eyes—but, I stray. O unhappy Calypso, what do you want? To destroy an innocent, whom you yourself cast into this abyss of woes? It is I who put the fatal flame to the bosom of chaste Telemachus. What innocence, what virtue, what horror of vice, what courage against shameful pleasures! Was it necessary to poison his heart? He would have forsaken me. Oh well . . . mustn't he forsake me, or else I must see him full of scorn for me, no longer living but for my rival? No, indeed, I only suffer what I well merited. Leave, Telemachus, go beyond the seas. Leave Calypso without consolation, unable to bear life, nor to find death. Leave her inconsolable, covered with shame, hopeless, with your prideful Eucharis."

She was speaking like this alone in her grotto. But suddenly she left impetuously.

"Where are you, O Mentor?" she said. "Is this how you support Telemachus against the vice to which he succumbs? You sleep while Love keeps vigil against you. I can no longer tolerate this craven indifference you show. Do you always tranquilly watch the son of Odysseus dishonor his father and neglect his high destiny? Is it to you or to me that his parents have entrusted his conduct? It is me who seeks the means of healing his heart, and you, you do nothing? There are, in the most remote part of this forest, great poplars suitable for constructing a vessel. It is there that Odysseus made the one in which he got off this island. You will find at the same spot a deep cavern, where there are all the instruments necessary to plane and join all the pieces of a vessel."

No sooner had she spoken these words than she repented them. Mentor did not waste a moment. He went into that cavern, found the instruments, felled the poplars, and, in a single day, readied a vessel in sailing condition; for the might and skill of Athena do not need a great amount of time to achieve the greatest works. Calypso found herself in a terrible state of mind. On the one hand, she wanted to see if Mentor's work was advancing. On the other, she could not resolve herself to quit the hunt where Eucharis would have been in complete liberty with Telemachus. Jealousy never permitted her to lose sight of the two lovers, but she tried to turn the hunt away from the side where she knew Mentor was building the vessel. She heard the blows of the axe and the hammer. She listened. Each blow made her shudder. But, at the same time, she feared this reverie robbing her of seeing some sign or some glance from Telemachus to the young nymph.

Meanwhile, Eucharis was saying to Telemachus in a teasing tone, "Are you not afraid that Mentor faults you for having come on the hunt without him? O how you are to be pitied for living under so harsh a master! Nothing can soften his austerity. He feigns to be hostile to every pleasure. He cannot tolerate you enjoying any of them. He makes the most innocent things a crime to you. You were able to depend on him when you were not in a state to lead yourself, but after having shown so much wisdom, you should no longer allow yourself to be treated like a child."

These artful words pierced Telemachus' heart and filled it with spite for Mentor, whose yoke he wanted to shake off. He feared seeing him again and he said nothing to Eucharis, troubled as he was. At last, toward nightfall, the hunt having passed from one side to another in a perpetual constraint, they returned through a corner of the forest somewhere near the spot where Mentor had worked all day. Calypso glimpsed the finished vessel in the distance. Her eyes instantly covered over with a thick cloud, like that of death. Her trembling knees gave way under her. A cold sweat broke out over all the limbs of her body. She was compelled to lean on one of the nymphs who surrounded her and Eucharis, holding out her hand to support her, was repulsed as Calypso cast her a terrifying look.

Telemachus, who saw this vessel but did not see Mentor because he had already retired, having finished his work, asked the goddess whose vessel it was and for what it was intended. At first, she could not answer. But finally she said, "It is to send Mentor back that I had it made. You will no longer be impeded by this severe friend, who is opposed to your happiness and who would be jealous if you became immortal."

"Mentor abandons me—I am done for!" Telemachus cried out. "O Eucharis, if Mentor forsakes me, I only have you!" These words escaped him in a frenzy of emotion. He saw the wrong he had done in saying them, but he had not been free to think about the meaning of his words. All the nymphs, stunned, remained silent. Eucharis, blushing and lowering her eyes, remained behind, completely taken aback, not daring to show herself. But while shame was on her face, joy was at the bottom of her heart. Telemachus no longer understood himself and could not believe he had spoken so indiscreetly. What he had done seemed like a dream to him, but a dream from which he remained confused and distressed.

Calypso, more furious than a lioness whose cubs had been snatched, ran through the forest without following any path, and not knowing where she was going. Finally, she found herself at the entrance to her grotto where Mentor was waiting for her.

"Get off my island," she said, "O foreigners, who came to trouble my repose. Get this young fool far away from me! And you, imprudent old man, you will feel what the wrath of a goddess can do if you do not take him away from here this instant. I no longer want to see him. I no longer want to tolerate any of my nymphs speaking to him nor looking at him. I swear by the waters of the Styx—oath that makes the gods themselves tremble. But be informed, Telemachus, that your woes are not ended. Ingrate, you will only get off my island to be prey to new misfortunes. I will be avenged. You will lament Calypso, but in vain. Poseidon, still angry with your father who offended him in Sicily, and solicited by Aphrodite whom you scorned on the island of Cyprus, prepares other tempests for you. You will see your father, who is not dead. But you will see him without knowing him. You will only reunite with him in Ithaca after having been the plaything of the cruelest fortune. Go. I conjure the celestial powers to avenge me. May you, in the middle of the seas, suspended on the peak of a rock and struck by lightning, invoke in vain Calypso, whom your torture will fill with joy!"

Having said these words, her agitated mind was already poised to make contrary resolutions. Love recalled into her heart the desire to detain Telemachus. *May he live*, she said to herself, *may he stay here. Perhaps he will sense at last all that I have done for him. Eucharis would not know, as I do, how to give him immortality. O too-blind Calypso, you betrayed yourself through your oath. Here you are committed, and the waters of the Styx, by which you swore, no longer permit you any hope.*

No one heard these words, but they saw painted on her face the Furies and all the pestilent venom of the black Cocytus seemed to exude from her heart.

~

Telemachus was seized with horror by it. Calypso realized it (for what does jealous love not guess?) and Telemachus' horror redoubled the frenzy of the goddess. Like a maenad, who fills the

BOOK VI

air with her howls and causes them to reverberate off the high mountains of Thrace, she runs through the woods with a spear in hand, calling all her nymphs and threatening to pierce all those who will not follow her. They run in droves, frightened by this threat. Even Eucharis moves forward, tears in her eyes, regarding from afar Telemachus, to whom she no longer dared to speak. The goddess shudders in seeing Eucharis alongside her and, far from being appeased by the submissiveness of this nymph, she feels a new furor, seeing that affliction enhances Eucharis' beauty.

~

Meanwhile, Telemachus had stayed alone with Mentor. He embraces his knees; for he dared not embrace him otherwise, nor look at him. He sheds a torrent of tears. He wants to speak; his voice fails him. Words fail him even more. He knows neither what he should do, nor what he is doing, nor what he wants. At last he cries out, "O my true father, O Mentor, deliver me from so many evils! I can neither abandon you nor follow you. Deliver me from so many evils, deliver me from myself—give me death."

Mentor embraces him, consoles him, encourages him, teaches him to bear up, without indulging his passion, and says to him, "Son of the wise Odysseus whom the gods have so loved, and still love, it is as a result of their love that you suffer such horrible evils. The one who has not felt his weakness and the violence of his passions is not yet wise, for he does not yet know himself and does not know how to distrust himself. The gods have led you, as if by the hand, just to the brink of the abyss in order to show you all its depth without allowing you to fall in. Understand now what you would never have understood if you had not experienced it. Someone would have spoken to you of the betrayals of love, that flatters in order to ruin and that, under an appearance of sweetness, hides the most dreadful bitterness.

"This child came full of spells, amidst Laughter, Games, and Graces. You saw him. He captured your heart, and you took pleasure in allowing him to capture it. You sought pretexts to ignore the wound in your heart. You sought to deceive me and to flatter yourself. You feared nothing. See the fruit of your temerity. You are now asking for death, and it is the only hope that remains to you. The distraught goddess resembles an infernal Fury. Eucharis burns with a fire more cruel than all the pains of death. All those jealous nymphs are ready to tear each other apart. Voila. That is what the traitor Love does, who appears so sweet. Recall all your courage. Realize to what extent the gods love you, since they open so fine a path to let you flee Love and see your dear homeland again. Calypso herself is compelled to chase you out. The vessel is ready. What delays us quitting this island, where virtue cannot live?"

Saying these words, Mentor took him by the hand and dragged him toward the shore. Telemachus barely followed him, always looking back. He gazed at Eucharis, who was distancing herself from him. Unable to see her face, he looked at her beautiful, knotted hair, her flowing gown, and her noble gait. He would have wanted to be able to kiss the traces of her steps. Even when he lost sight of her, he still listened carefully, imagining he heard her voice. Though absent, he saw her. Her living image was painted before his eyes.

He even believed he spoke to her, no longer knowing where he was, and he was unable to listen to Mentor.

Finally, returning to himself as from a deep sleep, he says to Mentor, "I am resolved to follow you, but I have not yet bade farewell to Eucharis. I would rather die than abandon her ungratefully like this. Wait so that I may see her one last time to give her an eternal farewell. At least tolerate that I may tell her, 'O nymph, the cruel gods, the gods jealous of my happiness, compel me to depart. But they will instead prevent me from living rather than from remembering you forever.' O my father, either allow me this last consolation, which is so just, or snatch life from me at this moment. No, I want neither to stay on this island, nor abandon myself to love. Love is not in my heart. I only feel friendship and gratitude for Eucharis. It suffices for me to tell her farewell one more time, and I will depart with you without delay!"

"How I pity you," Mentor responded. "Your passion is so furious that you do not sense it. You believe to be tranquil and you ask for death! You dare to say you are not vanquished by love, and you cannot tear yourself away from the nymph you love. You only see, you only hear her. You are blind and deaf to all the rest. A man whom fever renders frenetic says, 'I am not sick.' O blind Telemachus, you were ready to renounce Penelope, who is waiting for you, Odysseus whom you will see in Ithaca where you must reign in the glory and the high destiny that the gods have promised you through so many miracles that they have done in your favor.

"You renounced all those good possessions to live dishonored alongside Eucharis. Do you still say that love does not attach you to her? What is it then that distresses you? Why do you want to die? Why did you speak before the goddess with such abandon? I do not accuse you of bad faith, but I deplore your blindness. Flee, Telemachus, flee—one can only vanquish love in fleeing it. Against such an enemy, true courage consists of fearing and fleeing, but fleeing without deliberating and without giving oneself the time to ever look back.

"You have not forgotten the cares that you have cost me since your childhood and the perils which you got out of through my counsel. Either believe me or suffer that I abandon you. If you knew how much it hurts me to see you racing to your ruin! If you knew all that I have suffered while I dared not speak to you; the mother who brought you into the world suffered less in the pains of childbirth. I kept quiet. I swallowed my pain. I choked back my sighs, to see if you would return to me. O my son, my dear son, relieve my heart; return to me what is more dear to me than my being. Return to me Telemachus, whom I lost. Return you to yourself. If the wisdom in you surpasses love, I live and I live happily, but if love sweeps you away in spite of wisdom, Mentor can no longer live."

While Mentor was speaking so, he continued along his path toward the sea, and Telemachus, who was not yet strong enough to follow him on his own, was already strong enough to allow himself to be led without resistance. Athena, always hidden beneath the figure of Mentor, was invisibly covering Telemachus with her aegis and spreading a divine ray around him, causing him to feel a courage that he had not experienced since he had arrived on this island. Finally, they arrived at a part of the island where the seashore was steep. It was a rock always buffeted by the foaming waves. They looked from this height to see whether the vessel that Mentor had prepared was still in the same place. But they beheld a sad spectacle.

~

Love was extremely piqued to find that this strange old man was not only insensitive to his shafts but was even abducting Telemachus. He cried with spite and went to find Calypso roving in the gloomy forests. She could not see him without groaning, and she felt that he would reopen all the scars of her heart. Love said to her, "You are a goddess, and you allow yourself to be vanquished by a weak mortal who is captive on your island! Why are you allowing him to leave?"

"O wretched Love," she answered, "I no longer want to listen to your pernicious counsel. It is you who pulled me from a sweet and profound peace to fling me into an abyss of woes. It is done. I swore by the waters of the Styx that I would allow Telemachus to depart. Even Zeus, father of the gods, with all his might, would not dare to break so formidable an oath. Telemachus is getting off my island. Get off too, pernicious child. You have done more evil to me than he!"

Love, wiping away his tears, smiled mockingly and malignantly. "In truth," he said, "that is a great obstacle. Leave it to me. Follow your oath. Do not oppose Telemachus' departure. Neither your nymphs nor I have sworn by the waters of the Styx to let him depart. I will inspire a plan in them to burn that vessel that Mentor made with such precipitation. His diligence, which caught us by surprise, will be useless. He will be surprised, in turn, and there will no longer remain to him any means of snatching Telemachus away from you."

These flattering words caused hope and joy to slip deep into Calypso's bosom. What a refreshing zephyr does on the banks of a stream to relax the languishing flocks that the summer blaze consumes, so did this discourse appease the goddess's despair. Her face became serene, her eyes softened, the dark worries that were gnawing at her heart momentarily fled far from her. She stopped, she smiled, she caressed playful Love and, in caressing him, she prepared herself for new pains.

Love, satisfied in having persuaded her, went to persuade the nymphs as well, who were roaming and dispersed all over the mountains like a flock of sheep that the rage of famished wolves put in flight far from the shepherd. Love gathers them and says, "Telemachus is still in your hands. Hasten to burn that vessel, which the brazen Mentor built in order to flee."

Quickly, they light torches. They run along the shore. They shudder. They howl. They shake their disheveled hair like maenads. Already the flame soars. It devours the vessel, which is of a dry wood, coated with resin. Swirls of smoke and flame rise to the clouds.

Telemachus and Mentor spot the fire from the top of the cliff and hear the screams of the nymphs. Telemachus was tempted to rejoice with them, for his heart was not yet healed, and Mentor noticed that his passion was like a fire poorly put out, which emerges from time to time from beneath the ashes and rises again from live sparks.

"Well . . . here I am," said Telemachus, "back in my chains. There no longer remains any hope of us quitting this island."

Mentor saw well that Telemachus was going to fall back into all his weaknesses, and that there was not a moment to lose. He spied in the distance, amidst the swells, a stalled vessel, which dared not approach the island, for every pilot knew that the island of Calypso was inaccessible to all mortals. Immediately, wise Mentor, pushing Telemachus who was seated on the edge of the cliff, hurls him into the sea and leaps in with him. Telemachus, startled by this violent fall, drank bitter water and became the toy of the waves. But, returning to himself and seeing Mentor, who was holding out his hand to help him swim, he no longer thought of anything but distancing himself from the fatal island.

The nymphs, who had believed they held them captive, loosed screams full of fury, no longer able to prevent their flight. Calypso, inconsolable, reentered her grotto, which she filled with her howls. Love, who saw his triumph change into a shameful defeat, rose up to the middle of the air, fluttering his wings, and flew into the grove of Idalium, where his cruel mother was waiting for him. The child, even more cruel, only consoled himself by laughing with her at all the evils he had done.

As Telemachus distanced himself from the island, he felt with pleasure his courage born again, along with his love for virtue.

"I am experiencing," he shouted out, telling Mentor, "what you told me and what I could not believe for lack of experience—one only overcomes vice in fleeing it. O my father, how the gods have loved me in giving me your help! I merited being deprived of it and being abandoned to myself. I no longer fear the seas, the winds, or the tempests. I no longer fear anything but my passions. Love is itself more to be feared than all shipwrecks."

END OF BOOK VI

THE ADVENTURES OF
TELEMACHUS
SON OF ODYSSEUS

BOOK VII

T he stalled vessel toward which they advanced was a Phoenician vessel going to Epirus. Those Phoenicians had seen Telemachus on the Egyptian voyage but could hardly recognize him amid the waves. When Mentor was close enough to the vessel to make his voice heard, he cried out in a loud voice, raising his head above the water: "Phoenicians, so helpful to all nations, do not deny life to two men who expect it of your humanity. If respect for the gods touches you, receive us onto your vessel. We will go wherever you go."

The one who was in command answered, "We will joyfully receive you. We are not ignorant of what one must do for strangers who appear so unfortunate."

Straightaway, they received them onto the vessel. Barely were they boarded when, no longer able to breathe, they remained still, for they had swum for a long time and with effort, fighting against the surf. Little by little, they regained their strength. They were given other garments because theirs were weighed down with water that soaked them and streamed from all sides. When they were in a state to speak, all those Phoenicians pressing round them wanted to know of their adventures.

The one in command said to them, "How were you able to get onto that island you left? It is, they say, possessed by a cruel goddess, who never suffers one landing there. It is even rimmed with frightful rocks against which the sea madly fights, and one could not approach it without wrecking."

Mentor answered, "We were cast there. We are Greek. Our homeland is the island of Ithaca, neighboring Epirus, where you are headed. Even if you would not wish to put in at Ithaca, which is on your route, it will suffice that you carry us to Epirus. We will find friends there who will help us to make the short crossing that remains, and we will forever owe you for the joy of seeing again what we have of the most dear in the world."

So then, it was Mentor who spoke and Telemachus, keeping silent, let him speak, for the errors he had made on the island of Calypso had greatly increased his wisdom. He distrusted himself; he felt the need to always follow the wise counsel of Mentor, and when he could not speak to him to ask for his advice, he at least consulted his eyes and tried to guess all his thoughts.

The Phoenician commander, settling his eyes on Telemachus, believed to remember having seen him, but it was a confused memory that he could not sort out.

"Suffer," he said, "that I ask you if you remember having seen me another time, as it seems to me that I remember having seen you. Your face is not unknown to me. It struck me immediately, but I do not know where I have seen you. Your memory, perhaps, will aid mine."

Then Telemachus answered with an astonishment mixed with joy, "I am, in seeing you, as you are with regard to me—I saw you, I recognized you, but I could not recall if it was in Egypt or in Tyre."

Then this Phoenician, like a man who awakes in the morning, and who, little by little, recalls from a distance the fugitive dream that disappeared upon awakening, suddenly exclaimed, "You are Telemachus, whom Narbal took in friendship when we were returning from Egypt! I am his brother, whom he will undoubtedly have spoken of often. I left you in his hands after the Egyptian expedition. I had to go beyond all the seas into the famous Baetica, near the Pillars of Heracles. Consequently, I only caught sight of you, and it should not be astonishing if I had so much difficulty recognizing you at first."

"I see indeed that you are Adoam. I only caught a glimpse of you then, but I knew of you through conversations with Narbal. O what joy to be able to learn through you news of a man who will always be so dear to me. Is he still in Tyre? He did not suffer some cruel treatment from the suspicious and barbarous Pygmalion?"

Adoam answered, interrupting him, "Know, Telemachus, that favorable Fortune entrusts you to a man who will take every kind of care of you. I will take you back to the island of Ithaca before going on to Epirus, and Narbal's brother will have no less friendship for you than Narbal himself."

Having spoken so, he noticed that the wind he was waiting for was beginning to blow. He had the anchors raised, set the sails, and plowed the sea by dint of oars. Straightaway, he took Telemachus and Mentor aside, to talk with them.

"I am going," he said, looking at Telemachus, "to satisfy your curiosity. Pygmalion is no more. The just gods have delivered the earth from him. As he trusted no one, no one could trust him. The good contented themselves with groaning and fleeing his cruelties, unable to resolve themselves to do him any harm. The wicked believed they could only assure their lives by ending his. There was not one Tyrian who was not at risk each day of being the object of his distrust. His very guards were more exposed than the others. As his life was in their hands, he feared them more than all the rest of men. At the least suspicion, he sacrificed them to his safety. So, by dint of seeking his safety, he could no longer find it. Those who were the keepers of his life were in a continual peril through his distrust, and they could only get out of so horrible a state by preventing, through the death of the tyrant, his cruel suspicions.

"The impious Astarbe, of whom you have heard spoken so often, was the first to resolve the loss of the king. She passionately loved a very rich young Tyrian named Joazar. She hoped to put him on the throne. To succeed in this scheme, she persuaded the king that the eldest of his two sons, named Phadael, impatient to succeed his father, had conspired against him. She found false witnesses to prove the conspiracy. The wretched king had his innocent son killed. The second, named Baleazar, was sent to Samos under the pretext of learning the mores and sciences of Greece. But in reality, it was because Astarbe convinced the king that he must drive him away for fear that he might form liaisons with the malcontents. Barely had he departed, when those who steered the vessel, having been corrupted by this cruel woman, took measures to wreck during the night. They saved themselves by swimming to foreign barges that were waiting for them, and they flung the young prince to the bottom of the sea.

"Meanwhile, Astarbe's amours were unknown only to Pygmalion, and he imagined that she would only ever love him alone. This prince, so distrustful, was thus filled with a blind confidence in this wicked woman. It was love that blinded him so excessively. At the same time, avarice caused him to seek pretexts to kill Joazar, for whom Astarbe was so passionate. He only thought of stealing the riches of that young man.

"But while Pygmalion was prey to distrust, love and avarice, Astarbe hastened to take his life. She believed he had perhaps discovered something of her infamous amours with that young man. Besides, she knew that avarice alone would suffice to carry the king to a cruel act against Joazar. She concluded that there was not a moment to lose to prevent it: she saw the principal officers of the palace ready to dip their hands in the blood of the king; she heard some new conspiracy spoken of every day. But she feared confiding in anyone who might betray her. In the end, it seemed safest to poison Pygmalion.

"He ate most often all alone with her and prepared all he should eat himself, only able to trust his own hands. He confined himself to the most remote part of his palace so as to better hide his distrust and to never be observed when he prepared his meals. He no longer dared to seek any pleasures of the table. He could not resolve himself to eat any of the things he did not know how to prepare himself. So, not only all the meats cooked with rich sauces by the cooks, but even wine, bread, salt, milk, and all the other usual foods could not be of use to him. He only ate fruits that he had picked himself in his garden, or vegetables, which he had sown and cooked. Furthermore, he never drank any water other than what he drew for himself from a spring that was locked up in a part of his palace to which he always kept the key. Even though he seemed so filled with confidence in Astarbe, he did not fail to take precautions. He always had her eat and drink before him everything that should serve as his meal so that he could not be poisoned without her, and she would have no hope of living longer than him. But she took an antidote that an old woman—even more wicked than she and who was the confidante of her amours—supplied her, after which she no longer feared poisoning the king.

"This is how she went about it. At the moment when they were beginning their meal, this old woman, of whom I spoke, suddenly made a noise at a door. The king, who always believed that someone was going to murder him, is troubled and runs to this door to see if it is closed well enough. The old woman withdraws. The king remains taken aback, not knowing what he should think of what he had heard. He does not dare, however, open the door to find out.

Astarbe reassures him, flatters him, and presses him to eat. She had already tossed the poison into his golden cup while he was going to the door. Pygmalion, according to his custom, had her drink first. She drank without fear, trusting the antidote. Pygmalion also drank, and a short time afterward he fell into a faint.

"Astarbe, who knew him to be capable of killing her over the slightest suspicion, began to rend her garments, pull out her hair, and loose lamentable wails. She embraced the dying king, she held him tightly in her arms, she drenched him in a torrent of tears—for tears cost nothing to this artful woman. Finally, when she saw that the king's forces were drained, and that he was in the throes of death, for fear of him coming round and wanting her to die with him, she passed from caresses and the most tender marks of friendship to the most horrific fury. She threw herself on him and smothered him. Then, she snatched from his finger the royal ring, removed the diadem from him, and had Joazar enter, to whom she gave the one and the other.

"She believed that all those who had been attached to her would not fail to follow her passion and that her lover would be proclaimed king. But those who had been the most eager to please her, being of low and mercenary minds, were incapable of sincere affection. Besides, they lacked courage and feared the enemies that Astarbe attracted. In the end, they feared the haughtiness, the dissimulation, and the cruelty of this impious woman even more. Each, for his own safety, desired she perish.

"Meanwhile, the entire palace is filled with a dreadful tumult. Everywhere, cries can be heard of those saying, 'The king is dead.'

Some are frightened. Others run to arms. All appear troubled in the aftermath yet delighted by this news. Rumor causes it to fly from mouth to mouth throughout the great city of Tyre, and not a single man is found who laments the king. His death is the deliverance and the consolation of all the people.

"Narbal, struck by so terrible a blow, deplored as a good man the misfortune of Pygmalion, who had betrayed himself in delivering himself over to the impious Astarbe, and who had preferred being a terrifying and monstrous tyrant to being, according to the duty of a king, the father of his people. Narbal thought of the welfare of the state and hastened to rally all the good people to oppose Astarbe, under whom they would have seen a reign even more harsh than the one they saw end.

"Narbal knew that Baleazar had not drowned when he was flung into the sea. Those who assured Astarbe that he was dead spoke so believing that he was. But, thanks to the cover of darkness, he saved himself by swimming, and Cretan fishermen, touched with compassion, had received him onto their barge. He had not dared return to the kingdom of his father, suspecting that they had wanted to slay him, and fearing the cruel jealousies of Pygmalion as much as the artifices of Astarbe. For a long time, he remained wandering and disguised on the edge of the sea in Syria, where the Cretan fishermen had left him. He was even obliged to guard a flock to earn his living. Finally, he found a means of letting Narbal know the state he was in. He believed he could confide his secret and his life to a man of such proven virtue. Narbal, poorly treated by the father, never stopped loving the son and watching out for his interests. But he only looked after them in order to keep him from ever failing in what he owed his father, and he enlisted him to suffer his bad fortune patiently.

"Baleazar had summoned Narbal: 'If you judge that I can come and find you, send me a golden ring, and I will immediately understand that it is time to join you.'

"Narbal did not judge it appropriate, while Pygmalion was alive, to have Baleazar come. He would have risked everything, the life of the prince and his own, as difficult as it was to protect oneself from the rigorous searches of Pygmalion. But, as soon as that wretched king had met an end worthy of his crimes, Narbal hastened to send the golden ring to Baleazar. Baleazar immediately departed and arrived at the gates of Tyre during the time that all the city was in turmoil to know who would succeed Pygmalion. Baleazar was easily recognized by the principal Tyrians and by all the people. They loved him, not for love of the late king, his father, who was universally hated, but because of his gentleness and his restraint. Even his long misfortunes gave him something of a radiance that enhanced all his good qualities and touched the hearts of all the Tyrians in his favor.

"Narbal assembled the leaders of the people, the elders who formed the council, and the priests of the great Phoenician goddess. They bowed to Baleazar as their king and had him proclaimed by heralds. The people responded with a thousand acclamations of joy. Astarbe heard them from the depths of the palace where she was shut up along with her cowardly and infamous Joazar. All the wicked who had served her during Pygmalion's lifetime had abandoned her—for the wicked fear the wicked, distrust them, and do not wish to see them in positions of influence. Corrupt men know well how much their kind would abuse authority, and how violent they would be. But as for the good, the wicked are more adapting because at least they hope to find in them restraint and indulgence. There only remained around Astarbe certain accomplices to her most dreadful crimes who could only expect torture. They stormed the palace. Those scoundrels dared not resist for long and only thought to flee. Astarbe, disguised as a slave, wanted to escape into the crowd, but a soldier recognized her. She was taken, and they had great difficulty keeping her from being ripped apart by the enraged people. They had already begun dragging her through the mud. But Narbal pulled her from the hands of the rabble. Then she asked to speak to Baleazar, hoping to dazzle him with her charms and make him hope that she would reveal important secrets to him. Baleazar could not refuse listening to her. At first she displayed, along with her beauty, a sweetness and a modesty capable of touching the angriest hearts. She flattered Baleazar through the most delicate and insinuating praises. She represented to him how much Pygmalion had loved her. She beseeched him on Pygmalion's ashes to have mercy on her. She invoked the gods, as if she had sincerely venerated them. She shed torrents of tears. She threw herself at the knees of the new king. But then, she did her utmost to render suspect and odious to him all the servants most attached to him. She accused Narbal of having entered into a conspiracy against Pygmalion and of having tried to suborn the peoples in order to make himself king to the detriment of Baleazar. She added that he wanted to poison this young prince. She invented similar calumnies against all the other Tyrians who love virtue. She hoped to find in the heart of Baleazar the same distrust, and the same suspicions, that she had seen in that of the king, his father. But Baleazar, no longer able to tolerate the black malignity of this woman, interrupted her and called the guards. They put her in prison.

"The wisest elders were commissioned to examine all her deeds. They discovered with horror that she had poisoned and smothered Pygmalion. The entire course of her life seemed a continuous chain of monstrous crimes. They were going to condemn her to the torture meant to punish the greatest crimes in Phoenicia: being burned to death over a low flame. But when she realized that there no longer remained any hope for her, she became like a Fury out of the Underworld. She swallowed the poison that she always carried in order to kill herself should they want to make her suffer long tortures. Those who were guarding her saw that she was suffering violent pain. They wanted to help her, but she never wanted to answer them and she motioned that she wanted no relief. They spoke to her of the just gods that she had provoked. Instead of showing shame and repentance for what her wrongdoings merited, she glared at the sky with scorn and arrogance, as if to insult the gods.

"Rage and impiety were painted on her dying face. One no longer saw any remnant of that beauty that had caused the misfortune of so many men. All her charms were rubbed out. Her lifeless eyes rolled into her head and cast fierce looks. A convulsive movement contorted her lips and her mouth gaped horrifically. Her entire face, drawn and shrunken, grimaced hideously. A livid pallor and a mortal chill had seized her entire body. Sometimes she seemed to come round, but it was only to let loose howls. Finally, she expired, leaving filled with horror and fright all those who witnessed it. Undoubtedly, her impious mānes descended into those sad places where the cruel Danaids eternally draw water into porous vessels, where Ixion forever turns his wheel, where Tantalus, scorched with thirst, cannot swallow the water that flees from his lips, where Sisyphus uselessly rolls a rock that tumbles again without ceasing, and where Tityus will eternally feel, in his ever-regenerating entrails, a vulture gnawing away at them.

"Baleazar, delivered from this monster, rendered thanks to the gods through countless sacrifices. He began his reign with conduct completely opposite that of Pygmalion. He applied himself to making commerce—which was languishing more and more every day—flourish again. He has taken Narbal's counsel with regard to the most important affairs of state, and yet is not governed by him—for he wants to see everything himself; he listens to all the different opinions that they want to offer him, and then he decides what seems the best to him. He is loved by the peoples. In possessing their hearts, he possesses more treasures than his father had amassed through his cruel avarice, for there is no family who would not give him all that they have of property should he find himself in a pressing need. In this way, what he leaves them is more his than if he took it away from them. He does not need to take precautions for his personal safety, for he always has around him the most sure guard, which is the love of the peoples. There is not one of his subjects who does not fear losing him and who would not risk his own life to preserve that of so good a king. He lives happily, and all his people are happy along with him. He fears overburdening his peoples. His peoples fear not offering him a large enough portion of their goods. He leaves them in abundance, and this abundance renders them neither unruly nor insolent, for they are hard-working, devoted to commerce, steadfast in preserving the purity of the old laws. Phoenicia has ascended back to the height of her grandeur and glory. It is to her young king that she owes such prosperity. Narbal governs under him.

"O Telemachus, if he could see you now, with what joy would he shower you with presents! What pleasure it would be for him to send you back magnificently into your homeland! Am I not happy to do that which he would want to be able to do himself, going into the island of Ithaca to put the son of Odysseus on the throne so that he reigns as wisely there as Baleazar reigns in Tyre?"

After Adoam had spoken so, Telemachus, enchanted by the story this Phoenician had just recounted, and even more by the marks of friendship he had received from him in his misfortune, embraced him tenderly. Then, Adoam asked him by what adventure he had gotten onto the island of Calypso. Telemachus recounted to him in turn the story of his departure from Tyre, his passage into the island of Cyprus, the manner by which he had found Mentor again, their voyage to Crete, the public games for the election of a king after the flight of Idomeneus, the anger of Aphrodite, their shipwreck, the pleasure with which Calypso had received them, the jealousy of this goddess of one of her nymphs, and the action of Mentor, who had flung his friend into the sea as soon as he saw the Phoenician vessel.

After these conversations, Adoam had a magnificent meal served, and, to bear witness to a greater joy, he brought together all the pleasures one could enjoy. During the meal, which was served by young Phoenicians dressed in white and crowned with flowers, they burned the most exquisite perfumes of the East. All the rowing benches were filled with flutists. Achitoas interrupted them from time to time with the sweet harmony of his voice and his lyre, worthy of being heard at the table of the gods and delighting the ears of Apollo himself. The Tritons, the Nereids, all the deities who obey Poseidon, even the sea monsters, came out of their damp and deep grottos to come in droves around the vessel, entranced by this melody. A troupe of young Phoenicians of a rare beauty and dressed in fine linen whiter than snow danced the dances of their country for a long time, followed by those of Egypt and, finally, those of Greece. From time to time, trumpets reverberated over the water to distant shores. The silence of the night, the calm of the sea, the trembling light of the moon spread over the surface of the waters, the dark blue of the skies sprinkled with shining stars, served to render this spectacle even more beautiful.

Telemachus, of a keen and sensitive nature, was enjoying all these pleasures, but he dared not deliver his heart over to them. Since he had so shamefully experienced, on the island of Calypso, how quick youth is to become inflamed, every pleasure, even the most innocent, frightened him. All was suspect to him. He looked at Mentor. He searched his face and his eyes for what he should think of all these pleasures.

Mentor was glad to see him in this dilemma and pretended not to notice. Finally, touched by Telemachus' restraint, he said to him, smiling, "I understand what you fear. You are laudable for this fear. But you must not push it too far. No one would ever wish more than me for you to enjoy pleasures, but pleasures that neither impassion nor soften you. They should be pleasures that relax you and that you enjoy while in possession of yourself, but not pleasures that sweep you away. I wish sweet and moderate pleasures for you that do not rob you of reason and that never make you like an enraged beast. Now it is appropriate for you to unwind from all your difficulties. Enjoy, in deference to Adoam, the pleasures that he offers you. Rejoice, Telemachus, rejoice. Wisdom has nothing of austerity or affectation. It is what gives true pleasure. It alone knows how to season pleasures to make them pure and lasting. It knows how to mix games and laughter with grave and serious business. It prepares for pleasure through work and relaxes from work through pleasure. Wisdom is not ashamed of appearing playful when necessary."

While speaking, Mentor took up a lyre and played it so artfully that Achitoas, jealous, allowed his to fall from spite. His eyes sparked, his distressed face changed color. Everyone would have seen his pain and his shame had Mentor's lyre not captured the hearts and souls of all there. They hardly dared to breathe for fear of disturbing the silence and missing something of that divine song. They continually feared that he would finish too soon.

Mentor's voice had no effeminate sweetness. Rather it was supple, strong, and impassioned even the least things.

First, he sang the praises of Zeus, father and king of the gods and men, who, with a nod of his head, rattles the universe. Then he represented Athena who came out of the head of Zeus, that is to say wisdom, that this god shapes within himself and that comes out of him in order to instruct docile men. Mentor sang these truths in a tone so religious and so sublime that the entire assembly believed themselves transported to the heights of Olympus before Zeus, whose gaze is more piercing than his thunder. Afterward, he sang of the misfortune of young Narcissus, who, becoming so madly in love with his own beauty that he incessantly gazed at himself on the banks of a spring, was consumed with pain, and was changed into a flower that bears his name. Finally, he also sang of the gruesome death of beautiful Adonis, whom a wild boar ripped apart and whom Aphrodite, passionate for him, could not bring back to life by complaining bitterly to heaven.

All those listening to him could not hold back their tears, and each felt an indescribable pleasure in weeping. When he had ceased singing, the stunned Phoenicians looked at each other. One said, "It is Orpheus. That is how, with a lyre, he tamed the ferocious beasts and enraptured the woods and the rocks. That is how he enchanted Cerberus, how he suspended the torments of Ixion and the Danaids, and how he touched the inexorable Hades so as to extract the beautiful Eurydice from the Underworld."

Another exclaimed, "No, it is Linus, the son of Apollo."

Another responded, "You are wrong. It is Apollo himself."

BOOK VII

Telemachus was hardly less surprised than the others, for he had never thought Mentor would know how, with so much perfection, to sing and to play the lyre.

Achitoas, who had had time to hide his jealousy, began to praise Mentor, but he blushed while praising him and he could not finish his speech. Mentor, who saw his distress, spoke up as if he had wanted to interrupt him and tried to console him by giving him all the praises he merited. Achitoas was not consoled, for he felt Mentor surpassed him even more in his modesty than in the enchantments of his voice.

Meanwhile, Telemachus said to Adoam, "I remember that you spoke to me of a voyage you had made into Baetica after we were parted in Egypt. Baetica is a country of which such wonders are told that one can hardly believe them. Deign to inform me if all they say of it is true."

"I would be glad," responded Adoam, "to depict to you this famous country worthy of your curiosity and which surpasses all that Rumor trumpets of it." Immediately, he began in this way:

"The Baetis river runs through a fertile country and under a gentle sky that is always serene. The country took the name of the river that flows into the great Ocean somewhat near the Pillars of Heracles and from that place where the furious sea, breaking its dikes, once separated the land of Tharsis from great Africa. This country seems to have preserved the delights of the golden age. The winters there are warm, and the rigorous Northwinds never blow. The blazing heat of summer is always tempered by refreshing zephyrs, which come to soften the air toward the middle of the day. So, all year round is just a happy marriage of springtime and autumn, who seem to hold each other's hand. The land in the vales and in the flat countrysides bear a double harvest each year. There, the trails are fringed with laurel trees, pomegranate trees, jasmine, and other trees, always green and always blooming. The mountains are covered with flocks that supply fine wools sought after by all the known nations. There are several gold and silver mines in this beautiful country. But the inhabitants, simple, and happy in their simplicity, do not even deign to count silver and gold among their riches. They only esteem what truly serves the needs of man.

"When we began to trade with these peoples, we found the gold and the silver among them employed for the same uses as iron, such as the blades of plows, for example. As they did no commerce outside, they had no need of any money. They are almost all shepherds or plowmen. Few artisans are seen in this country, for they only want to tolerate the arts that serve the true necessities of men. Even so, most of the men in this country, being devoted to agriculture or to driving flocks, do not fail to exercise the arts necessary for their simple and frugal life.

"The women spin this beautiful wool and make a fine cloth of a marvelous white from it. They make the bread, prepare the meals, and this work is easy for them, for one sees in this country fruits or milk, and rarely beef. They use the hide of their sheep to make a light shoe for themselves, their husbands, and their children. They make tents, some of which are of waxed pelts and others of stripped tree bark. They make, they wash all the garments of the family and keep the homes in an admirable orderliness and cleanliness. Their garments are easy to make, for in this gentle climate, one only wears a piece of fine and light cloth that is not tailored and that each of them arranges in long folds around the body for modesty, giving it the shape they desire.

"The men have no other arts to exercise, outside of the cultivation of land and the driving of flocks, than the art of working with wood and iron. Nevertheless, they hardly make use of iron, except for the instruments needed for plowing. All the arts having to do with architecture are useless to them, for they never build houses. 'That is,' they say, 'attaching oneself too much to the land, to build a dwelling on it that lasts so much longer than us. It suffices to protect oneself from the assaults of the air.'

"As for all the other arts esteemed by the Greeks, the Egyptians, and all other well-governed peoples, they detest them as inventions of vanity and softness. When you speak to them of the peoples who have the art of making superb buildings, gold and silver furnishings, fabrics embellished with embroidery and precious stones, exquisite perfumes, delicious dishes, musical instruments of enchanting harmony, they respond in these terms: 'Those people are unfortunate indeed, to have employed so much work and cleverness to corrupt themselves. That superfluity softens, intoxicates, torments those who possess it. It tempts those who are deprived of it to want to acquire it through injustice and violence. Can one call 'good' a superfluity that only serves to render men bad? The men of these lands, are they healthier and more robust than us? Do they live longer? Are they more united among themselves?

Do they lead a life more free, more tranquil, more cheerful? On the contrary, they must be jealous of one another, gnawed at by a craven and black envy, always tormented by ambition, by fear, by avarice, incapable of pure and simple pleasures since they are slaves to so many false necessities on which they make all their happiness depend.'

"This is how these wise men speak," continued Adoam, "who only learned wisdom in studying simple nature. They are horrified by our politesse, and it must be confessed that theirs is great in its lovable simplicity. They live all together without dividing the lands. Each family is governed by its chief, who is the true king over them. The father of the family has the right to punish each of his children or grandchildren who does a bad deed. But before punishing them, he takes the opinion of the rest of the family. These punishments almost never happen, for the innocence of the mores, good faith, obedience, and a horror of vice live in this happy land.

"It seems that Astraea, who they say retreated into the sky, is still here below hidden among these men. Judges are not needed among them, for their own conscience judges them. All properties are common. The fruits of the trees, the vegetables of the land, the milk from the flocks are riches so abundant that people so sober and restrained have no need of dividing them. Each family, roaming in this beautiful country, carries their tents from one place to another when they have consumed the fruits and exhausted the grazing land in the spot where they were. So, they have no interest in supporting one against another, and they all love each other with a brotherly love that nothing troubles. It is the curtailment of vain riches and deceptive pleasures that preserves this peace, this union, and this liberty for them. They are all free and all equal.

"There is no distinction to be found among them other than that which comes from the experience of the wise old men or the extraordinary wisdom of some young men that equals the old men steeped in virtue. Fraud, violence, perjury, trials, wars never make their cruel and pestilent voices heard in this country cherished by the gods. Never has human blood reddened this land; barely do you see that of lambs flow. When one speaks to these peoples of bloody battles, rapid conquests, the overthrow of states that are seen in other nations, they cannot be astonished enough.

"'What!' They say. 'Men, are they not mortal enough, without giving themselves, and even each other, an early death? Life is so short! And it seems that it appears too long for them! Are they on earth to rip each other apart and render each other mutually unhappy?'

"Moreover, these peoples of Baetica cannot understand how we so admire conquerors who subjugate great empires.

"'What madness,' they say, 'to put one's happiness in governing other men, the governance of whom is so difficult if one wants to govern them with reason and according to justice. But why take pleasure in governing them in spite of themselves? It is all a wise man can do in wanting to subject himself to governing a docile people with whom the gods have charged him, or a people who beg him to be their father and their shepherd. But to govern peoples against their will, that is to make yourself very miserable in order to have the false honor of holding them in slavery. A conqueror is a man whom the gods, annoyed with mankind, have given the earth in their anger to ravage kingdoms, spread fright, misery, despair everywhere, and to make as many slaves as there are free men. A man who seeks glory, will he not find enough of it in wisely leading what the gods have placed in his hands? Does he think that he can only merit praise in becoming violent, unjust, haughty, usurping, tyrannical over all his neighbors? War must only ever be considered in order to defend his liberty. Happy is the one who, not being the slave of another, does not have the mad ambition to make another his slave! Those great conquerors, who are depicted to us with so much glory, resemble those rivers overflowing their banks that look majestic, yet ravage all the fertile countryside that they should only water.'"

After Adoam had given this portrayal of Baetica, Telemachus, enchanted, posed various questions to him out of curiosity.

"These people, do they drink wine?"

"They hardly drink any," resumed Adoam, "for they have never wanted to make any. It is not that they lack grapes. No land bears more delicious ones. But they are content to eat the grape like other fruits, and they fear wine as the corrupter of men.

"'It is a type of poison,' they say, 'that enrages. It does not kill man, but it renders him beastly. Men can preserve their health and their strength without wine; with wine, they run the risk of ruining their health and of losing good mores.'"

Then Telemachus said, "I would very much like to know what laws regulate marriages in this nation."

"Each man," answered Adoam "can have only one wife, and he must keep her as long as she lives. The honor of men in this country depends as much on their fidelity with regard to their wives as the honor of wives depends, among other peoples, on their fidelity to their husbands. Never were a people so honest, or so jealous of purity. There, the wives are beautiful and pleasant, yet natural, modest, and hard-working. There, the marriages are peaceful, fruitful, unstained. The husband and wife seem to no longer be but a single person in two different bodies. The husband and wife together share all the domestic cares. The husband puts all the outside affairs in order while the wife confines herself to her housework; she unburdens her husband; she seems to be made to please only him. She wins his confidence and enchants him less by her beauty than by her virtue. This true enchantment in their companionship lasts as long as their lives. Sobriety, moderation, and the pure mores of this people give a long life to them, exempt from maladies. There, one sees old men of a hundred, a hundred twenty years, who still have cheerfulness and vigor."

"It remains for me to know," added Telemachus, "what they do to avoid war with other neighboring peoples."

"Nature," said Adoam, "has separated them from other peoples, on the one side by the sea, and on the other by the high mountains of the north. Besides, the neighboring peoples respect them because of their virtue. Often, other peoples, unable to agree among themselves, have taken them as judges of their differences and have entrusted to them the lands and cities they were disputing over. As this wise nation has never done any violence, no one is distrustful of it. They laugh when one speaks to them of kings who cannot sort out the borders of their states among themselves.

"'Can they fear,' they say, 'that land is lacking to men? There will always be more of it than they will be able to cultivate. As long as there remains open and uncultivated lands we would not even want to defend ours against neighbors who would want to seize it.'

"Neither pridefulness, nor haughtiness, nor bad faith, nor the desire to extend their dominion are found throughout the inhabitants of Baetica. So, their neighbors never have anything to fear from such a people, and they cannot hope to make themselves feared by them; that is why they leave them in repose. This people would abandon their country or deliver themselves over to death rather than accept servitude. Therefore, they are as difficult to subjugate as they are incapable of wanting to subjugate others. This is what causes a profound peace between them and their neighbors."

Adoam finished this discourse by recounting the manner in which the Phoenicians conduct their commerce in Baetica.

"These peoples," he said, "were astonished when they saw coming across the waters of the sea strange men who came from so far. They allowed us to found a city on the island of Gibraltar. They even received us with kindness and gave us part of all that they had without wanting any payment from us. Moreover, they offered to liberally give us all that remained of their wools after they had made provision for their use and, indeed, they sent us a rich present of them. It is a pleasure for them to give their superfluity to foreigners.

"As for their mines, they had no difficulty abandoning them to us: they were useless to them. It seemed to them that men were hardly wise to go seeking through so much work, in the bowels of the earth, that which can neither render them happy nor satisfy any true need.

"'Do not dig,' they told us, 'so deep into the earth. Be contented to plow it. It will give you true goods that will nourish you. You will draw from it fruits that are worth more than gold and silver, since men only want gold and silver to buy the foods which sustain their life.'

"We had often wanted to teach navigation to them and bring the young men of their country into Phoenicia. But they never wanted their children to learn to live like us.

"'They would learn,' they told us, 'to need all the things that have become necessities to you. They would want to have them. They would abandon virtue in order to obtain them through evil skills. They would become like a man who has good legs and who, losing the habit of walking, finally accustoms himself to the need of always being carried like a sick person.'

"As for navigation, they admire it because of the cleverness of this art, but they believe it is a pernicious art. 'If those people,' they say, 'sufficiently have in their country that which is necessary for life, what are they going to seek in another? That which suffices the needs of nature, is it not sufficient for them? They would merit shipwreck since they seek death amidst the tempests in order to assuage the avarice of merchants and to flatter the passions of other men.'

Telemachus was delighted to hear these discourses of Adoam, and he rejoiced that there were still in the world a people who, in following simple nature, were so wise and so happy together.

"O how distant those mores are," he said, "from the vain and ambitious mores of the peoples whom we believe the wisest! We are so spoiled that we can barely believe that such natural simplicity could truly be. We look upon the mores of those people as a beautiful fable, and they must look upon ours as a horrific dream."

END OF BOOK VII

THE ADVENTURES OF
TELEMACHUS
SON OF ODYSSEUS

BOOK VIII

While *Telemachus and Adoam were talking so*, forgetting sleep and not noticing the night was already in the middle of its course, a hostile and deceiving deity was distancing them from Ithaca, which their pilot, Acamas, was seeking in vain. Poseidon, though favorable toward the Phoenicians, could no longer bear that Telemachus had escaped the tempest that had flung him against the rocks of the island of Calypso. Aphrodite was even more irritated to see this young man, triumphant, having vanquished Love and all his spells. In the frenzy of her pain, she quit Cythera, Paphos, Idalium, and all the honors that are rendered to her on the island of Cyprus. She could no longer stay in those places where Telemachus had scorned her empire. She ascended toward brilliant Olympus where the gods were assembled alongside the throne of Zeus.

From there they behold the celestial bodies wheeling under their feet. They can see the sphere of the earth like a little mass of mud. The immense seas appear to them as mere drops of water from which this morsel of mud is a bit sodden. The greatest kingdoms are, to their eyes, only a little sand that covers the surface of this mud. The countless peoples and the mightiest armies are like mere ants disputing over a blade of grass on this morsel of mud. The immortals laugh at the most serious affairs that agitate weak mortals, and they appear as child's play to them. What men call grandeur, glory, power, deep politics, seem to these supreme deities as only misery and weakness.

It is in that place, so elevated above earth, that Zeus set his immovable throne. His eyes pierce into the abyss and light up the deepest recesses of hearts. His gentle and serene gaze spreads calm and joy throughout the universe. On the contrary, when he shakes his locks, he rattles Heaven and Earth. Even the gods, dazzled by the glorious rays that surround him, only approach him with trembling. All the celestial deities are at that moment alongside him. Aphrodite presents herself to him with all the enchantments that blossom in her bosom. Her flowing robe had more brilliance than all the colors with which Iris drapes herself in the midst of the gloomy clouds when she comes to promise frightened mortals the end of tempests and to announce the return of beautiful weather. Her robe was knotted with that famous belt on which the Graces appear. The hair of the goddess was casually gathered behind with a golden braid. All the gods were startled by her beauty, as if they had never seen her, and their eyes were dazzled by it, like those of mortals are when Phoebus, after a long night, comes to shine on them with his rays. They looked at each other with astonishment, and their eyes always came back to Aphrodite. But they saw that the eyes of that goddess were bathed in tears, and a bitter pain was painted on her face. Meanwhile, she advanced toward the throne of Zeus with a soft and light step, like the rapid flight of a bird that parts the immense space of the air. Regarding her with complaisance, he gave her a gentle smile and rising, he embraced her.

"My dear daughter," he said to her, "what troubles you? I cannot see your tears without being touched by them. Do not fear opening up your heart to me. You know my affection and my complaisance."

Aphrodite answered him in a voice sweet, but cutoff by deep sighs, "O father of the gods and men, you who see all, can you not know what causes my difficulty? Athena is not satisfied having knocked to its foundations the superb city of Troy, which I defended, and having taken revenge on Paris, who had preferred my beauty to hers. She leads round all the lands and round all the seas the son of Odysseus, that cruel destroyer of Troy. Telemachus is accompanied by Athena. That is what keeps her from appearing here in her rank with the other deities. She led that brash young man onto the island of Cyprus to outrage me. He scorned my might. Not only did he not design to burn incense on my altars, but he expressed horror for the feasts that are celebrated in my honor. He closed his heart to all my pleasures. In vain, Poseidon, to punish him at my request, whipped up the winds and the waves against him. Telemachus, cast by a horrible shipwreck onto the island of Calypso, triumphed over Love himself, whom I had sent onto the island to touch the heart of that young Greek. Neither his youth, nor the spells of Calypso, nor her nymphs, nor the flaming shafts of Love were able overcome the artifices of Athena. She snatched him from that island. Here I am, foiled. A child triumphs over me."

Zeus, to console Aphrodite, said to her, "It is true, my daughter, that Athena defends the heart of this young Greek against all the arrows of your son, and that she prepares for him a glory that no young man has ever merited. I am annoyed that he would have scorned your altars. But I cannot subject him to your might. I consent, for the love of you, that he will still roam by sea and by land, that he will live far from his homeland, exposed to all sorts of evils and dangers. But the destinies neither permit that he should perish, nor that his virtue should succumb to the pleasures with which you flatter men. Console yourself then, my daughter. Be content to hold in your empire so many other heroes and so many immortals."

In saying these words, he smiled at Aphrodite, a smile filled with charm and majesty. A shard of light like the most piercing lightning bolt leapt from his eyes. Kissing Aphrodite affectionately, he spread the scent of ambrosia with which Olympus was perfumed. The goddess could not keep from being sensitive to this caress from the greatest of the gods. Despite her tears and her pain, one saw joy spreading over her face. She lowered her veil to hide her blushing cheeks and the embarrassment in which she found herself. The entire assembly of gods applauded the words of Zeus, and Aphrodite, without wasting a moment, went to find

Poseidon to devise with him the means of exacting vengeance on Telemachus.

She recounted to Poseidon what Zeus had said to her.

"I already knew," responded Poseidon, "the immutable order of the destinies. But if we cannot fling Telemachus into the abyss amidst the swells of the sea, at least we will spare no effort to make him wretched and delay his return to Ithaca. I cannot consent to cause the Phoenician vessel on which he embarked to perish. I love the Phoenicians. They are my people. No other nation in the universe grows my empire like them. It is through them that the sea became the link to the society of all the peoples of the earth. They honor me through continual sacrifices on my altars. They are just, wise, and hardworking in commerce. They spread convenience and abundance everywhere. No, goddess, I cannot suffer that one of their vessels wrecks. But I will make it so that the pilot will lose his way and distance himself from Ithaca, where he intends to go."

Aphrodite, content with this promise, laughed malignantly and returned in her flying chariot to the flowery fields of Idalium, where the Graces, Games, and Laughter bore witness to their joy in seeing her again, dancing round her on the flowers that perfume this enchanting place.

Poseidon quickly sent a deceiving deity resembling Dreams, except that Dreams only deceive during sleep whereas this deity bewitches the senses of those who keep vigil. This maleficent god, surrounded by a countless horde of winged Lies that flitted around him, spilled a subtle and magical liquor over the eyes of the pilot Acamas, who was attentively considering, by the light of the moon, the course of the stars and the shoreline of Ithaca, whose craggy cliffs he already beheld fairly close to him. At that same moment, the pilot's eyes no longer revealed anything real to him. A false sky and a feigned land were presenting themselves to him. The stars seemed as if they had changed their course, and they were retracing their steps. All Olympus seemed to be moving by new laws. Even the land was changed. A false Ithaca always presented itself to the pilot to distract him as he was distancing himself from the real one. The more he advanced toward that deceptive image of the shore of the island, the more that image recoiled. It always fled before him, and he did not know what to think of that flight. Sometimes, he imagined he already heard the noise that is made in a port. He was already preparing, according to the orders he had received, to secretly land on a small island alongside the large one in order to hide Telemachus' return from Penelope's suitors who were conspired against him. Sometimes, he feared the reefs with which this seacoast is rimmed, and he seemed to hear the horrible bellowing of the waves breaking apart against those reefs. Then, suddenly, he noticed that the land appeared to be even more distant. The mountains were, to his eyes at that distance, merely tiny clouds that sometimes obscure the horizon when the sun sets. Thus, Acamas was stunned, and the impact of the deceitful deity, who bewitched his eyes, caused him to experience a certain seizure that had been unknown to him up until then. He was even tempted to believe that he was no longer on watch, and that he was under the illusion of a dream. Meanwhile, Poseidon ordered the Eastwind to blow, in order to cast the ship onto the coasts of

BOOK VIII

Hesperia. The wind obeyed with so much violence that the ship soon arrived on the shore that Poseidon had marked.

Already Dawn had announced the day. Already the stars, which fear the rays of the Sun, and which are jealous of them, had gone to hide their somber fires in the Ocean, when the pilot cried out, "At last, I can no longer doubt it, we are almost touching the island of Ithaca. Telemachus, rejoice. In an hour, you will be able to see Penelope again and perhaps find Odysseus remounted on his throne."

At this cry, Telemachus, who was motionless in the arms of Sleep, awakes, rises, climbs up to the helm, embraces the pilot and, with his eyes still barely open, stares at the nearby coast. He groans, not recognizing the shoreline of his homeland.

"Alas! Where are we?," he said. "That is not my dear Ithaca. You are wrong, Acamas, you know this coast poorly, so distant from your country."

"No, no," responded Acamas, "I cannot be wrong regarding the shoreline of this island. How many times have I entered your harbor? I know it even down to the smallest rocks in it. The shore of Tyre is hardly better in my memory. Recognize that mountain that is approaching. See that cliff that rises up like a tower. Do you not hear the waterfall crashing against those other rocks, while it seems to threaten the sea with its fall? But do you not notice the temple of Athena that splits the cloud? There it is, the fortress, and the house of Odysseus your father."

"You are mistaken, O Acamas. I see on the contrary, a coast somewhat raised, but uniform. I behold a city that is not Ithaca. O gods, is it thus that you toy with men?"

While Telemachus was speaking, Acamas' eyes were suddenly changed. The spell broke. He saw the shoreline such as it truly was and recognized his mistake.

"I confess it, O Telemachus!" he cried out. "Some hostile deity had bewitched my eyes. I believed to see Ithaca, and its entire image presented itself to me, but at this moment it disappears like a dream. I see another city. It is undoubtedly Salentum, that Idomeneus, fugitive from Crete, just founded in Hesperia. I spy walls that are rising and are not yet completed. I see a port that is not yet entirely fortified."

While Acamas was noticing the various newly built works in this emerging city and Telemachus was deploring his misfortune, the wind that Poseidon caused to blow pushed them at full sail into a natural harbor, where they were sheltered and very near the port.

Mentor, who was ignorant of neither the vengeance of Poseidon nor the cruel artifice of Aphrodite only smiled at Acamas' mistake. When they were in this natural harbor, Mentor said to Telemachus, "Zeus tests you, but he does not desire your ruin. On the contrary, he only tests you in order to open up the path of glory to you. Remember the labors of Heracles. Always have before your eyes those of your father. Whoever does not know how to suffer does not have a great heart. You must, through your patience and through your courage, weary cruel Fortune, whom it pleases to persecute you. I fear less for you the most dreadful disgraces of Poseidon than I feared the flattering caresses of the goddess who kept you on her island. What delays us? Let us enter into this harbor. Here are a friendly people. They are Greek where we arrive. Idomeneus, so poorly treated by Fortune, will have pity for the wretched."

Straightaway, they entered the port of Salentum, where the Phoenician vessel was received without difficulty because the Phoenicians are at peace and in commerce with all the peoples of the universe.

Telemachus marveled at that emerging city, resembling a young plant that, having been nourished by the sweet dew of the night, feels, since the morn, the rays of the sun that come to embellish it; it grows, it opens up its tender buds, it stretches its green leaves, it blooms its fragrant blossoms with a thousand new colors. At each moment one looks at it, one finds a new brilliance. In this way, Idomeneus' new city was flourishing on the shores of the sea. Each day, each hour, it grew magnificently, and it showed from afar, to foreigners out to sea, new architectural adornments that rose to the sky. The entire coast reverberated with the cries of workers and the blows of hammers. Stones were suspended in the air by cranes with ropes. All the chiefs animated the people to work as soon as Dawn appeared, and King Idomeneus, giving orders everywhere himself, made the works move forward with an incredible haste.

Barely had the Phoenician vessel arrived when the Cretans gave Telemachus and Mentor all the marks of sincere friendship. They hastened to advise Idomeneus of the arrival of the son of Odysseus.

"The son of Odysseus!" he exclaimed, "Odysseus, that dear friend, that wise hero through whom we finally overthrew the city of Troy! May they bring him here, and may I show him how much I loved his father!"

Straightaway, they present Telemachus, who asks for hospitality, telling him his name. Idomeneus answered him with a gentle and smiling face.

"Even if they had not told me who you are, I believe I would have recognized you. Voila, Odysseus himself. Voila, his eyes full of fire, from which the gaze was so firm. Voila, his air, cold and reserved at first, that hid so much vivacity and charm. I even recognize that sly smile, that casual manner, that smooth-talk, plain and insinuating, that persuaded without one having time to distrust it. Yes, you are the son of Odysseus, but you will also be mine. O my son, my dear son, what adventure leads you onto this shore? Is it to seek your father? Alas, I have no news of him; Fortune persecuted us, him and me. He had the misfortune of being unable to find his homeland again, and I had that of finding mine full of the anger of the gods against me."

While Idomeneus was saying these words, he was staring at Mentor like a man whose face was not unknown to him but for whom he could not find the name.

Meanwhile, Telemachus responded to him, tears in his eyes, "O King, forgive me the pain that I would not know how to hide, at a time when I should only bear witness to joy and gratitude for your goodness. By the regret you show me for the loss of Odysseus, you inform me yourself of feeling the misfortune of being unable to find my father. I have already been seeking him for a long time throughout the seas. The provoked gods do not permit me to either see him again, or to know if he shipwrecked, or to be able to return to Ithaca, where Penelope languishes in the desire to be delivered from her suitors. I had thought to find you on the island of Crete. I learned of your cruel destiny there, and I did not think I would be obliged to approach Hesperia, where you founded a new kingdom. But Fortune, who toys with men, and who keeps me roaming throughout countries far from Ithaca, has finally cast me onto your coasts. Among all the woes that Fortune has caused me, it is this one that I bear most willingly. If she distances me from my homeland, at least she causes me to know the most generous of all the kings."

At those words, Idomeneus embraced Telemachus tenderly and, leading him into his palace, said to him, "So who is, then, this prudent old man who accompanies you? It seems to me that I have seen him often another time."

"He is Mentor," replied Telemachus, "Mentor, Odysseus' friend, to whom he entrusted my childhood. Who would be able to tell you all that I owe him?"

Immediately, Idomeneus advances and holds out his hand to Mentor.

"We saw each other once before," he said. "Do you remember the voyage you made to Crete, and the good counsel that you gave me? But then the ardor of youth and the taste for vain pleasures swept me away. It was necessary that my misfortunes instruct me in order to teach me what I did not want to believe. Would to the gods that I had believed you, O wise old man. But I notice with astonishment that you have hardly changed over so many years. It is the same fresh face, the same upright build, the same vigor. Only your hair is a little whiter."

"Great King," responded Mentor, "if I were a flatterer, I would say the same to you, that you have preserved that flower of youth that glowed on your face before the siege of Troy. But I would prefer to displease you than to wound the truth. Besides, I see by your wise discourse that you do not like flattery and that one hazards nothing in speaking to you with sincerity. You are indeed changed, and I would have had difficulty recognizing you. I clearly conceive the cause of it; it is that you have suffered much in your misfortune, but you have gained much in suffering since you have acquired wisdom. A man must console himself easily for the wrinkles that come to his face while the heart trains and fortifies itself in virtue. Furthermore, know that kings always wear themselves out more than other men. In adversity, the mental difficulties and the travails of the body cause them to age before their time. In prosperity, the delights of a soft life wear them out even more than all the travails of war. Nothing is so unhealthy as the pleasures in which one cannot moderate oneself. Hence it is that kings, not only in peace but even in war, always have difficulties and pleasures that cause old age to come before the age when it should naturally come. A life sober, restrained, simple, exempt from restlessness and passions, orderly, and hard-working retains in the limbs of a wise man lively youth, which, without those precautions, is always ready to fly away on the wings of time."

Idomeneus, enchanted by Mentor's discourse, would have listened to him for a long time had someone not come to advise him of a sacrifice which he must make to Zeus. Telemachus and Mentor followed him, surrounded by a large crowd of people who were considering with eagerness and curiosity these two foreigners. The Salentines were saying to one another, "These two men are indeed different. The young one has a certain something of keenness and affability. All the charms of beauty and youth are spread over his face and his entire body. But that beauty has nothing of softness or femininity; along with this tender flower of youth, he appears vigorous, robust, hardened to work. But this other one, though much older, has still lost none of his strength. His mien appears, at first, less lofty, and his face less charming, but when one looks at him closely, one finds in his simplicity signs of wisdom and virtue, along with a nobility that astounds. When the gods descended to earth to communicate with mortals, undoubtedly they took on such figures of foreigners and travelers."

Meanwhile, they arrive at the temple of Zeus which Idomeneus, of the bloodline of this god, had adorned with much magnificence. It was surrounded by a double row of mottled marble columns. The capitals were of silver. The temple was all inlaid with marble, along with bas-reliefs that represented Zeus changed into a bull, the ravishing of Europa, and his passage into Crete across the waves. They seemed to respect Zeus, even though he was in an unknown form. Then one saw the birth and the youth of Minos. Finally, that wise king giving, at a more advanced age, laws to his entire island to render it forever flourishing. There, Telemachus also noticed the principal adventures of the siege of Troy, where Idomeneus had acquired the glory of a great captain. Among those representations of combat, he searched for his father. He recognized him taking the horses of Rhesus, whom Diomedes had just killed;

then, fighting with Great Ajax over the arms of Achilles before all the assembled chiefs of the Greek army; lastly, emerging from the fatal horse to spill the blood of so many Trojans. Telemachus recognized him instantly by those famous deeds of which he had often heard spoken and which Nestor himself had recounted to him. Tears streamed from his eyes. He changed color. His face looked distressed. Idomeneus saw it, even though Telemachus turned away to hide his distress.

"Do not be ashamed," Idomeneus said to him, "of allowing us to see how touched you are by the glory and misfortunes of your father."

Meanwhile, the people were assembling in droves beneath the vast porticos formed by the double row of columns which surrounded the temple. There were two troupes of young boys and young girls, who were singing verses of praise to the god who holds the thunderbolt in his hands. These children, chosen from the most pleasant faces, had long hair floating on their shoulders. Their heads were wreathed with roses and perfumed. They were all dressed in white. Idomeneus sacrificed to Zeus a hundred bulls to render him favorable in a war that he had undertaken against his neighbors. The blood of the victims steamed on all sides. One saw it streaming into deep cups of gold and silver.

The old man Theophanes, friend of the gods and priest of the temple, kept, during the sacrifice, his head covered with a tip of his purple robe. Afterward he consulted the entrails of the victims, which still palpitated. Then, placing himself on the sacred tripod, "O gods," he cried out, "who then are these two foreigners that

BOOK VIII

heaven sends to these places? Without them, the war undertaken would be ill-fated to us, and Salentum would tumble in ruin before having been raised on the foundations. I see a young hero, whom Wisdom leads by the hand. It is not permitted for a mortal mouth to say more of it."

Saying these words, his look was fierce and his eyes sparkling. He seemed to be seeing other things than those which appeared before him. His face was ablaze. He was distressed and beside himself, his hair stood on end, his mouth frothing, his arms raised and unmoving. His stirring voice was louder than any human voice. He was out of breath, and unable to keep contained within him the divine spirit that was shaking him.

"O happy Idomeneus!" he cried out again, "what do I see! What misfortunes avoided! What sweet peace within! But without, what combats! What victories! O Telemachus, your travails surpass those of your father. The proud enemy groans in the dust under your glaive. Brass gates, the inaccessible ramparts fall at your feet. O great goddess, may his father . . . O young man, you will see at last . . ."

At these words, speech dies on his lips, and he remains, as if in spite of himself, in a silence full of astonishment.

All the people are frozen with fear. Idomeneus, trembling, dares not ask him to finish. Even Telemachus, startled, barely understands what he just heard; barely can he believe that he had heard those lofty predictions. Mentor is the only one whom the divine spirit did not astound.

"You hear," he said to Idomeneus, "the plan of the gods. Against whatever nation you have to fight, victory will be in your hands, and you will owe to the young son of your friend the good fortune of your armies. Do not be jealous of him, only profit from what the gods give you through him."

Idomeneus, having not yet recovered from his astonishment, sought words in vain. His tongue remained still.

Telemachus, quicker to react, said to Mentor, "So much promised glory does not touch me. But what can, then, those last words mean, 'you will see . . .'? Is it my father, or only Ithaca? Alas! What did he not complete? He left me more in doubt than I was. O Odysseus, O my father, would it be you, you yourself, that I should see? Would it be true? But I flatter myself. Cruel oracle, you take pleasure in toying with an unhappy wretch. One more word, and I would have been overflowing with happiness!"

Mentor said to him, "Respect what the gods reveal, and do not undertake to reveal what they want to hide. A brazen curiosity merits being confounded. It is through a wisdom full of goodness that the gods hide from weak men their destiny in an impenetrable night. It is useful to foresee what depends on us in order to do it well. But it is no less useful to ignore what does not depend on our cares, and what the gods desire to do with us."

Telemachus, touched by these words, restrained himself with much difficulty. Idomeneus, who had recovered from his astonishment, began for his part to praise great Zeus, who had sent young Telemachus and wise Mentor to him in order to render him victorious over his enemies. After they had had a magnificent meal following the sacrifice, he spoke to the two foreigners in private.

BOOK VIII

"I confess that I did not yet know enough the art of reigning when I returned to Crete after the siege of Troy. You know, dear friends, the misfortunes that deprived me of reigning on that great island, since you assure me that you have been there since I departed. Even happier would I be had the cruelest strikes of Fortune served to instruct me and to render me more moderate! I traversed the seas as a fugitive whom the vengeance of the gods and men pursue. All my past grandeur only served to make my fall more shameful and more unbearable. I came to seek refuge with my household gods on this deserted coast where I found only uncultivated lands covered with brambles and thorns, forests as old as the earth, cliffs almost inaccessible, where ferocious beasts retreat. I was reduced to being glad to possess—along with a small number of soldiers and companions, who were happy to follow me in my misfortunes—this savage land, and to make it my homeland, no longer able to hope to ever see that happy island again, where the gods had caused my birth to have me reign there.

"'Alas!' I told myself, 'What a change! What a horrific example I am to kings! I must be held up to all those who reign in the world to instruct them through my example. They imagine themselves having nothing to fear because of their elevation above the rest of men. Ho! It is their elevation itself that causes them to have everything to fear. I was feared by my enemies and loved by my subjects. I commanded a mighty and bellicose nation. Rumor had carried my name into the most distant countries. I reigned on a fertile and delightful island. A hundred cities gave me a tribute of their riches every year. These peoples recognized me as being of the bloodline of Zeus, born in their country. They loved me as the grandson of wise Minos, whose laws rendered them so mighty and so happy. What was missing from my happiness, other than knowing how to enjoy it with moderation? But my pridefulness, and the flattery that I listened to, toppled my throne. Thus will fall all kings who deliver themselves over to their desires and to the counsel of flattering minds.

"Throughout the day, I tried to display a face, cheerful and full of hope, in order to sustain the courage of those who had followed me. 'Let us build,' I said to them, 'a new city that consoles us for all that we have lost. We are surrounded by peoples who have given us a beautiful example for this enterprise. We see Tarentum, which is rising up fairly close to us. It is Phalantus, along with his Lacedaemonians, who founded this new kingdom. Philoctetes gives the name of Petelia to a great city that he built on the same coast. Metapontum is yet a similar colony. Will we do less than all these foreigners roaming like us? Fortune is no more rigorous to us.'

"While I tried to ease, through these speeches, the difficulties of my companions, I was hiding in the depths of my heart a mortal pain. It was a consolation to me that the light of day forsook me, and that the night came to wrap me in her shadows so as to deplore, in freedom, my miserable destiny. Two torrents of bitter tears flowed from my eyes, and sweet Sleep was unknown to them. The following day, I would begin my work again with a new ardor. Voila, Mentor, that is what causes you to find me so aged."

BOOK VIII

After Idomeneus had finished recounting his difficulties, he asked Telemachus and Mentor for their succor in the war in which he found himself engaged.

"I will send you back to Ithaca," he said to them, "as soon as the war is ended. In the meantime, I will have vessels depart for all the most distant coasts to learn news of Odysseus. In whatever place in unknown lands that the tempest or the anger of some deity has cast him, I will know well how to retrieve him from it. Would to the gods that he still lives. As for you, I will send you back along with the best vessels that have ever been built on the island of Crete. They are made of timber felled on the veritable Mount Ida, where Zeus was born. This sacred wood would not know how to perish in the waves. The winds and the rocks fear it and respect it. Even Poseidon, in his greatest wrath, would not dare to whip up the ocean waves against it. Be assured, then, that you will return happily to Ithaca, without difficulty, and that no hostile deity will be able to make you wander any longer on so many seas. The trip is short and easy. Send the Phoenician vessel back that brought you here and only think to acquire the glory of establishing the new kingdom of Idomeneus in order to mend all his misfortunes. It is at this price, O son of Odysseus, that you will be judged worthy of your father. Even if the rigorous destinies have already caused him to descend into the gloomy kingdom of Hades, all of enchanted Greece will believe to see him again in you."

At these words, Telemachus interrupted Idomeneus.

"Let us send the Phoenician vessel back. What delays us in taking up arms to attack your enemies? They have become ours.

If we were victorious fighting in Sicily for Acestes, a Trojan and enemy of Greece, will we not be even more ardent and more favored by the gods when we fight for one of the Greek heroes who overthrew the city of Priam? The oracle that we just heard does not permit us to doubt it."

End of Book VIII

THE ADVENTURES OF
TELEMACHUS
SON OF ODYSSEUS

BOOK IX

M*entor, regarding with a gentle* and tranquil eye Telemachus, who was already filled with a noble ardor for combat, spoke thus:

"I am glad, son of Odysseus, to see so fine a passion for glory in you, but remember that your father only acquired so great a glory among the Greeks at the siege of Troy in showing himself to be the wisest and the most moderate among them. Achilles, though invincible and invulnerable, though he brought terror and death wherever he fought, could not take the city of Troy. He fell himself at the foot of the walls of that city, and she triumphed over Hector's murderer. But Odysseus, in whom prudence led valor, brought the flame and the sword into the midst of the Trojans, and it is to his hands that we owe the fall of those tall and superb towers which threatened all of confederated Greece for ten years.

As far as Athena is above Ares so does a discreet and foresighted valor surpass a boiling and fierce courage. Let us begin, then, by informing ourselves of the circumstances of this war that must be sustained. I refuse no peril; but I believe, O Idomeneus, that you must first explain to us if your war is just, then against whom you wage it, and lastly what your military forces are to hope for a favorable outcome."

Idomeneus answered, "When we arrived on this coast, we found a savage people who roved in the forests, living off their hunt and the fruits that the trees bear. These peoples, who are called Mandurians, were horrified seeing our vessels and our arms. They retreated into the mountains, but, as our soldiers were curious to see the country and wanted to hunt deer, they encountered those fugitive savages. Then the chiefs of those savages said to them, 'We have abandoned the gentle shores of the sea in order to cede them to you. There only remain to us the almost inaccessible mountains. At the least, is it not just that you leave us there in peace and liberty? We find you roaming, dispersed, and weaker than us. It would only be up to us to slit your throats and even to deny your companions the knowledge of your misfortune. But we do not want to dip our hands into the blood of those who are men as well as us. Go, remember that you owe your life to our sentiments of humaneness. Never forget that it is from a people whom you call uncouth and savage that you receive this lesson in moderation and generosity.'

"Those among our own, who were sent back in this way by those barbarians, returned to camp and recounted what had happened to them. Our soldiers were stirred up by it. They were ashamed to see that Cretans owed their lives to that troop of fugitive men, who appeared to them to resemble bears more than men. They went out hunting them in a greater number than the former ones and with all sorts of arms. Soon they encountered the savages and attacked them. The combat was cruel. Shafts flew from both sides like hail falls in the countryside during a storm. The savages were compelled to retreat into their craggy mountains where our men dared not engage them.

"Soon after, those peoples sent my way two of their wisest old men to ask for peace. They brought presents. They were the hides of ferocious beasts they had killed and fruits of the country. After having given me their presents, they spoke so:

"'O king, we hold, as you see, in one hand the sword and in the other an olive branch.' (Indeed, they held one and the other in their hands.) 'Here, peace and war—choose. We would prefer peace. It is for the love of it that we had no shame in ceding to you the gentle shores of the sea, where the sun renders the land fertile and produces so many delicious fruits. Peace is sweeter than all those fruits. It is for peace that we retreated into those tall mountains always covered with ice and snow, where one never sees either the flowers of spring or the rich fruits of autumn. We are horrified by this brutality that, under the fine names of ambition and glory, madly ravages provinces and sheds the blood of men, who are all brothers. If that false glory touches you, we are far from envying you; we feel sorry for you and we pray to the gods to preserve us from a like fury. If the sciences that the Greeks learn with so much care, and if the politesse, on which they pride themselves, only inspire this detestable injustice in them, we believe ourselves only too fortunate not to have these advantages. We will glory in always being ignorant and barbaric, yet just, humane, loyal, selfless, accustomed to satisfying ourselves with little and to scorning the vain delicateness that causes one to need so much. What we esteem, it is health, frugality, liberty, vigor in body and mind. It is love of virtue, reverential awe of the gods, good character with respect to our kin, attachment to our friends, fidelity to everyone, moderation in prosperity, steadfastness in misfortunes, courage to always boldly tell the truth, horror of flattery. There, these are the peoples we are offering you as neighbors and allies. If the provoked gods blind you to the point of causing you to refuse peace, you will learn, but too late, that those who love, through moderation, peace, are the most formidable in war.'

"While these old men were speaking so, I could not weary of looking at them. They had long and scruffy beards; shorter hair, but white, thick eyebrows; keen eyes; a steady gaze and countenance; a speech, grave and full of authority; simple and ingenuous manners. The furs that served them for garments, being knotted at the shoulder, allowed one to see arms more sinewy and muscles more developed than those of our athletes. I answered these two envoys that I would desire peace. We sorted out together in good faith several conditions. We prayed for all the gods to witness, and I sent those men back to their dwellings with presents.

"But the gods, who had chased me from the kingdom of my ancestors, were not yet weary of persecuting me. Our hunters, who could not yet have been alerted to the peace that we had just made, encountered, that very day, a large troop of those barbarians, who were accompanying their envoys as they returned from our camp. They attacked them with fury, killing a number of them and pursuing the rest into the wood. Voila, the war reignited.

"These barbarians believe they can no longer trust either our promises or our oaths. In order to be more mighty against us, they call to succor them the Locrians, the Apulians, the Lucanians, the Bruttians, the peoples of Crotona, of Neritus and of Brindisi. The Lucanians come with chariots armed with sharp scythes. Among the Apulians, each is covered with the hide of some ferocious animal he has killed; they bear clubs full of fat knots and garnished with iron tips. They are almost the size of giants, and their bodies are rendered so robust through arduous exercise, to which they are devoted, that the very sight of them terrifies. The Locrians, coming from Greece, are still in touch with their origins and are more humane than the others, but they have joined together the exacting discipline of Greek troops, the vigor of barbarians, and the habit of leading a hard life, all of which renders them invincible. They carry light shields which are made of wicker work and covered with skins. Their swords are long. The Bruttians are light runners, like the stag and the fallow deer. It is believed that even the most tender grass is not trampled under their feet, barely do they leave in the sand any trace of their step. One sees them suddenly melt down upon their enemies and then disappear with an equal rapidity. The peoples of Crotona are adroit at archery. An ordinary man among the Greeks could not draw a bow such as is commonly seen with the Crotoniates, and, if they ever apply themselves to our games, they will bring home the prize. Their arrows are dipped in the sap of certain poisonous weeds that come, it is said, from the banks of the Avernus and of which the poison is mortal. As for those of Neritus, of Brindisi, and of Messapia, they only share strong bodies and an artless valor. The screams they loose to the sky at the sight of their enemies are dreadful. They use the slingshot fairly well, and they obscure the air with a hail of hurled stones, but they fight without order. Voila, Mentor, what you desired to know. You now know the origin of this war, and who our enemies are."

After this enlightenment, Telemachus, impatient for combat, believed there was nothing left to do but to take up arms. Mentor still restrained him and said to Idomeneus, "How does it come about, then, that even the Locrians, peoples out of Greece, unite with the barbarians against Greeks? How does it come about that so many colonies flourish on this same seacoast without having the same wars to sustain as you? O Idomeneus, you say that the gods are not yet weary of persecuting you, and me, I say that they have not yet finished instructing you. The many misfortunes that you have suffered have not yet taught you what must be done to prevent war. What you recount yourself of the good faith of these barbarians suffices to show that you would have been able to live in peace with them. But haughtiness and pridefulness attract the most dangerous wars. You would have been able to give them hostages and take some from them. It would have been easy to send, along with their ambassadors, some of your chiefs to conduct them back safely. Since this war renewed, you should have still been able to appease them by representing to them that they were attacked for want of knowing about the alliance that had just been sworn to. It would have been necessary to offer them all the assurances they would have asked for and to establish rigorous penalties against all those of your subjects who would have failed to keep the alliance. But what has happened since the beginning of this war?"

"I believed," responded Idomeneus, "that we could not, without baseness, search for those barbarians who hastily assembled all their men of fighting age and implored succor from all the neighboring peoples to whom they rendered us suspect and odious. It seemed to me that the most assured position was to quickly capture certain passages in the mountains, which were poorly guarded. We took them without difficulty, and in doing so positioned ourselves to desolate those barbarians. I had towers raised there, from where our troops can overwhelm with shafts all the enemies who come from the mountains into our country. We are able to enter into theirs, and to ravage, when it pleases us, their principal dwellings. Through this means, we are in a position to resist, with unequal forces, that countless multitude of enemies that surround us. Furthermore, peace between them and us has become very difficult. We would not know how to abandon these towers to them without exposing ourselves to their incursions, and they regard them as citadels which we want to use to reduce them to servitude."

Mentor responded to Idomeneus, "You are a wise king, and you want the truth revealed to you without any softening. You are not like those weak men who fear seeing it, and who, lacking courage to mend their ways, only use their authority to sustain the errors they have made. Know, then, that those barbarous people gave you a marvelous lesson when they came to ask you for peace. Was it through weakness that they asked for it? Did they lack courage or resources against you? You see well that the answer is no, since they are so warlike and supported by so many formidable neighbors. Why did you not imitate their moderation? Now a false modesty and a false glory have cast you into this misfortune. You feared rendering the enemy too proud, and you did not fear rendering him too powerful in uniting so many peoples against you through a haughty and unjust conduct. Of what use are these towers that you vaunt so, if not to put all of your neighbors in the necessity of perishing, or perishing yourself in order to preserve yourself from an imminent servitude? You only raised these towers for your assurance, and it is through these towers that you are in so great a peril. The surest rampart of a state is justice, moderation, good faith, and the assurance—where your neighbors are concerned—that you are incapable of usurping their lands. The strongest walls can tumble through various unforeseen accidents. Fortune is capricious and inconstant in war. But the love and confidence of your neighbors, when they have felt your moderation, make it so that your state cannot be vanquished and is almost never attacked. Even when an unjust neighbor should attack it, all the others, interested in their own preservation, will quickly take up arms to defend it. This support from so many peoples, who find their true interests in sustaining yours, would render you much more powerful than these towers that render your woes irremediable. If you had thought from the beginning to avoid the jealousy of all your neighbors, your emerging city would flourish in a happy peace, and you would be the arbiter of all the nations of Hesperia.

"Let us step back now to examine how we can mend the past through the future. You had begun to tell me that there are on this coast various Greek colonies. These peoples should be disposed to helping you. They have not forgotten either the great name of Minos, son of Zeus, or your travails at the siege of Troy, where you distinguished yourself so many times among the Greek princes with regard to the common quarrel of all Greece. Why are you not thinking to put these colonies on your side?"

"They are all," answered Idomeneus, "resolved to remain neutral. It is not that they would not have some inclination to help me, but the overly grand brilliance that this city has had since its birth terrified them. These Greeks, as well as the other peoples, feared that we would have designs on their liberty. They thought that after having subjugated the barbarians of the mountains, we would push our ambition further. In a word, all are against us. Even those who do not wage open war against us desire our abasement, and jealousy leaves us no ally."

"Bizarre ending!" resumed Mentor. "In wanting to look too mighty, you ruin your might, and, while you are, on the outside, the object of the fear and hatred of your neighbors, you are, on the inside, draining yourself through the efforts necessary to sustain such a war. O wretched and doubly-wretched Idomeneus, whom even misfortune has only been able to half instruct! Will you still need a second downfall to learn to anticipate the woes that threaten the greatest kings? Leave it to me and just recount to me in detail which Greek cities, then, are refusing your alliance."

"The main one," answered Idomeneus, "is the city of Tarentum. Phalantus founded it three years ago. He gathered in Laconia a great number of young men born of women who had forgotten their husbands, absent during the Trojan war. When the husbands returned, those women only thought to appease them and to disavow their wrongdoings. Those numerous youths, who were born outside of wedlock, no longer knowing either father or mother, lived with an unbounded licentiousness. The severity of the laws repressed their disorder. They united under Phalantus, bold, intrepid, ambitious chief, who knows how to win hearts through his artifices. He came onto this coast with those young Laconians. They made of Tarentum a second Lacedaemon. On another side, Philoctetes, who had so great a glory at the siege of Troy, in carrying the arrows of Heracles, has raised in this neighborhood the walls of Petelia, less mighty, to tell the truth, but more wisely governed than Tarentum. Lastly, we have near here the city of Metapontum, which wise Nestor founded along with his Pylians."

"What, you have Nestor in Hesperia, and you have not known how to engage him in your interests, Nestor, who saw you so many times fighting against the Trojans, and with whom you have a friendship!"

"I lost it," replied Idomeneus, "through the artifice of those peoples, who have nothing barbaric about them other than the name. They had the address of persuading him that I wanted to make myself the tyrant of Hesperia."

"We will set him straight," Mentor said. "Telemachus saw him in Pylos before he would have come to found his colony and before we would have undertaken our great voyages in search of Odysseus. He will not yet have forgotten that hero, nor the marks of affection that he gave to his son Telemachus. But the main thing is to heal his distrust. It is through the umbrage taken by your neighbors that this war ignited and it is through dissipating this umbrage that this war can be put out. Once again, leave it to me."

At these words, Idomeneus, embracing Mentor, was touched with tenderness and unable to speak. Finally, he barely pronounced these words:

"O wise old man sent by the gods to mend all my errors, I confess that I would be irritated with any other who would have spoken to me as freely as you. I confess that there is only you alone who would be able to oblige me to seek peace. I had resolved to perish or to vanquish all my enemies. But it is right to believe your wise counsel rather than my passion. O fortunate Telemachus, who can never go astray like me since you have such a guide! Mentor, you are the master. All the wisdom of the gods is in you. Athena herself would not be able to give more salutary counsel. Go, promise, conclude, give all that is mine. Idomeneus will approve all that which you judge appropriate to do."

While they were reasoning so, a confused noise was suddenly heard of chariots, horses whinnying, men loosing horrific howls, and trumpets filling the air with a bellicose sound. Someone cries out, "Here are the enemies who made a great detour to avoid the guarded passages. Here they are, coming to besiege Salentum!" The old men and the women looked dismayed. "Alas, was it necessary to quit our dear homeland, fertile Crete, and follow a luckless king across so many seas to found a new city that will be reduced to ashes like Troy?"

From the top of the newly built walls, they saw in the vast countryside, glinting in the sun, the helmets, cuirasses, and shields of the enemies. Their eyes were dazzled by them. They also saw bristling pikes that covered the land, as if it were covered by an abundant crop that Demeter prepares in the countryside of Enna in Sicily during the heat of summer to reward the plowman for all his troubles. Already they noticed chariots armed with sharp scythes. They easily distinguished each people coming to this war.

Mentor ascended onto a high tower to see better. Idomeneus and Telemachus followed him closely. No sooner had he arrived there than he spotted on one side Philoctetes and on another Nestor with Pisistratus his son. Nestor was easy to recognize in his venerable old age.

"What then!" Mentor exclaimed. "You thought, O Idomeneus, that Philoctetes and Nestor were content to not assist you. Here they are, they have taken up arms against you. And if I am not mistaken, those other troops that march in such good order with so much slowness are the Lacedaemonian troops commanded by Phalantus. All are against you. There is no neighbor on this coast of whom you have not made an enemy without wanting to."

Saying these words, Mentor hastily descends from this tower; he advances toward a gate of the city on the side where the enemies were advancing. He has it opened, and Idomeneus, surprised by the

BOOK IX

majesty with which he does these things, dares not even ask him what his design is. Mentor motions with his hand so that no one thinks of following him. He goes before the enemies, astonished to see a lone man presenting himself to them. He showed them, from a distance, an olive branch as a sign of peace, and when he was within range to make himself heard, he asked them to assemble all the chiefs. Quickly the chiefs assembled, and he spoke thus:

"O generous men assembled from so many nations that flourish in rich Hesperia, I know that you only came here in the common interest of liberty. I laud your zeal. But suffer that I represent to you an easy means of preserving the liberty and glory of all your peoples, without shedding human blood.

"O Nestor, wise Nestor whom I spied in this assembly, you are not ignorant of how calamitous war is, even to those who undertake it with justice and under the protection of the gods. War is the greatest of the evils with which the gods afflict men. You will never forget what the Greeks suffered for ten years outside wretched Troy. What divisions among the chiefs! What caprices of Fortune! What carnage of the Greeks at the hands of Hector! What woes in all the most powerful cities, caused by the war during the long absence of their kings! In returning, some shipwrecked at the promontory of Caphereus; others found a gruesome death even in the very bosom of their spouses. O gods, it is in your anger that you armed the Greeks for that glorious expedition. O Hesperian peoples, I pray the gods never give you a victory so ill-fated. Troy is in ashes, it is true. But it would be worth more to the Greeks were she still in all her glory and craven Paris still enjoyed his infamous amours with Helen in peace. Philoctetes, so wretched and abandoned for so long on the island of Lemnos, do you not fear finding similar woes in a similar war? I know that the people of Laconia have also felt the troubles caused by the long absence of the princes, captains, and soldiers who went against the Trojans. O Greeks, who passed into Hesperia, all of you have only passed here through a series of misfortunes, which were the aftermath of the Trojan war."

After speaking so, Mentor advanced toward the Pylians, and Nestor, who had recognized him, also advanced to receive him. "O Mentor," he said, "it is with pleasure that I see you again. It was many years ago that I saw you for the first time in Phocis. You were only fifteen years old, and I foresaw then that you would be as wise as you have been afterward. But by what adventure have you been driven to these places? What are then the means that you have to end this war? Idomeneus has compelled us to attack him. We only asked for peace. Each of us had a pressing interest to desire it. But we were no longer able to find any security with him. He violated all his promises with regard to his closest neighbors; peace with him would not be a peace—it would only serve him to dissipate our league, which is our only resource. He has demonstrated to all the peoples his ambitious design to enslave them, and he left us no means of defending our liberty than in trying to overthrow his new kingdom. Through his bad faith, we are reduced to slaying him or receiving the yoke of servitude from him. If you find some expedient to arrange things in such a way that we can trust him and be assured of a good peace, all the peoples that you see here will gladly forsake their arms, and we will joyfully avow that you surpass us in wisdom."

Mentor responded, "Wise Nestor, you know that Odysseus has entrusted his son, Telemachus, to me. This young man, impatient to discover the destiny of his father, stayed with you in Pylos, and you received him with all the attentions that he could expect from a loyal friend of his father. You even gave him your son to guide him. He then undertook long voyages on the sea. He saw Sicily, Egypt, the island of Cyprus, that of Crete. The winds, or rather the gods, cast him onto this coast as he was wanting to return to Ithaca. We arrived here just in time to spare you the horrors of a cruel war. It is no longer Idomeneus, it is the son of wise Odysseus, it is I who answers to you for all these things that will be promised to you."

While Mentor was speaking so with Nestor amidst the confederated troops, Idomeneus and Telemachus, along with all the armed Cretans, were regarding them from atop the walls of Salentum. They were attentive to note how Mentor's discourse would be received, and they would have wanted to be able to hear the wise discussions of those two old men. Nestor had always passed for the most experienced and the most eloquent of all the kings of Greece. It was he who moderated, during the siege of Troy, the boiling wrath of Achilles, the arrogance of Agamemnon, the pride of Ajax, and the impetuous courage of Diomedes. Sweet persuasion flowed from his lips like a stream of honey. The sound of his voice alone caused him to be heard by all those heroes: all fell silent as soon as he opened his mouth, and there was only he who could appease in the camp fierce Discord. He was beginning to feel the insults of trembling old age, but his words were still filled with strength and sweetness. He recounted events of the past to instruct the youth through his experience, but he recounted them with charm, though with a little slowness. This old man, admired by all Greece, seemed to have lost all his eloquence and all his majesty as soon as Mentor appeared with him. His old age appeared wilted and beaten-down alongside that of Mentor, in whom the years seemed to have respected the strength and the vigor of his temperament. Mentor's speech, though grave and simple, had a vivacity and an authority that were beginning to lack in the other. All that he said was brief, precise, and taut. Never did he repeat himself. Never did he recount anything but the facts necessary for the affair that must be decided. If he was obliged to speak several times of the same thing in order to instill it or to persuade, it was always through new turns and through relatable comparisons. He even had a certain something of complaisance and playfulness, when he wanted to adapt to the needs of others and to insinuate some truth to them. These two men, so venerable, were a touching spectacle to so many assembled peoples.

While all the allied enemies of Salentum were throwing themselves on top each other in droves in order to see them more closely and to try to hear their wise discourse, Idomeneus, and all of his people were striving to discover, through their avid and eager gaze, what their gestures and the looks on their faces signified.

Meanwhile, Telemachus, impatient, steals away from the multitude that surrounds him. He runs to the gate by which Mentor had left. He has it opened with authority. Presently, Idomeneus, who believes him at his side, is stunned to see him running to the middle of the campaign and that he is already alongside Nestor. Nestor recognizes him and hastens, but with a heavy and halting step, to receive him. Telemachus throws himself at his neck and holds him tightly in his arms, without speaking. Finally, he cries out, "O my father! I am not afraid to call you such. The misfortune of not finding my real father, and the kindnesses you have made me feel, give me the right to use so tender a name. My father, my dear father, I see you again. So, may I also see Odysseus again! If something could console me in being deprived of him, it would be finding in you another like him."

Nestor could not, at these words, hold back his tears, and he was touched by a secret joy, seeing those that streamed with a marvelous charm down Telemachus' cheeks. The beauty, the sweetness, and the noble assurance of this young stranger, who so recklessly crossed through so many enemy troops, stunned all the allies.

"Is he not," they were saying, "the son of this old man who came to speak to Nestor?"

"Undoubtedly, it is the same wisdom in the two ages of life so far apart. In the one, it is only just beginning to bud; in the other, it abundantly bears the ripest fruits."

Mentor, who had been pleased to see the tenderness with which Nestor had just received Telemachus, profited from this happy disposition.

"Voila," he said to him. "The son of Odysseus, so dear to all Greece, so dear to even you, O wise Nestor. Here, I deliver him to you, as a hostage, and as the most precious gage that one could give you of the fidelity of Idomeneus' promises. You judge well that I would not want that the loss of the son should follow that of the father and that the unhappy Penelope would be able to reproach Mentor for having sacrificed her son to the ambition of the new king of Salentum. With this gage, which he himself has just offered, and which the gods, admirers of peace, send to you, I begin, O peoples assembled from so many nations, to make propositions to you to establish a solid peace forever."

At the name of peace, a confused noise is heard from rank to rank. All those different nations quaked with wrath and believed time was being wasted as the combat was delayed. They imagined that they were only making all these speeches to ramp down their fury and to allow their prey to escape. The Mandurians especially were impatiently tolerating that Idomeneus would hope to deceive them once again. They often undertook to interrupt Mentor, for they feared that his speeches, filled with wisdom, would detach their allies. They were beginning to distrust all the Greeks who were in the assembly. Mentor, perceiving it, hastened to increase this distrust in order to cast division into the minds of all those peoples.

"I confess," he said, "that the Mandurians have cause to complain and to ask for some reparation for the wrongs they have suffered. But, also, it is not just that the Greeks, who build colonies on this coast, should be suspect and odious to the former peoples of their country. On the contrary, the Greeks must be united among themselves and well-treated by others. It is only necessary that they be restrained and that they never undertake to usurp the lands of their neighbors. I know that Idomeneus has had the misfortune of causing you to take umbrage, but it is easy to heal all your distrust—Telemachus and I, we offer ourselves as hostages who will answer to you for the good faith of Idomeneus. We will remain in your hands until the things that will be promised you are faithfully accomplished.

"What irritates you, O Mandurians," he shouted out, "it is that the Cretan troops have seized the passages of your mountains by surprise, and that, in so doing, they are in a position to enter in spite of you, as often as they please, into the country where you retreated so as to leave them the flat country along the shore of the sea. These passages that the Cretans fortified with tall towers full of armed men are then the real subject of the war. Answer me. Is there still any other?"

Then the chief of the Mandurians advanced and spoke thus:

"What have we not done to avoid this war? The gods are our witnesses that we only renounced peace when peace escaped us, without recourse, through the restless ambition of the Cretans and through the impossible position they put us of having to rely on their oaths to us. Foolish nation that has reduced us, in spite of ourselves, to the frightful necessity of taking a position of despair against it and of no longer being able to seek our salvation but in its destruction! As long as they preserve these passages, we will always believe they want to usurp our lands and put us in servitude. If it is true that they now only think of living in peace with their neighbors, they would be content with what we have ceded to them, without difficulty, and they would not endeavor to preserve entries into a country against whose liberty they would form no ambitious design. But you do not know them, O wise old man. It is through a great misfortune that we learned to know them. Cease, O beloved man of the gods, delaying a just and necessary war, without which Hesperia will never be able to hope for a continual peace. O ungrateful, deceptive and cruel nation that the provoked gods sent alongside us to trouble our peace and to punish us for our wrongdoings! But after having punished us, O gods, you will avenge us! You will be no less just against our enemies than against us."

At these words, all the assembly appeared stirred up; it seemed that Ares and Enyo were going from rank to rank, reigniting in their hearts the fury of combat that Mentor was trying to put out. Thus, he resumed speaking, "If I only had promises to make to you, you could refuse to rely on them, but I am offering you things certain and present. If you are not content to have Telemachus and myself as hostages, I will have twelve of the noblest and most valiant Cretans given to you. It is also just that you would give hostages from your side, for Idomeneus, who sincerely desires peace, desires it without fear and without abasement. He desires peace, as you say yourselves that you have desired it, through wisdom and moderation, but not through the love of a soft life or through weakness at the sight of the dangers with which war threatens men. He is ready to perish or to vanquish. But he prefers peace to the most brilliant victory. He would be ashamed to fear being vanquished. But he fears being unjust, and he is not ashamed to want to mend his errors. Arms in hand, he offers you peace. He does not want to impose high-handed conditions on it, for he makes no case for a forced peace; he wants a peace in which all the parties are content, that ends all jealousies, appeases all resentments, and heals all distrusts—in a word, Idomeneus is of the sentiment where I am sure you would like him to be. It is only a question of persuading you of it. Persuasion will not be difficult if you want to listen to me with an open and tranquil mind.

"Listen, then, O peoples full of valor, and you, O chiefs so wise and so united, listen to what I offer you on behalf of Idomeneus. It is not right that he would be able to enter into the lands of his neighbors; neither is it right that his neighbors would be able to enter into his. He consents that the passages, which have been fortified by tall towers, be guarded by neutral troops. You, Nestor, and you, Philoctetes, you are of Greek origin. But on this occasion, you have declared yourselves against Idomeneus. So then, you cannot be suspected of being too favorable to his interests. What touches you, it is the common interest of the peace and liberty of Hesperia. May you yourselves be the custodians and guardians of those passages that are causing the war. You have no less interest in preventing the ancient peoples of Hesperia from destroying Salentum, new colony of the Greeks similar to those that you founded, than in preventing Idomeneus from usurping the land of his neighbors. Keep the balance between the one and the other. Instead of bringing iron and fire to a people that you should love, reserve for yourself the glory of being the judges and mediators. You will say to me that these conditions would seem wonderful to you if you could assure yourselves that Idomeneus will carry them out in good faith, but I am going to satisfy you.

"There will be, for reciprocal security, hostages, of whom I have spoken, just until all the passages are put into the custody of your hands. When the salvation of all Hesperia, when that of Salentum itself, and of Idomeneus will be at your discretion, will you be content? Who will you distrust after that? Will it be yourselves? You dare not put your trust in Idomeneus, and Idomeneus is so incapable of deceiving you that he wants to trust you. Yes, he wants to entrust you with the peace of mind, the liberty, the lives of all his people and of himself. If it is true that you only desire a good peace, here is what presents itself to you and what removes all pretext to back away. Once again, do not imagine that fear reduces Idomeneus to making these offers. It is wisdom and justice that commit him to take this position without putting himself in difficulty, should you impute to weakness what he does through virtue.

"In the beginning, he made errors, and he puts his glory in recognizing them through the offers which he provides you. It is weakness, it is vanity, it is gross ignorance of his own interest to hope to be able to hide his errors in affecting to sustain them with pride and haughtiness. The one who confesses his errors to his enemy, and who offers to mend them, demonstrates thereby that he has become incapable of committing them and that the enemy has everything to fear from a conduct so wise and so steadfast unless he makes peace. Be very wary of tolerating that he put you in the wrong in turn. If you refuse the peace and justice that comes to you, peace and justice will be avenged. Idomeneus, who should fear finding the gods provoked against him, will turn them from him against you. Telemachus and I, we will fight for the good cause. I take all the gods of Heaven and of the Underworld as witnesses of the just proposals I make to you now."

Finishing these remarks, Mentor raised his arms to show to so many peoples the olive branch which was, in his hand, the sign of peace. The chiefs, who regarded him closely, were stunned and dazzled by the divine fire that glowed in his eyes. He appeared with a majesty and an authority that is above all that one sees in the greatest among mortals. The enchantment of his sweet and forceful words captured their hearts. They were like those magical words that suddenly, in the deep silence of the night stop, in the middle of Olympus, the moon and the stars, calm the angry sea, silence the winds and the waves, and suspend the course of rushing rivers. Mentor was, in the midst of these furious peoples, like Dionysus when he was surrounded by tigers who, forgetting their cruelty, came, through the power of his sweet voice, to lick his feet and submit to his caresses. At first, there was a profound silence throughout the army. The chiefs were looking at each other, unable to resist this man nor to comprehend who he was. All the troops, stock-still, had their eyes attached to him. They dared not speak for fear that he would still have something to say and they would keep him from being heard. Though nothing could be added to the things he had said, they wished that he had spoken longer. Everything he had said remained as if engraved in every heart. In speaking so, he made himself loved. He made himself believed. Each person was avid and held in suspense to gather even the least words that emerged from his mouth.

Finally, after a fairly long silence, a dull noise was heard that spread little by little. It was no longer that confused noise of peoples quaking in their indignation. It was, on the contrary, a sweet and favorable murmur. One already beheld on their faces an indescribable serenity and mellowness. The Mandurians, so angry, felt their weapons falling from their hands. Fierce Phalantus with his Lacedaemonians was startled to find his heart of iron soften. The others began to yearn for that happy peace that had just been shown them. Philoctetes, more sensitive than the others through the experience of his misfortunes, could not hold back his tears. Nestor, unable to speak in the emotional state where Mentor's discourse had put him, embraced Mentor tenderly, and all those peoples at once, as if there had been a signal, quickly cried out, "O wise old man, you disarm us! *Peace! Peace!*"

Nestor, a moment after, wanted to begin a speech, but all the impatient troops feared that he wanted to present some difficulty.

"*Peace! Peace!*," they shouted out again. Silence could only be imposed on them in making all the chiefs of the army cry out along with them, "*Peace! Peace!*"

Nestor, seeing clearly that he was not free to make a follow-up speech, contented himself in saying, "You see, O Mentor, the power of the word of a good man. When wisdom and virtue speak, they calm all passions. Our just resentments turn into friendship and into the desire for a lasting peace. We accept it, such as you offer it." At the same time, all the chiefs shook hands in a sign of consent.

Mentor ran toward the city gate to have it opened and to summon Idomeneus out of Salentum without precaution. Meanwhile, Nestor embraced Telemachus, saying, "O lovable son of the wisest of all the Greeks, may you be as wise and more fortunate than he. Have you discovered nothing of his destiny? The memory of your father, whom you resemble, served to smother our indignation."

Phalantus, though harsh and fierce, though he had never seen Odysseus, could not help being touched by his misfortunes and by those of his son. They were already pressing Telemachus to recount his adventures when Mentor returned with Idomeneus and all the Cretan youth who followed him.

At the sight of Idomeneus, the allies felt their wrath reigniting, but the words of Mentor put out that fire ready to explode.

"What delays us in concluding this holy alliance, to which the gods will be the witnesses and the defenders? May they avenge it, if ever some impious one dares to violate it, and may all the horrible evils of war, far from crushing faithful and innocent peoples, come down on the perjurious and execrable head of the ambitious one who would trample underfoot the sacred rights of this alliance. May he be detested by the gods and men. May he never enjoy the fruit of his perfidy. May the infernal Furies, beneath the most hideous figures, come to incite his rage and his despair. May he fall dead with no hope of sepulcher. May his body be the prey of dogs and vultures, and may he be, in the Underworld, in the deepest abyss of Tartarus, forever tormented more rigorously than Tantalus, Ixion, and the Danaids. May rather, this peace be unshakable like the rocks of Atlas that hold up the sky. May all the peoples revere it and enjoy its fruits from generation to generation. May the names of those who have sworn to it be in the mouths of our last descendants with love and veneration. May this peace, based on justice and on good faith, be the model of all peace that will be made in the future by all the nations of the world. And, may all the peoples, who want to render themselves happy in reuniting together, think to imitate the people of Hesperia!"

At these words, Idomeneus and the other kings swear to peace on the conditions marked. They give twelve hostages from each side. Telemachus wants to be in the number of hostages given by Idomeneus, but they cannot consent to Mentor being one because the allies wish for him to remain alongside Idomeneus in order to answer for his conduct and that of his counselors, just until the complete execution of the things promised.

They sacrificed, between the city and the enemy army, a hundred heifers, white as snow, and as many bulls of the same color, whose horns were gilded and adorned with garlands. The dreadful bellowing of the victims that fell under the sacred knife was heard reverberating to the neighboring mountains. Steaming blood streamed from all sides. An exquisite wine flowed with abundance for libations. The haruspices consulted the entrails, which still palpitated. The sacrificing priests burned on the altars an incense that formed a thick cloud, the good scent of which perfumed all the countryside. Meanwhile, the soldiers of the two sides, ceasing to look at each other with an enemy eye, began to talk about their adventures. They were already unwinding from their travails, and tasting, in advance, the sweetness of peace.

Several of those who had followed Idomeneus at the siege of Troy recognized those of Nestor, who had fought in the same war. They embraced each other with affection, and mutually recounted all that had befallen them since they had ruined that superb city, which was the ornament of all Asia. They were already bedded down on the grass, crowning themselves with flowers and drinking together the wine that was brought from the city in large vessels to celebrate so happy a day.

Suddenly, Mentor said to the kings and to the captains assembled, "Henceforth, under various names and under various chiefs, you will no longer make but one single people—this is how the just gods, admirers of the men that they have formed, want the eternal bond of their perfect concord to be. All humankind is only one family dispersed over the face of all the earth. All peoples are brothers and must love each other as such. Woe betide those impious ones who seek a cruel glory in the blood of their brothers, which is their own blood. War is sometimes necessary, it is true; but it is the shame of humankind that it is inevitable on certain occasions. O kings, do not say that one must wish for war in order to attain glory—true glory is not found outside of humaneness. Whoever prefers his own glory to sentiments of humanity is an arrogant monster, and not a man. He will only ever attain a false glory, for the true is only found in moderation and goodness. Men may flatter him in order to satisfy his mad vanity; but they will always say of him in secret, when they want to speak sincerely, 'He merited glory all the less because he desired it with an unjust passion.' Men should not esteem him, since he has esteemed men so little, and he has spilled their blood prodigiously for a brutal vanity. Happy the king who loves his people; who is loved by them; who trusts his neighbors, and who has their trust; who, far from waging war with them, stops them from having it among themselves; and who makes all the foreign nations envy the happiness that his subjects have in having him as king.

"Think, then, of reassembling together from time to time, O you who govern the mighty cities of Hesperia. Every three years have a general assembly, where all the kings who are present here meet to renew the alliance through a new oath, to reaffirm the promised friendship, and to deliberate about all the common interests. As long as you are united, you will have inside this beautiful country peace, glory, and abundance; outside, you will always be invincible. There is only Discord, coming out of the Underworld to torment men, that can trouble the felicity that the gods prepare for you."

Nestor responded to him, "You see, by the ease with which we made peace, how distant we are from wanting to wage war through vainglory or through an unjust avidity to grow bigger to the detriment of our neighbors. But what can one do when he finds himself alongside a violent prince who knows no other law than his own interest and who wastes no occasion to invade the lands of other states? Do not think that I am speaking of Idomeneus. No, I no longer have this thought of him. It is Adrastus, king of the Daunians, of whom we have everything to fear. He scorns the gods and believes that all men who are on the earth were only born to serve his glory through their servitude. He does not want subjects to whom he would be king and father. He wants slaves and worshipers; he has divine honors rendered to him. Up until now, blind Fortune has favored his most unjust enterprises. We were hastening to attack Salentum to rid ourselves of the weaker of our enemies, who was only beginning to establish itself on this coast so as to then turn our arms against that other, more powerful enemy. He has already taken several cities of our allies. Those of Croton have lost two battles against him. He uses all sorts of means to satisfy his ambition. Military might and artifice, all are the same to him, provided he crushes his enemies. He has amassed great treasures. His troops are disciplined and warlike. His captains are experienced. He is well served. He unceasingly keeps vigil himself over all those who act by his orders; he severely punishes the least errors and liberally rewards the services rendered to him. His valor sustains and animates that of all his troops. He would be an accomplished king if justice and good faith ruled his conduct. But he fears neither the gods nor the reproach of his conscience. He even counts his reputation for nothing. He regards it as a vain phantom that only arrests weak minds. He only counts, as a solid and real good, the advantage of possessing great riches, of being feared, and of trampling underfoot all humankind. Soon, his army will appear on our lands, and if the union of so many peoples does not put us in a state to resist him, all hope of liberty will be taken away from us. It is in the interest of Idomeneus, as well as our own, to oppose this neighbor who cannot suffer any liberty in his neighborhood. If we are vanquished, Salentum would be threatened with the same misfortune. Let us hasten then, all together, to prevent it."

While Nestor was speaking so, they were advancing toward the city, for Idomeneus had urged all the kings and all the principal chiefs to enter in order to pass the night there."

END OF BOOK IX

THE ADVENTURES OF
TELEMACHUS
SON OF ODYSSEUS

BOOK X

Meanwhile, *all the armies* of the allies pitched their tents, and the countryside was already covered with rich pavilions of all sorts of colors, where the tired Hesperians awaited sleep. When the kings along with their entourages had entered into the city, they looked astonished that, in so little time, one could have built so many magnificent buildings and that the hindrance of so great a war had not impeded this nascent city from growing and embellishing itself so suddenly.

They marveled at the wisdom and vigilance of Idomeneus, who had founded so beautiful a kingdom, and each concluded that, peace being made with him, the allies would be more mighty if he entered into their league against the Daunians. They proposed to Idomeneus that he enter in with them. He could not reject so just a proposition and promised troops. But, as Mentor was not ignorant of all that is needed to render a state flourishing, he realized that Idomeneus' military forces could not be as great as they appeared. He took him in private and spoke to him thus:

"You see that our attentions have not been useless to you. Salentum is saved from the misfortunes that threatened it. It is up to you to raise the glory of it to the sky and to equal the wisdom of Minos, your grandfather, in the governance of your peoples. I continue to speak freely to you, assuming that you desire it and that you detest all flattery. While those kings lauded your magnificence, I was thinking to myself of the temerity of your conduct."

At the word "temerity," Idomeneus' expression changed; his eyes clouded, he reddened, and he hardly needed to interrupt Mentor to show his resentment. Mentor said to him in a modest and respectful tone, yet free and bold,

"This word 'temerity' shocks you, I see well. Anyone other than me would have been wrong to use it, for kings must be respected and their delicateness handled, even in correcting them of it. Truth alone wounds them enough, without adding strong terms to it. But, I thought that you would be able to tolerate my speaking to you without softening so as to reveal your error to you. My design was to accustom you to hearing things called by their names and to realize that when others give you counsel about your conduct, they will never dare to tell you all they are thinking. You must, if you do not want to be deceived by them, understand still more that they will not tell you of things that will be disadvantageous to you. As for me, I am quite willing to soften my words, according to your need, but it is useful to you that a man without self-interest, and inconsequential, use straight talk with you in private. No one else will ever dare to speak like this to you. You will see the truth only halfway, and in beautiful wrapping."

At these words Idomeneus, already recovered from his former quick temper, appeared ashamed of his delicateness.

"You see," he said to Mentor, "what the habit of being flattered does. I owe you for the salvation of my new kingdom. There is no truth that I would not believe myself fortunate to hear from your mouth, but have mercy on a king whom flattery has poisoned and who could not, even in his misfortunes, find men generous enough to tell him the truth. No, I have never found anyone who loved me enough to want to displease me in telling me the whole truth."

Saying these words, tears came to his eyes and he embraced Mentor tenderly. Then, this wise old man said, "It is with pain that I find myself compelled to say harsh things to you, but can I betray you in hiding the truth from you? Put yourself in my place. If you have been deceived up until now, it is that you were willing to be; it is that you feared counselors too sincere. Have you sought out the most selfless people, and the most suitable to contradict you? Have you taken care to draw out the people least eager to please you, the most selfless in their conduct, the most capable of condemning your passions and your unjust sentiments? When you have found flatterers, have you scattered them? You, were you distrustful of them? No, indeed, you have not done what those who love the truth, and who merit knowing it do. Let us see if you will now have the courage to allow yourself to be humbled by the truth that condemns you.

"I was saying, then, that what attracts so much praise to you only merits being reprimanded. While you had so many enemies on the outside who were threatening your kingdom, still poorly established, you only thought to build magnificent works on the inside of your new city. It is this that has cost you so many bad nights, as you have confessed to me yourself. You drained your riches. You did not think of either increasing your population or of cultivating the fertile lands of this coast. Was it not necessary to regard these two things as the two essential foundations of your power, *to have lots of good men, and well cultivated lands to feed them?* An extended peace was necessary in the beginning to favor the proliferation of your people. You should have only thought of agriculture and the establishment of the wisest laws. A vain ambition has pushed you to the brink of the precipice. By dint of wanting to appear grand, you thought to ruin your real grandeur.

"Hasten to mend these errors. Suspend all your grand works. Renounce this splendor that will ruin your new city. Allow your peoples to breathe in peace. Apply yourself to putting them in abundance, in order to facilitate marriages. Know that you are only king to the extent that you have peoples to govern, and that your power should be measured not by the stretch of lands that you occupy, but by the number of men who inhabit those lands and who will be bound to obey you. Possess a good land, though average in stretch, covered with countless peoples, hard-working and disciplined. Make it so that these peoples love you. You are more mighty, more happy, more filled with glory than all the conquerors who ravage so many kingdoms."

"What will I do then with regard to these kings?" responded Idomeneus. "Shall I confess my weakness to them? It is true that I neglected agriculture, and even commerce, which is so easy for me on this coast. I only thought of building a magnificent city. Must I then, my dear Mentor, dishonor myself in the assembly of so many kings and reveal my imprudence? If I must, I desire it. I will do it without hesitating, whatever it costs me; for you have taught me that a true king, who is made for his peoples, and who owes himself entirely to them, must prefer the salvation of his kingdom to his own reputation."

"This sentiment is worthy of the father of the peoples," resumed Mentor. "It is to this goodness and not to the vain magnificence of your city that I recognized in you the heart of a true king. But, your honor must be handled carefully for the very interest of your kingdom. Leave it to me. I will make these kings understand that you are committed to reestablishing Odysseus, if he is still alive, or at least his son, to royal power in Ithaca, and that you want to chase out, through military force, all Penelope's suitors. They will have no difficulty understanding that this war demands numerous troops. So then, they will consent to your only giving them, at first, a weak help against the Daunians."

At these words, Idomeneus looked like a man relieved of a crushing burden. "You know, dear friend, of my honor and the reputation of this emerging city, whose depletion you will conceal from all my neighbors. But how does it look to say that I want to send troops to Ithaca to reestablish Odysseus, or at least Telemachus, his son, while Telemachus himself is enlisted to go to war against the Daunians?"

"Do not be troubled," replied Mentor. "I will say nothing but the truth. The vessels that you send to establish your commerce will go along the coast of Epirus. They will do two things at once: one, call back to your coast the foreign merchants, that the overly-high taxes distanced from Salentum; the other, seek news of Odysseus. If he is still alive, he must not be far from these seas that divide Greece from Italy, and it is assured that he was seen with the Phaeacians. Even though there may no longer be any hope of seeing him again, your vessels will render a significant service to his son; they will spread in Ithaca and throughout the neighboring countries the terror of the name of the young Telemachus, who is believed dead like his father; Penelope's suitors will be stunned to learn that he is ready to return with the succor of a mighty ally; the Ithacans will not dare to shake off the yoke; Penelope will be consoled and will continue refusing to choose a new spouse. In this way, you will serve Telemachus while he will be in your place with the allies of this coast of Italy against the Daunians."

At these words, Idomeneus cried out, "Lucky the king who is supported by wise counsel! A wise and faithful friend is worth more to a king than victorious armies. But doubly lucky the king who senses his good fortune and who knows how to profit from it through making good use of wise counsel! For often it happens that one distances from his confidence the wise and virtuous men whose virtue they fear, in order to lend an ear to flatterers whose treason they do not fear. I have myself fallen into this error, and I will recount to you all the woes that have come to me through a false friend who flattered my passions in the hope that I would in turn flatter his."

Mentor easily made the allied kings understand that Idomeneus must take charge of Telemachus' affairs while Telemachus would go with them. They were satisfied with having in their army the young son of Odysseus along with one hundred young Cretans that Idomeneus gave to accompany him. They were the flower of the young nobility that this king had brought over from Crete.

Mentor had counseled him to send them into this war. "You must attend, during peacetime, to multiply the people. But, for fear of the entire nation softening and falling into an ignorance of warfare, you must send the young nobility into foreign wars. That suffices to maintain the entire nation in an emulation of glory, in the love of arms, in the scorn for struggles and for death itself, lastly, in the experience with military art."

The allied kings departed Salentum content with Idomeneus and enchanted by the wisdom of Mentor. They were filled with joy that they were bringing Telemachus with them. This one could not moderate his pain when it was necessary to separate from his friend. While the allied kings were making their farewells and swearing to Idomeneus that they would keep an eternal alliance with him, Mentor held Telemachus tightly in his arms and felt himself soaked with his tears.

"I am numb," Telemachus said, "with joy to be going to acquire glory, and I am only touched with the pain of our separation. I seem to see that woeful time again when the Egyptians snatched me from your arms and distanced me from you, without leaving me any hope of seeing you again."

Mentor responded to these words with gentleness to console him. "This is a very different separation—it is willing; it will be short. You are going to seek victory. You must, my son, love me with a love that is less tender and more courageous. Accustom yourself to my absence; you will not always have me. It must be wisdom and virtue rather than the presence of Mentor that inspires in you what you must do."

In saying these words, the goddess, hidden beneath the figure of Mentor, covered Telemachus with her aegis. She filled him with the spirit of wisdom and foresight, intrepid valor, and gentle restraint, which are so rarely found together.

"Go," said Mentor, "into the midst of the greatest perils, every time that it is useful for you to go. A prince dishonors himself even more in avoiding the dangers in combat than in never going to war. The courage of the one who commands others must not be in doubt. If it is essential for a people to preserve its chief or its king, it is even more essential for them to not find him with a dubious reputation about valor. Remember that the one who commands must be the model to all others. His example must animate the entire army. So fear no danger, O Telemachus, and perish in combat rather than have your courage doubted. Flatterers—who will be the most eager to prevent you from exposing yourself to peril on necessary occasions—will be the first to say, in secret, that you lack heart, should they find you easy to stop on those occasions.

"But also, do not go seeking perils uselessly. Valor can only be a virtue to the extent it is ruled by prudence. Otherwise, it is a senseless scorn for life and a brutal ardor. Fiery valor has nothing sure about it. The one who does not have possession of himself in danger is more hot-headed than brave. He needs to be beside himself in order to rise above fear because he cannot surmount it through the natural disposition of his heart. In that state, if he does not flee, at the very least he is distressed. He loses the freedom of his mind, which he needs to give good orders, to profit from opportunities, to overthrow the enemy, and to serve his homeland. If he has all the ardor of a soldier, he does not have the discernment of a captain. He does not even have the true courage of a simple soldier, for the soldier must preserve in combat the presence of mind and the restraint needed to obey. The one who brashly takes risks disrupts the order and discipline of the troops, sets an example of temerity, and often risks the entire army to great misfortunes; those who prefer their vain ambition to the safety of the common cause merit punishments and not rewards. Be very careful then, my dear son, of seeking glory with impatience. The true means of finding it is to tranquilly wait for the favorable opportunity. Virtue makes itself revered all the more to the extent that it reveals itself to be more natural, more modest, more hostile to all flamboyance. It is as the need to expose yourself to peril increases that you must have fresh reserves of foresight and courage, which are ever-increasing.

"Furthermore, remember that you must not attract the envy of anyone. For your part, do not be jealous of the success of others. Praise them for all that merits some praise, but praise with discernment, saying the good with pleasure, hiding the bad and only thinking on it with sorrow.

"Do not make a decision in front of all those old captains who have all the experience that you cannot have. Listen to them with deference. Consult them, beg the most able to instruct you, and do not be ashamed to attribute to their instruction all the good that you will do.

"Lastly, never listen to the discourses by which someone will want to incite your distrust or your jealousy of other chiefs. Speak to them with confidence and genuineness. If you think they have missed something in your regard, open up your heart to them; explain to them all your reasons. If they are capable of sensing the nobility of this conduct, you will enchant them and draw from them all that you will have had cause to expect from them. If, on the contrary, they are not reasonable enough to take an interest in your sentiments, you will learn for yourself what unreasonableness there is to be tolerated in them, you will take measures so as not to commit yourself any longer than the war's end, and you will have nothing to reproach yourself for. But above all, never tell certain flatterers, who sow division, about the difficult issues that you believe to have against the army chiefs with whom you will be."

"I will stay here," continued Mentor, "to assist Idomeneus in his need to strive for the happiness of his peoples and to complete having him mend the errors that his poor counsel and flatterers caused him to commit in the establishment of his new kingdom."

Then, Telemachus could not keep from expressing to Mentor some surprise and even some scorn for Idomeneus' conduct. But Mentor corrected him in a severe tone,

"Are you surprised," he said to him, "that the most estimable men are still men and still show some remnants of the foibles of humanity amidst the innumerable traps and impediments inseparable from the kingship? Idomeneus, it is true, has been nourished on ideas of splendor and haughtiness, but what philosopher would have been able to protect himself from flattery had he been in his place? It is true that he allowed himself to be thwarted by those who have had his confidence. But the wisest kings are often deceived, whatever precautions they take not to be. A king cannot do without ministers who unburden him and in whom he trusts, since he cannot do everything. Besides, a king knows much less than the private individuals do of the men who surround him. They are always masked alongside him. They exhaust all sorts of artifices to deceive him. Alas, dear Telemachus, you will experience it only too much. One does not find in men either the virtues or the talents that one seeks in them. No matter how hard we study them and dig deep, we are disappointed every day. There never comes an end to making the best men do what you need them to do for the public good. They have their hardheadedness, their incompatibilities, their jealousies. One hardly persuades them nor corrects them.

"The more peoples one has to govern, the more ministers are needed to do through them what one cannot do himself; and the more one needs men to whom authority is entrusted, the more one is exposed to being mistaken in such choices. The one who is a merciless critic of kings today would govern tomorrow much worse than them and would make the same errors, along with infinitely greater ones if one entrusted the same power in him. The private station, should a man combine it with a little wit to speak well, covers over all natural faults, highlights dazzling talents, and makes a man appear worthy of every position from which he is far removed. But it is authority that puts all talents to a severe test and reveals great faults.

"Grandeur is like certain glasses that enlarge every object. All faults appear to grow in those high places where the least things have great consequences and where the slightest errors have violent repercussions. The entire world is busy observing a single man at all hours and judging him with extreme rigor. Those who judge him have no experience in the position he holds; they do not appreciate the difficulties of it, and they no longer desire him to be a man as much as they demand perfection of him.

"A king, however good and wise he may be, is still a man. His mind has limits, and his virtue has them too. He has moods, passions, habits, of which he is not entirely the master. He is obsessed over by self-interested and artful people. He does not find the help he seeks. He falls each day into some miscalculation, at times through his passions, and at times through those of his ministers. No sooner has he mended an error than he falls into another. Such is the condition of the most enlightened and the most virtuous kings. The longest and best reigns are too short and too imperfect to mend in the end what one has spoiled, without wanting to, in the beginning. Kingship carries with it all these miseries. Human impotence succumbs under so crushing a burden. One must pity kings and excuse them. Are they not to be pitied for having to govern so many men, whose needs are infinite and who give so much difficulty to those who want to govern them well? Frankly speaking, men are greatly to be pitied in having to be governed by a king who is only a man like them, for it would require gods to redress men. But kings are to be pitied no less, being only men—that is to say, weak and imperfect—in having to govern this countless multitude of corrupt and deceiving men."

Telemachus retorted, "Idomeneus lost through his error the kingdom of his ancestors in Crete, and, without your counsel, he would have lost a second one in Salentum."

"I confess," resumed Mentor, "that he made great errors. But seek in Greece and all the better governed countries a king who has not made inexcusable errors. The greatest men have, in their temperament and the character of their mind, faults that lead them astray, and the most laudable are those who have the courage to know and to mend their waywardness. Do you think that Odysseus, the great Odysseus, your father, who is the model for the kings of Greece, would not have his weaknesses and his faults too? If Athena had not led him step by step, how many times would he have succumbed in the perils and the predicaments where Fortune toyed with him! How many times did Athena have to restrain or redress him in order to always lead him to glory by the path of virtue! Do not even expect, when you see him reigning with so much glory in Ithaca, to find him without imperfections. You will see them in him, undoubtedly. Greece, Asia, and all the islands of the sea admired him despite those faults; a thousand marvelous qualities make them forget. You will be only too happy to be able to admire him too and to study him unceasingly as your model.

"Accustom yourself then, O Telemachus, to only expect of the greatest men that which humanity is capable of doing. Youth, inexperienced, delivers itself over to a presumptuous criticism, which disgusts it with all the models it needs to follow and throws it into an incurable indocility. Not only must you love, respect, imitate your father, though he may not be perfect, but also you must have a high esteem for Idomeneus despite all that I have corrected in him. He is naturally sincere, upright, fair, open-handed, beneficent. He is the model of valor. He detests fraud when he knows of it, and he freely follows the true leanings of his heart. All his apparent talents are great and proportionate to his rank. His simplicity in confessing his wrong, his sweetness, his patience in allowing me to say the harshest things, his courage to publicly mend his errors and, in so doing, put himself above all the criticism of men show a truly great soul. Good fortune or the counsel of others can preserve a very mediocre man from certain errors, but there is only an extraordinary virtue that can push a king, so long seduced by flattery, to mend his wrong. It is even more glorious to pick oneself up again in this way than to have never fallen. Idomeneus has made the errors that almost all kings make. But almost no king does, in order to correct himself, what he just did. As for me, I could not weary of admiring him in the very moments when he permitted me to contradict him. Admire him too, my dear Telemachus: it is less for his reputation than for your own usefulness that I give you this counsel."

Mentor made Telemachus sense, through this discourse, how dangerous it is to be unjust in letting oneself indulge in a rigorous critique against other men, and particularly against those who are charged with the predicaments and difficulties of governing. Then he said to him, "It is time that you depart. Farewell. I will wait for you. O my dear Telemachus, remember that those who fear the gods have nothing to fear from men. You will find yourself in the most extreme perils. But know that Athena will not abandon you."

At these words, Telemachus thought he felt the presence of the goddess, and he would have even recognized that it was her speaking in order to fill him with confidence, had the goddess not recalled the notion of Mentor to him by saying, "Do not forget, my son, all the cares that I took during your childhood to render you wise and courageous like your father. Do nothing that would not be worthy of his great examples and of the maxims of virtue that I have tried to inspire in you."

The sun was already rising and gilding the summits of the mountain when the kings went out of Salentum to rejoin their troops. These troops, camped around the city, began to march under their commanders. One saw on all sides the glinting iron of raised pikes. The brilliance of the shields dazzled the eyes. A cloud of dust rose up to the clouds. Idomeneus, along with Mentor, led the allied kings into the countryside and drew away from the walls of the city. Finally they separated after having given, on both sides, marks of a true friendship, and the allies no longer doubted that peace would last when they knew the goodness in Idomeneus' heart, which had been represented to them so very differently than what it was; it is that they had judged him, not by his own natural sentiments, but by the flattering and unjust counsel to which he had delivered himself.

~

After the army had departed, Idomeneus led Mentor throughout the quarters of the city.

"Let us see," said Mentor, "how many men you have, not only in the city but even in the neighboring countryside. Let us make a count of them. Let us also examine how many plowmen you have among those men. Let us see how much your lands bear, in average years, of wheat, wine, oil, and other useful things. We will know by this path if the land supplies something to feed all its inhabitants, and if it even produces something to make a useful commerce of its surplus with foreign countries. Let us also examine how many vessels you have, and sailors. That is how your might must be judged."

He went to visit the port and boarded each vessel. He informed himself of the countries where each vessel was going for commerce; what merchandise it carried there, that which it took in return; what the expenses of the vessel were during the voyage; the loans that the merchants made to each other; the companies they formed among each other, so as to know if they were equitable and faithfully observed; and lastly, the risks of shipwreck and other misfortunes of commerce, to prevent the ruin of the merchants, who, through avidity for gain, often undertook things that were beyond their forces.

He wanted all bankruptcies punished severely, because those who are exempt of bad faith are almost never exempt of temerity. At the same time, he made rules to arrange things in such a way that it would be easy to never go bankrupt. He established magistrates to whom the merchants rendered an account of their assets, profits, expenses, and enterprises. It was never permitted for them to risk the goods of others, and they could only risk half of their own. Moreover, they formed companies for the enterprises that they could not do alone, and the policies of those companies were inviolable through the rigor of the penalties imposed on those who did not follow them. Outside of that, freedom of commerce was complete. Far from interfering with it through taxes, they promised a reward to all merchants who could attract to Salentum the commerce from some new nation.

So, the peoples soon came rushing there in droves from all parts. The commerce of this city was like the ebb and flow of the sea. Treasures swept in like the tides coming one on top of another. All was brought in and all went out freely. All that came in was useful. All that went out left, in going out, other riches in its place. Severe justice presided in the port amidst so many nations. Franchise, good faith, candor seemed, from the top of those superb towers, to call merchants from the most distant lands. Each of those merchants, whether he came from the eastern shores where the sun emerges each day from the bosom of the ocean waters, whether he came from the part of that great sea where the sun, wearied from her course, goes to extinguish her fires, lived as peacefully in security in Salentum as in their homeland.

As for the interior of the city, Mentor visited every warehouse, every artisanal boutique, and every public square. He prohibited all merchandise from foreign countries that could introduce luxury and softness. He regulated the dress, the nourishment, the furnishings, the grandeur and ornamentation of the homes for all the different stations. He banned all ornamentations of gold and silver, and he said to Idomeneus, "I only know of a single means of rendering your people modest in their spending—it is for you yourself to give the example. It is necessary that you have a certain majesty in your appearance. But your authority will be noticed enough by your guards and by the principal officers who surround you. Be content with a habit of very fine wool, tinted purple. May the principals of the state, after you, be dressed in the same wool, and may the only difference consist in the color and in a light gold embroidery that you will have on the hem of your habit. The different colors will serve to distinguish the different stations without needing gold, silver, or precious stones. Sort out the stations by birth. In the first rank, put those who are of a nobility more ancient and more brilliant. Those who have the merit and authority over employees will be content enough to come after those ancient and illustrious families who have been in possession of first honors for so long. Men who do not have the same nobility will cede to them without difficulty, provided you do not accustom them to forgetting their origins through an overly rapid and large fortune and you praise the moderation of those who are modest in prosperity. The distinction the least exposed to envy is that which comes from a long line of ancestors. As for virtue, it will be excited enough and there will be enough eagerness to serve the state provided you give crowns and statues for beautiful deeds, and it would be a beginning of nobility for the children of those who will have done them.

"The persons of the first rank after you will be dressed in white with a gold fringe at the bottom of their habit. They will have a gold ring on their finger and a gold medal with your portrait on their neck. Those of the second rank will be dressed in blue, they will wear a silver fringe, along with the ring, and no medal; the third, in green, without the ring and without the fringe, but with the medal; the fourth, in a sunrise yellow; the fifth, in a pale red or rose; the sixth, in linen gray; and the seventh, who will be the last of the people, in a mix of yellow and white. Voila, there you have the habits for the seven different stations of free men. All the slaves will be dressed in gray-brown. In this way, without any expense, each will be distinguished according to his station, and all the arts that only serve to maintain flamboyance will be banished from Salentum. All the artisans who would be employed in these pernicious arts will serve either in necessary arts, which are few in number, or in commerce or agriculture. No changes will ever be tolerated, either in regard to the nature of the fabrics or in the form of the habits; for it is unworthy that men, destined for a serious and noble life, amuse themselves in inventing pretentious jewelry, or that they permit their wives, to whom those amusements would be less shameful, to ever fall into this excessiveness."

Mentor, like an able gardener who prunes his fruit trees of useless branches, tried thereby to prune the useless flamboyance that corrupted mores. He brought all things back to a noble and frugal simplicity. He regulated in the same way the nourishment of the citizens and slaves.

"What a shame," he said, "that the most elevated men have their grandeur consist in rich sauces by which they soften their souls and imperceptibly ruin the health of their bodies! They should have their happiness consist in their moderation, in their authority to do good to other men, and in the reputation that their good deeds should procure for them. Sobriety renders the simplest foods very agreeable. It is sobriety that yields, along with the most vigorous health, the purist and most constant pleasures. You must, then, limit your meals to the best meats, but prepared with no rich sauces. It is an art for poisoning men, that of stirring their appetite beyond their true need."

Idomeneus understood well that he had been wrong to allow the inhabitants of his new city to soften and corrupt their mores in violating all the laws of Minos on sobriety. But wise Mentor pointed out to him that the laws themselves, though renewed, would be useless if the example of the king did not give them an authority that could not come from anywhere else. Straightaway Idomeneus put his table in order, where he only admitted excellent bread, wine of the country that is strong and agreeable but in extremely small quantity, along with plain meats such as he had eaten along with the other Greeks at the siege of Troy. No one dared to complain of a rule that the king imposed on himself, and each corrected himself in this way from the profusion and the delicateness where they were beginning to plunge with regard to meals.

Mentor then cut back on the soft and effeminate music, which corrupted all the youth. He condemned with no less severity the manic music, which intoxicated hardly any less than wine and which produced mores filled with frenzy and impudence. He limited all music to the feasts at the temples so as to sing there the praises of the gods and heroes who had exemplified the rarest virtues.

Also, he only allowed the temples to have grand architectural adornments, such as columns, pediments, porticos. He gave models of a simple and gracious architecture in order to build, in an average space, a cheerful and comfortable home for a large family, such that it was turned out in a healthy aspect, the lodgings were spread out one from another, orderliness and cleanliness would be easily preserved there, and the maintenance would cost little. He wanted each house of any consequence to have a salon and small peristyle, along with small bedrooms for every free person. Yet, he adamantly prohibited the superfluous multitude and magnificence of lodgings. These various models of houses, according to the grandeur of the families, served to embellish a part of the city at little cost and to render it harmonious; whereas another part, already completed according to the caprice and the flamboyance of private individuals, had, despite its magnificence, a disposition less agreeable and less comfortable. This new city was built in very little time because the neighboring coast of Greece supplied good architects, and they had a very large number of masons from

Epirus and several other countries come, on condition that after having completed their work, they would establish themselves around Salentum, they would take lands from there to clear, and they would serve to populate the countryside.

Painting and sculpture seemed to Mentor arts that he was not allowed to abandon. But he wanted tolerated in Salentum only a few men attached to these arts. He established a school where teachers of an exquisite taste presided, who examined the young students.

"There must not be," he said, "anything of baseness and weakness in these arts which is not absolutely necessary. Consequently, only young people of a genius with much promise and who tend toward perfection should be accepted. Others are born for less noble arts, and they will be more usefully employed in the ordinary needs of the republic. Sculptors and painters must only be employed," he said, "in order to preserve the memory of great men and great deeds. It is in the public buildings or in the tombs that one should preserve the representations of all that which has been done with an extraordinary virtue in serving the homeland."

Nevertheless, the moderation and frugality of Mentor did not prevent him authorizing all the great structures destined for horse and chariot races, for wrestling matches, for those of boxing, and for all the other exercises that cultivate bodies in order to render them more upright and vigorous.

He cut back a prodigious number of merchants who sold fabrics manufactured in distant lands; embroideries of an excessive price; gold and silver vases with figures of gods, men, and animals;

lastly, liquors and perfumes. He even desired the furnishings of each house to be simple and made in a manner to last a long time in such a way that the Salentines, who complained loudly of their poverty, would begin to sense how much superfluous wealth they had. But it was deceptive wealth that impoverished them, and they actually became wealthy as they had the courage to divest themselves of it. *It is enriching oneself,* they said to themselves, *to scorn such riches that drain the state, and to diminish one's needs by reducing them to the true necessities of nature.*

Mentor hastened to visit the arsenals and all the warehouses to learn whether the armaments and all the other things necessary for war were in good condition.

"For you must always be ready to wage war," he said, "in order to never be reduced to the misfortune of waging it."

He found that several things were lacking everywhere. Straightaway, workers were assembled to work in iron, steel, and brass. One saw rising blazing furnaces, swirls of smoke and flames like those subterranean fires that Mount Etna vomits. The hammer resounded on the anvil that groaned under the redoubled blows. The neighboring mountains and shores of the sea reverberated with them. One would have believed to be on that island where Hephaestus, animating the Cyclops, forges thunderbolts for the father of the gods, and, through a wise foresight, one saw during a profound peacetime all the preparations for war.

Then Mentor went out of the city with Idomeneus and found a large stretch of fertile land that remained uncultivated. Others were only half-cultivated through the negligence and poverty of the plowmen, who, lacking men, also lacked the courage and manpower to bring agriculture to its perfection.

Mentor, seeing that desolated countryside, said to the king, "The land here is only asking to enrich its inhabitants. But the inhabitants are missing from the land. Let us take then all those superfluous artisans who are in the city, and whose professions would only serve to disrupt the mores, to have them cultivate these plains and these hills. It is true that it is a misfortune that all those men trained in the arts that require a sedentary life may not be trained for physical work, but here is a means to remedy that. The vacant lands must be divided among them, and they must call to their aid neighboring peoples who will do under them the hardest, toughest work. Those people will do it, provided they are promised suitable rewards for the produce of the very lands they clear. They will be able, afterward, to possess a part of them and to thereby be incorporated into your people, who are not numerous enough. Provided they are hard-working and law-abiding, you will not have better subjects, and they will increase your might. Your artisans of the city, transplanted into the countryside, will raise their children to work and to have a taste for the country life. Moreover, all the masons from foreign countries working to build your city are committed to clearing a part of your lands, to becoming plowmen, and incorporated into your people as soon as they have completed their work in the city. These workers are delighted to commit to spending their life under a dominion that is now so sweet. As they are robust and hard-working, their example will serve to incite hard work in the artisans transplanted from the city to the countryside with whom they will mingle. Afterward, the entire country will be populated with vigorous families devoted to agriculture.

"Furthermore, do not be pained about the proliferation of this people. They will soon become countless, provided you facilitate marriages. The manner of facilitating marriages is very simple. Almost all men have the inclination to marry. There is only destitution that keeps them from it. If you do not burden them with taxes, they will live with their wives and children without difficulty, for the Earth is never ungrateful; she always nourishes with her fruits those who cultivate her attentively. She only refuses her bounty to those who fear giving her their efforts. The more children the plowmen have, the richer they are if the prince does not impoverish them; for their children, from their earliest youth, begin to help them. The youngest drive sheep to the pastures, the others, who are bigger, already handle large herds. The oldest plow with their father. Meanwhile, the mother of the family prepares a simple meal for her husband and their dear children, who must return tired from the work of the day. She attends to milking her cows and her ewes, and streams of milk are seen to flow. She builds a great fire around which the entire family, innocent and peaceful, takes pleasure in singing all evening while awaiting sweet sleep. She prepares cheeses, chestnuts, and fruits preserved in the same freshness as if they had just been picked. The shepherd returns with his flute and sings to the gathered family new songs he has learned in neighboring hamlets. The plowman returns with his plow, and his tired oxen walk, necks hanging low, with a slow and halting step despite the goad that prods them. All the woes of work end with the day. The poppies that Sleep, by order of the gods, spreads over the land, appeases all the dark worries with their spells, and hold all nature in a sweet enchantment; each sleeps without anticipating the difficulties of the morrow.

"Happy are those men without ambition, without distrust, without artifice, provided the gods give them a good king who does not trouble their innocent joy! But what horrible inhumanity to snatch from them, for designs filled with flamboyance and ambition, the sweet fruits of their land, which they only hold through generous nature and the sweat of their brow. Nature alone will draw from her fruitful womb all that which is necessary for an infinite number of modest and hard-working men. But it is the pridefulness and softness of certain men that put so many others in a frightful poverty."

"What will I do," said Idomeneus, "if those peoples I scatter about these fertile countrysides neglect to cultivate them?"

"Do," Mentor answered, "the complete opposite of what is commonly done. Princes, avid and without foresight, only think to charge taxes to those among their subjects who are the most vigilant and the most clever in profiting from their possessions; it is because they hope to be paid more easily by them. At the same time, they charge those that laziness renders more destitute less. Reverse this evil order that overburdens the good, that rewards vice, and that introduces a negligence as ill-fated to the king himself as to the entire state. Put taxes, fines, and even, if you must, other rigorous penalties on those who neglect their fields, just as you would punish soldiers who abandon their posts in war.

On the contrary, give favors and exemptions to families who, in proliferating, increase proportionately the cultivation of their lands. Soon, the families will proliferate, and everyone will be animated to work. It will even become honorable. The profession of the plowman will no longer be scorned and no longer be overburdened with so many woes. The plow will be honored again, handled by the victorious hand that would have defended the homeland. It will be no less excellent to cultivate the inheritance received from one's ancestors during a happy peacetime than to have generously defended it during the difficulties of war. All the countryside will flourish again. Demeter will be crowned with golden grains; Dionysus, stamping the grapes under his feet, will cause streams of wine sweeter than nectar to flow from the mountainside. Deep vales will reverberate with the concerts of shepherds, who, along the clear streams, will join their voices with their flutes, while their bounding flocks graze on the grass and among the flowers without fear of wolves.

"Will you not be only too happy, O Idomeneus, to be the source of so much good and to cause to live in the shade of your name so many peoples in such lovable repose? This glory, is it not more touching than that of ravaging the land, of spreading everywhere—almost as much at home as amidst the victories in vanquished foreign lands—carnage, distress, horror, languor, dismay, cruel hunger, and despair? O happy the king loved enough by the gods, and with a heart great enough, to undertake to be in this way the delight of the peoples, and to display to all the centuries so enchanting a spectacle during his reign! The entire land, far from protecting itself from his might through combat, will come to his feet to beg him to reign over it."

Idomeneus responded, "But when the peoples are in peace and abundance like this, the delights will corrupt them, and they will turn the strengths I have given them against me."

"Do not fear that inconvenience. It is a pretext that is always alleged to flatter spendthrift princes who want to overburden their people with taxes. The remedy is easy. The laws that we just established with regard to agriculture will render their life laborious and, in their abundance, they will have only what is needed because we are curtailing all the arts that supply the superfluous. This very abundance will be diminished by the facilitation of marriages and by the great proliferation of families. Each family, being numerous and having little land, will need to cultivate it through unrelenting work. It is softness and idleness that render the peoples insolent and rebellious. They will have bread and quite amply, to tell the truth. But they will only have bread and fruits from their own land earned by the sweat of their brow. To keep your people in this moderation, you must sort out, from the present, the stretch of land that each family will be able to possess. You know that we have divided all your people into seven classes according to different stations. Each family, in each class, must only be permitted to be able to possess the stretch of land absolutely necessary to feed the number of persons of which it is comprised. This rule being inviolate, the nobles will not be able to make acquisitions over the poor. Everyone will have lands. But each will have very little of it and will thus be incited to cultivate it well. If, in the long term, lands are lacking here, you will form colonies, which will augment this state.

"I even believe that you must take care to never allow wine-growing to become too widespread in your kingdom. If too many vines are planted, they must be pulled up. Wine is the source of the greatest woes among peoples. It causes maladies, quarrels, seditions, idleness, disgust for work, the disorder of families. May wine be, therefore, reserved as a kind of remedy, or as a very rare liqueur which is only used for sacrifices or for extraordinary feasts. But do not expect to have such an important rule observed if you do not make yourself the example of it.

"Furthermore, you must inviolably keep the laws of Minos for the education of children. Public schools must be established where they teach the reverential awe of the gods, love of homeland, respect of the laws, the preference for honor over pleasures and even over life itself. There must be magistrates who watch over the families and over the mores of private individuals. Watch over them yourself, you who are only king, that is to say, shepherd of the people, in order to watch over your flock night and day. By doing so, you will prevent an infinite number of disorders and crimes. Those which you are unable to prevent, severely punish at the outset. It is a clemency to make examples up front that staunch the course of iniquity. Through a little blood appropriately spilled, one spares much afterward and puts himself in a position of being respected, without using rigor often.

"But what a detestable maxim to believe to only find his safety in the oppression of his peoples! Not to instruct them, not to guide them to virtue, never making them love it, to push them through terror to the point of despair, to put them in the dreadful necessity of either never being able to breathe freely or shaking off the yoke of your tyrannical domination—is that the true means of reigning without trouble; is that the true path that leads to glory?

"Remember that the countries where the domination of the sovereign is most absolute are those where the sovereigns are less mighty. They take, they ruin everything, they alone possess the entire state, but also the entire state languishes: countrysides are covered with weeds and almost deserted, cities diminish each day, commerce dries up. The king, who cannot be king all alone and who is only great through his peoples, annihilates himself little by little through the heartless annihilation of his peoples from whom he draws his riches and his might. His state is drained of money and men—that latter loss is the greatest and the most irreparable. His absolute power makes as many slaves as he has subjects. They flatter him, they pretend to worship him, they tremble at the least of his regards. But wait for the slightest revolution. This monstrous might, pushed to an overly violent excessiveness, will not know how to last—it has no resource in the hearts of the peoples. It has wearied and irritated all the bodies of state; it compels all the limbs of that body to yearn for a change. At the first blow dealt him, the idol topples, shatters, and is trampled underfoot. Scorn, hate, fear, resentment, distrust—in a word, all the passions reunite against an authority so odious. The king, who, in his vain prosperity, did not find a single man bold enough to tell him the truth, will not find, in his misfortune, any man who deigns either to excuse him or to defend him against his enemies."

After these discourses, Idomeneus, persuaded by Mentor, hastened to distribute the vacant lands, filling them with all of the unnecessary artists and executing all that had been resolved. He only reserved for the masons the lands that he had intended for them and that they could only cultivate after the end of their work for the city. Already the reputation of the gentle and moderate government of Idomeneus attracts in droves from every direction peoples coming to incorporate themselves into his own, in pursuit of their happiness under so lovable a dominion. Already those countrysides, covered with brambles and thorns for so long, promise rich harvests and fruits unknown until then. The earth opens her womb to the blade of the plow and prepares her riches to reward the plowman. Hope shines again from all sides. In the vales and on the hillsides are seen flocks of sheep that bound over the grass, and great herds of oxen and heifers that make the tall mountains echo with their bellowing. These herds serve to fertilize the countryside. It is Mentor who found the means of having these herds. Mentor counseled Idomeneus to make a trade with the Peucetians, a neighboring peoples, of all the superfluous things that they no longer wanted to tolerate in Salentum for these herds that the Salentines were lacking.

At the same time, the city and surrounding villages were filled with a beautiful youth who had languished in misery for a long time, and who had not dared marry for fear of increasing their woes. When they saw how Idomeneus was embracing humanitarian sentiments and that he desired to be their father, they no longer feared famine and the other scourges with which heaven afflicts earth; only cries of joy and the songs of shepherds and plowmen who were celebrating their weddings were then heard. One would have believed to see the god Pan along with a throng of Satyrs and Fauni mingling among the Nymphs and dancing to the sound of the flute in the shade of the wood. All was tranquil and laughing. But the joy was restrained, and the pleasures only served to relax them from long travails. They were more alive and more pure-hearted from it.

The old men, astonished to see what they had not dared hope for after so long a lifetime, were crying through an exceeding joy mixed with tenderness; they raised their trembling hands toward the sky, and said: "Bless, O great Zeus, the king, who resembles you and who is the greatest gift that you have made to us. He was born for the good of mankind. Render unto him all the goods that we receive from him. Our descendants, coming from these marriages that he favors, will owe everything to him up to their birth, and he will truly be the father of all his subjects."

The young men and the young girls that they married could only burst out in joy, singing the praises of the one from whom this joy so sweet had come to them. Their mouths, and even more their hearts, were unceasingly filled with his name. They believed themselves to be happy to see him; they feared losing him. His loss would have been the desolation of each family.

Then Idomeneus avowed to Mentor that he had never felt pleasure as touching as that of being loved and of making so many people happy.

BOOK X

"I would never have believed it," he said. "It seemed to me that all the grandeur of princes only consisted in making themselves feared, that the rest of men were created for them, and all that which I had heard said of kings who had been the love and the delight of their peoples appeared a pure fable to me. I recognize the truth in it now. But, I must recount to you how my heart has been poisoned since my earliest childhood about the authority of kings. It is what has caused all the misfortunes of my life."

Then Idomeneus began this narration.

End of Book X

THE ADVENTURES OF
TELEMACHUS
SON OF ODYSSEUS

BOOK XI

"Protesilas, *who is a little older than me*, was the one of all the young men that I liked the most. His keen and bold nature suited my taste. He joined in my pleasures. He flattered my passions; he made me suspicious of another young man, whom I also liked and who was named Philocles. This one had reverence for the gods and a great yet restrained soul. He put his grandeur not in elevating himself, but in vanquishing himself and doing nothing base. He spoke to me freely about my faults, and even when he dared not speak to me, his silence and the sadness of his expression made me hear well enough what he wanted to reproach me for.

"In the beginning, this sincerity pleased me, and I often professed to him that I would listen to him with confidence all my life to preserve myself from flatterers. He told me all that I should do in order to walk in the footsteps of my grandfather, Minos, and to render my kingdom happy. He did not have as profound a wisdom as you, O Mentor. But his maxims were good; I recognize it now. Little by little, the artifices of Protesilas, who was jealous and full of ambition, made me disgusted with Philocles. This one, Philocles, was not eager to please, and he allowed the other to prevail. He contented himself in always telling me the truth, when I wanted to hear it. It was my welfare, and not his fortune, that he sought.

"Protesilas persuaded me, gradually, that Philocles' was a grievous and lofty mind who criticized all my deeds, who asked me for nothing because he had the pridefulness to want nothing from me and to aspire to the reputation of a man who is above all honors. He added that this young man, who spoke to me so liberally about my faults, was speaking of them to others with the same liberty, and he quite implied that he hardly esteemed me and that, in belittling my reputation so, he wanted, through the brilliance of an austere virtue, to open up the path to the kingship for himself.

"At first, I could not believe that Philocles would want to dethrone me. There is in real virtue a candor and genuineness that nothing can fake, and in which one cannot be mistaken, provided one is attentive to it. But the firmness of Philocles against my weaknesses was beginning to weary me. The complaisance of Protesilas and his inexhaustible cleverness in inventing new pleasures for me made me feel even more impatiently the austerity of the other. Meanwhile, Protesilas, unable to tolerate that I would not believe all that he was telling me against his enemy, took the position to no longer speak of him to me and to persuade me through something stronger than all words. Here is how he succeeded in deceiving me. He counseled me to send Philocles to command the vessels that should attack those of Carpathus, and, to convince me of it, he said to me, '"You know that I am not suspect in the praises that I give him. I confess that he has courage and genius for warfare. He will serve you better than another, and I prefer the interest of your service to all my resentments against him.'"

"I was delighted to find this uprightness and fairness in the heart of Protesilas, to whom I had entrusted the administration of my greatest affairs. I embraced him in a transport of joy, and I believed myself only too fortunate in having given all my trust to a man who appeared, in this way, above all passion and all self-interest. But, alas, how worthy princes are of compassion! This man knew me better than I knew myself. He knew that kings are usually distrustful and distracted—distrustful through the continual experience they have with the artifices of corrupt men, by whom they are surrounded; distracted because pleasures sweep them away and they are accustomed to having people charged with thinking for them, without them taking on the difficulty of it. He understood, therefore, that he would have no great difficulty making me distrustful and jealous of a man who would not fail to do great deeds. Above all, his absence made it very easy for Protesilas to set traps for him.

"Philocles, in departing, foresaw what could happen to him. 'Remember,' he said to me, 'that I will no longer be able to defend myself, that you will only listen to my enemy, and that in serving you at the peril of my life, I run the risk of having no other reward than your indignation.'

"'You are mistaken,' I said to him, 'Protesilas does not speak of you like you speak of him. He lauds you, he esteems you, he believes you worthy of the most important posts. If he began to speak against you to me, he would lose my confidence. Fear nothing, go, and only think of serving me well.'

"He departed and left me in a strange situation. I must confess to you, Mentor, that I saw clearly how necessary it was for me to have several men whom I might consult and that nothing was worse, either for my reputation or for the outcome of affairs, than to deliver myself over to only one. I had experienced that the wise counsel of Philocles had saved me from several dangerous errors where the haughtiness of Protesilas would have caused me to fall. I quite felt that there was in Philocles a foundation of probity and equitable maxims, which did not make themselves felt in the same way in Protesilas. But I had allowed Protesilas to take on a certain decisive tone, to which I could almost no longer fight back. I was tired of always finding myself between two men whom I was unable to reconcile, and in this weariness, I preferred through weakness to hazard something at the expense of affairs and to breathe freely. I would not have dared to admit to myself so shameful a reason for the decision I had made, but this shameful reason which I dared not unwrap did not fail to secretly act in the bottom of my heart and to be the true motive for everything I did.

"Philocles overtook the enemy, brought home a total victory, and hastened to come back in order to prevent the wicked machinations he had to fear. However, Protesilas, who had not yet had time to deceive me, wrote to him that I desired he raid the island of Carpathus to profit from the victory. Indeed, he had persuaded me that I could easily conquer this island. But, he made it such that several essential things were lacking to Philocles in this enterprise, and he subjected him to certain orders which caused various unexpected setbacks in the execution. Meanwhile, he made use of a very corrupt attendant whom I had alongside me and who was observing even the slightest things so as to render an account of them to Protesilas, even though they seemed to hardly see each other and to never agree on anything. This attendant, named Timocrates, came one day to tell me, in great secrecy, that he had uncovered a very dangerous affair.

"'Philocles,' he told me, 'wants to use your naval army to make himself king of the island of Carpathus. The chiefs of the troops are attached to him. All the soldiers are won over by his largesse and even more by the pernicious licentiousness in which he allows the troops to live. He is puffed up by his victory. Here is a letter that he wrote to one of his friends about his project to make himself king. One can no longer doubt it after so evident a proof.'

"I read this letter, and it appeared to me to be from the hand of Philocles. However, someone had perfectly imitated his handwriting, and it was Protesilas who had done it along with Timocrates. This letter cast me into a strange shock. I reread it incessantly and could not persuade myself that it was from Philocles as I passed over in my troubled mind all the touching marks that he had given me of his selflessness and his good faith. However, what could I do? How could I resist a letter, in which I believed to be certain of recognizing Philocles' handwriting?

"When Timocrates saw that I could no longer resist his artifice, he pushed it even further.

"'Dare I,' he said to me hesitatingly, 'point out to you a word in this letter? Philocles says to his friend that he is able to speak in confidence to Protesilas about a thing that he only designates with a cipher. Assuredly, Protesilas entered into Philocles' scheme, and they reconciled at your expense. You know that it is Protesilas who pressed you to send Philocles against the Carpathians. For some time, he has ceased speaking against him to you as he once did so often. On the contrary, he lauds him. He excuses him on every occasion. They have been seeing each other somewhat civilly for a while. Undoubtedly, Protesilas has taken steps, along with Philocles, to share the conquest of Carpathus with him. You see yourself that he wanted this enterprise to be done against all the rules, and that he risks having your naval army perish in order to satisfy his ambition. Do you think he would have wanted to make us of Philocles' ambition in this way if they were still adversarial? No, indeed, it can no longer be doubted that these two men are reunited so as to rise together to a great authority and, perhaps, to overthrow the throne on which you reign. In speaking to you so, I know that I am exposing myself to their resentment, if, despite my sincere advice, you still leave your authority in their hands. But what does it matter, provided that I tell you the truth?'

"Those last words of Timocrates made a great impression on me. I no longer doubted the treason of Philocles, and I distrusted Protesilas as his friend. Meanwhile, Timocrates was incessantly saying to me, 'If you wait until Philocles has conquered the island of Carpathus, there will no longer be time to stop his schemes. Hasten to imprison him while you still can.'

"I was horrified by the profound dissimulation of men. I no longer knew who to trust. After having uncovered Philocles' treason, I no longer saw any men on earth whose virtue could reassure me. I was resolved to destroy this perfidy at the earliest. But I feared Protesilas, and I did not know how to do it with regard to him. I feared finding him guilty, and I also feared trusting him. Finally, in my distress, I could not keep from telling him that Philocles had become suspect to me. He appeared surprised by it; he represented his upright and moderate conduct to me; he exaggerated his services—in a word, he did everything that he must to persuade me that he was on very good terms with Philocles.

"On the other hand, Timocrates did not waste a minute to point out this harmonious relationship and to oblige me to lose Philocles while I could still protect myself from him. See, my dear Mentor, how unfortunate and exposed kings are to being the plaything of other men, even while other men appear trembling at their feet. I thought to make a deep political strike and to disconcert Protesilas by secretly sending Timocrates to the naval army to kill Philocles. Protesilas pushed his dissimulation to the limit and deceived me all the more as he effortlessly appeared as the sort of man who lets himself be deceived. Timocrates departed, then, and found Philocles sufficiently hampered in his raid. He lacked everything, for Protesilas, not knowing if the supposed letter would be able to destroy his enemy, wanted to have at the same time another resource ready for the poor outcome of an enterprise about which he had given me so much hope and which would not fail to make me angry with Philocles. This one was sustaining that very difficult war through his courage, his genius, and the love that his troops had for him. Although everyone in the army recognized that this raid was brash and calamitous for the Cretans, each was striving to make it succeed as if they saw their life and their happiness attached to the outcome. Each was content to risk his life at all hours under a chief so wise and so applied to making himself loved.

"Timocrates had everything to fear in wanting to slay this chief in the midst of an army that loved him with so much passion—but furious ambition is blind. Timocrates found nothing difficult when it came to satisfying Protesilas, with whom he imagined himself having absolute governance over me after the death of Philocles. Protesilas could not bear a good man, the mere sight of whom was a hidden reproach for his crimes and who could, in opening my eyes, overturn his projects.

"Timocrates assured himself of two captains who were incessantly alongside Philocles. He promised them great rewards from me, and then he said to Philocles that he had come on my behalf to tell him secret things which he must only confide to him in the presence of those two captains. Philocles shut himself up with them and Timocrates. Then Timocrates thrusts a knife at Philocles. The thrust slipped and barely pierced the skin. Philocles, not surprised, grabbed the knife from him, used it against him and against the two others. At the same time, he shouted, troops came running, knocked down the door, and delivered Philocles from the hands of these three men who, being distressed, had attacked him weakly.

BOOK XI

They were taken and, so great was the indignation of the army, they would have immediately been ripped apart had Philocles not stopped the multitude. Then he took Timocrates in private and gently asked him what had obliged him to commit so black a deed. Timocrates, who feared that they would kill him, hastened to show him the order I had given him in writing to murder Philocles and, as traitors are always cowardly, he only thought to save his life in revealing to Philocles all the treason of Protesilas. Philocles, frightened to see so much malice in men, took a position full of restraint. He declared to all the army that Timocrates was innocent, he kept him safe, sent him back to Crete, and deferred the command of the army to Polymenes, whom I had named in my handwritten order to take command when Philocles had been murdered. Lastly, he exhorted the troops to the loyalty that they owed me and passed during the night in a light boat that he drove onto the isle of Samos, where he lives tranquilly in poverty and solitude, working to make statues to earn his living, no longer wanting to hear deceiving and unjust men speak, but above all kings whom he believes the most unhappy and the most blind of all men."

At this spot Mentor stopped Idomeneus. "Well then, did it take you long to uncover the truth?"

"No, I comprehended, little by little, the artifices of Protesilas and Timocrates. They even had a falling out, for the wicked have great difficulty remaining united. Their division ended up showing me the depths of the abyss into which they had flung me."

"Well then," resumed Mentor, "did you not make the decision to rid yourself of them both?"

"Alas," replied Idomeneus, "is it, my dear Mentor, that you are ignorant of the weakness and the predicament of princes? When they have once delivered themselves over to corrupt and bold men, who have the art of making themselves essential, they can no longer hope for any freedom. Those whom they scorn the most are those whom they treat the best and lavish with benefits. I was horrified by Protesilas, and I was leaving all authority to him. Strange delusion! I knew I was glad to recognize it, but I did not have the strength to take back the authority that I had abandoned to him. Besides, I found him accommodating, complaisant, clever in flattering my passions, ardent with regard to my interests. Lastly, I had a reason to excuse myself for my weakness: it was that I did not know real virtue. For want of knowing how to choose good men who might conduct my affairs, I believed that there were none of them on earth and that probity was a fine phantom. *What does it matter, I told myself, if one makes a great row in order to get out of the hands of one corrupt man only to fall into those of some other, who will be neither more selfless nor more sincere than he?* Meanwhile, the naval army commanded by Polymenes returned. I was no longer thinking of conquering the island of Carpathus, and Protesilas could not dissimulate so profoundly that I would not discover how afflicted he was to learn that Philocles was safe in Samos."

Mentor interrupted Idomeneus again to ask him if he had continued, after so black a treason, to entrust all his affairs to Protesilas.

"I was," Idomeneus answered him, "too hostile to affairs and too distracted to be able to pull myself from his hands. I would have had to upset the order that I had established for my convenience and to instruct a new man. That is what I never had the strength to undertake. I preferred to close my eyes so as not to see the artifices of Protesilas. I only consoled myself by making it understood to certain confidantes that I was not ignorant of his bad faith. In this way, I imagined myself only half-deceived, since I knew that I was being deceived. I even made Protesilas aware from time to time that I bore his yoke with impatience. I took particular pleasure in contradicting him, in reprimanding him publicly for something he had done, in deciding against his sentiment. But, as he knew my haughtiness and my laziness, he was not bothered by all my grievances. He stubbornly returned to the attack. At times he used an insistent manner, at other times he used suppleness and insinuation. Above all, when he perceived that I was upset with him, he redoubled his attentions so as to supply me with new amusements likely to soften me up or to have me embark on some affair where he would have the opportunity to make himself essential and to show off his zeal for my reputation.

"Although I was on guard against him, this manner of flattering my passions always swept me away; he unburdened me in my predicaments; he caused everyone to tremble through my authority. In the end, I could not resolve myself to lose him. But, in maintaining him in his rank, I put all the good people in no position to represent my true interests to me. From that moment on, no free speech was heard in my councils. Truth distanced itself from me. Ruin, which prepares the downfall of kings, punished me for having sacrificed Philocles to the cruel ambition of Protesilas.

Even those who had the most zeal for the state, and for my person, believed themselves dispensed with setting me straight after so terrible an example. I myself, my dear Mentor, I feared the truth piercing the cloud and reaching me in spite of the flatterers, for, no longer having the strength to follow it, its light importuned me. I felt, deep inside, that it would have caused me cruel remorse, being unable to pull myself from so ill-fated a commitment. My softness and the ascendancy that Protesilas had gradually gained over me plunged me into some despair of ever getting my freedom back. I neither wanted to see so shameful a state of affairs nor to allow others to see it. You know, dear Mentor, the vain haughtiness and the false glory in which kings are raised. They never want to be wrong. In order to cover up one error, they must make a hundred of them. Rather than confessing that he is mistaken and having the difficulty of recovering from his mistake, he must be allowed to be wrong all his life. That is the state of affairs of weak and distracted princes; it was precisely mine when I had to depart for the siege of Troy.

"In departing, I left Protesilas as master of affairs. He conducted them in my absence with haughtiness and inhumanity. The entire kingdom of Crete groaned under his tyranny. But no one dared to summon me over the oppression of the peoples. They knew that I feared seeing the truth and that I abandoned to the cruelty of Protesilas all those who undertook to speak against him. But the less they dared to make a noise, the more violent the evil was. In the aftermath of the siege of Troy, he compelled me to dismiss the valiant Meriones, who had followed me with so much glory.

He had become jealous of him, as with all those I loved and who demonstrated some virtue. You must know, my dear Mentor, that all my misfortunes came from that. It is not the death of my son that caused the revolt of the Cretans so much as it was the vengeance of the gods, angered by my weaknesses, and the hatred of the peoples that Protesilas had attracted to me. When I spilled the blood of my son, the Cretans, weary of a rigorous government, had exhausted all their patience, and the horror of that last act only made them show on the outside what had been deep in their hearts for a long time.

"Timocrates followed me to the siege of Troy and secretly rendered an account through his letters to Protesilas of all he was able to discover. I indeed felt that I was in captivity. But I tried not to think about it, despairing of remedying it. When the Cretans, upon my arrival, revolted, Protesilas and Timocrates were the first to flee. They would have undoubtedly abandoned me had I not been compelled to flee myself almost as quickly as they. Count on it, my dear Mentor, that men who are insolent during prosperity are always weak and trembling in disgrace. Their heads spin as soon as absolute authority escapes them. One sees them to be as groveling as they had been haughty, and it is in an instant that they pass from one extreme to the other."

Mentor said, "But how does it come about then, knowing these two wicked men so well, that you still keep them alongside you, as I see? I am not surprised they would have followed you, having nothing better to do for their interests. I even understand that you did a generous act in giving them asylum in your new settlement.

But why do you still deliver yourself over to them after so many cruel experiences?"

"You do not know," answered Idomeneus, "how useless all experiences are to princes, soft and distracted, who live without reflection. They are dissatisfied with everything, and they do not have the courage to redress anything. So many years of habit were shackles that bound me to these two men, and they obsessed over me at all hours. Since I have been here, they have thrown me into all the excessive expenditures that you have seen; they drained this nascent state; they attracted this war to me which was going to crush me without you—I would have soon experienced in Salentum the same misfortunes that I felt in Crete. But you have finally opened my eyes and have inspired in me the courage that I lacked to get myself out of servitude. I do not know what you have done in me, but since you have been here, I feel myself another man."

Mentor then asked Idomeneus what Protesilas' conduct was in this changeover of affairs.

"Nothing is more artful," resumed Idomeneus, "than what he has done since your arrival. At first, he did his utmost to cast, indirectly, some distrust in my mind. He said nothing against you, but I saw various people who came to warn me that these two foreigners were to be greatly feared. 'The one,' they were saying, 'is the son of the deceitful Odysseus, the other is a man cloaked and of a profound mind. They are accustomed to wandering from kingdom to kingdom. Who knows if they have not formed some design on this one? These adventurers themselves recount that they have caused great troubles in every country they have passed through. This is a nascent state, and poorly reinforced. The least movements could topple it.'

"Protesilas said nothing. But he tried to have me glimpse the danger and the excessiveness of all these reforms that you were having me undertake. He took me through my own self-interest. 'If you put the people in abundance,' he said, 'they will no longer work, they will become proud, disobedient, and will always be ready to revolt. There is only weakness and misery that renders them supple and that keeps them from resisting authority.'

"Often, he tried to take back his former authority in order to drag me along, and he shrouded it under a pretext of zeal for my service.

"'In wanting to unburden the peoples,' he said, 'you diminish the royal might, and in doing so, you do an irreparable wrong to the peoples themselves, for they need to be kept low for their own peace of mind.'

"To all that, I responded that I would know well how to keep the peoples in their duty, in making myself loved by them, in relaxing none of my authority even though I unburdened them, in punishing all the guilty with firmness, lastly, in giving to the children a good education and to all the people an exact discipline, in order to hold them in a simple, sober, and hard-working life.

"'Ho! What's this!' I said, 'Can one not subjugate a people without causing them to die of hunger? What inhumanity! What a brutal politic! How many peoples do we see treated kindly and very faithfully by their princes! What causes revolts—it is the ambition and the restlessness of the elites of a state when they are given too much license and their passions are allowed to expand without limits; it is the multitude of the elites and the hangers-on who live in softness, in luxury, and in idleness; it is the overly great abundance of men devoted to war, who have neglected all the useful occupations, which must be taken up in times of peace; lastly, it is the despair of poorly treated peoples, it is the harshness, the haughtiness of kings and their softness that render them incapable of watching over all the members of the state in order to anticipate troubles. Voila, that is what causes revolts and not the bread that is left to the plowman to eat in peace after he has earned it by the sweat of his brow.'

"When Protesilas saw that I was unwavering in these maxims, he took a position completely opposite that of his past conduct. He began to follow those maxims that he had been unable to destroy. He pretended to appreciate them, to be convinced of them, to be obliged to me for having shed light on them. He goes beyond all that I could wish for to unburden the poor. He is the first to represent their needs to me and to cry out against excessive expenditures. You know yourself that he praises you, he shows confidence in you, and he does his utmost to please you. As for Timocrates, he is beginning to no longer get on so well with Protesilas. He had thought to become independent. Protesilas is jealous of him, and it is in part through their differences that I discovered their perfidy."

Mentor, smiling, responded to Idomeneus, "What then! You have been weak to the point of allowing yourself to be tyrannized for so many years by two traitors, whose treason was well known to you?"

BOOK XI

"Ah, you do not know," responded Idomeneus, "what power artful men have over a weak and distracted king who has delivered himself over to them for all his affairs. Besides, I have already told you that Protesilas now enters into all your views for the public good."

Mentor resumed the discourse with a grave air. "I see only too well how much the wicked prevail over the good alongside kings. You are a terrible example of it. So you say that I have opened your eyes about Protesilas, and they are still closed with regard to leaving the governance of your affairs to this man unworthy of living. Know that the wicked are not men incapable of doing good. They do it indifferently, the same as evil, when it can serve their ambition—doing evil costs them nothing because no sentiment of goodness nor any principle of virtue holds them back. But they also do good without difficulty because their corruption carries them to do it in order to look good and to deceive the rest of men. Strictly speaking, they are not capable of virtue though they appear to practice it. But they are capable of adding to all their other vices the most horrible of vices, which is hypocrisy. As much as you would absolutely desire to do good, Protesilas will be ready to do it along with you to preserve authority, but should he sense even a little laxity in you, he will spare no effort to cause you to tumble into waywardness again and to freely resume his deceptive and fierce nature.

"Can you live with honor and with peace of mind, while such a man obsesses over you at all hours and while you know the wise and loyal Philocles is poor and dishonored on the island of Samos?

You recognize well, O Idomeneus, that deceptive and bold men who are in their presence drag weak princes along. But you should add that princes have still another misfortune that is no less bad; it is that of easily forgetting the virtue and services of a man pushed away. The multitude of men who surround princes is the reason they never have any men who make a deep impression on them. They are only struck by the one who is present and who flatters them. All the rest soon fade away. Above all, virtue touches them little because virtue, far from flattering them, contradicts them and condemns them in their weaknesses. Must you be astonished that they are not loved since they are not lovable, and they love nothing but their grandeur and their pleasure?"

After having said these words, Mentor persuaded Idomeneus that he must, at the earliest, dismiss Protesilas and Timocrates in order to recall Philocles. The only difficulty that was stopping the king was that he feared the severity of Philocles.

"I confess," he said, "that I cannot help but fear his return a little, even though I love and esteem him. I have been, since my earliest youth, accustomed to praises, eagerness, and indulgences, which I would not know how to hope to find in this man. As soon as I did something he did not approve of, his sad air signaled well enough that he condemned me. When he was in private with me, his manners were respectful and restrained, but dry."

"Do you not see," responded Mentor, "that princes spoiled by flattery find dry and austere all that is free and ingenuous? They even go so far as to imagine that one is not zealous for service to them and does not love their authority as soon as one does not have a servile heart and is not ready to flatter them in the most unjust use of their power. All free and liberal speech seems haughty, critical, and seditious to them. They become so delicate that everything that is not flattering wounds and provokes them. But let us go further. I assume that Philocles actually is dry and austere. His austerity, is it not more valuable than the pernicious flattery of your counselors? Where will you find a man without faults? And the fault of telling you the truth too boldly, is it not the one that you must fear the least? What I am saying, is it not a necessary fault in order to correct yours, and to vanquish the distaste for truth, where flattery has made you fall? You need a man who only loves the truth and you, who loves you more than you know how to love yourself, who would tell you the truth despite you, who enforces your cutbacks, and this essential man—it is Philocles. Remember that a prince is only too happy when a single man emerges under his reign with this generosity, that he is the most precious treasure of the state, and that the greatest punishment that must be feared from the gods is losing such a man should the prince render himself unworthy of him for want of knowing how to make use of him.

"As for the faults of good people, you must know how to recognize them, and never stop making use of them: redress them; never deliver yourself over blindly to their indiscreet zeal. But listen to them favorably; honor their virtue, demonstrate to the public that you know how to distinguish it; above all, be very wary of continuing to be as you have been up until now. Princes who have been spoiled as you were, content with despising corrupt men, never stop employing them with confidence and lavishing them with benefits. On the other hand, they pride themselves in also knowing virtuous men, but they only give them vain accolades, not daring to entrust posts to them, nor to accept them into their inner circle, nor to shower benefits on them."

Then, Idomeneus said that he was ashamed to have so long delayed freeing the oppressed innocent and punishing those who had deceived him. Mentor had no difficulty convincing the king to lose his favorite, for as soon as one has managed to render the favorites suspect and importune to their masters, princes, weary and embarrassed, only seek to be rid of them. Their friendship vanishes, their services are forgotten—the downfall of their favorites cost them nothing, provided they no longer see them.

Straightaway, the king secretly ordered Hegesippe, who was one of the principal officers of his house, to take Protesilas and Timocrates, conduct them safely to the island of Samos, leave them there, and bring Philocles back from that place of exile. Hegesippe, surprised by this order, could not keep from crying with joy.

"It is now," he said to the king, "that you are going to enchant your subjects. Those two men have caused all your misfortunes and all those of your peoples. For twenty years they have made all the good people groan, and barely did one even dare to groan, so cruel was their tyranny. They crushed all those who undertook to go to you through a channel other than theirs."

Then Hegesippe revealed to the king a great number of perfidies and inhumanities committed by those two men, of which the king had never heard spoken because no one dared to accuse them. He even recounted to him what he had uncovered of a secret conspiracy to slay Mentor. The king was horrified by all he saw.

~

Hegesippe hastened to seize Protesilas in his house. It was less grand but more comfortable and more pleasant than that of the king. The architecture was of better taste. Protesilas had decorated it with an expenditure drawn from the blood of the destitute. He was, at that time, in a salon of marble alongside his baths, casually lying on a bed of purple with a gold embroidery. He appeared weary and drained from his work. His eyes and eyebrows showed a certain something of agitation, somberness, and fierceness. The most elite men of the state were arranged on carpets around him, composing their expressions from that of Protesilas, of whom they observed even the slightest nod. Barely had he opened his mouth when everyone cried out to admire what he was going to say. One of the principals of the group was recounting to him with ridiculous exaggeration what Protesilas had personally done for the king. Another was assuring him that Zeus, having deceived his mother, had given life to him and he was the son of the father of the gods. A poet had just sung verses assuring that Protesilas, instructed by the Muses, had equaled Apollo in all his intellectual works. Another poet, even more base and more impudent in his verses, was calling him the inventor of fine arts and the father of the peoples whom he rendered happy. He depicted him holding in his hand the horn of plenty.

Protesilas was listening to all these praises with a dry, distracted, and disdainful air, like a man who knows well that he merits still greater ones, and he is only too gracious in allowing himself be praised. There was one flatterer who took the liberty of speaking in his ear to tell him something amusing against the policies that Mentor was trying to establish. Protesilas smiled. All the assembly laughed, though most could not yet know what had been said. But as Protesilas soon regained his severe and haughty air, each fell back into fear and silence. Several nobles were seeking the moment when Protesilas would be able to turn their way and listen to them. They looked fidgety and awkward; it is that they had to ask him for favors. Their suppliant posture spoke for them. They appeared as submissive as a mother at the foot of the altars as she asks the gods for the healing of her only son. They looked content, touched with tender feelings, full of admiration for Protesilas, even though they all held against him an implacable rage in their hearts.

At that moment, Hegesippe enters, seizes Protesilas' sword, and declares to him on behalf of the king that he is going to take him to the island of Samos. At these words, all the arrogance of that favorite tumbled like a rock that detaches from the summit of a steep mountain. There he is, hurling himself, trembling and distraught, at Hegesippe's feet. He cries, he hesitates, he stammers, he trembles, he embraces the knees of this man whom he did not deign an hour before to honor with one of his looks. All those who were showering him with praise, seeing him lost without recourse, changed their flattery into ruthless insults.

Hegesippe did not want to allow him the time to make his final farewells to his family nor to take certain secret writings. All was seized and carried to the king. Timocrates was arrested at the same time, and his surprise was extreme, for he believed that, having turned against Protesilas, he could not be wrapped up in his ruin.

~

They depart in a vessel that had been readied. They arrive at Samos. Hegesippe leaves these two wretches there and, to top off their wretchedness, he leaves them together. There, they furiously reproach each other for the crimes they had committed, which were the cause of their downfall. They find themselves without hope of seeing Salentum again, condemned to live far from their wives and their children; I do not say far from their friends, for they did not have any.

They led them into a strange land where they should no longer have any other resource to live than their work, those two who had spent so many years in delights and splendor. Like two ferocious beasts, they were always ready to rip each other apart.

Meanwhile, Hegesippe asked in what part of the island Philocles lived. They told him that he lived somewhat far from the city on a mountain, where a grotto served him as a home. Everyone spoke to him admiringly of this foreigner.

"Since he has been on this island," they said to him, "he has offended no one. Each is touched by his patience, his work, his tranquility. Having nothing, he always appears content. Even though he is far from affairs here, without property and without authority, he does not fail to oblige those who merit it, and he has a thousand clever skills to please all his neighbors."

Hegesippe advances toward this grotto. He finds it empty and open, for the poverty and simplicity of Philocles' mores made it so that, in going out, he had no need to shut his door. A mat of thick bulrush served him as a bed. Rarely did he light a fire, because he ate nothing cooked. He lived off freshly picked fruits during the summer and dates and dried figs in the winter. A clear spring that formed a sheet of water in tumbling from a rock quenched his thirst. In his grotto, he had only the instruments needed for sculpture, and some books, which he read at certain hours, not to sharpen his wit, nor to content his curiosity, but to instruct himself while relaxing from his work and to learn to be good. As for sculpture, he only applied himself to it in order to exercise his body, flee idleness, and earn his living without needing anyone.

Hegesippe, upon entering the grotto, marveled at the works which were begun. He noticed a Zeus whose serene expression was so full of majesty that one easily recognized him for the father of gods and men. On another side appeared Ares with a tough and menacing pride. But that which was most touching—it was an Athena animating the arts. Her expression was noble and gentle, her build tall and free; she was in an act so lifelike that one would have been able to believe that she was going to walk.

Hegesippe, having taken pleasure in seeing these statues, came out of the grotto and saw in the distance under a tall tree Philocles, reading on the lawn. He goes toward him, and Philocles, spotting him, does not know what to think. *Is that not Hegesippe there*, he said to himself, *with whom I lived for so long in Crete? But what is the likelihood he would come onto an island so remote? Would this be his shade, which would come after his death from the banks of the Styx?*

While he was in this doubt, Hegesippe arrived so near him that he could not help but recognize him and embrace him.

"Is it you, then," he said, "my dear and old friend? What chance, what tempest has cast you onto this shore? Why have you abandoned the island of Crete? Is it a disgrace similar to mine that has snatched you from our homeland?"

Hegesippe answered, "It is not a disgrace; on the contrary, it is the favor of the gods that leads me here."

Straightaway, he recounted to him the long tyranny of Protesilas, his plots with Timocrates, the misfortunes into which they had precipitated Idomeneus, the downfall of this prince, his flight along the coasts of Italy, the founding of Salentum, the arrival of Mentor and Telemachus, the wise maxims with which Mentor had filled the mind of the king, and the disgrace of the two traitors. He added that he had brought them to Samos, to suffer there the exile that they had caused Philocles to suffer, and he ended by telling him that he had orders to conduct him to Salentum where the king, who knew his innocence, wanted to entrust his affairs to him and to shower him with goods.

"Do you see," Philocles responded to him, "that grotto more suited to hiding wild beasts than to being inhabited by men? For so many years, I have enjoyed more sweetness and peace of mind there than in the golden palaces on the island of Crete. Men no longer deceive me, for I no longer see men. I no longer hear their flattering and poisonous discourses. I no longer need them. My hands, hardened from work, easily give me the simple nourishment that is necessary. I only need, as you see, a light cloth to cover me.

No longer having needs, enjoying a profound calm, and a sweet liberty, which the wisdom in my books teaches me to make good use of, what else would I go seeking among jealous, deceitful, and inconstant men? No, indeed, my dear Hegesippe, do not envy me my happiness. Protesilas betrayed himself in wanting to betray the king and to lose me. But he did me no evil. On the contrary, he did me the greatest good. He delivered me from the tumult, and from the servitude of affairs. I owe my cherished solitude and all the innocent pleasures that I enjoy here to him.

"Return, O Hegesippe, return to the king, help him to bear the miseries of grandeur, and do alongside him what you would desire that I do. Since his eyes, so long shut to the truth, have finally been opened by this wise man you call Mentor, may he retain him at his side. As for me, after my shipwreck, it does not suit me to quit the harbor where the tempest has fortunately tossed me just to put myself at the mercy of the winds again. O how kings are to be pitied, O how those who serve them are worthy of compassion! If they are wicked, how much do they cause men to suffer and what torments are prepared for them in gloomy Tartarus. If they are good, what difficulties will they not have to vanquish, what traps to avoid, what evils to endure! Once again, Hegesippe, leave me in my fortunate poverty."

While Philocles was speaking so, with much vehemence, Hegesippe was regarding him with astonishment. He had seen him once in Crete when he governed over the greatest affairs, thin, languishing, and drained; for his ardent and austere nature consumed him in his work. He could not see, without indignation, vice go unpunished. He wanted a certain exactness in affairs that one never finds in them. Thus, his posts were destroying his delicate health. But in Samos, Hegesippe saw him stout and vigorous. Despite the years, glowing youth was renewed on his face; a sober, tranquil, and hard-working life had caused something of a new temperament in him.

"You are surprised to see me so changed," Philocles said, smiling. "It is my solitude that has given me this freshness and this perfect health. My enemies have given me what I would never have been able to find in the greatest fortune. Do you want me to lose true goods to chase after false ones, and to plunge myself into my old miseries again? Do not be more cruel than Protesilas. At least, do not envy me the happiness which I hold from him."

Then, Hegesippe represented to him, but uselessly, all that he thought suitable to touch his heart.

"Are you, then, insensitive to the pleasure of seeing your relatives and your friends again, who yearn for your return and whom the mere hope alone of embracing you fills with joy? But you, who reveres the gods, and who loves your duty, do you count serving your king as nothing, helping him in all the good things that he wants to do, and rendering so many peoples happy? Is one permitted to abandon oneself to an uncivilized philosophy, to preference oneself over all the rest of humankind, and to prefer one's peace of mind to the happiness of one's fellow citizens? Moreover, they will think that it is through resentment that you no longer want to see the king. If he had wanted to harm you, it was because he did not know you. It is not the true, the good, the just Philocles that he had wanted to slay. It was a man very different from you that he wanted to punish. But now that he knows you, and he no longer takes you for another, he feels all his old friendship revived in his heart. He is waiting for you; he is already holding out his arms to embrace you. In his impatience, he counts the days and the hours. Will you have so hard a heart as to be inexorable to your king and to all your most affectionate friends?"

Philocles, who had at first been touched with tenderness upon recognizing Hegesippe, resumed his austere air while listening to this discourse. Like a rock against which the winds fight in vain, and on which all the ocean waves go to crash, howling, he remained unmoved, and neither pleas nor reasoning found any opening to enter into his heart. But, at the moment when Hegesippe was beginning to despair of winning him over, Philocles, having consulted the gods, beheld through the flight of birds, through the entrails of sacrifices, and through various other presages that he should follow Hegesippe. Then he no longer resisted. He prepared to depart, but it was not without lamenting the wilderness where he had spent so many years.

"Alas, must I forsake you, O lovable grotto, where peaceful Sleep came every night to relax me from the work of the day? Here the Fates spun for me, in the midst of my poverty, days of gold and silk."

He bowed down, weeping, to worship the Naiad who had quenched his thirst for so long with her clear water, and the Nymphs who inhabited all the neighboring mountains. Echo heard his laments and, with a sad voice, repeated them to all the country deities.

BOOK XI

Afterward, Philocles went to the city with Hegesippe to embark. He thought that the wretched Protesilas, filled with shame and resentment, would not want to see him. But he was mistaken, for corrupt men have no shame, and they are always ready for all sorts of baseness. Philocles was hiding modestly for fear of being seen by this poor wretch. He feared increasing Protesilas' misery in displaying to him the prosperity of an enemy who was going to rise up on his ruins. But Protesilas was seeking Philocles with eagerness. He wanted to inspire pity in him and to enlist him to ask the king that he be able to return to Salentum. Philocles was too sincere to promise to work toward having him recalled, for he knew better than anyone how pernicious his return would have been. But he spoke to him very gently, showed him compassion, tried to console him, exhorted him to appease the gods through pure mores and through a great patience in his woes. As he had learned that the king had taken from Protesilas all his property unjustly acquired, he promised him two things that he would faithfully execute afterward. One was to take care of his wife and children, who had remained in Salentum in dreadful poverty, exposed to public indignation. The other was to send to Protesilas on this distant island some monetary aid to soften his misery.

Meanwhile, the sails swell with a favorable wind. Hegesippe, impatient, hastens to have Philocles depart; Protesilas watches them embark. His eyes remain attached and fixed from the shore. They follow the vessel, which plows the waters and which the wind always distances. Even when he can no longer see it, he still repaints the image of it in his mind. Finally, distressed, furious, delivered over to his despair, he pulls out his hair; rolls in the sand; reproaches the gods for their rigor; calls, in vain, to his aid cruel Death, who, deaf to his pleas, does not deign to deliver him from so many woes; and he does not have the courage to deliver himself.

~

Meanwhile, the vessel, favored by Poseidon and the winds, soon arrived in Salentum. The king was told that it was already entering the harbor. Immediately, he ran out, along with Mentor, to welcome Philocles. He embraced him tenderly, bearing witness to a visible regret for having persecuted him so unjustly. This confession, far from appearing a weakness in a king, was regarded by all the Salentines as the effort of a great soul, who rises above his own wrongdoings by courageously confessing them in order to mend them. Everyone was crying with joy at seeing again the good man who had loved the people and hearing the king speak with so much wisdom and goodness. Philocles, with a respectful and modest air, received the accolades of the king and was impatient to steal away from the acclamations of the people. He followed the king to the palace. Soon, Mentor and he were in the same confidence as if they had spent their lives together, even though they had never seen each other; for the gods, who have refused to the wicked eyes to know the good, have given to the good something to recognize one another. Those who have the taste for virtue cannot be together without being united through the virtue that they love.

Soon, Philocles asked the king to let him retire near Salentum in a solitude where he continued to live in poverty, as he had lived in Samos. The king went with Mentor to see him almost every day in his wilderness. It is there that they examined the means of firming up the laws and giving a solid shape to the government for the public happiness. The two main things that they examined were the education of the children and the manner of living during peace.

As for the children, Mentor said, "They belong less to their parents than to the republic. They are the children of the people. They are the hope and the strength of them. It is not the time to correct them once they are corrupted. It is a small thing to exclude them from posts when one sees that they have become unworthy of them. It is much better to prevent evil than to be reduced to punishing it.

"The king," he added, "who is the father of all his people, is even more particularly the father of all the youth, who are the flower of all the nation. It is in the flower that the fruits must be prepared. May the king not disdain, then, overseeing and having overseen the education that is given to the children. May he hold steadfast, then, to have the laws of Minos observed, which command that children be raised with a scorn for pain and for death; that honor be placed in fleeing delights and riches; that injustice, mendacity, ingratitude, and softness pass for infamous vices; that they are taught from their earliest childhood to sing the praises of the heroes, who have been loved by the gods, who have performed generous deeds for their homeland, and whose courage has shone in combat. May the enchantment of music seize their souls, in order to render their mores sweet and pure. May they learn to be tender with regard to their friends, loyal to their allies, fair to all men, even with regard to their most cruel enemies; may they fear death and torment less than the slightest reproach from their consciences. If, at an early age, one fills children with these great maxims and causes them to enter into their hearts through the sweetness of song, there will be few children who are not enflamed with the love of glory and virtue."

Mentor added that it was capital to establish public schools to accustom youth to the toughest exercises of the body and to avoid the softness and idleness that corrupt the most beautiful natures. He wanted a great variety of games and events that would animate all the people but would, above all, exercise the body to make it adroit, supple, and vigorous. He added prizes to excite a noble emulation. But what he wished for the most with regard to good mores is that the young people marry at an early age, and that their relatives, without any view to self-interest, would allow them to choose wives agreeable in body and mind to whom they could grow attached.

But while they were preparing, in this way, the means of keeping the youth pure, innocent, hard-working, docile, and passionate for glory, Philocles, who loved warfare, said to Mentor, "It is in vain that you busy the young people with all these exercises if you allow them to languish in a continual peace where they will gain no experience with warfare, nor any need to put their valor to the test. In doing so, you will gradually weaken the nation. Courage will wane, delights will corrupt mores, other bellicose peoples will have no difficulty vanquishing them, and for having wanted to avoid the woes that war drags after it, they will fall into a dreadful servitude."

Mentor responded, "The woes of war are even more horrific than you think. War drains a state and always puts it in danger of perishing, even when you bring home the greatest victories. With whatever advantages you begin it, you are never sure of ending it without being exposed to the most tragic reversals of fortune. No matter what superior military forces you enlist in combat, the least miscalculation, a panic terror, a mere nothing, snatches from you the victory that was already in your hands and conveys it to the enemy. Even when you hold victory in the camp, as if shackled, you would destroy yourself in destroying your enemies: you depopulate your country, you leave the lands practically uncultivated, you disrupt commerce. But what is still worse, you weaken the best laws, and you allow mores to be corrupted. The youth no longer devote themselves to scholarship. Pressing need makes it so that you have to tolerate a pernicious licentiousness in the troops. Justice, polity, all suffer from this disorder. A king who sheds the blood of so many men and who causes so much unhappiness to acquire a little glory or to extend the borders of his kingdom is unworthy of the glory that he seeks and merits losing what he possesses for having wanted to usurp that which does not belong to him.

"But here are the means of exercising the courage of a nation in times of peace. You have already seen the exercises of the body that we are establishing, the prizes that will excite emulation, the maxims of glory and virtue with which the hearts of children will be filled, almost from the cradle, through the song of great heroic deeds. Add to these aids that of a sober and hard-working life. But that is not all. As soon as a people allied with your nation are at war, you must send the flower of your youth, particularly those in whom you notice a genius for war and who will be the most suitable to profit from the experience. In so doing, you will preserve a high reputation among your allies. Your alliance will be sought after; they will fear losing it. Without having war at home at your expense, you will always have a war-ready and intrepid youth. Although you have peace at home, you will not fail to treat with the greatest honors those who have the talent for warfare, for the true means of keeping war far away and preserving a long peace—it is to cultivate the armies; it is to honor the excellent men in this profession; it is to always have in the army those who were trained in foreign countries and who know the military forces, the discipline, and the methods of the warfare of neighboring peoples; it is to be not only incapable of waging war through ambition but equally incapable of fearing war through softness. Then, being always ready to wage war in necessity, you arrive at almost never having it.

"As for the allies, when they are ready to wage war against each other, it is up to you to make yourself the mediator. By doing so, you acquire a glory more solid and more sure than that of conquerors. You gain the love and esteem of foreigners. They all need you. You reign over them through trust, just as you reign over your subjects through authority. You become the custodian of secrets, the arbiter of treaties, the master of hearts. Your reputation flies throughout the most distant countries. Your name is like a delightful perfume that wafts from country to country to the most distant peoples. In this state, should a neighboring people attack you against the rules of justice, they find you war-ready, prepared, but what is even

BOOK XI

stronger, they find you loved and succored; all your neighbors call to arms for you, and are persuaded that your preservation makes for public safety. That is a rampart much more assured than all the walls of the cities and than all the best fortified places. That is true glory. But how few kings there are who know how to seek it and who do not distance themselves from it. They run after a deceiving shadow and leave true honor behind them for want of knowing it."

After Mentor had spoken in this way, Philocles, astonished, was staring at him; then he cast his eyes on the king and was enchanted to see how avidly Idomeneus was gathering, in the depths of his heart, all those words that emerged, like a river of wisdom, from the lips of this foreigner.

Athena, in the figure of Mentor, thus established in Salentum all the best laws and the most useful maxims of government, less to cause the kingdom of Idomeneus to flourish than to show Telemachus, when he returned, a visible example of what a wise government can do to render the peoples happy and to give to a good king a lasting glory.

END OF BOOK XI

THE ADVENTURES OF
TELEMACHUS
SON OF ODYSSEUS

BOOK XII

Meanwhile, *Telemachus was demonstrating* his courage in the perils of war. Upon departing Salentum, he applied himself to gaining the affection of the old captains, whose reputation and experience were of the highest rank. Nestor, who had already seen him in Pylos, and who had always loved Odysseus, treated him as if he were his own son. He gave him training that he bolstered with various examples. He recounted to him all the adventures of his youth and all the most remarkable things he had witnessed of the heroes of past ages. The memory of this wise old man, who had lived to see three generations of men, was like a history of ancient times engraved on brass or marble.

Philoctetes did not have the same inclination for Telemachus as Nestor at first. The hate that he had nurtured for so long in his heart for Odysseus distanced him from Odysseus' son, and he could only see with difficulty all that it seemed the gods were preparing in favor of this young man to render him equal to the heroes who had overthrown the city of Troy.

But in the end, Telemachus' restraint vanquished all of Philoctetes' resentments. He could not defend himself from loving that sweet and modest virtue. He often took Telemachus aside and said to him, "My son (for I no longer fear calling you such), your father and I, I confess, we have been enemies for a long time. I even confess that after we had brought down the lofty city of Troy, my heart was not yet appeased, and when I saw you, I had difficulty loving the virtue in the son of Odysseus. I have often reproached myself for it. But in the end, virtue, when it is sweet, unaffected, ingenuous, and modest, overcomes all."

Then, Philoctetes gradually promised to recount to him what had ignited in his heart so much hate for Odysseus. "I must," he said, "take up my story from the top. I followed everywhere the great Heracles, who delivered the Earth from so many monsters and before whom the other heroes were only like weak reeds alongside a great oak, or like the least of birds in the presence of the eagle. His woes and mine came from a passion that causes all the most dreadful disasters. It is Love. Heracles, who had vanquished so many monsters, could not vanquish that shameful passion, and the cruel infant Eros toyed with him. He could not think back without blushing with shame about how he had once forgotten his glory to the point of trailing alongside Omphale, queen of Lydia, like the most cowardly and effeminate of all men, so much had he been swept away by a blind love.

BOOK XII

"A hundred times he confessed to me that this part of his life had tarnished his virtue and almost blotted out the glory from all his labors. Nevertheless, O gods, such is the weakness and inconstancy of men! They expect everything of themselves and resist nothing. Alas! The great Heracles fell back into the snares of love that he had so often detested. He loved Deianira. He would have been only too happy had he been constant in this passion for one woman, who was his wife! But soon the youthfulness of Iole, on whose face the Graces were painted, delighted his heart. Deianira burned with jealousy. She thought back to that fatal tunic which the centaur Nessus had left her when he was dying as an assured means of reawakening Heracles' love every time that he appeared to neglect her for the love of some other. That tunic, filled with the venomous blood of the centaur, contained the poison from the arrows with which that monster had been pierced. You know that the arrows of Heracles, who killed that perfidious centaur, had been dipped in the blood of the Hydra of Lerna, and that this blood poisoned those arrows in a way that all the wounds they made were incurable.

"Heracles, having donned that tunic, soon felt the devouring fire, which slipped into the marrow of his bones. He loosed horrible screams with which Mount Oeta resounded and caused to reverberate in all the deepest valleys; even the sea appeared stirred by them. The most furious bulls, who would have bellowed in their fights, would not have made a noise as dreadful. The unfortunate Lichas, who had brought this tunic to him on Deianira's behalf, having dared to approach him, Heracles, racked with pain, took him, spun him, just as a slinger spins with his slingshot the stone that he wants to hurl far from him. So Lichas, launched from the top of the mountain by the mighty hand of Heracles, fell into the swells of the sea, where he was instantly changed into a rock that still keeps the human shape and that, always buffeted by the angry waves, horrifies wise pilots from afar.

"After this misfortune of Lichas, I believed I could no longer trust Heracles. I thought to hide in the deepest caverns. I saw him effortlessly uproot with one hand the tall pines and old oaks that had for several centuries scorned the winds and the tempests. With the other hand, he tried in vain to snatch from his back the fatal tunic. It clung to his skin, as if incorporated into his limbs. As he tore at it, he also tore his skin and his flesh; his blood streamed and soaked the ground. Finally, his virtue overcoming his pain, he cried out, 'You see, O my dear Philoctetes, the evils that the gods make me suffer. They are just. It is I who offended them. I violated conjugal love. After having vanquished so many enemies, I cravenly let myself be vanquished by the love of a beautiful foreigner. I am perishing, and I am content to perish, to appease the gods.

'But alas dear friend, where did you flee? The excessive pain made me commit, it is true, a cruelty against that wretched Lichas, for which I reproach myself. He did not know what poison he presented to me. He did not merit what I made him suffer. But do you think that I could forget the friendship I owe you and could want to snatch life from you? No, no, I will not cease loving Philoctetes. Philoctetes will receive in his bosom my soul ready to soar. It is he who will gather my ashes. Where are you then,

BOOK XII

O my dear Philoctetes, Philoctetes, the only hope that remains to me here below!'"

"At these words, I hasten to run to him. He holds out his arms to me and wants to embrace me. But he draws back, for fear of igniting in my bosom the cruel fire with which he himself is burned.

"'Alas,' he said, 'even this consolation is no longer permitted me.'

"Speaking so, he assembles all those trees he has just felled. He makes of them a pyre on the summit of the mountain. He tranquilly ascends onto the pyre. He lays out the skin of the Nemean lion, which had covered his shoulders for so long when he was going from one end of the earth to the other to slay monsters and deliver the unfortunate. He leans on his club and orders me to light the fire of the pyre. My hands, trembling and seized with horror, could not refuse him this cruel office, for life was no longer for him a present from the gods so much as it was gruesome to him. I even feared that the excessiveness of his pain might carry him to do something unworthy of that virtue that had astounded the universe.

"As he saw that the flame of the pyre was beginning to take, he cried out, 'It is now, my dear Philoctetes, that I put to the test your true friendship! Since you love my honor more than my life, may the gods render honor to you. I leave you that which I have of the most precious on earth, those arrows dipped in the blood of the Hydra of Lerna. You know that the wounds they make are incurable. By them you will be invincible, as I have been, and no mortal will dare to fight against you. Remember that I die faithful to our friendship and never forget how dear you have been to me. But, if it is true that you are touched by my woes, you can give me one last consolation: promise me never to reveal to any mortal either my death, or the place where you will have hidden my ashes.'

"I promised it to him—alas, I even swore it—while drenching his pyre with my tears. A ray of joy appeared in his eyes, but instantly a swirl of flames that engulfed him smothered his voice and nearly stole him from my sight. I still saw him a little, nevertheless, through the flames with an expression as serene as if he would have been wreathed with flowers and covered with perfumes in the joy of a delicious feast in the midst of all his friends.

"The fire soon consumed all that there was of earthliness and mortality in him; soon there remained nothing at all of that which he had received at birth from his mother Alcmena. But he preserved, by the command of Zeus, that subtle and immortal nature, that celestial flame that is the true principle of life and that he had received from the father of the gods. Thus, he went with them, under the golden vaults of shining Olympus, to drink nectar where the gods gave him as a spouse the lovely Hebe, the goddess of youth. She poured the nectar into the cup of the great Zeus before Ganymede received that honor. As for me, I found an inexhaustible source of pain in those arrows that he had given me to elevate me above all the heroes.

"Soon, the leagued kings undertook with Menelaus to exact vengeance on the infamous Paris, who had abducted Helen, and to overthrow Priam's empire. The oracle of Apollo caused them to understand that they must not hope to end that war happily unless they had the arrows of Heracles.

BOOK XII

"Odysseus, your father, who was always the most enlightened and the most clever in all the councils, charged himself with persuading me to go with them to the siege of Troy and to bring those arrows that he believed I had. It had already been a long time since Heracles had appeared on earth. One no longer heard of any new exploit of this hero. Monsters and scoundrels began to appear again with impunity. The Greeks did not know what to think of him—some were saying he was dead; others were maintaining he had gone just below the frozen Great Bear to subdue the Scythians.

"But Odysseus maintained that he was dead and undertook to make me confess it. He came to find me at a time when I still could not console myself of having lost the great Alcides. He had great difficulty coming up to me, for I could no longer bear the sight of men. I could not suffer someone snatching me from those deserts of Mount Oeta where I had seen my friend perish. I only thought of repainting the image of this hero and weeping at the sight of those sad places. But sweet and powerful persuasion was on the lips of your father. He appeared almost as afflicted as me. He shed tears, he knew how to gradually win my heart and lure my trust. He softened me toward the Greek kings who were going to fight for a just cause and who could not succeed without me. He could never, however, wrest from me the secret of Heracles' death, which I had sworn to never tell. But he did not doubt that he was dead, and he pressed me to reveal to him the spot where I had hidden his ashes. Alas, I was horrified of perjuring myself in telling him a secret that I had promised the gods to never tell. But I was weak enough to elude my oath, not daring to violate it. The gods punished me for it. I struck the ground with my foot at the spot where I had placed Heracles' ashes.

"Afterward, I went to join the leagued kings who received me with the same joy as they would have received Heracles himself. As I was passing into the island of Lemnos, I wanted to demonstrate to all the Greeks what my arrows could do. Preparing to shoot a fallow deer that was leaping into a wood, I allowed, accidentally, the arrow to fall from the bow onto my foot, and it caused a wound that I still feel. Instantly, I experienced the same pains that Heracles had suffered. Night and day, I filled the island with my screams. A black and corrupt blood oozing from my cut infected the air, and spread in the encampment of the Greeks a stench capable of suffocating the most vigorous men. The entire army was horrified to see me in this extremity. Each concluded that it was a torture that was sent to me by the just gods.

"Odysseus, who had enlisted me into this war, was the first to abandon me. I have recognized since that he did it because he preferred the common interest of Greece, and victory, to all the reasons of friendship or of individual welfare. They could no longer make sacrifices in the camp, so much did the horror of my cut, its infection, and the violence of my screams disturb the entire army. But at the moment when I saw myself abandoned by all the Greeks through Odysseus' counsel, that politic seemed to me filled with the most horrific inhumanity and the blackest betrayal. Alas, I was blind and did not see that it was right that the wisest of men would be against me, the same as the gods whom I had provoked.

BOOK XII

"I remained, throughout almost all the siege of Troy, alone, without help, without hope, without relief, delivered over to horrific pains on that deserted and wild island where I only heard the noise of the ocean waves crashing against the rocks. I found, in the midst of that solitude, an empty cavern in a rock, with two peaks raised toward the sky, resembling two heads. From that rock emerged a clear spring. This cavern was the retreat of ferocious beasts whose fury I was exposed to night and day. I amassed some leaves on which to sleep. The only goods left for me were a roughly worked wooden pot and some worn rags with which I wrapped my cut to stop the bleeding and which I also used to clean it. There, abandoned by men and delivered over to the anger of the gods, I passed my time piercing with my arrows doves and other birds that flew around that rock. When I had killed some bird for my nourishment, I had to painfully drag myself along the ground to gather my prey. In this way my hands prepared something to nourish myself.

"It is true that the Greeks, in departing, left me some provisions, but they did not last long. I lit a fire with stones. That life, as dreadful as it was, would have seemed sweet to me, far from ungrateful and deceptive men, had the pain not crushed me and had I not incessantly passed over and over again in my mind my sad adventure. *What!* I said, *to pull a man out of his homeland, as the only man who can avenge Greece, and then to abandon him on this deserted island during his sleep!*

"For it was during my sleep that the Greeks departed. Judge what was my surprise, and how many tears I shed upon awakening, when I saw the vessels plowing the waters. Alas, searching in every direction on that wild and terrible island, I found only pain.

"On this island, there is neither port, nor commerce, nor hospitality, nor men who land there willingly. One only sees the unfortunates that tempests have cast onto the island, and one can only hope for any company from shipwrecks. Even still, those who came to this place dared not take me to bring me back—they feared the anger of the gods and that of the Greeks.

"For ten years I suffered shame, pain, hunger. I fed a cut that was devouring me. Even hope was extinguished in my heart. Suddenly, returning from seeking medicinal plants for my cut, I spotted in my cave a young man, handsome and charming, yet proud and of a heroic build. It seemed to me that I was seeing Achilles, so much did he have his traits, his look, and his walk. His age alone made me realize that it could not be him. I noticed on his face both compassion and discomfort. He was touched to see with what difficulty and what slowness I dragged myself along. The piercing and painful cries that I made echo along that shoreline touched his heart.

"'O stranger,' I said to him from some distance, 'what misfortune has driven you onto this uninhabited island? I recognize the Greek dress, this dress that is still so dear to me. O how I long to hear your voice and to find on your lips that tongue that I learned in childhood and that I could no longer speak to anyone for so long in this solitude! Do not be frightened to see a man so wretched. You must pity him.'

"Barely had Neoptolemus said, 'I am Greek,' when I cried out, 'O sweet words after so many years of silence and pain without consolation! O my son, what misfortune! What tempest! Or rather, what favorable wind drove you here to end my woes?'

"He answered me, 'I am from the island of Scyros. I am returning there. They say that I am the son of Achilles. You know all.'

"Words so curt did not satisfy my curiosity. I said, 'O son of a father whom I so loved, dear nursling of Lycomedes, how did you come here then? Where are you coming from?'

"He answered that he was coming from the siege of Troy.

"'You were not,' I said to him, 'from the first expedition.'

"'And you?' he said. 'Were you from it?'"

"So I answered, 'You do not know, I see well, either the name of Philoctetes, or his misfortunes. Alas, woeful as I am! My persecutors insult me in my misery. Greece is ignorant of what I suffer; my pain increases. The Atreidae put me in this state. May the gods render such a state to them.' Then, I recounted to him the manner by which the Greeks had abandoned me. As soon as he had listened to my complaints, he made his to me.

"'After the death of Achilles . . .'

"Immediately I interrupted him, 'What? Achilles is dead! Forgive me, my son, if I disrupt your story with the tears that I owe your father.'

"Neoptolemus responded, 'You console me in interrupting me. How sweet it is for me to see Philoctetes mourn my father!' Neoptolemus, resuming his discourse, said to me:

"'After the death of Achilles, Odysseus and Phoenix came to seek me, assuring that they could not, without me, overthrow the city of Troy. They had no difficulty taking me, for my grief over the death of Achilles, and the desire to inherit his glory in that celebrated war enlisted me enough to follow them.'

"'I arrive at Sigeum. The army assembles around me. Each swears he is seeing Achilles again, but alas, he was no more. Young and inexperienced, I believed I could expect everything of those who were giving me so much praise. Immediately I ask the Atreidae for my father's armor. They answer me cruelly, 'You will have the rest of what belonged to him. But as for his armor, it is destined for Odysseus.' Instantly, I am distraught, I weep, I lose my temper, but Odysseus, without emotion, says, 'Young man, you were not with us in the perils of this long siege. You have not merited such arms, and you already speak too proudly! You will never have them.' Stripped unjustly by Odysseus, I am going back to the isle of Scyros, less indignant with Odysseus than with the Atreidae. May whoever is their enemy be the friend of the gods. O Philoctetes, I have told all.'

"Then, I asked Neoptolemus how Great Ajax, son of Telamon, had not stopped that injustice.

"'He is dead,' he answered."

"'He is dead!', I cried out, 'And Odysseus did not die—on the contrary, he flourishes in the army.' Then, I asked him for news of Antilochus, the son of wise Nestor, and of Patroclus, so cherished by Achilles.

"'They are dead too,' he told me.

"Immediately, I cried out again, 'What, dead! Alas, what are you telling me! Cruel war harvests the good and spares the wicked. Odysseus is alive then. Thersites is also undoubtedly. This is what the gods do, and we still praise them!'

"While I was in that fury against your father, Neoptolemus continued to deceive me. He added these sad words, 'Far from the Greek army, where evil prevails over good, I am going to live contentedly on the wild island of Scyros. Farewell, I am departing. May the gods heal you.'

"Quickly I said, 'O my son, I conjure you by the mānes of your father, by your mother, by all that you have of the most dear on earth, to not leave me alone in these woes that you see. I am not ignorant of how much I will be a burden to you, but there would be shame in abandoning me. Throw me in the bow, in the stern, into the bilge even, wherever I would inconvenience you the least. There are only great hearts who know how much glory there is in being good. Do not leave me in a wilderness where there is no vestige of man; take me into your homeland or into Euboea, which is not far from Mount Oeta, Trachis, and the agreeable banks of the river Spercheios. Render me to my father. Alas, I fear he is dead. I had summoned him to send me a vessel—either he is dead, or indeed those who had promised me to tell him did not do it. I resort to you, O my son. Remember the fragility of things human. He who is in prosperity ought to fear abusing it and come to the aid of the unfortunate ones.'

"Voila, that is what the excessiveness of my pain caused me to say to Neoptolemus. He promised to take me away. Then I cried out again, 'O happy day! O lovable Neoptolemus, worthy of the glory of his father. Dear comrades of this voyage, suffer that I would say farewell to this sad dwelling. See where I lived. Understand what I suffered. No other could have suffered it. But necessity has taught me, and it teaches men what they would never be able to know otherwise. Those who have never suffered know nothing. They know neither good nor evils. They are ignorant of men. They are ignorant of themselves.' Having spoken so, I grabbed my bow and my arrows.

"Neoptolemus begged me to suffer he kiss them, those arms so famous, and consecrated by the invincible Heracles.

"I answered, 'You may do all. It is you, my son, who today renders to me the light, my homeland, my father stooped with old age, my friends, myself. You may touch those arms and boast of being the only one among the Greeks who has merited touching them.' Quickly, Neoptolemus enters my grotto to marvel at my arms.

"At that moment, a cruel pain seizes me. It distresses me. I no longer know what I am doing. I demand a sharp glaive to cut my foot, I cry out, 'O Death so desired, why do you not come! O young man, burn me this instant, as I burned the son of Zeus. O ground! O ground! Receive a dying man, who can no longer get up.'

"From this onslaught of pain, I suddenly fall, according to my habit, into a deep drowsiness. A heavy sweat began to relieve me; a black and corrupt blood oozed from my cut. During my sleep, it would have been easy for Neoptolemus to take my arms and depart. But he was the son of Achilles and was not born to deceive. Awakening, I recognized his discomfort; he was sighing like a man who does not know how to dissimulate, and who is acting against his heart.

"'Do you want to overtake me?' I said to him, 'What is it, then?'

"'You must,' he answered, 'follow me to the siege of Troy.'

"I retorted, 'Ah, what did you say, my son? Give me back that bow. I am betrayed. Do not snatch life from me.'

"Alas, he said nothing. He looked at me tranquilly. Nothing touched him.

"'O shores! O promontories! O ferocious beasts! O steep cliffs! It is to you that I complain, for I only have you to whom I can complain. You are accustomed to my wails. Must I be betrayed by the son of Achilles? He takes the sacred bow of Heracles away from me; he wants to drag me into the Greek camp in order to triumph over me. He does not see that it is to triumph over a dead man, a shade, a vain image. O if he would have attacked me in my prime! But even now, it is only by surprise. What will I do? Give back, my son, give back. Be like your father, like yourself. What do you say? You say nothing! O savage rock, I come back to you naked, miserable, abandoned, without nourishment! I will die in this cave alone. No longer having my bow to kill the beasts, the beasts will devour me. What does it matter? But, my son, you do not appear wicked. Some counsel pushes you. Give back my arms. Go away.'

"Neoptolemus, tears in his eyes, said very softly, 'Would to the gods had I never left Scyros.'

"At that moment, I cry out, 'Ho! What do I see? Is it not Odysseus?'

"Instantly, I hear his voice, and he answers me, 'Yes, it is I.'

"Had the somber kingdom of Hades opened up and I had seen the gloomy Tartarus, which even the gods fear to glimpse, I would not have been gripped, I confess, with a greater horror.

"I cried out again. 'O land of Lemnos, I take you as witness! O Sun, you see him, and you suffer him!'

"Odysseus responds without emotion, 'Zeus desires it, and I execute it.'

"'Dare you,' I said to him, 'name Zeus? Do you see this young man, who was not born for fraud, and who suffers in executing what you oblige him to do?'

"'It is not in order to deceive you,' Odysseus said to me, 'nor to harm you, that we come. It is to deliver you, to heal you, to give you the glory of overthrowing Troy, and to take you back to your homeland. It is you, and not Odysseus, who is the enemy of Philoctetes.'

"Then I said to your father all that furor could inspire in me, 'Since you abandoned me on this shore,' I told him, 'why not leave me here in peace? Go seek the glory of combat and every pleasure. Enjoy your happiness with the Atreidae. Leave me my misery and my pain. Why take me away? I am no longer anything. I am already dead. Why do you not still believe today, as you once believed, that I would not know how to depart, that my screams, and the infection of my cut would disturb the sacrifices? O Odysseus, author of my woes, may the gods . . . But the gods do not listen to me—on the contrary, they incite my enemy. O soil of my homeland that I will never see again, O gods, if there still remains someone among you who has any justice at all, have mercy on me, punish, *punish* Odysseus! Then, I will believe myself healed.'

"While I was speaking so, your father, tranquil, regarded me with an air of compassion, like a man who, far from being provoked,

BOOK XII

bears and excuses the distress of a wretch that Fortune provoked. I saw him, like a boulder on the summit of a mountain toys with the fury of the winds and allows their rage to wane while it remains unmoved. So your father, remaining silent, waited for my anger to wane, for he knew that one must only attack the passions of men, to reduce them to reason, when they begin to weaken through a kind of weariness. Then, he said these words to me:

"'O Philoctetes, what have you done with your reason and your courage? This is the moment to make use of them. If you refuse to follow us to fulfill the grand plans of Zeus for you, farewell; you are unworthy of being the liberator of Greece and the destroyer of Troy. Remain in Lemnos. These arms that I carry away will bring me a glory that was destined for you. Neoptolemus, let us depart. It is useless to speak to him. Compassion for a single man must not cause us to abandon the salvation of all Greece.'

"Then, I felt like a lioness whose cubs have just been snatched. She fills the forests with her roars.

"'O cavern,' I said, 'never will I forsake you! You will be my tomb. O sojourn of my pain! No more nourishment, no more hope! Who will give me a glaive to impale myself? O, if the birds of prey could take me away! I would no longer pierce them with my arrows. O precious bow, bow consecrated by the hands of the son of Zeus! O dear Heracles, if there still remains in you some feeling, are you not indignant? This bow is no longer in the hands of your faithful friend. It is in the impure and deceiving hands of Odysseus. Birds of prey! Ferocious beasts no longer flee this cavern! My hands no longer have arrows. Wretched, I can no longer harm you. Come take me away. Or rather may the thunderbolt of merciless Zeus crush me.'

"Your father, having attempted all other means to persuade me, judged in the end that it was best to give my arms back to me. He motioned to Neoptolemus, who quickly gave them to me. Then, I said, 'Worthy son of Achilles, you show that you are—but leave me to pierce my enemy.'

"Straightaway I wanted to draw my arrow against your father, but Neoptolemus stopped me, saying, 'Anger distresses you and keeps you from seeing the unworthiness of the deed you want to do.'

"As for Odysseus, he appeared as tranquil against my arrows as against my insults. I felt touched by that intrepidness and that patience. I was ashamed for having wanted in that former outburst to use my arms to kill the one who had had them given back to me. But as my resentment was not yet appeased, I was inconsolable to owe my arms to a man who I hated so.

"Meanwhile, Neoptolemus was saying to me, 'Know that the divine Helenus, son of Priam, having left the city of Troy by the command and inspiration of the gods, has unveiled the future to us. "The unfortunate Troy will fall,' he said, 'but it can only fall after it will have been attacked by the one who holds the arrows of Heracles. That man can only heal when he is before the walls of Troy. The children of Asclepius will heal him.'

"At that moment, I felt my heart split. I was touched by the naïveté of Neoptolemus and by the good faith with which he had given back my bow. But I could not yet resolve myself to see the day when it would be necessary to cede to Odysseus, and a wicked shame held me in suspense. *Will I be seen*, I said to myself, *with Odysseus and the Atreidae? What will one think of me!*

"While I was in this uncertainty, I suddenly hear a voice, superhuman; I see Heracles in a brilliant cloud. He was surrounded with rays of glory. I easily recognized his somewhat rugged features, his robust body, and his natural mannerisms. But he had a loftiness and a majesty that had never appeared so grand in him when he was subduing monsters. He said to me, 'You hear, you see Heracles. I have quit high Olympus to announce the commands of Zeus to you. You know through what labors I acquired immortality. You must go with the son of Achilles to walk in my footsteps on the path to glory. You will heal. You will pierce with my arrows Paris, author of so many woes. After the taking of Troy, you will send the rich spoils to your father, Poias, on Mount Oeta. Those spoils will be placed on my tomb as a monument of the victory owed to my arrows. And you, O son of Achilles, I declare to you that you cannot vanquish without Philoctetes, nor Philoctetes without you. Go then, like two lions who seek their prey together. I will send Asclepius to Troy to heal Philoctetes. Above all, O Greeks, love and observe religion. The rest dies; it never dies.'

"After hearing those words, I cried out, 'O happy day! Sweet light! You finally reveal yourself after so many years. I am obeying you; I am departing after having bowed to these places. Farewell, dear cave. Farewell nymphs of these damp meadows. I will no longer hear the dull noise of the surf of this sea. Farewell shores where so many times I suffered the assaults of the air. Farewell promontory, where Echo repeated my wails so many times. Farewell sweet springs that were so bitter to me. Farewell O land of Lemnos, allow me to depart happily since I go where the will of the gods and my friends call me.

"So we departed. We arrived at the siege of Troy. Machaon and Podalirius, through the divine science of their father Asclepius, healed me, or at least put me in the state where you find me. I no longer suffer, I have found all my vigor again, but I am a little crippled. I made Paris fall like a timid young doe that a hunter pierces with his shafts. Soon Ilium was reduced to ashes. You know the rest. Nevertheless, I still had somewhat of an aversion for the wise Odysseus in thinking back on those woes, and his virtue could not appease that resentment. But the sight of a son who resembles him, and whom I cannot help loving, touches my heart, even for the father."

END OF BOOK XII

THE ADVENTURES OF
TELEMACHUS
SON OF ODYSSEUS

BOOK XIII

W*hile Philoctetes was recounting* his adventures in this way, Telemachus had remained in suspense and motionless. His eyes were attached on that great man who was speaking. All the different passions that had agitated Heracles, Philoctetes, Odysseus, Neoptolemus appeared in turn on the naïve face of Telemachus as they were represented in the course of that narration. Sometimes he cried out and interrupted Philoctetes without thinking to; sometimes he appeared to be dreamy like a man who thinks deeply about the course of affairs. When Philoctetes depicted the discomfort of Neoptolemus, who did not know how to dissimulate, Telemachus seemed to be in the same discomfort and, at that moment, one would have taken him for Neoptolemus.

Meanwhile, the army of the allies marched in good order against Adrastus, king of the Daunians, who scorned the gods and only sought to deceive men. Telemachus faced great difficulties with regard to comporting himself well among so many kings jealous of one another. He had to render himself suspect to no one and make himself loved by all. His nature was good and sincere, but hardly welcoming. He was barely aware of what could please others. He was not attached to riches, yet he did know how to give. So, with a heart noble and inclined to good, he appeared neither obliging, nor sensitive to friendship, nor open-handed, nor appreciative for the attentions given him, nor alert to distinguish merit. He followed his taste without reflection.

His mother Penelope had nurtured him, despite Mentor, in a haughtiness and a pride that tarnished all that there was of the most lovable in him. He regarded himself as being of another nature than the rest of men. Others seemed to him only put on earth by the gods to please him, to serve him, to anticipate all his desires, and to attribute everything to him as to a deity. The good fortune of serving him was, according to him, a high enough reward for those who served him. Nothing should ever be impossible when it concerned satisfying him, and the least delays provoked his ardent nature.

Those who would have seen him in his natural state would have judged that he was incapable of loving anything other than himself, that he was only sensitive to his glory and to his pleasure. But this indifference for others and this constant attention to himself only came from the constant frenzy into which he was thrown by

BOOK XIII

the violence of his passions. He had been indulged by his mother since the cradle, and he was a great example of the misfortune of those who are of high birth. The rigors of Fortune that he had felt since his earliest youth had not been able to moderate this impetuosity and this haughtiness. Stripped of everything, abandoned, exposed to so many evils, he had lost none of his pride; it always rose again, just as the supple palm unceasingly rises again, no matter the effort one makes to lower it.

While Telemachus was with Mentor, these faults did not appear, and they diminished every day. Like a spirited steed that bounds in the vast meadows that neither cliffs, nor precipices, nor fast mountain streams stop, that only knows the voice and the hand of a single man capable of taming it, Telemachus, full of a noble ardor, could only be held back by Mentor alone. Moreover, just one of his looks could stop him suddenly in his greatest impetuosity; he immediately understood what that look signified; he immediately recalled into his heart all the sentiments of virtue. Wisdom, in an instant, rendered his expression soft and serene. Poseidon, when he raises his trident and threatens the heaving waves, does not appease more suddenly the black tempests.

When Telemachus found himself alone, all those passions, pent-up like a mountain stream arrested by a strong dike, resumed their course. He could not tolerate the arrogance of the Lacedaemonians and Phalanthus, who was at their head. That colony, which had come to found Tarentum, was comprised of young men born during the siege of Troy who had not had any education. Their illegitimate birth, the dissoluteness of their mothers, the licentiousness in which they had been raised, gave them a certain something of fierceness and barbarity. They resembled a troop of brigands rather than a Greek colony.

Phalanthus, on every occasion, sought to contradict Telemachus. He often interrupted him in the assemblies, scorning his counsels like those of an inexperienced young man. He made fun of him, treating him as weak and effeminate. He pointed out his slightest errors to the chiefs of the army. He tried to sow jealousy everywhere and to render Telemachus' pride odious to all the allies.

~

One day, Telemachus having taken several Daunians prisoner, Phalanthus claimed that those captives should belong to him because, he said, it was he who, at the head of the Lacedaemonians, had defeated that enemy troop and Telemachus, finding the Daunians already vanquished and fleeing, had no other difficulty than that of letting them live and leading them into camp. Telemachus sustained, on the contrary, that it was he who had kept Phalanthus from being vanquished and who had brought home the victory over the Daunians. They both went to defend their cause in the assembly of the allied kings. Telemachus lost his temper to the point of threatening Phalanthus. They would have fought on the spot had they not been stopped.

Phalanthus had a brother named Hippias, famous throughout the army for his valor, for his strength, and for his prowess. Polydeuces, the Tarentins said, did not fight better at boxing; Castor could not have surpassed him in driving a horse. He had nearly the size and strength of Heracles. The entire army feared him, for he was even more quarrelsome and more brutal than he was strong and valiant. Hippias, having seen with what haughtiness Telemachus had threatened his brother, hastily goes to take the prisoners to bring them to Tarentum without waiting for the judgment of the assembly. Telemachus, whom someone came to tell in secret, left quaking with rage. Just like a wild boar, frothing at the mouth, that seeks the hunter by whom he was wounded, he was seen roving through the camp, seeking the eyes of his enemy and brandishing the spear with which he wanted to pierce him. Finally he encounters him, and, seeing him, his fury redoubles. It was no longer that wise Telemachus instructed by Athena under the figure of Mentor. It was a frenzied lunatic or an enraged lion.

Straightaway, he shouts at Hippias, "Halt! O most cowardly of all men! Halt! We will see if you can take from me the spoils of those I vanquished. You will not drive them to Tarentum. Go! Descend this instant to the gloomy banks of the Styx!"

He spoke and hurled his spear, but he hurled it with so much fury that he could not gage his mark. The spear did not touch Hippias. Quickly, Telemachus took his sword, of which the cross guard was gold, that Laertes had given him when he departed Ithaca as a measure of his tender affection. Laertes had used it with much glory when he was young, and it had been stained with the blood of several famous captains of the Epirotes in a war in which Laertes was victorious. No sooner had Telemachus drawn that sword than Hippias, who wanted to profit from the advantage of his strength, lunged to snatch it from the hands of the young son of Odysseus. The sword snaps in their hands. They seize and grip each other. There they are, like two cruel beasts seeking to rip each other apart; fire shines in their eyes; they press, they back off, they duck, they rise again, they lunge at each other, they are thirsty for blood. There they are, grappling foot to foot, hand to hand; those two intertwined bodies seemed only one. But Hippias, who was older, seemed to overwhelm Telemachus, whose tender youth was less muscular. Telemachus, already out of breath, felt his knees buckling. Hippias, seeing him rattled, redoubled his efforts. The son of Odysseus was done for. He was going to bear the pain of his temerity and his hot-headedness, had not Athena—who was watching over him from afar, and who was only leaving him in this extreme peril to instruct him—determined the victory in his favor.

She did not quit the palace of Salentum, but she sent Iris, swift messenger of the gods. Iris, flying on light wings, ripped through the immense space of the air, leaving behind a long trail of light that painted a cloud of a thousand different colors. She only sets down on the shore of the sea where the countless army of allies was encamped. She sees in the distance the quarrel, the ardor, and the efforts of the two fighters; she shudders at the sight of the danger the young Telemachus was in. She approaches, wrapped in a light cloud she had formed from delicate mists. At the moment when Hippias, feeling all his strength, believed himself victorious, she covered the young nursling of Athena with the aegis that the wise goddess had entrusted to her.

Immediately, Telemachus, whose forces were drained, begins to come alive. As he comes alive, Hippias is troubled. He feels a certain something of the divine that stuns him and is weighing

BOOK XIII

down on him. Telemachus presses him and attacks, sometimes in one spot, sometimes in another: he rattles him, he leaves him no time to steady himself. Finally, he throws him to the ground and falls on him. A great oak of Mount Ida, that the ax has hacked by a thousand blows, with which the entire forest reverberates, does not make a more horrible noise in falling; the ground groans from it, all that surrounds it is rattled by it.

Meanwhile, wisdom had returned with force within Telemachus. No sooner had Hippias fallen under him than the son of Odysseus realized the error he had made in attacking so the brother of one of the allied kings whom he had come to help. Confusedly, he recalled the wise counsel of Mentor. He was ashamed of his victory and understood how much he had merited being defeated. At that moment, Phalanthus, carried away with fury, came running to the aid of his brother. He would have run Telemachus through with the spear he carried had he not feared piercing Hippias also, whom Telemachus held under him in the dust. The son of Odysseus could have effortlessly taken the life of his enemy, but his anger was appeased, and he no longer thought of anything but mending his error by showing restraint.

He rises, saying, "O Hippias, it suffices for me to have taught you to never scorn my youth. Live. I admire your strength and your courage. The gods have protected me; cede to their might. Let us no longer think of anything but fighting together against the Daunians."

As Telemachus was speaking so, Hippias got up, covered with dust and blood, filled with shame and rage. Phalanthus dared not take the life of the one who had just given it so generously to his brother. He was unsettled and beside himself. All the allied kings come running. They lead to one side Telemachus, to another Phalanthus and Hippias, who, having lost his pride, dared not lift his eyes. The entire army could not be more astonished that Telemachus—at so tender an age, when men do not yet have their full strength—would have been able to take down Hippias, resembling in size and strength those giants, children of the earth, who once dared to chase the immortals from Olympus.

But the son of Odysseus was quite far from enjoying the pleasure of this victory. While they could not weary of admiring him, he withdrew into his tent, ashamed of his error, and no longer able to bear himself. He groaned over his quick temper. He recognized how unjust and unreasonable he was in his fits of anger. He found a certain something of vainness, weakness, and lowness in this unbounded and unjust haughtiness. He recognized that true greatness is only in restraint, justice, modesty, and humaneness. He saw it, but he dared not hope to correct himself of it after so many relapses. He was grappling with himself, and was heard roaring like an enraged lion. He remained shut up alone in his tent for two days, unable to resolve himself to reenter into any society and punishing himself. *Alas,* he said, *dare I see Mentor again? Am I the son of Odysseus, the wisest and most patient of men? Did I come to bring division and disorder into the army of the allies? Is it their blood or that of the Daunians, their enemies, that I should shed? I was brash; I did not even know how to hurl my spear. I exposed myself, in a fight with Hippias, to unequal forces. I should have expected only death* from it, along with the shame of being vanquished. But what would that matter! I would no longer be, no, I would no longer be that brash Telemachus, that young fool, who does not profit from any counsel. My shame would end with my life. Alas! If I could at least hope to no longer do what I am sorry for having done! Too happy would I be, only too happy! But perhaps before the end of the day I will make, and will want to make, the same mistakes again for which I now have so much shame and horror. O ill-fated victory! O praises that I cannot suffer, and that are cruel reproaches of my madness!

While he was alone, inconsolable, Nestor and Philoctetes came to find him. Nestor wanted to point out to him the wrong he had done, but this wise old man, quickly recognizing the young man's desolation, changed his grave reproaches to words of tenderness to ease his despair.

The allied princes were halted by this quarrel, and they could only march toward the enemy after reconciling Telemachus with Phalanthus and Hippias. They feared at all hours that the troops of the Tarentins would attack the hundred young Cretans who had followed Telemachus into this war. All was in turmoil through the error of Telemachus alone, and Telemachus, who saw so many evils present and perils still to come, of which he was the author, abandoned himself to a bitter pain. All the princes were in an extreme predicament. They dared not have the army march for fear that, in the march, Telemachus' Cretans and Phalanthus' Tarentins would fight each other. It was difficult enough restraining them within the camp where they were closely guarded. Nestor and Philoctetes were incessantly coming and going from Telemachus' tent to that of the implacable Phalanthus, who only breathed vengeance. The sweet eloquence of Nestor and the authority of the great Philoctetes could not moderate that savage heart that was still incessantly provoked by the raging diatribes of his brother Hippias. Telemachus was much more meek, but he was despondent through a pain that nothing could console.

While the princes were in this unrest, all the troops were filled with dismay. The entire camp seemed like a house desolated, having just lost the father of the family—the support of all his kin and the sweet hope of his grandchildren.

In this disorder and consternation of the army, a horrifying noise is suddenly heard of chariots, arms, whinnying of horses, the screams of men—some victorious and animated by carnage, others fleeing, or dying, or wounded. A whirlwind of dust forms a thick cloud that shrouds the sky and envelops the entire camp. Soon, the dust combines with a thick smoke, obstructing the air and stifling the breath. A dull sound was heard, like that of the swirl of flame that Mount Etna vomits up from the bottom of its blazing bowels when Hephaestus, along with his Cyclops, forges thunderbolts there for the father of the gods. Horror seizes hearts.

Adrastus, vigilant and tireless, had surprised the allies. He had hidden his march from them and had been informed of theirs. For two nights, he had made incredible haste to go around a nearly inaccessible mountain of which the allies had seized all the passes. Holding those narrow passes, they believed themselves to be in complete safety and even claimed, through these passes that they occupied, to be able to fall upon their enemy behind the mountain once the troops they were awaiting had come.

Adrastus, who scattered silver by the handful in order to know his enemy's secrets, had learned of their resolution, for Nestor and Philoctetes, those two captains otherwise so wise and so experienced, were not so tight-lipped in their enterprises. Nestor, in his declining age, took too much pleasure in recounting what could draw some praise to him. Philoctetes by nature spoke less, but he was temperamental, and if the least thing excited his quick temper, he could be made to say what he had resolved to keep quiet. Artful people had found the key to his heart so as to draw the most important secrets from it: he only had to be provoked. Then, hot-headed and beside himself, he exploded with threats and boasted of having the sure means to attain what he wanted. If one merely appeared to doubt those means, he thoughtlessly hastened to explain them, and the most intimate secret escaped from the bottom of his heart. Just as a precious yet cracked vase from which flows all the most delicious liquors, the heart of this great captain could hold nothing.

Traitors, corrupted by Adrastus' silver, did not fail to play on the weaknesses of these two kings. They incessantly flattered Nestor through vain praises. They recalled his past victories to him, admired his foresight, never wearied of applauding him. On the other hand, they set continual traps for the impatient temper of Philoctetes; they only spoke to him of difficulties, setbacks, dangers, inconveniences, irremediable errors. As soon as his irascible nature was inflamed, wisdom abandoned him, and he was no longer the same man.

Telemachus, despite the faults we have seen, was much more prudent in keeping a secret. He was accustomed to it through his misfortunes and from having, since his childhood, to hide himself from the suitors of Penelope. He knew how to keep a secret without telling any lie. He did not even have that certain reserved and mysterious air that secretive people usually have; he did not appear burdened by the weight of a secret he was obliged to keep. One always found him free, natural, open, like a man who wears his heart on his sleeve. But, while saying all that could be said without consequence, he knew how to stop precisely and without affectation at the things that could draw some suspicion and broach his secret. In so doing, his heart was impenetrable and inaccessible. Even his best friends only knew what he believed useful to reveal to them in order to draw wise counsel from them, and there was only Mentor alone with whom he showed no reserve. He confided in other friends, but to varying degrees, and in proportion to what he had experienced of their friendship and their wisdom.

Telemachus had often noticed that the resolutions of the council were spreading a little too much in the camp. He had warned Nestor and Philoctetes of it. But these two men, so experienced, did not pay enough attention to such salutary advice. Old age no longer has any suppleness; longtime habits hold it as if shackled; it no longer has hardly any resources against its faults. Just as trees whose rough and knotty trunks have hardened by the number of years and can no longer be straightened, men of a certain age can almost no longer bend away from certain habits that have aged with them and that have entered into the marrow of their bones.

BOOK XIII

Often, they recognize them, but too late. They bemoan them in vain, and tender youth is the only age when man is still able to correct himself on his own.

There was a Dolope in the army named Eurymachus, flattering, insinuating, knowing how to adapt to all the tastes and inclinations of the princes, inventive and clever in finding new ways to please them. To hear him tell it, nothing was ever difficult. Ask him for his opinion? He divined that which would be the most agreeable. He was pleasing, mocking of weak people, complaisant with those he feared, able to season a delicate praise, which would be well received by the most modest of men. He was serious with the serious, playful with those who were of a playful humor. It cost him nothing to take on all sorts of shapes. Sincere and virtuous men, who are always the same, and who submit to the rules of virtue, would never know how to be as agreeable to princes whose passions dominate them.

Eurymachus knew warfare; he was capable in affairs; he was an adventurer who had given himself over to Nestor and who had gained his confidence. He drew from the depths of Nestor's heart, somewhat vain and sensitive to praise, all that he desired to know from him. Although Philoctetes did not confide in Eurymachus, anger and impatience did in him what trust did in Nestor. Eurymachus only had to contradict him, for in provoking him, he discovered everything.

This man had received great sums from Adrastus to send him all the plans of the allies. The king of the Daunians had a certain number of defectors in the army who were obliged to escape from the camp of the allies and return to his, one after another. As there was some important affair to make known to Adrastus, Eurymachus had one of these defectors depart. The deception could not easily be discovered because these defectors did not carry letters. If they were overtaken, nothing was found that could render Eurymachus suspect. Meanwhile, Adrastus was apprised of all the undertakings of the allies. No sooner had a resolution been made in council than the Daunians did precisely what was necessary to impede its success. Telemachus did not tire of seeking the cause for this and inciting the distrust of Nestor and Philoctetes, but his attention was useless—they were blind.

In council, they had resolved to wait for the numerous troops that were to come, and they had a hundred vessels advance secretly during the night to conduct these troops more swiftly from a very rough seacoast where they should arrive, to the spot where the army was encamped. Meanwhile, they believed themselves safe, because their troops held the narrow passes of the neighboring mountain, which is an almost inaccessible coast of the Apennines. The army was encamped on the banks of the Galesus river, fairly close to the sea. This delightful countryside is abundant in grazing land and all the produce that can feed an army.

Adrastus was behind the mountain, and they counted on him being unable to pass over it. But as he knew that the allies were still weak, that they were waiting for large reinforcements, that vessels were waiting for the arrival of the troops that should come, and that the army was divided by Telemachus' quarrel with Phalanthus, they hastened to make a great detour. He hurriedly came day and night along the edge of the sea and passed by trails that were always believed to be absolutely impassable. Thus, boldness and obstinate work overcome the greatest obstacles; thus, there is almost nothing impossible for those who know how to dare and to suffer; thus, those who sleep, figuring that difficult things are impossible, merit being surprised and crushed.

At daybreak, Adrastus surprised the hundred vessels that belonged to the allies. As these vessels were poorly guarded and wary of nothing, he seized them without resistance and used them to transport his troops with an incredible haste to the mouth of the Galesus. Then he hurriedly went up the length of the river. Those who were in the forward posts around the encampment, toward the river, believed that these vessels were bringing the troops they were awaiting. They immediately let loose great cries of joy. Adrastus and his soldiers descended before they could recognize them: they fell upon the allies, who were suspecting nothing; they found the allies in a camp completely open, without order, without chiefs, without weapons.

The side of the camp they attacked first was that of the Tarentins, where Phalanthus commanded. The Daunians entered with so much vigor, that this Lacedaemonian youth, being surprised, could not fight back.

While they search for their weapons and hamper each other in this confusion, Adrastus sets fire to the camp. Quickly, the flame rises from the pavilions and ascends to the clouds. The noise from the fire is like that of a torrent that floods an entire countryside and sweeps along in its swift current great oaks with their deep roots, crops, barns, stables, and flocks. The wind impetuously pushes the flame from pavilion to pavilion, and soon the entire camp is like an ancient forest that an ember has set ablaze.

Phalanthus, who sees the peril more closely than any other, is unable to remedy it. He realizes that all the troops are going to perish in this inferno if they do not hasten to abandon the camp. But he also understands how much the disorder of this retreat is to be feared before a victorious enemy. He begins to get his Lacedaemonian youth out, still half-unarmed. But Adrastus does not allow them to breathe. From one side, a troop of adroit archers pierce Phalanthus' soldiers with countless arrows. From the other, sling-shooters hurl a hail of fat stones. Adrastus himself, sword in hand, marching at the head of a troop chosen from the most intrepid Daunians, pursues, by the glow of the fire, the troops who are fleeing. He reaps with his sharp blade all that have escaped the fire. He swims in blood, and he cannot slake himself of carnage. Lions and tigers do not equal his fury, when they slay the shepherds along with their flocks. Phalanthus' troops succumb and courage abandons them. Pale Death, driven by an infernal Fury whose head bristles with serpents, freezes the blood in their veins. Their numb limbs stiffen, and their buckling knees deny them even the hope of flight.

Phalanthus, to whom shame and despair still give a remnant of fortitude and vigor, raises his hands and eyes toward the sky. He sees fall at his feet his brother Hippias under the strikes of the lethal hand of Adrastus. Hippias, stretched out on the ground, rolls in the dust; a black and bubbling blood flows out like a stream from the deep wound that crosses his side; his eyes close to the light; his furious soul flees with all his blood. Phalanthus himself, completely covered with the blood of his brother, and unable to help him, finds himself enveloped by a horde of enemies endeavoring to strike him down; his shield is pierced with a thousand shafts. He is wounded in many parts of his body. He can no longer rally his fugitive troops. The gods see him, and they have no mercy on him.

Zeus, in the midst of all the celestial deities, watched from the heights of Olympus this carnage of the allies. At the same time, he consulted the immutable destinies and saw all the chiefs for whom the thread must this very day be cut by the scissors of the Fates. Each of the gods was attentive to discover on the face of Zeus what would be his will. But the father of gods and men said to them in a gentle and majestic voice, "You see to what extremity the allies are reduced. You see Adrastus who strikes down all his enemies. But this spectacle is very deceptive. The glory and prosperity of the wicked is fleeting. Adrastus, unbelieving and odious through his bad faith, will not bring home a complete victory. This misfortune is only happening to the allies to teach them to mend their ways and to better keep their enterprises secret. Here wise Athena prepares a new glory for her young Telemachus, in whom she delights.

Then, Zeus ceased speaking. All the gods continued to watch the combat in silence.

Meanwhile, Nestor and Philoctetes were advised that a part of the camp had already burned, that the flame, pushed by the wind, was still advancing, that their troops were in disorder, and that

Phalanthus could no longer sustain the efforts of the enemy. Barely do these calamitous words strike their ears and they are already running to arms, assembling the captains, and ordering them to hasten to get out of the camp to evade this inferno.

Telemachus, who had been despondent and inconsolable, forgets his pain. He takes up his armor, precious gift from wise Athena, who, appearing in the figure of Mentor, pretended to have received them from an excellent craftsman of Salentum, but who had had them made by Hephaestus in the steaming caverns of Mount Etna.

These arms were polished like glass and shining like the rays of the sun. On it, one saw Poseidon and Pallas disputing over who would have the glory of giving their name to an emerging city. Poseidon with his trident was striking the ground, and one saw emerging from it a spirited horse; fire leapt from his eyes, and froth from his mouth. His mane floated with the wind. His supple and muscular legs pranced with vigor and lightness; he was not walking, he was lunging with his hind legs, but with so much quickness that he left no trace of his steps. One believed to hear him whinny.

On the other side, Athena was giving the inhabitants of her new city the olive, fruit of the tree that she had planted. The branch on which its fruit hung represented sweet peace, along with abundance, preferable to the turmoil of war for which that horse was the image. The goddess remained victorious through her simple and useful gifts, and superb Athens bore her name.

One also saw Athena gathering round her all the fine arts, who were tender, winged infants. They took refuge around her, being

BOOK XIII

horrified by the brutal fury of Ares who ravages everything, like bleating lambs take refuge under their mother at the sight of a famished wolf, who, with his gaping and inflamed maw, pounces to devour them. Athena, with a disdainful and provoked expression, was confounding, through the excellence of her work, the foolish temerity of Arachne, who had dared to dispute her over the perfection of tapestries. One saw that poor wretch, whose extended limbs were disfiguring and changing into those of a spider.

On another side appeared Athena again, who, in the war of the giants, served as counsel to Zeus himself and supported all the other stunned gods. Lastly, she was represented with her lance and her aegis on the banks of the Xanthus and the Simois, leading Odysseus by the hand, reanimating the fugitive troops of Greece, standing up to the efforts of the most valiant Trojan captains, and the redoubtable Hector himself, finally, having Odysseus enter that fatal machine which ought, in a single night, topple Priam's empire.

On another side, this shield represented Demeter in the fertile countrysides of Enna that are in the middle of Sicily. The goddess is seen gathering the peoples scattered hither and yon, seeking their nourishment through hunting or picking wild fruit that falls from the trees. She was demonstrating to those crude men the art of softening the land and drawing from its fruitful womb their nourishment. She was presenting a plow to them and having oxen yoked to it. One saw the land opened up in furrows by the blade of the plow. Then one spied golden crops which covered those fertile countrysides. The reaper, with his scythe, was cleaving the sweet produce of the land and was rewarded for all his troubles. Iron, destined elsewhere to destroy everything, only seemed used in this place to prepare abundance and to cause every pleasure to sprout.

Nymphs, crowned with flowers, danced together in a meadow on the banks of a stream, alongside a grove. Pan played the flute. Fauni and coltish Satyrs frolicked in a corner. Dionysus appeared there also, wreathed with ivy, leaning with one hand on his thyrsus, and holding with the other a vine festooned with green leaves and several clusters of grapes; his was a soft beauty with a certain nobleness, passionate and languishing. He was just as he appeared to the unhappy Ariadne, when he found her alone, abandoned and lost in pain on an unknown shore.

Lastly, one saw on all sides numerous people: old men carrying the first of their produce into the temples, young men returning to their spouses, weary from the work of the day; wives going to welcome them, leading by the hand their little children whom they caressed. Shepherds were also seen, seeming to be singing, and some of them were dancing to the sound of the chalumeaux—all represented peace, abundance, delights; all appeared laughing and happy. One even saw wolves frolicking in the pastures amidst the sheep. The lion and the tiger, having forsaken their ferocity, were grazing with the tender lambs. A little shepherd was driving them together under his crook. This lovable painting recalled all the charms of the golden age.

Telemachus, having donned this divine armor, instead of taking his regular sword-belt, took the terrifying aegis that Athena had sent him, entrusting it to Iris, the swift messenger of the gods. Iris had removed his sword-belt without him noticing and had given him in its place this aegis, redoubtable to the gods themselves.

In this state, he runs out of the camp to avoid the flames. He summons to him in a loud voice all the chiefs of the army, and this voice already reanimates all the distraught allies. A divine fire flashes in the eyes of the young warrior. He always appears gentle, always free and tranquil, always attentive to giving orders just like a wise old man attentive to sorting out his family and teaching his children. But he is swift and rapid in the execution, like an impetuous river that not only rolls its foamy waves with haste but even sweeps along its course the heaviest vessels with which it is charged.

Philoctetes, Nestor, the chiefs of the Mandurians, and other nations, sense in the son of Odysseus a certain authority to which they must all cede; the experience of the old men fails them; the counsel and wisdom are taken away from all the commanders; even jealousy, so natural to men, is extinguished in their hearts. All are silent, all admire Telemachus, all fall in line to obey him without questioning it, as if they were accustomed to it. He advances and ascends a hill, from where he observes the disposition of the enemy. Then, suddenly, he judges that they must hasten to take them by surprise in the disorder where they have put themselves in burning the camp of the allies. He hurriedly makes the turn, and all the most experienced captains follow him. He attacks the Daunians from behind at a time when they believed the army of the allies to be enveloped in the flames of the blaze. This surprise attack distresses them. They fall under the hand of Telemachus like leaves in the last days of autumn fall in the forests, when a proud Northwind bringing back winter causes the trunks of the old trees to groan and shakes all the branches. The ground is covered with the men that Telemachus strikes down. With his spear, he pierces the heart of Iphicles, the youngest of Adrastus' children; this one dared to stand against him in combat to save the life of his father, who he thought would be overtaken by Telemachus. The son of Odysseus and Iphicles were both handsome, vigorous, full of prowess and courage, of the same size, the same sweetness, the same age. Both were cherished by their parents. But Iphicles was like a flower that blossoms in a field and that must be cut down by the blade of the reaper's scythe. Then, Telemachus strikes down Euphorion, the most famous of all the Lydians coming from Etruria. Finally, his glaive pierces Cleomene, newly married, who had promised his spouse to bring her the rich spoils of his enemy and who should never see her again.

Adrastus quakes with rage, seeing the death of his dear son, that of several captains, and victory escaping from his hands. Phalanthus, almost slain at his feet, is like a sacrifice, throat half-slit, that gets away from the sacred knife and flees far from the altar. It would have taken Adrastus only an instant to finish off the Lacedomonian.

Phalanthus, drowning in his own blood and that of the soldiers who are fighting alongside him, hears the shouts of Telemachus, who is advancing to come to his rescue. In that instant, life is returned to him; the cloud that already covered his eyes dissipates. The Daunians, sensing this unforeseen attack, abandon

Phalanthus to repulse a more dangerous enemy. Adrastus is like a tiger from whom the shepherds, banded together, snatch the prey that it was ready to devour. Telemachus seeks him in the melee and wants to instantly end the war by delivering the allies from their implacable enemy.

But Zeus did not want to give the son of Odysseus a victory so swift and so easy. Even Athena desired that he would have to suffer evils even longer to better learn how to govern men. The unbeliever Adrastus was thus preserved by the father of the gods so that Telemachus would have the time to acquire more glory and more virtue. A cloud that Zeus gathered in the air saved the Daunians. A horrifying thunderclap declared the will of the gods. One would have thought that the eternal vaults of high Olympus were going to crash down on the heads of weak mortals. Flashes of lightning split the cloud from one pole to the other, and in an instant when their eyes were dazzled by their piercing fires, everything fell back into the dreadful darkness of the night. An abundant rain that fell in an instant served to separate the two armies.

Adrastus profited from the succor of the gods, without being touched by their might, and merited by this ingratitude being reserved for a more cruel vengeance. He hastened to have his troops pass between the half-burned camp and a marsh that extended to the river. He did it with so much cleverness and swiftness that this retreat demonstrated how much resourcefulness and presence of mind he had. The allies, animated by Telemachus, wanted to pursue him, but thanks to this storm, he escaped them like a bird with a light wing escapes the nets of the hunters.

The allies no longer thought of anything but reentering their camp and mending their losses. Reentering the camp, they saw what war has of the most lamentable: the sick and wounded, being unable to drag themselves out of the tents, were unable to save themselves from the fire. They appeared half-burnt, loosing to the sky, in plaintive and dying voices, painful shrieks. Telemachus' heart was pierced by them. He could not hold back his tears. He averted his eyes several times, gripped with horror and compassion. He could not witness, without shuddering, those bodies still alive and committed to a long and cruel death. They looked like the flesh of the sacrifices that one burns on the altars, the odor of which spreads in every direction.

"Alas," Telemachus cried out, "here they are then, here are the evils that war drags along after it! What blind fury pushes wretched mortals! They have so few days to live on earth. Those days are so miserable. Why hurry a death already so near? Why add so much dreadful desolation to the bitterness with which the gods have filled this life that is so short? Men are all brothers, yet they tear each other apart. Ferocious beasts are less cruel than them. Lions do not wage war with lions, nor tigers with tigers. They only attack animals of a different species. Man alone, despite his reason, does what animals without reason would never do.

But still, why these wars? Is there not enough land in the universe to give every man more of it than he can cultivate? How much deserted land is there? Humankind would not know how to fill it. What then! A false glory, a vain title of conqueror that a prince wants to acquire, ignites war in immense countries! So then, a single man, given to the world by the anger of the gods, brutally sacrifices so many other men to his vanity—all must perish, all swim in blood, all be devoured by flames. He who escapes the sword and fire cannot escape hunger, even more cruel, so that a single man, who toys with the whole of human nature, finds in this general destruction his pleasure and his glory. What monstrous glory!

Can one abhor too much and scorn too much the men who have so forgotten humanity? No, indeed. Very far from being demigods, they are not even men, and they should be an execration to all the centuries in which they believed that they would be admired. O how kings must be wary of the wars they undertake! They must be just. That is not enough though—they must be necessary for the public good; the blood of a people must only be spilled in order to save that people in extreme need. But flattering counsel, false ideas of glory, vain jealousies, unjust avidity that cloaks itself in beautiful pretexts, lastly, insensitive commitments nearly always drag kings into wars where they make themselves wretched, where they risk everything unnecessarily, and where they do as much evil to their subjects as to their enemies." Thus reasoned Telemachus.

But he was not content to deplore the evils of war; he tried to soften them. He was seen going into tents to help the sick and dying himself: he gave them silver and remedies; he consoled and encouraged them through discourses full of friendliness. Those whom he could not visit himself, he had visited by others.

Among the Cretans who were with him, there were two old men, one of whom was named Traumaphilus and the other Nosophugus. Traumaphilus had been at the siege of Troy with Idomeneus and had learned from the children of Asclepius the divine art of healing cuts. He spread into the deepest and most infected wounds a fragrant liqueur that consumed the dead and corrupt flesh without needing to make any incision and quickly formed new flesh healthier and finer than the former.

As for Nosophugus, he had never seen the children of Asclepius, but he had received, through the intermediary Meriones, a sacred and mysterious book that Asclepius had given his children. Besides, Nosophugus was a friend of the gods; he had composed hymns in honor of the children of Leto; every day he offered the sacrifice of a white and unstained ewe to Apollo, by whom he was often inspired. No sooner had he seen a sick person than he knew by his eyes, by the color of his complexion, by the conformation of his body, and by his breathing the cause of his sickness. At times, he gave remedies that caused sweating, and he demonstrated through the success of the sweats how much perspiration facilitates, diminishes, disconcerts, or re-establishes all the workings of the body. At times he gave, for the aches of languor, certain brews that, bit by bit, fortified the vital organs and rejuvenated men by softening their blood. But he assured that it was for want of virtue and courage that men so often needed medicine.

"It is a shame," he said, "with regard to men, that they have so many maladies, for good mores produce health. Their intemperance," he said again, "changes into deadly poisons the foods intended to preserve life. Pleasures, taken without moderation, abridge the days of men more than remedies can prolong them. The poor are less often sick for want of nourishment than the rich become sick from taking too much of it. Foods that flatter the taste too much, and that cause one to eat beyond need, poison them instead of nourishing. Remedies are themselves true evils that make use of nature and that must be used only in pressing need. The great remedy, which is always innocent, and is always useful: it is sobriety, it is temperance in all pleasures, it is tranquility of the mind, and it is exercising the body. In doing so, one causes a soft and temperate blood and dissipates all the superfluous black bile."

Thus, wise Nosophugus was less admirable for his remedies than for the diet that he counseled to prevent maladies and to render remedies unnecessary.

These two men were sent by Telemachus to visit all the sick in the army. They healed many of them through their remedies, but they healed even more of them through the care they took to have them waited on properly; for they applied themselves to keeping them clean, to prevent poor air through this cleanliness, and to keep them on a diet of strict sobriety in their convalescence.

All the soldiers, touched by these aids, rendered thanks to the gods for having sent Telemachus into the army of the allies.

"He is not a man," they were saying. "He is undoubtedly some beneficent deity beneath a human figure. At least, if he is a man, he resembles less the rest of men than the gods. He is only on earth to do good. He is even more lovable through his gentleness and through his goodness than through his valor! O if we could have him as king! But the gods reserve him for some people more fortunate that they cherish, and for whom they wish to renew the golden age."

Telemachus, while he was going nightly to visit the quarters of the camp as a precaution against Adrastus' ruses, heard these praises, which were not suspect of flattery like those that flatterers often give in front of princes, assuming they have neither modesty nor delicateness and one only has to praise them without measure to capture their favor. The son of Odysseus could only appreciate that which was true; he could not tolerate praises other than those which were given of him in private, far from him, and that he truly merited. His heart was not insensitive to them. He felt that pleasure so sweet and so pure that the gods have attached to virtue alone, and that the wicked, for want of having experienced it, can neither conceive of nor believe in. But he did not abandon himself to this pleasure. Instantly, all the errors he had made crowded into his mind. He did not forget his innate haughtiness and his indifference toward men. He had a secret shame of being born so harsh, yet appearing so human.

He gave back to wise Athena all the glory that was given to him and that he did not believe to merit himself. "It is you," he said, "O great goddess, who gave Mentor to me in order to instruct me and to correct my poor nature. It is you who gives me the wisdom to profit from my errors in order to distrust myself. It is you who holds back my impetuous passions. It is you who causes me to feel the pleasure of relieving the unfortunate—without you, I would be hated and worthy of being so; without you, I would make irreparable errors; I would be like a child, who, not sensing his weakness, quits his mother and tumbles at the first step."

~

Nestor and Philoctetes were astounded to see Telemachus become so gentle, so attentive to oblige men, so officious, so helpful, so ingenious with regard to anticipating needs. They did not know what to think. They no longer recognized in him the same man. What surprised them more was the care he took of Hippias' funeral. He went himself to retrieve his bloody and disfigured body from the spot where it was hidden under a pile of corpses. He shed pious tears over him, saying, "O great shade, you now know how much I esteemed your valor! It is true that your pride provoked me, but your faults came from an ardent youth. I know how much this age needs one to forgive it. We would have been genuinely united afterward. I was wrong for my part. O gods, why rob me of him before I could have forced him to love me?"

Afterward, Telemachus had the body washed in fragrant liqueurs, then by his order they prepared a pyre. The tall firs, groaning under the blows of the ax, fall, rolling from the top of the mountains. The oaks, those old children of the Earth, who seem to threaten the skies, tall poplars, elms, whose heads are so green and adorned with a thick foliage, beech trees, which are the honor of the forests, tumble onto the banks of the river Galesus. There rises up with orderliness a pyre that resembles a regular building. The flame begins to appear. A swirl of smoke ascends to the sky.

The Lacedaemonians advance with a slow and lugubrious step, holding their pikes reversed and their eyes downcast. Bitter pain is painted on those faces so fierce, and tears flow abundantly. Then, they saw Pherecides coming, old man less beaten-down by the number of years than by the pain of surviving Hippias, whom he had raised since his childhood. He lifted his hands and his eyes bathed in tears toward the sky. Since Hippias' death, he had refused all nourishment. Sweet Sleep could neither weigh down his eyelids nor suspend for a moment his searing pain. He marched with a trembling step, following the crowd and not knowing where he was going.

No word left his lips, for his heart was too gripped by pain; it was a silence of despair and despondence. But when he saw the pyre lit, he suddenly appeared furious, and he cried out, "O Hippias, Hippias, I will no longer see you! Hippias is no more, and I still live! O my dear Hippias, it is me, cruel, pitiless me, who taught you to scorn Death. I believed that your hands would close my eyes, and that you would gather my last sigh. O cruel gods, you prolong my life to have me see the death of Hippias! O dear child whom I nurtured and who cost me so many cares, I will see you no more! But I will see your mother, who will die of sadness while reproaching me for your death. I will see your young wife striking her breast, pulling out her hair, and I will be the cause of it. O dear shade! Call me onto the banks of the Styx. The light is odious to me. It is you alone, my dear Hippias, who I want to see again. Hippias, Hippias, O my dear Hippias! I still live only to render the last rites to your ashes."

Meanwhile, they saw the body of young Hippias laid out as they bore him in a coffin ornamented with purple, gold, and silver. Death, which had extinguished his eyes, had not been able to blot out all his beauty, and the Graces were still half-painted on his pale face. They saw floating round his neck, whiter than snow but leaning on his shoulder, his long black hair—more beautiful than that of Atys or Ganymede—which was going to be reduced to ashes. They noticed in his side the deep wound through which all his blood had flowed, and had caused him to descend into the gloomy kingdom of Hades.

Telemachus, sad and despondent, followed the body closely and tossed flowers to it. When they had arrived at the pyre, the young son of Odysseus could not watch the flame penetrating the cloth that wrapped the body without shedding new tears.

"Farewell," he said, "O magnanimous Hippias! for I dare not call you my friend. Be at peace, O shade who merited so much glory. If I did not love you, I would envy your good fortune. You are delivered from the miseries where we still are, and you have left them by the most glorious path. Alas, how happy I would be to end the same. May the Styx not stop your shade, may the Elysian Fields be open to it, may winged Rumor preserve your name throughout the centuries, and may your ashes rest in peace."

Barely had he said these words, intermingled with sighs, when the entire army heaved a cry. They were touched by Hippias, of whom they recounted great deeds and the pain of his death, recalling all his good qualities, and forgetting the faults that an impetuous youth and a poor education had imparted to him. Yet they were even more touched by the tender sentiments of Telemachus.

"Is this," they were saying, "that young Greek so proud, so haughty, so disdainful, so intractable? Here he is, grown gentle, humane, tender. Undoubtedly, Athena, who so loved his father, loves him too. Undoubtedly, she made the most precious gift to him that the gods can make to men in giving him, along with wisdom, a heart sensitive to friendship."

The body was already consumed by the flames. Telemachus himself doused the still-steaming ashes with perfumed liquors. Then he had them put into a golden urn that he rimmed with flowers, and he carried that urn to Phalanthus. This man was stretched out, pierced with various wounds, and, in his extreme weakness, he glimpsed near him the gloomy Gates of the Underworld.

Traumaphile and Nosophugus, sent by the son of Odysseus, had already given him all the aids of their art. They recalled, little by little, his soul ready to soar. New spirits were gradually bringing him back to life; a gentle and penetrating force, a balm of life, was insinuating itself from vein to vein to the depths of his heart. An agreeable warmth stole him from the icy hands of Death. At that moment, the stupor ceasing, grief followed. He began to feel the loss of his brother, which he had not, until then, been in a state to feel.

"Alas," he said, "why do they take such great care to make me live? Would it not be better for me to die and follow my dear Hippias? I saw him perish right alongside me. O Hippias, the sweetness of my life, my brother, my dear brother, you are no more. I will no longer be able to see you, nor hear you, nor embrace you, nor tell you my troubles, nor console you in yours. O gods, enemies of men! There is no longer any Hippias for me. Is it possible? But is it not a dream? No, it is only too true. O Hippias, I lost you.

I saw you die, and I must still live as long as necessary to avenge you. I want to sacrifice to your mānes cruel Adrastus, stained with your blood."

While Phalanthus was speaking so, the two divine men tried to ease his grief for fear that it would increase his aches and impede the effect of the remedies. Suddenly, he spied Telemachus, who appeared before him. At first, his heart was fighting two opposing passions. He held onto the resentment from all that had passed between Telemachus and Hippias. The grief from the loss of Hippias rendered this resentment even more acute. On the other hand, he could not ignore that he owed the preservation of his life to Telemachus, who had pulled him, bloody and half dead, from the hands of Adrastus. But when he saw the golden urn where the ashes, so dear, of his brother Hippias were contained, he shed a torrent of tears; he immediately embraced Telemachus, unable to speak to him, and finally said to him in a listless voice, choked off by sobs, "Worthy son of Odysseus, your virtue forces me to love you. I owe you the remainder of this life that is going to be extinguished, but I owe you something that is even more dear to me. Without you, the body of my brother would have been the prey of vultures. Without you, his shade, deprived of sepulcher, would have roamed unhappily on the banks of the Styx, forever repulsed by the merciless Charon. Must I owe so much to a man whom I hated so? O gods, reward him, and deliver me from a life so wretched! As for you, O Telemachus, render me the last rites that you rendered my brother, so that your glory lacks for nothing."

At these words, Phalanthus remained exhausted and beaten-down by an excess of pain. Telemachus took up a position alongside him, without daring to speak to him and waited until he regained his strength. Soon Phalanthus, rallying from this faint, took the urn from Telemachus' hands, kissed it several times, wet it with his tears, and said, "O cherished, O precious ashes, when will mine be contained with you in this same urn? O shade of Hippias, I am following you into the Underworld. Telemachus will avenge us both."

Meanwhile, Phalanthus' aches diminished day by day through the care of the two men who had the science of Asclepius. Telemachus was unceasingly with them alongside the patient so as to render them more attentive to advancing his healing, and the entire army admired the heartfelt goodness with which he helped his greatest enemy even more than the valor and wisdom he demonstrated in saving, in battle, the army of the allies.

At the same time, Telemachus showed himself to be tireless in the roughest travails of war. He slept little, and his sleep was often interrupted either by the warnings that he received at all hours of the night as in the day, or by the rounds he made to every quarter of the camp, which he never did twice at the same hour so as to better surprise those who were not as vigilant. He often came back to his tent covered with sweat and dust. His nourishment was plain, and he lived like the soldiers in order to set the example of sobriety and patience. The army having few rations in this camp, Telemachus judged it suitable to stop the grumbling of the soldiers by voluntarily enduring the same inconveniences as they. His body, far from weakening from a life so arduous, strengthened and hardened each day. He was beginning to lose those tender charms that are like the flower of early youth. His complexion became more tanned and less delicate, his limbs less soft and more muscular.

End of Book XIII

THE ADVENTURES OF
TELEMACHUS
SON OF ODYSSEUS

BOOK XIV

Meanwhile, *Adrastus*, whose troops had been considerably weakened in combat, had withdrawn behind the Aulon mountain to await various reinforcements and to try to surprise his enemies again, like a hungry lion, who, having been put off by a sheepfold, turns back into the somber forest and reenters his cavern where he sharpens his teeth and his claws, awaiting the favorable moment to slay the whole flock.

Telemachus, having taken care to put in place an exacting discipline throughout the camp, no longer thought of anything but executing a plan that he had conceived and that he concealed from all the chiefs of the army. For a long time, he was agitated during the night by dreams that portrayed his father Odysseus to him. This dear image always came back at the end of the night, before Dawn came to chase from the skies with her nascent fires the inconstant stars, and from the earth sweet Sleep trailed by flitting Dreams. At times, he believed he saw Odysseus nude, on a happy island, on the banks of a river, in a meadow adorned with flowers and surrounded by nymphs, who were tossing him garments to cover himself; at times, he believed he heard him speaking in a palace resplendent with gold and ivory, where men crowned with flowers were listening to him with pleasure and admiration. Often, Odysseus would suddenly appear to him at feasts, where joy burst forth amidst the delights and where one heard the tender harmony of a voice along with a lyre sweeter than the lyre of Apollo and all the voices of the Muses.

Telemachus, awakening, was saddened by those dreams so agreeable. "O my father, O my dear father Odysseus," he cried out, "the most dreadful dreams would be sweeter to me! These images of felicity lead me to believe that you have already descended into the resting place of blissful souls, whose virtue the gods reward with an eternal tranquility. I believe I see the Elysian Fields. O how cruel it is to no longer hope. What then, O my dear father, I will never see you! Never will I embrace the one who loved me so and whom I seek with so much difficulty. Never will I hear that mouth speak, from which wisdom came! Never will I kiss those hands, those dear hands, those victorious hands, which slew so many enemies! They will not punish the foolish suitors of Penelope, and Ithaca will never rise again from its ruin! O gods, enemies of my father, you send me these sinister dreams to wrench all hope from my heart. It is to wrench life from me. No, I can no longer live in this uncertainty.

"What am I saying! Alas! I am only too certain that my father is no more. I am going to seek his shade as far as the Underworld. Theseus indeed descended there, Theseus, that impious man who wanted to outrage the infernal deities, and me, I am going there, driven by piety. Heracles descended there. I am not Heracles, but it is a fine thing to dare to imitate him. Indeed, through the story of his misfortunes, Orpheus touched the heart of that god whom they depict as inexorable. He procured from him the return of Eurydice among the living. I am more worthy of compassion than Orpheus, for my loss is greater. Who would be able to compare a young girl like a hundred others to the wise Odysseus, admired by all of Greece? Come now! We die if we must—why fear Death when one suffers so in life? O Hades, O Persephone, I will soon experience whether you are as pitiless as they say! O my father, after having crossed over lands and seas in vain to find you, I am finally going to see if you are in the gloomy domain of the dead. If the gods refuse my possessing you on earth, in the light of the sun, perhaps they will not refuse me seeing your shade at least in the kingdom of the night."

Saying these words, Telemachus soaked his bed with his tears. Straightaway, he rose and sought, by the light, to ease the searing pain those dreams had caused him. But it was an arrow that had pierced his heart and that he carried with him everywhere.

~

In that pain, he undertook to descend to the Underworld through a famous spot not too distant from the camp. They called it Acherontia because there was, in that spot, a dreadful cavern through which one descended onto the banks of the Acheron, by which even the gods fear to swear. The city was on a cliff, posed like a nest at the top of a tree. At the foot of that cliff was found the cavern, which timid mortals dared not approach. Shepherds attended to turn their flocks away from it. The sulfuric vapor from the Stygian marsh unceasingly exhaled through this opening, causing the air to reek. All around neither grass nor flowers grew. One never felt the gentle zephyrs there, nor the nascent charms of springtime, nor the rich gifts of autumn. The arid land languished there.

One only saw there some barren brushes and macabre cypresses. For a distance all around even, Demeter refused her golden crops to the plowmen; Dionysus seemed to promise his sweet fruits in vain, the clusters of grapes shriveling instead of ripening. The sad Naiads did not make a clear water flow: their currents were always bitter and cloudy. Birds never sang in this land bristling with brambles and thorns, and they found no grove in which to retreat. They went to sing their love songs under a gentler sky. One only heard the cawing of crows and the lugubrious voice of the owls. Even the grass was bitter there, and the flocks that grazed it did not feel the sweet joy that made them leap. The bull fled the heifer, and the shepherd, dejected, forgot about his musette and his flute.

From that cave emanated, from time to time, a thick black smoke that caused a kind of night to descend in the middle of the day. Then the neighboring peoples redoubled their sacrifices to appease the infernal deities. But often men in their prime and in their most tender youth were the only victims that those cruel deities took pleasure in sacrificing through a calamitous contagion.

It is there that Telemachus resolved to search for the path to the gloomy dwelling of Hades. Athena, who watched over him unceasingly, and who covered him with her aegis, had rendered Hades favorable to him. Even Zeus, at the prayer of Athena, had commanded Hermes—who descended each day to the Underworld to deliver a certain number of dead to Charon— to tell the king of the shades that he would allow the son of Odysseus to enter into his empire.

Telemachus steals away from the camp during the night. He walks by the light of the moon, and he invokes that mighty deity who—being in the sky the shining star of the night, and on earth the chaste Artemis—is in the Underworld, the redoubtable Hecate. This deity listened favorably to his wishes because his heart was pure, and he was driven by the pious love that a son owes his father.

No sooner was he alongside the entrance of the cavern than he heard the subterranean empire bellow. The ground trembled under his feet. The sky armed itself with lightning and fire that seemed to fall to earth. The young son of Odysseus felt his heart stirred and his whole body was covered with an icy sweat, but his courage sustained him. He lifted his eyes and hands to the sky.

"Great gods," he cried out, "I accept these presages which I believe happy ones. Complete your work."

He spoke, and redoubling his steps, he boldly presented himself. Immediately, the thick smoke, which rendered the opening of the cavern fatal to all animals as soon as they approached it, dissipated.

The poisonous odor ceased for a short time. Telemachus enters alone, for what other mortal would have dared to follow him? Two Cretans, who had accompanied him up to a certain distance from the cavern, and to whom he had confided his plan, remained trembling and half-dead somewhat far from there in a temple, making vows and no longer hoping to see Telemachus again.

Meanwhile, the son of Odysseus, sword in hand, plunges into the terrifying darkness. Soon he perceives a weak and gloomy light such as one sees during the night on Earth. He notices light shades flitting round him, and he scatters them with his sword. Then he sees the sad banks of the marshy river, whose muddy and dormant water only formed eddies. He beheld on that bank a countless horde of dead deprived of sepulcher, who present themselves in vain to the merciless Charon. This god, whose eternal old age is always sad and sorrowful, yet full of vigor, threatens them, repulses them, and admits aboard his craft the young Greek. Entering, Telemachus hears the wails of a shade who could not console himself.

"What is then," he said to him, "your misfortune? Who were you on Earth?"

"I was," this shade answered, "Nabopharsan, king of superb Babylon. All the peoples of the East trembled at the mere sound of my name. I had myself venerated by the Babylonians in a temple of marble, where I was represented by a statue of gold before which they burned night and day the most precious perfumes of Ethiopia. Never did anyone dare to contradict me without being punished straightaway. Each day, they invented new pleasures to render life more delightful to me. I was still young and robust. Alas, what prosperities still remained for me to enjoy on the throne! But a woman whom I loved, who did not love me, indeed made me feel that I was not a god; she poisoned me. I am no longer anything. Yesterday, my ashes were put into a golden urn with pomp. They wept, they pulled out their hair, they pretended to want to throw themselves into the flames of my pyre to die with me. They still go to wail at the foot of the superb tomb where my ashes were placed, but no one laments me. The memory of me is horrifying even to my family, and here below, I already suffer horrific treatment."

Telemachus, touched by this spectacle, said to him, "Were you truly happy during your reign? Did you feel that sweet peace, without which the heart always remains gripped and withered in the midst of delights?"

"No," answered the Babylonian. "I do not even know what you mean. Wise men vaunt that peace as the only good. As for me, I never felt it. My heart was unceasingly agitated by new desires, fear, and expectation. I tried to distract myself by stirring my passions. I attended to maintain this intoxication so as to make it continual. The least interval of tranquil reason would have been too bitter to me. There, you see, that is the peace that I possessed. Every other appeared a fable and a dream to me. There, you see, those are the good things that I lament."

As he was speaking so, the Babylonian wept like a cowardly man who had been softened through prosperity, and who is not accustomed to constantly bearing a misfortune. He had alongside him some slaves that had been executed in order to honor his funeral service. Hermes had delivered them to Charon along with their king and had given them an absolute power over this king whom they had served on Earth. Those shades of slaves no longer feared the shade of Nabopharsan. They held him shackled and inflicted the cruelest indignities on him. One said to him, "Were we not men as well as you? How were you foolish enough to believe yourself a god, and was it not necessary to remind yourself that you were of the race of other men?"

Another, to insult him, said, "You were right in not wanting to be taken for a man, for you were a monster without humanity."

Another said to him, "Well! Where are your flatterers now? You no longer have anything to give, wretch. You can no longer do any harm. Here you are, having become a slave to your very slaves. The gods have been slow to do justice, but in the end they do it."

At these harsh words, Nabopharsan threw himself face down on the ground, tearing out his hair in an excess of rage and despair. But Charon said to the slaves, "Pull him up by his chain. Lift him up despite himself; he will not even have the consolation of hiding his shame. All the shades of the Styx must be witnesses to it in order to justify the gods who tolerated this unbeliever reigning on Earth for so long. It is only now, O Babylonian, that your pains begin. Prepare yourself to be judged by the inflexible Minos, judge of the Underworld."

During this speech of the terrifying Charon, the craft was already touching the bank of the empire of Hades. All the shades came running to consider this living man, who appeared amongst the dead on the craft. But at the moment when Telemachus set foot on land they fled, like the shadows of the night that the least light of day dissipates. Charon, displaying to the young Greek a brow less wrinkled and eyes less fierce than usual, said to him, "Mortal, cherished by the gods, since they have given you entry into this kingdom of the night, inaccessible to other living souls, hasten to go where the destinies call you. Go, by this somber trail, to the palace of Hades, whom you will find on his throne. He will permit you entry into the places of which he has forbidden me to reveal the secret to you."

Straightaway, Telemachus moves forward with great strides. He sees on all sides shades flitting, more numerous than the grains of sand that cover the shores of the sea, and in the agitation of that infinite multitude he is gripped by a divine horror, observing the profound silence of those vast spaces. His hair stands on end when he lands in the dark dwelling of merciless Hades. He feels his knees buckling, his speech fails him, and it is with difficulty that he can utter these words to the god:

"You see, O terrifying deity, the son of the unfortunate Odysseus. I come to ask you if my father has descended into your empire or if he is still roaming the Earth."

Hades was on a throne of ebony. His face was pale and severe, his eyes hollow and gleaming, his brow wrinkled and menacing. The sight of a living man was odious to him, just as the light offends the eyes of animals accustomed to only coming out of their retreats during the night. At his side appeared Persephone who alone attracted his regard, and who seemed to soften his heart a bit. She possessed a beauty forever fresh. But she appeared to have combined with those divine charms something of the harshness and cruelty of her spouse.

At the foot of the throne was Death, pale and devouring, with his sharp scythe that he unceasingly sharpened. Round him flitted Dark Worries; cruel Distrusts; Vengeances, all disgusting with blood and covered with cuts; unjust Hates; Avarice, gnawing at herself; Despair, ripping herself apart with her own hands; fanatical Ambition, upending everything; Betrayal, wanting to feast on blood and only able to savor the evils she has done; Envy, spilling her mortal venom round her, and twisting, enraged, in her impotence to do harm; Impiety, who hollows out a bottomless abyss where she hopelessly flings herself; hideous Specters, phantoms who represent the dead to terrorize the living; frightful Dreams; Insomnias as cruel as sad dreams—all these sinister images surrounded proud Hades and filled the palace where he dwells. He answered Telemachus in a low voice that made the depths of Erebus groan.

"Young mortal, the destinies had you violate this sacred asylum of the shades. Follow your high destiny. I will not tell you where your father is. It suffices that you are free to seek him. Since he was a king on Earth, you only have to pass through from one side, the area of the gloomy Tartarus, where wicked kings are punished, and on the other, the Elysian Fields, where good kings are rewarded. But you can only go from here to the Elysian Fields after having passed through the Tartarus. Hasten to go and get out of my empire."

Instantly, Telemachus seems to fly through those empty and vast spaces so much does he long to know if he will see his father, and he wants to distance himself from the horrible presence of the tyrant who holds in fear the living and the dead. He soon spies near him the gloomy Tartarus. A thick and dark smoke was emanating from it, the pestilent odor of which would bring death if it spread into the domain of the living. This smoke blanketed a river of fire and swirls of flame, the noise of which, like that of the most impetuous mountain streams when they plunge from the highest cliffs into the depths of the abysses, made it so that nothing could be heard distinctly in these grim places.

Telemachus, secretly animated by Athena, fearlessly enters into this pit. Immediately, he spots a great number of men who had lived in the lowest classes and who were being punished for having sought riches through fraud, treason, and cruelties.

He noticed many impious hypocrites who, pretending to love religion, used it only as a fine pretext to satisfy their ambition and to toy with credulous men. These men, who had abused virtue itself—even though it is the greatest gift of the gods—were punished as the most heinous of all men. Children who had slain their fathers and mothers, wives who had dipped their hands in the blood of their husbands, traitors who had delivered over their homelands after having violated every oath would suffer pains less cruel than these hypocrites. The three judges of the Underworld desired it so, and here is their reasoning: it is that hypocrites are not content in being wicked, like the rest of impious men; they still want to pass for good, and, through their false virtue, they make it so that men no longer dare to trust in the true. The gods, whom they mocked, and whom they rendered despicable to men, take pleasure in using all their might to avenge their insults.

Alongside these hypocrites appeared other men, whom the common man would hardly think culpable, and who divine vengeance pursues mercilessly. They are the ingrates, the liars, the flatterers who have lauded vice, the malignant critics who have tried to sully the purest virtue, lastly, those who have rashly judged things without knowing them in depth and who, in so doing, have harmed the reputation of the innocent. But, among all these ingrates, the one who is punished as the blackest is the one who comes down against the gods.

"What then!" Minos said. "One passes for a monster when he lacks gratitude for his father or a friend, from whom he received some help, and one is glorified for being ungrateful toward the gods, from whom he has life and every good that comes from it? Does one not owe his birth to them more than to the father and mother from whom he was born? The more all those crimes are unpunished and excused on Earth, the more they are in the Underworld the object of an implacable vengeance, from which nothing escapes."

Telemachus, seeing the three judges who were seated, and who were condemning a man, dared to ask them what his crimes were. Quickly, the condemned, speaking up, cried out, "I have never done any evil. I put all my pleasure into doing good. I was magnificent, open-handed, just, compassionate. What, then, can one reproach me for?"

Then Minos said to him, "You are reproached for nothing with regard to men, but did you not owe less to men than to the gods? What is, then, this justice of which you boast? You failed in no obligation to men, who are nothing. You were virtuous, but you related all your virtue to yourself and not to the gods who had given it to you, for you wanted to enjoy the fruit of your own virtue and confine it to yourself. You were your deity. But the gods, who created everything and who created nothing but for themselves, cannot renounce their rights. You forgot them. They will forget you. They will deliver you over to yourself, since you wanted to be yours and not theirs. Seek therefore now, if you can, your consolation in your own heart. Here you are, forever separated from the men you wanted to please. Here you are, alone with yourself, who was your idol. Learn that there is no true virtue without the respect and love for the gods, to whom all is owed. Your false virtue, which has long dazzled men easy to deceive, will be confounded. Men, only judging vices and virtues by what shocks them or by what conveniences them, are blind not only about good but about evil. Here, a divine light upends all their superficial judgments. It often condemns what they admire and justifies what they condemn."

At these words, this philosopher, as if struck by a lightning bolt, can not bear himself. The complacency that he had once had in contemplating his moderation, his courage, and his generous inclinations changes into despair. The sight of his own heart, enemy of the gods, becomes his torture. He sees himself and he cannot cease seeing himself. He sees the vanity of the judgments of men, whom he had wanted to please in all his deeds. It causes a total revolution within him, as if all his entrails are turned upside-down. He no longer finds himself the same; all support is lacking in his heart. His conscience, the testimony of which had been so sweet to him, rises up against him and bitterly reproaches him for the waywardness and the delusion of all his virtues, which did not have the worship of the divine as the principal and final end. He is distressed, dismayed, filled with shame, remorse, and despair.

The Furies do not torment him because it suffices for them to have delivered him over to himself, and that his own heart avenged enough the scorned gods. He seeks the gloomiest places to hide from the other dead, unable to hide from himself. He seeks the darkness and cannot find it. An importune light pursues him everywhere. Everywhere, the piercing rays of Truth go to avenge the truth that he neglected to follow. All that he has loved becomes odious to him, as being the source of his woes, which can never end. He says to himself, *O fool! So, I knew neither the gods, nor men, nor myself! No, I knew nothing, since I never loved the one and true good. My every step was wayward; my wisdom was only madness; my virtue was only an impious and blind pridefulness. I was myself my idol.*

Finally, Telemachus spied the kings who were condemned for having abused their power. On one side, an avenging Fury was presenting a mirror to them that reflected all the deformity of their vices to them; there they saw and could not stop seeing their crude vanity and avidity for the most ridiculous praises, their harshness with regard to men, whose felicity they were obliged to make, their insensitivity to virtue, their fear of hearing the truth, their inclination for cowardly and flattering men, their distractedness, their softness, their indolence, their misplaced distrust, their splendor and their excessive magnificence founded on the ruin of the peoples, their ambition to attain a little vainglory with the blood of their citizens and, lastly, their cruelty that seeks each day new delights among the tears and despair of so many wretches. They saw themselves unceasingly in this mirror. They found themselves more horrible and more monstrous than either the Chimera vanquished by Bellerophon, or the Hydra of Lerna slain by Heracles, or even Cerberus, though he vomits from his three bleating maws a black and venomous blood, which is capable of infecting the entire race of living mortals on Earth.

At the same time, on the other side, another Fury insultingly repeated to them all the praises their flatterers had given them during their lifetime and presented another mirror to them, in which they saw themselves as the flattery had depicted them. The opposition of those two portraits so contrary was the torture for their vanity. One noticed that the most wicked among those kings were those who had been given the most magnificent praises during their lifetime, because the wicked are more feared than the good, and they immodestly demand the most craven flatteries of the poets and orators of their time.

One hears them wailing in those dark shadows, where they can only see the insults and the derisions which they have to suffer. They have nothing around them that does not repulse them, that does not contradict them, that does not confound them; whereas on Earth they toyed with the lives of men and claimed that all was created in order to serve them, in Tartarus, they are delivered over to all the caprices of certain slaves who make them feel, in their turn, a cruel servitude. They serve with pain, and there remains no hope to them of ever being able to ease their captivity. They are, under the blows of these slaves, who have become their merciless tyrants, like an anvil under the strikes of the Cyclops' hammers, when Hephaestus presses them to work in the blazing furnaces of Mount Etna.

There, Telemachus makes out pale, hideous, and dismayed faces. It is a black sadness that gnaws at these criminals. They are horrified with themselves and can no more deliver themselves from this horror than from their own nature. They need no other punishment for their transgressions than their transgressions themselves. They see them unceasingly in all their enormity; they appear before them as horrible specters. They pursue them. To save themselves from them, they seek a death more powerful than that which separated them from their bodies. In the despair where they find themselves, they call to their rescue a death that can extinguish all feeling and all consciousness in them. They ask for the abysses to engulf them to rid themselves of the vengeful rays of Truth, which persecutes them. But they are reserved for a vengeance trickling down on them, drip by drip, that will never go dry.

Truth, which they had feared seeing, makes their torment. They see it and only have eyes to see it rising up against them. The sight of it pierces them, rips them apart, tears them from themselves. It is like the lightning bolt. Without destroying anything on the outside, it penetrates to the depths of the bowels. Like metal in a blazing furnace, the soul is melted by that avenging fire. It leaves nothing of consistence, yet it consumes nothing. It dissolves down to the first principles of life, and one cannot die. One is torn from oneself. One can no longer find either support or repose for a single instant. One no longer lives but through the rage one has against oneself and through a loss of all hope, which brings madness.

Among those sights that made Telemachus' hair stand on end, he saw several former kings of Lydia who were punished for having preferred the delights of a soft life to the work that must be inseparable from kingship in order to relieve the peoples.

These kings were reproaching each other for their blindness. One said to another who had been his son, "Did I not recommend to you often, during my old age, and before my death, to mend the evils I had done through my negligence?"

The son answered, "O wretched father, it is you who ruined me. It is your example that accustomed me to splendor, to pridefulness, to voluptuousness, to harshness toward men. In seeing you reign with so much softness, with so many craven flatterers around you, I was accustomed to loving flattery and pleasures. I believed that the rest of men were, with regard to kings, what horses and other beasts of burden are with regard to men; that is to say, animals to which one attaches importance only to the extent they render services and they give comfort and convenience. I believed it. It is you who made me believe it, and now I suffer so many woes for having imitated you."

To these reproaches they added the most dreadful curses and appeared animated with rage to rip each other apart.

Around those kings still flitted, like owls in the night, cruel Suspicions; vain Alarms; Distrusts who avenge the peoples for the harshness of their kings; Avarice, the insatiable thirst for riches; False Glory, ever tyrannical; and craven Softness that redoubles all the woes one suffers without ever being able to give solid pleasure.

One saw several of those kings severely punished, not for the evils they had done but for the good they should have done. All the crimes against the peoples that came from the negligence with which the laws were observed were imputed to the kings, who must only reign in order that the laws reign through their ministry. Also imputed to them was all the disorders that come from splendor, luxury, and all the other excesses that hurl men into a violent state, and into the temptation to scorn the laws in order to acquire possessions. Above all, they treated rigorously the kings who, instead of being good and vigilant pastors of the peoples, had only thought to ravage the flocks like devouring wolves.

But what dismayed Telemachus even more, it was seeing in this abyss of darkness and woes a great number of kings who had passed on Earth for fairly good kings. They had been condemned to the pains of Tartarus for having allowed themselves to be governed by wicked and artful men. They were punished for the evils that they had allowed done through their authority. Moreover, most of these kings had been neither good nor wicked, so much as their weakness had been great. They had never feared not knowing the truth; they had not had a taste for virtue and had not put their pleasure in doing good.

When Telemachus got out of those places, he felt relieved, as if a mountain had been lifted off his chest. He understood, by this relief, the wretchedness of those who were confined there without hope of ever getting out. He was horrified to see how much more rigorously kings were tormented than other culprits. *What then!* he said, *so many duties, so many perils, so many traps, so many difficulties involved in knowing the truth in order to protect oneself against others and against oneself. In the end, so many horrible torments in the Underworld after having been so agitated, so envied, so double-crossed in one short life. O fool, the one who seeks to reign! Happy the one who is confined to a private and peaceful station, where virtue is less difficult!*

Reflecting so, he was distressed within. He shuddered and fell into a dismay that made him feel something of the despair of those wretches whom he had just considered. But, as he distanced himself from that sad domain of darkness, horror and despair, his courage began, little by little, to be reborn. He breathed and already glimpsed in the distance the gentle and pure light of the resting place of the heroes.

There dwelt all the good kings who had, up until then, governed men wisely. They were separated from the rest of the just. As the wicked princes suffered in Tartarus infinitely more rigorous tortures than the other guilty of a private station, so did the good kings enjoy in the Elysian Fields a happiness infinitely greater than that of the rest of men who had loved virtue on Earth.

Telemachus advanced toward those kings, who were in fragrant groves on evergreen and blooming lawns. A thousand tiny brooks of a clear water flowed through these beautiful places and caused a delightful coolness to be felt there. An infinite number of birds made these groves resound with their sweet song. One saw the flowers of spring sprouting underfoot, together with the richest fruits of autumn hanging from the trees. There, never did one feel the blazing heat of the relentless dog days of summer; there, never did the dark Northwinds dare to blow, nor make the rigors of winter felt. Neither bloodthirsty War, nor cruel Envy, who bites with a venomous tooth and wears vipers entwined round her breasts and around her arms, nor Jealousies, nor Distrusts, nor Fear, nor vain Desires ever approach this happy resting place of peace. The day does not end there, and night, with its shadowy veils, is unknown.

A pure and gentle light radiates around the bodies of these just men and surrounds them with its rays like a vestment. This light is not like the somber light that gleams in the eyes of wretched mortals yet is only darkness. It is more of a celestial glory than a light; it penetrates more subtly the thickest bodies than the rays of the sun penetrate the purest crystal; it never dazzles—on the contrary, it fortifies the eyes and carries into the depths of the soul an indescribable serenity. It is from this light alone that these blissful men are nourished. It emerges from them, and it enters into them; it penetrates them and incorporates itself in them like food incorporates itself in us. They see it, they feel it, they breathe it, and it causes to be born in them an endless source of peace and joy. They are plunged into this abyss of joy like fish into the sea. They no longer desire anything. They have everything without having anything, for this taste of pure light appeases the hunger of their hearts, all their desires are sated, and their plenitude elevates them above all that which men, empty and starving, seek on Earth.

All the delights that surround them are nothing to them, because their overflowing bliss, which comes from within, leaves

BOOK XIV

them no sentiment for all that they see of delights without. They are like the gods who, sated with nectar and ambrosia, would not deign to nourish themselves on the coarse meats that one would present to them at the most exquisite table of mortal men.

All woes flee far from these tranquil places. Death, Malady, Poverty, Pain, Regrets, Remorse, Fears, even Hopes—which often exact as many difficulties as Fears—Divisions, Disgusts, Spites can have no entry here. The high mountains of Thrace that split the clouds with their brow, covered in snow and ice since the origin of the world, would be upended from their foundations, set down at the center of the Earth, before the hearts of these just men could even be stirred. They only pity the miseries that crush men living in the world, but it is a gentle and peaceful pity that distorts none of their immutable bliss. An eternal youth, an everlasting bliss, a wholly divine glory are painted on their faces, but their joy has nothing of coltish antics nor indecency. It is a gentle joy, noble, full of majesty. It is a sublime taste for truth and virtue that transports them. They remain without interruption, at every moment, in the same heart-stopping joy of a mother who sees her dear son again, whom she had thought dead, but this joy that soon slips away from the mother never flees from the hearts of these men; never does it languish for an instant; it is always renewing in them. They know the elation of intoxication without the trouble or blindness of it.

They talk about what they see and what they enjoy. They trample underfoot the effete delights and vain grandeurs of their former stations which they deplore. They gladly revisit those sad but short years when it was necessary to battle against each other and against the torrent of corrupt men in order to become good. They marvel at the succor of the gods, who led them as if by the hand to virtue through so many perils. A certain divineness unceasingly streams through their hearts, like a torrent of the divinity itself merging with theirs. They see, they enjoy, they are happy, and they feel as if they always will be. They sing all together the praises of the gods, and they are all together but a single voice, a single thought, a single heart. The same bliss ebbs and flows in these merged souls.

In this divine rapture, the centuries flow by more swiftly than hours among mortals, and nevertheless thousands and thousands of centuries flowing past take nothing away from their ever-renewing and ever-complete bliss. They reign all together, not on thrones that the hand of man can topple, but within themselves with an immutable power, for they no longer need to be formidable through a might borrowed from a vile and destitute people. They no longer wear those vain diadems, the brilliance of which hides so many Fears and Dark Worries. The gods themselves have crowned them with their own hands with crowns that nothing can sully.

Telemachus, who was seeking his father and who had feared finding him in these beautiful places, was so seized with this taste of peace and bliss that he would have wanted to find Odysseus there, and he was afflicted himself to be compelled to return afterward to the company of mortals. *It is here,* he said, *that true life is found, and ours is only a death.*

But what astonished him was having seen so many kings punished in Tartarus and seeing so few of them in the Elysian

BOOK XIV

Fields. He realized that there are few kings steadfast enough and courageous enough to resist their own might and to reject the flattery of so many people who excite all their passions. So, good kings are very rare, and most are so wicked that the gods would not be just if, after having tolerated their abuse of power during their life, they did not punish them after their deaths.

Telemachus, not seeing his father Odysseus among all these kings, sought at least the eyes of the divine Laertes, his grandfather. While he was uselessly seeking him, a venerable old man, full of majesty, approached him. His old age did not resemble that of men whom the weight of their years stoop on Earth. One only saw that he had been old before his death. It was a mixture of everything that old age has of gravity with all the charms of youth, for those charms bloom again even in the most broken-down old men at the moment when they are admitted into the Elysian Fields. This man advanced eagerly and regarded Telemachus with complaisance, as someone very dear to him. Telemachus, who did not recognize him, was at a loss and in suspense.

"I forgive you, O my dear son," the old man said, "for not recognizing me. I am Arcesius, the father of Laertes. I ended my days a little before Odysseus, my grandson, set out for the siege of Troy. So, you were still a small child then in the arms of your wet nurse. Since then, I have conceived of you great expectations. They were not deceiving, since I see you descended into the kingdom of Hades to seek your father and that the gods support you in this enterprise. O happy child, the gods love you and prepare for you a glory equal to that of your father. O happy me to see you again!

"Cease seeking Odysseus in these places. He still lives and he is preserved in order to raise up our house again on the island of Ithaca. Even Laertes, though the weight of the years has beaten him down, still enjoys the light and awaits his son to return to close his eyes. In this way, men pass like flowers that bloom in the morning and in the evening are wilted and trampled underfoot; generations of men flow by like the currents of a rapid river. Nothing can stop time, which drags along after it all that which appears the most fixed.

"You yourself, O my son, my dear son, you yourself, who now enjoys a youth so vibrant and ripe with pleasures, remember that this beautiful age is only a flower, which will be drying up almost as quickly as it blooms. You will see changing, imperceptibly, the laughing Graces and sweet pleasures that accompany you: fortitude, health, joy will vanish like a beautiful dream; there will only remain to you a sad memory of it. Old age, languishing and hostile to pleasure, will come to wrinkle your face, stoop your body, weaken your limbs, dry up the source of joy in your heart, disgust you with the present, cause you to fear the future, render you numb to everything except pain. This time appears distant to you. Alas, you are mistaken, my son. It hastens. There it is, arrived. What comes with so much swiftness is not far from you, and the present that flees is already far away, since it vanishes in the moment that we are speaking and can no longer approach again. Never count then, my son, on the present, but sustain yourself on the rugged and rough path of virtue through a view to the future.

"Prepare for yourself, through pure mores, and through the love of justice, a place in this happy resting place of peace. Soon, you will finally see your father retake authority in Ithaca. You were born to reign after him, but alas, O my son, how deceptive kingship is! When one regards it from afar, he sees only grandeur, brilliance, and delights. But up close, all is thorny. A private individual can, without dishonor, lead a gentle and obscure life. A king cannot, without dishonoring himself, prefer a gentle and idle life to the arduous functions of government. He owes himself to all the men he governs. He is never allowed to be his own. His least errors are of an infinite consequence, because they cause the unhappiness of the peoples, sometimes for several centuries. He must repress the audacity of the wicked, support innocence, dissipate defamations. It is not enough for him to do no harm; he must do all the possible good of which the state has need. It is not enough to do good oneself; he must even prevent all the evils that others would do if they were not held back. Fear then, my son, fear a condition so perilous; arm yourself with courage against yourself, against your passions, and against flatterers."

Saying these words, Arcesius appeared animated by a divine fire and showed Telemachus a face full of compassion for the woes that accompany kingship. "When kingship is taken on in order to satisfy oneself, it is a monstrous tyranny," he said. "When it is taken on to fulfill obligations and to lead a people, countless in number, just as a father leads his children, it is an overwhelming servitude that demands heroic courage and patience. Also, it is certain that those who have reigned with a sincere virtue possess here all that the power of the gods can give to render their bliss complete."

While Arcesius was speaking so, those words entered deep into Telemachus' heart; they were engraved there, just as an able artisan engraves in bronze with his chisel the indelible figures that he wants to display to the eyes of the most distant posterity. Those wise words were like a subtle flame that penetrated deep inside young Telemachus; he felt stirred and on fire; something of the divine seemed to melt his heart. What he carried into the most intimate part of himself was secretly consuming him. He could neither contain it, nor bear it, nor resist so violent an impact. It was an alive and delightful feeling, which was mixed with a torment capable of wrenching life from him.

Afterward, Telemachus began to breathe more freely. He recognized in Arcesius' face a great resemblance to Laertes. He even believed he vaguely remembered having seen in his father Odysseus traits of this same resemblance when Odysseus set out for the siege of Troy. This memory touched his heart. Sweet tears mixed with joy flowed from his eyes. He wanted to embrace this person so dear. Several times he tried uselessly; this vain shade eluded his embrace, just as a deceiving Dream steals away from the man who believes to possess it. At times the parched mouth of that sleeping man pursues a fugitive water; at times his lips stir to form words that his numb tongue cannot utter. His hands reach out with effort and take nothing. Thus, Telemachus cannot satisfy his affection; he sees Arcesius, he hears him, he speaks to him, he cannot touch him. Finally, he asks him who those men are whom he sees around him.

"You see, my son," the wise old man answered, "the men who have been the ornaments of their centuries: the glory and the happiness of humankind. You see the small number of kings who have been worthy of kingship, and who have faithfully done the work of the gods on Earth. These others whom you see somewhat near them but separated by that small cloud have much less glory; they are heroes, in truth, but the reward for their valor and their military expeditions cannot be compared to that of the wise, just, and beneficent kings. Among these heroes, you see Theseus whose face is a bit sad; he felt the misfortune of being too credulous with an artful woman, and he is still aggrieved in having so unjustly asked Poseidon for the cruel death of his son Hippolytus. He would have been happy had he not been so quick-tempered and so easy to provoke.

"You also see Achilles, leaning on his lance because of that wound he received on his heel at the hand of cowardly Paris, and which ended his life. If he had been as wise, just, and restrained as he was intrepid, the gods would have granted him a long reign. But they had pity on the Phthians and the Dolopes, over whom Achilles should naturally reign after Peleus. They did not want to deliver so many peoples over to the mercy of a man, hot-headed and easier to provoke than the stormiest sea. The Fates shortened the thread of his days; he was like a flower barely budding that the blade of the plow cuts and that droops before the end of the day when one had seen it sprout. The gods only wanted to use him, like the torrents and the tempests, to punish men for their crimes. They used Achilles to tear down the walls of Troy, to avenge the perjury of Laomedon and the unjust amours of Paris. After having so employed that instrument of their vengeances, they were appeased, and they refused the tears of Thetis to allow more time on Earth to this young hero, who was only suitable to trouble men and to overthrow cities and kingdoms.

"But do you see this other with that fierce expression? That is Ajax, son of Telamon and cousin of Achilles. You are not ignorant, undoubtedly, of his glory in combat. After the death of Achilles, he claimed that his arms could not be given to any other person than him. Your father did not believe that they should be ceded to him. The Greeks judged in favor of Odysseus. Ajax killed himself in despair. Indignation and fury are still painted on his face. Do not approach him, my son, for he would only think that you would want to insult him in his misfortune, and he is just to lament it. Do you not notice that he looks at us with difficulty, and that he enters brusquely into that somber grove because we are odious to him? You see on this other side Hector, who would have been invincible had the son of Thetis not been in the world at the same time.

"But there is Agamemnon passing by, who still bears on him the marks of the perfidy of Clytemnestra. O my son, I shudder to think of the misfortunes of that family of the impious Tantalus. The division of the two brothers, Atreus and Thyestes, filled that house with horror and blood. Alas, how much one crime lures others to it! Agamemnon, returning at the head of the Greeks from the siege of Troy, had not had time to enjoy in peace the glory that he had acquired. Such is the destiny of almost all conquerors. All those men whom you see were formidable in war, but they were not lovable and virtuous. Therefore, they are only in the second resting place of the Elysian Fields.

"As for the ones here, they have reigned with justice and have loved their peoples. They are friends of the gods. While Achilles and Agamemnon, full of their quarrels and their fights, still preserve their difficulties and their innate faults here, while they lament in vain the life that they lost, and grieve being only powerless and vain shades, these just kings—being purified by the divine light with which they are nourished—no longer have anything to desire for their happiness. They regard with compassion the restlessness of mortals, and the greatest affairs that agitate ambitious men appear child's play to them. Their hearts are sated with the truth and the virtue they draw from the source. They no longer have anything to suffer themselves: no more desires, no more needs, no more fears—all is ended for them, except their joy, which cannot end.

"Consider, my son, this old king Inachus who founded the kingdom of Argos. You see him with this old age, so sweet and so majestic. Flowers bloom under his feet. His light gait resembles the flight of a bird. He holds in his hand a lyre of ivory, and, in an eternal elation, he sings of the marvels of the gods. There exudes from his heart and from his mouth an exquisite perfume. The harmony of his lyre and voice would delight men and the gods. He is rewarded so for having loved the people that he gathered inside his new walls, and to whom he gave laws.

"On the other side, you can see, between those myrtles, Cecrops the Egyptian, who first reigned in Athens, a city consecrated to the goddess whose name it bears. Cecrops, bringing useful laws from Egypt, which were the source of letters and good mores for Greece, softened the fierce natures of the burgs of Attique and united them through the bonds of society. He was just, humane, compassionate; he left the peoples in abundance and his family in a common state, not wishing that his children would have authority after him, because he judged that others were more worthy of it.

"I must also show you, in this small valley, Erichthonius, who invented the use of silver for money. He did it with a view to facilitate commerce between the islands of Greece. But he foresaw the inconvenience attached to this invention. 'Apply yourselves,' he said to all peoples, 'to multiply at home all the natural riches, which are the true ones. Cultivate the land in order to have a great abundance of wheat, wine, oil, and produce. Have countless flocks that will nourish you with their milk and will cover you with their wool. In so doing, you will put yourself in a state to never fear poverty. The more children you have, the richer you will be, provided that you render them hard working—for the Earth is inexhaustible, and she increases her fruitfulness in proportion to the number of her inhabitants who attend to cultivate her. She pays them all liberally for their troubles, as opposed to becoming miserly and ungrateful to those who cultivate her negligently. Attach yourself, then, principally, to the true riches that satisfy the true needs of man. With regard to coined silver, you must in no case make more of it than is necessary either for the inevitable wars that must be sustained abroad, or for the commerce of necessary merchandise that is lacking in your country.' Still, Erichthonius would have wished that commerce was allowed to wane with regard to all the things that only serve to maintain luxury, vanity, and softness.

"The wise Erichthonius often said, 'I well fear, my children, having made you an ill-fated present in giving you the invention of money. I foresee that it will excite avarice, ambition, flamboyance; that it will maintain an infinite number of pernicious arts that will only soften and corrupt mores; that it will make you disgusted with the happy simplicity that brings all peace of mind and all assurance in life; lastly, that it will cause you to scorn agriculture, which is the foundation of human life, and the source of all real goods. But the gods are witnesses that I had a pure heart in giving you this invention, useful in and of itself.'

"In the end, when Erichthonius perceived that silver corrupted the peoples as he had foreseen, he withdrew in grief to a wild mountain where he lived to a great age, poor and far away from men, without wanting to meddle in the government of the cities.

"A short time after him there appeared in Greece the celebrated Triptolemus, to whom Demeter had taught the art of cultivating the lands and covering them every year with a golden crop. It was not that men did not already know about grain and the manner of multiplying it in sowing it. But they were ignorant of the perfection of plowing. Sent by Demeter, Triptolemus came, plow in hand, to offer the gifts of the goddess to all the peoples who would have enough courage to vanquish their natural sloth and dedicate themselves to an assiduous work. Soon, Triptolemus taught the Greeks to plow the Earth and fertilize it by splitting its womb apart. Soon, the ardent and tireless reapers made the yellow grains that covered the countrysides fall under their sharp sickles.

"Even the wild and ferocious peoples who were scattered hither and yon in the forests of Epirus and Aetolia, to feed on acorns, softened their mores and submitted themselves to the laws when they had learned how to grow crops and nourish themselves with bread. Triptolemus caused all the Greeks to feel the pleasure that there is in only owing their riches to their work and finding in their fields all that which is necessary to render life comfortable and happy. This abundance, so natural and so innocent, and which is attached to agriculture, reminded them of the wise counsel of Erichthonius. They scorned silver and all artificial riches, which are only riches in the imagination, which tempt men to seek dangerous pleasures, and which turn them away from the work where they would find all the real goods, along with pure mores, in complete liberty. They understood, then, that a fertile and well-cultivated field is the true treasure of a family wise enough to want to live frugally like their fathers had lived.

"Happy the Greeks if they had remained steadfast in these maxims so suitable to render them powerful, free, happy, and worthy of being so through a solid virtue. But alas, they are beginning to admire false riches. Little by little they neglect the true ones, and the Greeks degenerate from that marvelous simplicity.

"O my son, you will reign one day. Then, remember to lead men back to agriculture, honor this art, unburden those who apply themselves to it, and do not tolerate that men live idly or occupied by the arts that maintain luxury and softness. Those two men who have been so wise on Earth are here cherished by the gods. Notice my son, that their glory surpasses that of Achilles and the other heroes who only excelled in combat, as much as a sweet springtime is beyond icy winter and the light of the sun is brighter than that of the moon."

While Arcesius was speaking in this way, he perceived that Telemachus had always kept his eyes fixed on the edge of a small wood of laurel trees and a stream bordered with violets, roses, lilies, and several other fragrant flowers, whose vivid colors resembled that of Iris when she descends from the skies to earth to announce to some mortal the commands of the gods. It was the great king Sesostris whom Telemachus recognized in that beautiful place. He was a thousand times more majestic than he had ever been on his Egyptian throne. Rays of a soft light leapt from his eyes, and those of Telemachus were dazzled by them. Seeing him, one would have believed that he was drunk on nectar, so much had the divine spirit transported him beyond human reasoning to reward his virtues.

Telemachus said to Arcesius, "I recognize, O my father, Sesostris, that wise king of Egypt, whom I saw there not so long ago."

"There he is," responded Arcesius, "and you see, by his example, how magnificent the gods are in rewarding good kings. But you must know that all this bliss is nothing in comparison to that which he was destined, had an overly great prosperity not caused him to forget the rules of moderation and justice. His passion to put down the pridefulness and insolence of the Tyrians pushed him to take their city. That conquest gave him the desire to take others. He let himself be seduced by the vainglory of conquerors. He subjugated, or better said, he ravaged all of Asia.

"Upon his return to Egypt, he found that his brother had stolen the kingship and had distorted, through an unjust government, the best laws of the land. Thus, his great conquests only served to disrupt his kingdom. But what rendered him more inexcusable was that he was drunk with his own glory. He hitched to a chariot the loftiest of the kings he had vanquished. Afterward, he recognized his error and was ashamed of having been so inhumane. Such was the fruit of his victories. Voila, that is what conquerors do to their state and to themselves in wanting to usurp the states of their neighbors. That is what caused a king, otherwise so just and beneficent, to lose rank, and it is what diminished the glory that the gods had prepared for him.

"Do you not see this other, my son, whose wound appears so glaring? It is a king of Caria, named Dioclides, who sacrificed himself for his people in a battle because an oracle had told him that in the war of the Carians and Lycians, the nation whose king perished would be victorious.

"Consider this other one. He was a wise legislator who, having given his nation laws suitable to render them good and happy, made them swear that they would never violate any of those laws during his absence. After that, he departed, exiled himself from his homeland, and died poor in a foreign land in order to oblige his people through that oath to always keep such useful laws.

"This other that you see is Eunesimus, king of the Pylians and one of the ancestors of wise Nestor. In a plague that ravaged the land and covered the banks of the Acheron with new shades, he asked the gods to appease their anger by paying, with his death, for so many thousands of innocent men. The gods exalted him in having him find here true royalty of which all those on Earth are only vain shades.

"This old man, whom you see crowned with flowers, is the famous Belus. He reigned in Egypt, and he married Achinoe, daughter of the god Nilus, who hides the source of his waters and who enriches the lands he irrigates through his floods. Belus had two sons, Danaus, whose story you know, and Egyptius, who gave his name to that beautiful kingdom. Belus believed himself richer through the abundance where he put his people and through the love his subjects had for him than through all the tributes he would have been able to impose on them.

"These men, whom you believe dead, are living, my son, and it is the life that one miserably drags along on Earth that is only death— the names alone are changed. Would that the gods render you good enough to merit this happy life that nothing can ever end or trouble! Hasten, it is time to go seek your father. Before finding him, alas, you will see bloodshed! But what glory awaits you in the countrysides of Hesperia! Remember the counsel of wise Mentor, provided you follow it, your name will be great among all the peoples and throughout the centuries."

He spoke, and straightaway he led Telemachus to the Ivory Gate by which one can come out of the dark empire of Hades. Telemachus, tears in his eyes, parted from him, unable to embrace him, and leaving those gloomy places, he hurriedly returned toward the camp of the allies after rejoining on the way the two young Cretans who had accompanied him to the cavern and who no longer hoped to see him again.

END OF BOOK XIV

THE ADVENTURES OF
TELEMACHUS
SON OF ODYSSEUS

BOOK XV

Meanwhile, *the chiefs of the army gathered* to deliberate about whether or not it was necessary to capture Venuse. It was a fortified city that Adrastus had once taken from his neighbors, the Peucetians of Apulia. They had joined the league against him to demand justice for this invasion. Adrastus, to appease them, had put this city in the hands of the Lucanians for safekeeping. However, he had corrupted with silver not only the Lucanian garrison but also the one who commanded it, in such a way that the Lucanian nation had less effective authority than him in Venuse, and the Apulians, who had consented to the Lucanian garrison guarding Venuse, had been deceived in that negotiation.

A citizen of Venuse named Demophantes had secretly offered to deliver to the allies, at night, one of the gates to the city. This advantage was all the greater as Adrastus had put all his war and food provisions in a castle neighboring Venuse, which could not defend itself should Venuse be taken. Philoctetes and Nestor had already opined that they must take advantage of so fortuitous an opportunity. All the chiefs, swept away by their authority and dazzled by the usefulness of so easy an enterprise, applauded this sentiment. But Telemachus, upon his return, made the final efforts to deter them from it.

"I am not unaware," he said to them, "that if ever a man has merited being deceived and taken by surprise, it is Adrastus, the one who has deceived everyone so often. I see well that in overtaking Venuse, you would only be putting yourselves in possession of a city that belongs to you, since it belongs to the Apulians, who are one of the peoples in your league. I avow that you could do it with even more semblance of reason than Adrastus, who put this city in safekeeping and corrupted the commander and the garrison in order to enter into Venuse when he should judge it suitable. Lastly, I realize, like you, that if you were to take Venuse, you would be, from the following day, masters of the fortified castle, where all the preparations of war that Adrastus has assembled are kept, and thus you would end in two days this war so formidable.

"But is it not worth more to perish than to vanquish by such means? Must we repulse fraud through fraud? Will it be said that so many kings, in league with one another to punish the impious Adrastus for his deceptions, are deceivers like him? If we are permitted to do as Adrastus, he is not guilty, and we are wrong in wanting to punish him. What! The whole of Hesperia, supported by so many Greek colonies and heroes returned from the siege of Troy, does it not have other weapons against the perfidy and perjuries of Adrastus than perfidy and perjury?

"You swore by the things most sacred that you would leave Venuse in the hands of the Lucanians for safekeeping. The Lucanian garrison, you say, is corrupted by Adrastus' silver. I believe as you do. However, this garrison is still in the pay of the Lucanians. The garrison has not refused to obey them. It has kept, at least in appearance, neutrality. Neither Adrastus nor his troops have ever entered into Venuse. The treaty remains. Your oath is not forgotten by the gods. Will one keep his given word only when one lacks plausible pretext to violate it? Will one be loyal and faithful to oaths only when one has nothing to gain in violating them?

"If the love of virtue and reverential awe of the gods no longer touch you, at least be touched by your reputation and your self interest. If you show to the world this pernicious example of failing to keep your word and violating your oath to end a war, what wars will you not incite through that impious conduct? What neighbor will not be compelled to fear everything from you and to detest you? Who will be able henceforth, in the most pressing necessity, to trust you? What security will you be able to give, when you want to be sincere, that will mean something from you in persuading your neighbors of your sincerity? Will it be a solemn treaty? You will have trampled one underfoot! Will it be an oath? Hey! Will they not know that you count the gods for nothing whenever you hope to draw through perjury some advantage? Peace will then not have any more security than war with regard to you. All that comes from you will be received as a war, either feigned or declared. You will be the perpetual enemies of all those who have the misfortune of being your neighbors. All affairs that demand a reputation for probity and trust will become impossible for you. You will no longer have any resource to make your promises believed.

"Here is," added Telemachus, "an interest even more pressing that should strike you, should there remain in you some sentiment of probity and some foresight for your own interests: it is that a conduct so deceptive attacks from within your entire league and is going to ruin it. Your perjury is going to cause Adrastus to triumph."

At these words, the entire assembly, stirred up, asked him how he dared say that an action that would give a certain victory to the league could ruin it.

"How," he answered them, "will you be able to trust each other, once you break the only bond of society and trust, which is good faith? After you have posed as a maxim that one can violate the rules of probity and loyalty for a great interest, who among you will be able to trust another when this other will be able to find a great advantage for himself in failing to keep his word and deceiving you? Where will you be then? Who among you will not want to preempt the artifices of his neighbor through his own artifice? What becomes of a league of so many peoples when they are agreed among them, through a common deliberation, that one is allowed to overtake his neighbor and to violate the oath given? How great will your mutual distrust be, your division, your ardor to destroy each other? Adrastus will no longer need to attack you; you will rip each other apart all by yourselves. You will justify his perfidies.

"O wise and magnanimous kings, O you who command with so much experience over countless peoples, do not disdain to listen to the counsels of a young man. If you should fall into the most dreadful extremities where war sometimes precipitates men, you must pick yourself up again through your vigilance and through the efforts of your virtue—for true courage never allows itself to be beaten. But should you once break the barrier of honor and good faith, that loss is irreparable. You would no longer be able to reestablish either the trust needed for the success of all important affairs, or to bring men back to the principles of virtue, after you have taught them to scorn them. What do you fear? Do you not have enough courage to vanquish without deceiving? Your virtue, combined with the military forces of so many peoples, is it not sufficient for you? Let us fight, let us die if we must, rather than vanquish so unworthily. Adrastus, impious Adrastus, is in our hands, provided we are horrified of imitating his cowardice and bad faith."

When Telemachus had finished this speech, he felt that sweet persuasion had flowed from his lips and streamed into the depths of hearts. He noticed a profound silence in the assembly. Each was thinking, not of him nor of the charms of his words, but of the strength of the truth that made itself felt in the course of his reasoning. Astonishment was painted on their faces. Finally, a dull murmur was heard that spread little by little in the assembly. They were looking at one another, not daring to speak first. They waited for the chiefs of the army to declare themselves, and each had difficulty holding back his sentiments. Finally, grave Nestor uttered these words:

"Worthy son of Odysseus, the gods have caused you to speak, and Athena, who has so many times inspired your father, has put into your heart the wise and generous counsel that you have given. I do not regard your youth. I only consider Athena in all that you just said. You spoke for virtue. Without it, the greatest advantages are true losses. Without it, one soon attracts the vengeance of his enemies, the distrust of his allies, the horror of all good people, and the just anger of the gods. Let us then leave Venuse in the hands of the Lucanians and no longer think of anything but vanquishing Adrastus through our courage."

He spoke, and the entire assembly applauded those wise words. But in applauding, each, stunned, turned his eyes toward the son of Odysseus, and they believed to see shining in him the wisdom of Athena who inspired him. There soon arose another issue in the counsel of the kings from which he acquired no less glory.

~

Adrastus, always cruel and perfidious, sent into the camp a defector named Acanthus, who was to poison the most illustrious chiefs of the army. Particularly, he had orders to do his utmost to kill the young Telemachus, who was already the terror of the Daunians. Telemachus, who had too much courage and candor to be inclined to distrust, readily received with goodwill this wretch who had seen Odysseus in Sicily, and who recounted the adventures of this hero to him. He fed him and tried to console him in his unhappiness, for Acanthus complained of having been deceived and treated unworthily by Adrastus. But it was to feed and warm in his bosom a venomous viper ready to strike a mortal wound.

Another defector was overtaken, named Arion, whom Acanthus was sending to Adrastus to apprise him of the state of the camp of the allies and to assure him that he would poison the principal kings and Telemachus at a feast, which Telemachus was to give for them the next day. Arion, taken, confessed his treason. It was suspected that he was passing intelligence to Acanthus, for they were good friends. But Acanthus, profoundly dissimulating and intrepid, defended himself with so much art that one could neither convict him nor get to the bottom of the conspiracy. Several of the kings were of the opinion that it was necessary, when in doubt, to sacrifice Acanthus for the public safety.

"We must execute him," they were saying. "The life of a single man is nothing when it concerns assuring those of so many kings. What does it matter that an innocent should perish when it concerns the preservation of those who represent the gods among men?"

What an inhumane maxim. What a barbarous policy!" responded Telemachus. "What, you are so wasteful of human blood, O you who were established as shepherds of men, and who only command over them in order to preserve them as a shepherd preserves his flock! You are then cruel wolves and not shepherds. At least, you are only shepherds so as to shear and slay the flock instead of driving them to green pastures. According to you, a man is guilty as soon as he is accused. A suspicion merits death. The innocents are at the mercy of the envious and the slanderers. As tyrannical distrust grows in your hearts, more victims must be slain for you."

Telemachus said these words with an authority and a vehemence that swept hearts away and that covered the persons behind such craven counsel with shame. Afterwards, mellowing, he said to them, "As for me, I do not love life enough to want to live at this price. I prefer that Acanthus were wicked than that I was, and that he snatch my life from me through a betrayal than that I unjustly kill him myself when in doubt. But listen, O you, who, being established kings—that is to say, judges of the peoples—should know how to judge men with justice, prudence, and moderation, allow me to interrogate Acanthus in your presence."

Straightaway, he interrogates this man about his exchanges with Arion. He presses him about an infinite number of details. Several times he pretends to send him back to Adrastus as a defector worthy of being punished to observe whether he would be afraid of being sent back or not. But Acanthus' expression and voice remained tranquil, and Telemachus concluded from it that Acanthus [...].[1]

In the end, unable to draw the truth from the bottom of his heart, he said to him, "Give me your ring. I want to send it to Adrastus."

At this demand for his ring, Acanthus paled and was uncomfortable. Telemachus, whose eyes were always fixed on him, saw it. He took his ring. "I am going," he said to him, "to send it to Adrastus by the hands of a Lucanian named Polytropus, whom you know and who will seem to be going there secretly on your behalf. If we are able to uncover in this way that you pass intelligence to

---

[1] The author left this sentence incomplete in all manuscripts.

Adrastus, we will ruthlessly destroy you through the most cruel torments. If, on the contrary, you confess your wrongdoing up until now, we will pardon you for it, and we will be content to send you to an island in the sea, where you will lack for nothing."

Then Acanthus confessed everything, and Telemachus managed to get the kings to let him live because he had promised it to him. They sent him to one of the Echinades islands, where he lived in peace.

~

A short time later, a Daunian of an obscure birth but of a violent and bold temperament, named Dioscore, came into the camp of the allies at night offering to slit the throat of King Adrastus in his tent. He could do it—for one is master over the life of others when he no longer counts his own for anything. This man only breathed vengeance because Adrastus had abducted his wife, whom he loved madly, and who was equal in beauty to Aphrodite herself. He was resolved to either slay Adrastus and take back his wife, or to be slain himself. He had secret agreements to enter at night into the tent of the king and to be favored in his enterprise by several Daunian captains. But he believed he needed the allied kings to attack Adrastus' camp at the same time so that in the turmoil he could more easily abduct his wife and get away. But he was content to perish if he could not abduct her after having killed the king.

As soon as Dioscore had explained his plan to the kings, everyone turned to Telemachus as if to ask him for a decision. "The gods," he responded, "who have preserved us from traitors, forbid us from making use of them. Even if we did not have enough virtue to detest treason, our self-interest alone would suffice to reject it. As soon as we authorize it by our example, we will merit it turning against us. From that moment, who among us will be safe? Adrastus will well be able to evade the strike that threatens him and cause it to fall on the allied kings. The war will no longer be one war. Wisdom and virtue will no longer be of any use. One will no longer see anything but perfidy, treason, and assassinations. We will ourselves feel the sinister consequences of it, and we will merit them since we will have authorized the greatest of evils. I conclude, then, that the traitor must be sent back to Adrastus. I confess that this king does not merit it. But all Hesperia and all Greece have their eyes on us, and they merit that we maintain this conduct so that we may be esteemed by them. We owe to ourselves, and even more to the just gods, this horror of perfidy."

Straightaway, they sent Dioscore back to Adrastus, who shuddered at the peril in which he had been and who could not be more astonished by the generosity of his enemies—for the wicked cannot comprehend pure virtue. Adrastus admired, despite himself, what he had just seen and dared not praise it. This noble action of the allies brought back a shameful reminder of all his deceptions and all his cruelties. He sought to belittle the generosity of his enemies and was ashamed to appear ungrateful, as he owed his life to them—but corrupt men soon harden themselves against all that could touch them.

Adrastus, who saw that the reputation of the allies was rising every day, believed he was pressed to take some brilliant action against them. As he could do nothing virtuous toward them, he

BOOK XV

wanted to at least try to gain some great advantage over them through his weaponry, and he hastened to combat.

The day of combat having come, no sooner had Dawn opened to the sun the gates of the East, in a rose-strewn path, than young Telemachus, preempting—through his attentiveness—the vigilance of the oldest captains, tore himself from the arms of sweet Sleep and set all the officers in motion. His helmet, covered with flowing horsehair, already glinted on his head, and the cuirass on his back dazzled the eyes of the entire army. The handwork of Hephaestus had, apart from its natural beauty, the brilliance of the aegis that was concealed there. He held his lance with one hand; with the other, he pointed out the various positions that must be occupied.

Athena had put in his eyes a divine fire, and on his face a proud majesty, that already promised victory. He marched, and all the kings, forgetting their age and their dignity, felt themselves swept along by a superior force that made them follow in his footsteps; weak jealousy can no longer enter into their hearts; all cede to the one whom Athena invisibly leads by the hand. His actions had nothing of impetuosity or hastiness. He was gentle, tranquil, patient, always ready to listen to others and profit from their counsel; yet active, foresighted, attentive to the most distant needs, arranging everything suitably, awkward in nothing and not making others feel awkward, excusing errors, mending missteps, anticipating difficulties, never asking too much of anything from anyone, inspiring liberty and trust everywhere. Giving an order, it was in the plainest and simplest terms. He would repeat it to better instruct the man who should execute it. Telemachus saw in his eyes whether he had understood well. He then had him explain in common terms how he had understood his words and the principal goal of his undertaking. When he had thus tested the good sense of the one whom he was sending, and with whom he had shared his views, he only had him depart after having given him some token of esteem and trust to encourage him.

In this way, all those he sent were filled with ardor to please him and to succeed. But they were not troubled by fear that he would impute a poor outcome to them, for he excused all mistakes that did not come from evil intent.

The horizon appeared red and inflamed by the first rays of the sun. The sea was filled with the fires of the dawning day. The entire coast was covered with men, armor, horses, and chariots in motion. It was a confused noise, like that of the raging waves when Poseidon excites from the depths of his abysses the dark tempests. So Ares began, through the noise of the weapons and the shuddering apparatus of war, to sow rage in every heart. The countryside was filled with bristling pikes, like the grains that cover the fertile rows at harvest time. Already, a cloud of dust was rising that, little by little, stole the land and sky from the eyes of men. Confusion, horror, carnage, merciless death were advancing. Barely were the first shafts hurled when Telemachus, lifting his eyes and hands toward the sky, pronounced these words:

"O Zeus, father of the gods and men, you see on our side justice and peace, which we have not been ashamed to seek; it is with regret that we fight. We would desire to spare the blood of men. We do not even hate this enemy though he is cruel, perfidious, and sacrilegious. Witness and decide between him and us. If we must die, our lives are in your hands. If we must deliver Hesperia and slay the tyrant, it will be your might and the wisdom of Athena, your daughter, who will give us the victory. The glory of it will be owed to you. It is you who, scale in hand, rules the fate of combat. We fight for you, and, since you are just, Adrastus is more your enemy than ours. If your cause is victorious before the end of the day, the blood of an entire hecatomb of oxen will stream on your altars."

He spoke, and instantly he pushed his spirited and lathery chargers into the most pressing ranks of the enemy. He first encounters Periander the Locrian, covered with the skin of a lion he had killed in Cilicia while he was traveling there. He was armed like Heracles with an enormous club. His size and strength rendered him like the giants. As soon as he saw Telemachus, he scorned his youth and the beauty of his face.

"You are a fine one," he said, "effeminate youngster, to fight us for the glory of combat. Go, child, go among the shades to seek your father." Saying these words, he raises his heavy, knotty club armed with iron tips. It looks like a ship's mast. Each fears the blow of its fall. It threatens the head of the son of Odysseus. But he wheels away from the strike and hurls himself onto Periander with the swiftness of an eagle ripping through the air. The club, in falling, breaks a wheel of a chariot alongside that of Telemachus. At the same time, the young Greek pierces Periander in the throat with a shaft. The blood that flows in fat bubbles from his large gash chokes off his voice. His spirited horses, no longer feeling his failing hand

and the reins floating on their necks, carry him hither and yon. He falls beneath his chariot, eyes already closed to the light, and pale Death already being painted on his disfigured face. Telemachus pities him. He quickly gives his body to his attendants and keeps as a token of his victory the skin of the lion along with the club.

Then he seeks Adrastus in the melee, but in seeking him, he flings to the Underworld a horde of combatants: Hileus, who had harnessed to his chariot two chargers like those of the Sun and raised in the vast meadows that the Aufidus river waters; Demoleon, who in Sicily had once almost equaled Eryx in boxing; Crantor, who had been a host and friend of Heracles when that son of Zeus, passing into Hesperia, took the life of the infamous Cacus; Menecrates, who resembled, they say, Polydeuces in boxing; Hippocoon the Salapian, who imitated the address and smoothness of Castor in handling a horse; the famous hunter Eurymedes, always stained with the blood of bears and wild boars that he had killed in the snow-covered summits of cold Apennines, and who had been, they say, so dear to Artemis that she herself had taught him to shoot arrows; Nicostrates, victor over a giant who vomited fire in the cliffs of Mount Garganus; Cleanthes, who was to marry the young Pholoe, daughter of the river god Liris. She had been promised by her father to the one who would deliver her from a winged serpent which had been born on the banks of the river and was to devour her in a few days according to the prediction of an oracle. This young man, through an excess of love, devoted himself to killing the monster. He succeeded. But he would not be able to enjoy the fruit of his victory. While Pholoe, preparing herself for a sweet wedding, was impatiently waiting for Cleanthes, she learned that he had followed Adrastus into battle and that the Fates had cruelly cut short his days. She filled the wood and mountains along the river with her wails; she drowned her eyes in tears, pulled out her beautiful blond hair, forgot about the garlands of flowers she was accustomed to picking and accused heaven of injustice. As she did not cease crying day and night, the gods, touched by her laments and pressed by the prayers of the river, put an end to her grief. By dint of shedding so many tears, she was suddenly changed into a stream that flows into the bosom of the river and goes on to join its waters with those of the god, her father. But the water of this stream is still bitter, the grasses along the riverbank never flower, and one finds no other shade than that of the cypress on those sad banks.

Meanwhile, Adrastus, who learned that Telemachus was spreading terror on all sides, was eagerly seeking him. He hoped to easily vanquish the son of Odysseus at still so tender an age, and he led thirty Daunians of extraordinary strength, prowess, and audacity around him, to whom he had promised great rewards if they could, in combat, slay Telemachus by whatever manner it could be done. If Adrastus had encountered him at the beginning of the combat, undoubtedly those thirty men surrounding Telemachus' chariot, while Adrastus would have attacked him from the front, would have had no difficulty killing him. But Athena caused them to lose their way.

Adrastus believed to see and to hear Telemachus in a part of the sunken plain at the foot of a hill, where there was a horde of fighters. He runs, he flies, he wants to sate himself with blood. But, instead of Telemachus, he sees old Nestor, who, with a trembling hand, was haphazardly hurling some useless shafts. Adrastus, in his fury, wants to run him through, but a troop of Pylians threw themselves around Nestor. Then, a cloud of shafts obscured the air and covered all the fighters. One heard only the plaintive cries of the dying and the noise of the armor of those who fell in the melee. The Earth groaned under a pile of dead. Streams of blood flowed from all directions. Enyo and Ares, along with the infernal Furies, dressed in robes disgustingly covered with blood, passed their cruel eyes over this spectacle and incessantly renewed the rage in hearts. Those deities, enemies of men, repulsed far from both sides generous Pity, restrained Valor, and gentle Humanity. There was no longer anything in this confused heap of unremitting men, one on top of another, but Massacre, Vengeance, Despair, and brutal Fury. The wise and invincible Pallas herself, having seen it, shuddered and recoiled with horror.

Meanwhile, Philoctetes, marching with slow steps and holding in his hands the arrows of Heracles, hastened to go to Nestor's rescue. Adrastus, unable to reach the divine old man, had hurled his shafts at several Pylians, who bit the dust. He had already slain Ctesilas, so light in running that he barely left a trace of his steps in the sand, and who, in his own country, outran the most rapid currents of the Eurotas and the Alpheus. At his feet had fallen Euthyphro, more beautiful than Hylas and as ardent a hunter as Hippolytus; Pterelas, who had followed Nestor to the siege of Troy and whom Achilles himself had loved because of his courage and his fortitude; Aristogiton who, having bathed, they said, in the waters of the Achelous river, had secretly received from that god the virtue of taking on all sorts of shapes. Indeed, he was so supple and so quick in all his movements that he escaped the strongest hands. But Adrastus, with a strike of his lance, rendered him motionless and his soul fled instantly, along with his blood.

Nestor, who was seeing his most valiant captains fall under the hand of cruel Adrastus, just as the golden grains during harvest fall under the sharp scythe of a tireless reaper, forgot the danger to which he uselessly exposed his old age. His wisdom had forsaken him. He no longer thought of anything but keeping his eyes on Pisistratus, his son, who for his part, ardently sustained the fight to distance peril from his father. But the fatal moment had come when Pisistratus should cause Nestor to feel how unfortunate one often is to have lived too long.

Pisistratus dealt a lancing blow so violent against Adrastus that the Daunian ought to have succumbed. But he evaded it, and while Pisistratus, rattled by the missed strike he had delivered, gathered his lance, Adrastus impaled him with a javelin through the stomach. His entrails immediately began to spill out with a stream of blood. His complexion faded like a flower that the hand of a nymph has picked in the meadow. His eyes were already nearly extinguished, and his voice failing. Alcaeus, his governor, who was alongside him, supported him as he was going to fall and only had time to drag him into the arms of his father. There, he wanted to speak and give the last signs of his affection, but, in opening his mouth, he expired.

While Philoctetes spread around him carnage and horror to repulse the efforts of Adrastus, Nestor held tightly in his arms the body of his son. He filled the air with his cries and could not bear the light. "Wretch," he said, "to have been father, and to have lived so long! Alas, cruel destinies, why did you not end my life either at the hunt of the Caledonian boar, or on the voyage to Colchis, or at the first siege of Troy? I would have died with glory and without bitterness. Now, I drag along in a painful, scorned, and helpless old age. I no longer live but for my woes. I no longer feel anything but sadness. O my son, O my son, O dear son Pisistratus! When I lost your brother Antilochus, I had you to console me. I no longer have you. I no longer have anything, and nothing will console me. All is ended for me. Hope, sole solace for the pains of men, is no longer a good that regards me. Antilochus, Pisistratus, O dear children, I believe it is today that I lose you both. The death of the one reopens the scar that the other had made in the bottom of my heart. I will no longer see you. Who will close my eyes? Who will gather my ashes? O Pisistratus, you died like your brother, a courageous man. There is only I who cannot die."

In saying those words, he wanted to impale himself with a spear he held, but they stopped his hand. They wrested the body of his son from him, and as that luckless old man collapsed, they carried him into his tent, where, having regained his strength a bit, he wanted to return to combat. But they held him back despite himself.

Meanwhile, Adrastus and Philoctetes were seeking each other. Their eyes were gleaming like those of a lion and of a leopard who seek to rip each other apart in the countrysides watered by the

BOOK XV

Cayster. Threats, warlike Furor, and cruel Vengeance burst forth in their ferocious eyes. They bring certain death wherever they hurl their shafts. All the combatants regard them with fright. They see each other, and Philoctetes holds in his hand one of those terrifying arrows that have never missed their mark, and from which the wounds are incurable. But Ares, who favored the cruel and intrepid Adrastus, could not tolerate that he perish so soon. He wanted, through him, to prolong the horrors of war and to multiply the carnage. Adrastus was still obligated to the justice of the gods to punish men and to spill their blood.

At the moment when Philoctetes wants to attack him, he is wounded himself by a lance strike dealt him by Amphimachus, young Lucanian more handsome than the famous Nireus, whose beauty only ceded to that of Achilles among all the Greeks who fought at the siege of Troy. Barely had Philoctetes received the strike when he drew his arrow against Amphimachus. It pierced him through the heart. Immediately, his beautiful black eyes were extinguished and shrouded with the shadows of death. His lips, more ruby-red than the roses which rising Dawn scatters on the horizon, faded. A frightful pallor darkened his cheeks. That face, so tender and charming, was suddenly disfigured. Even Philoctetes pitied him. All the fighters groaned seeing that young man fall in his own blood, where he rolled, and his hair as beautiful as that of Apollo dragged in the dust.

Philoctetes, having vanquished Amphimachus, was compelled to withdraw from combat. He was losing his blood and his strength. Even his old wound, in the effort of combat, seemed ready to open again and to renew his pains, for the children of Asclepius, along with their divine science, had not been able to heal it completely. There he is, ready to tumble into a pile of bloody bodies that surround him. Archidamus, the most proud and most skillful of all the Oebalians, whom he had brought with him to found Petelia, removed him from combat at the moment when Adrastus would have effortlessly slain him at his feet. Adrastus no longer finds anything that dares to resist him nor to delay his victory. All fall, all flee; it is a torrent that, having overflowed its banks, sweeps along, in its furious currents, crops, flocks, shepherds, and villages.

Telemachus heard from afar the shouts of the victors, and he saw the disorder of his own who were fleeing before Adrastus like a herd of timid deer cross the vast countryside, the woods, the mountains, even the most rapid rivers, when they are pursued by hunters.

Telemachus groans. Indignation appears in his eyes. He quits the spot where he has fought for so long with so much danger and glory. He runs to support his troops. He advances, all covered with the blood from a multitude of enemies that he has laid in the dust. From a distance, he lets out a battle cry that makes itself heard by both armies. Athena had put something terrifying in his voice, which the neighboring mountains echoed back. Never did Ares make his cruel voice heard more loudly in Thrace when he called up the infernal Furies, War, and Death.

This cry of Telemachus brings courage and audacity into the hearts of his troops. It freezes the enemies with horror. Even Adrastus is ashamed of feeling troubled. I don't know how many fatal presages cause him to shudder. What animates him is more despair than tranquil valor.

Three times his trembling knees began to buckle under him. Three times he fell back without thinking what he was doing. A pallor of a ghastly faint and a cold sweat spread throughout his limbs. His voice, hoarse and hesitant, could not complete a single word. His eyes, full of a somber and gleaming fire, appeared to leap from his head. One saw him like Orestes, tormented by the Furies. All his movements were convulsive. Then he began to believe that there are gods. He imagined seeing them provoked and hearing a faint voice coming out of the depths of the abyss to call him into gloomy Tartarus. Everything gave him the feeling that a celestial and invisible hand, suspended over his head, was weighing down to smite him. Hope was extinguished in the bottom of his heart. His audacity dissipated just as the light of day disappears when the sun sets in the bosom of the waves and the earth wraps itself in the shadows of the night.

The impious Adrastus—too long tolerated on Earth; too long, if men had not had need of such a chastisement—the impious Adrastus was finally touching his last hour. He runs frantically before his inevitable fate. Horror, stinging Remorse, Dismay, Fury, Rage, Despair, march with him. Barely does he see Telemachus when he believes to see the Avernus opening up and swirls of flames coming out of the black Phlegethon ready to devour him. He screams, and his mouth remains open without him being able to utter a single word, just as a sleeping man, who, in a dreadful dream, opens his mouth and strives to speak but speech always fails him, and he seeks it in vain. With a trembling and precipitous hand, Adrastus hurls his spear at Telemachus. This one, intrepid, like a friend of the gods, covers himself with his shield. It seems that Victory, covering him with her wings, already holds a crown suspended above his head. Sweet and peaceful courage glow in his eyes. One would take him for Athena herself, so wise and steady does he appear in the midst of the greatest perils. The spear hurled by Adrastus is repelled by the shield. Then, Adrastus hastens to draw his sword to deny the son of Odysseus the advantage of hurling his spear in turn. Telemachus, seeing Adrastus, sword in hand, hastens to draw one too, dropping his useless spear.

When they saw the two of them fighting up close, all the other fighters silently lowered their weapons to watch them attentively, and they awaited from their combat the decision of the entire war. The two glaives, glinting like the lightning that comes from thunderbolts, cross each other several times and land useless blows on the polished armor that reverberates from them. The two fighters lunge, retreat, duck, suddenly rise again, and finally grapple. Ivy sprouting at the foot of an elm does not cling more tightly to the hard and knotted trunk with its intertwined branches up to the highest limbs of the tree than those two fighters grip one another.

Adrastus had not yet lost any of his strength; Telemachus did not yet have all of his. Adrastus makes several efforts to surprise his enemy and to rattle him. He tries to grab the sword of the young Greek, but in vain. At the moment he is seeking it, Telemachus lifts him off the ground and throws him to the sand. Then, that unbeliever, who had always scorned the gods, shows a cowardly fear of death. He is ashamed to ask for life and cannot keep himself from confessing that he desires it. He tries to stir Telemachus' compassion.

"Son of Odysseus," he finally said, "it is now that I know the just gods. They are punishing me as I merited. There is only misfortune that opens the eyes of men to see the truth. I see it: it condemns me. But may a wretched king cause you to remember your father, who is far from Ithaca, and touch your heart."

Telemachus, holding him under his knees, having the glaive already raised to pierce his throat, quickly responded,

"I only wanted victory and peace for the nations that I came to help. I do not like to spill blood. Live, then, O Adrastus, but live in order to mend your wrongdoings; give back all that you have usurped; reestablish calm and justice on the coast of the great Hesperia that you have soiled by so many massacres and betrayals. Live, and become another man. Learn, by your downfall, that the gods are just; that the wicked are wretched, that they deceive themselves in seeking felicity through violence, inhumanity, and mendacity; that, in the end, nothing is so sweet nor so happy as authentic and constant virtue. Give us as hostages your son Metrodorus, along with twelve principals of your nation."

At these words, Telemachus allows Adrastus to rise and extends his hand, not distrusting his bad faith. But Adrastus quickly hurls at him a second spear, very short, that he kept hidden. The spear was so sharp and hurled with so much address that it would have pierced Telemachus' armor had it not been divine. At the same time, Adrastus lunges behind a tree to avoid the pursuit of the young

Greek. Then Telemachus cries out, "Daunians, you see him. The victory is ours. The unbeliever only saves himself through betrayal. This one who does not fear the gods, fears death. On the contrary, the one who fears the gods, fears nothing but them."

Saying these words, he advances toward the Daunians and signals to his own, who were on the other side of the tree, to cut off the path of the perfidious Adrastus. Adrastus, fearful of being overtaken, pretends to retrace his steps and wants to strike down the Cretans who stand in his way. But suddenly Telemachus, swift as the thunderbolt that the hand of the father of the gods hurls from high Olympus onto the heads of the guilty, comes melting down on his enemy. He seizes him with a victorious hand. He topples him just like the trending Northwind pummels the tender crops that gild the countrysides. He no longer listens to him, though the unbeliever dares once again to try to abuse the goodness of his heart. He sinks his glaive, and hurries him into the flames of gloomy Tartarus, worthy punishment for his crimes!

No sooner was Adrastus dead than all the Daunians, far from deploring their defeat and the loss of their chief, were glad for their deliverance. They held out their hands to the allies in a sign of peace and reconciliation.

Metrodorus, Adrastus' son, whom his father had nurtured on maxims of dissimulation, injustice, and inhumanity, cowardly fled. But a slave, complicit in his infamies and cruelties, whom he had freed and showered with goods, and to whom he had entrusted his flight, only thought to betray him for his own interest. He killed him from behind while he was fleeing, severed his head, and brought it into the camp of the allies, hoping for a great reward for a crime that ended the war. But they were horrified by this scoundrel and they executed him.

Telemachus, having seen the head of Metrodorus, who was a young man of a marvelous beauty and of an excellent nature which pleasures and evil examples had corrupted, could not hold back his tears. "Alas," he cried out, "See, that is what the poison of prosperity does to a young prince. The more highborn and vivacious he is, the more he strays and is distanced from all sentiments of virtue. And now, I would have perhaps been the same, had the misfortunes into which I was born, thanks be to the gods, and Mentor's instruction not taught me to moderate myself."

The assembled Daunians asked, as the only condition of peace, that they be permitted to have a king for their nation who could blot out, through his virtues, the dishonor with which the impious Adrastus had covered the kingdom. They thanked the gods again for having struck down the tyrant. They came in droves to kiss the hand of Telemachus, which had been dipped in the blood of that monster, and their defeat was for them like a triumph.

Thus tumbled in a moment, without any recourse, that might that had threatened all the others in Hesperia, and that caused so many peoples to tremble, just as those terrains that appear firm and fixed, but that are sapped little by little from below. Over a long period, the flimsy work that attacks their foundations is mocked. Nothing appears weakened; all is smooth, nothing shakes. Meanwhile, all the underground supports are destroyed, bit by bit, until the moment when suddenly the terrain subsides and a chasm opens up. In this way, an unjust and deceptive might, whatever prosperity it procures through its violences, hollows out a precipice for itself under its feet. Fraud and inhumanity sap, bit by bit, all the most solid foundations of legitimate authority. One marvels at it, one fears it, one trembles before it, just until the moment when it is no more. It falls of its own weight, and nothing can lift it again, because it has destroyed with its own hands the true pillars of good faith and justice, which attract love and trust.

END OF BOOK XV

THE ADVENTURES OF
TELEMACHUS
SON OF ODYSSEUS

BOOK XVI

The chiefs of the army assembled the following day to grant a king to the Daunians. They took pleasure in seeing the two camps mingle together with such unexpected friendliness, and thereafter the two armies were no longer but one. Wise Nestor could not be found in this council because grief, combined with old age, had wilted his heart, just as the rain beats down and causes to languish, at night, a flower that was, that morning, during the dawning of the day, the glory and ornament of the green countryside. His eyes had become two fountains of tears that could not go dry; far from them fled sweet Sleep, which casts its spells on the most searing pains. Hope, which is the life of the heart of man, was extinguished in him. All nourishment was bitter to this luckless old man. Even the light was odious to him.

His soul no longer asked for anything but to quit his body and plunge into the eternal night of the empire of Hades. All his friends spoke to him in vain. His heart, failing, was disgusted by all friendship like a sick man is disgusted by the best foods. To all that one could say to him of the most touching things, he only responded with groans and sobs. From time to time, he was heard to say, "O Pisistratus, Pisistratus, Pisistratus, my son, you are calling me; I am following you. Pisistratus, you will render death sweet to me. O my dear son, I no longer desire any possession, other than seeing you again on the banks of the Styx."

He spent entire hours without uttering a single word, but wailing and raising his hands and eyes drowned in tears to the sky.

Meanwhile, the assembled princes awaited Telemachus, who was alongside the body of Pisistratus. He spread over his body flowers by the handful. He added exquisite perfumes as he shed bitter tears.

"O my dear comrade," he said, "I will never forget having seen you in Pylos, having followed you to Sparta, having found you again on the edge of the great Hesperia. I owe you a thousand cares. I loved you; you loved me too. I knew your valor. It would have surpassed that of many famous Greeks. Alas, it caused you to perish with glory, but it robbed the world of a nascent virtue that would have equaled that of your father. Yes, your wisdom and your eloquence at a mature age would have been like that of this old man, the admiration of all Greece. You already had that sweet insinuation that cannot be resisted when he speaks; that naïve way of recounting a story; that wise restraint, which is like magic in appeasing provoked spirits; that authority, which comes from prudence and the strength of good counsel. When you spoke, all lent an ear, all were rapt, all desired to find that you were right. Your speech, plain and humble, flowed gently into hearts like the dew on sprouting grass. Alas, so many good things that we possessed a few hours ago are taken from us forever. Pisistratus, whom I embraced this morning, is no more. There only remains to us a painful memory of him. At least if you had closed the eyes of Nestor before we closed yours, he would not see what he sees, he would not be the most wretched of all fathers."

After these words, Telemachus had the bloody cut, which was on Pisistratus' side, washed and he had him laid out on a bed of purple, where his drooping head, with the pallor of death, resembled a young tree that—having covered the ground with its shade, and pushed toward the sky its flowering branches —was hacked by the blade of a woodsman's ax: it no longer holds to its roots, nor to fertile mother Earth, who nourished the heartwood at her breast. It languishes, its verdure fades, it can no longer support itself. It falls, and its limbs, which hid the sky, drag in the dust wilted and dried—it is no longer anything but a trunk, felled and stripped of all its charms. Thus, Pisistratus, prey to Death, was already carried away by those who must put him on the fatal pyre.

Already the flame mounts to the sky. A Pylian troop, eyes downcast and filled with tears, their arms reversed, slowly lead it. The body is soon burned. The ashes are placed in a golden urn and Telemachus, who takes care of everything, entrusts this urn, like a great treasure, to Callimachus, who had been Pisistratus' governor.

"Keep," he said to him, "these ashes, sad but precious remains of the one whom you loved. Keep them for his father, but wait to give them to him when he will have enough strength to ask for them—what provokes pain in one moment eases it in another."

Then, Telemachus entered the assembly of the leagued kings, where each fell silent to listen to him as soon as they spotted him. He blushed from it, and they could not make him speak. The praises they gave him, through public acclamations, over all he had done, increased his shame. He would have wanted to be able to hide. It was the first time that he looked uncomfortable and uncertain.

Finally, he asked, as a favor, that they would no longer praise him. "It is not that I do not like them," he said, "particularly when they are given by such good judges of virtue, but it is that I fear liking them too much. They corrupt men. They fill them with themselves. They render them vain and presumptuous. One must merit them and shun them. The best praises resemble the false. The most wicked of all men, who are the tyrants, are those who have themselves praised by flatterers the most. What pleasure is there in being praised like them? Good praise is that which you will give me in my absence, should I be fortunate enough to merit it. If you truly believe me good, you must also believe that I want to be modest and to fear vanity. Spare me, then, if you esteem me, and do not praise me like a man in love with praise."

After speaking so, Telemachus no longer responded to those who continued to elevate him to the sky and, through an air of indifference, he soon stopped those accolades they were giving him. They began to fear annoying him in praising him. So, the praises ended, but the admiration increased. Everyone knew of the tenderness he had shown for Pisistratus and the cares he had taken to render the last rites to him. The entire army was more touched by those signs of the goodness of his heart than by all the wonders of wisdom and valor that emanated from him.

"He is wise, he is valiant," they said to each other in private. "He is a friend of the gods and the true hero of our age. He is above humanity. But all that is only admirable, all that only astonishes us. He is humane, he is good, he is a loyal and affectionate friend, he is compassionate, open-handed, beneficent, and gives himself entirely to those whom he ought to love. He is the delight of those who live with him. He has rid himself of his haughtiness, his indifference, and his pride. Voila, what is useful. That is what touches hearts. That is what softens us toward him and makes us sensitive to all his virtues. That is what causes us all to give our lives for him."

Barely were these discourses ended when they hastened to speak of the necessity of giving a king to the Daunians. Most of the princes who were in the council opined that the country must be divided among them as a conquered land. They offered Telemachus, for his part, the fertile country of Arpi that bears twice yearly the rich fruits of Demeter, the sweet presents of Dionysus, and the evergreen fruits of the olive tree consecrated to Athena.

"This land," they said to him, "should make you forget poor Ithaca with its huts, the frightful cliffs of Dulichium, and the wild woods of Zachynthus. Search no longer for your father, who must have perished in the waves of the promontory of Caphereus through the vengeance of Nauplius and the anger of Poseidon; nor for your mother, whom her suitors have possessed since your departure; nor for your homeland, whose land is not favored by heaven like that which we are offering you."

He listened patiently to these speeches, but the rocks of Thrace and Thessaly are no more deaf nor more insensitive to the pleas of hopeless lovers than Telemachus was to these offers.

"As for me," he responded, "I am touched by neither riches, nor delights. What does it matter if one possesses a greater stretch of land and commands a greater number of men? One only has more obstacles from it and less liberty. Life is full of enough misfortunes, even for the wisest and most moderate men, without still adding to it the difficulties of governing other men, who are indocile, restless, unjust, deceptive, and ungrateful. When a man wants to be master over men for the love of himself—only thinking of his own authority, his pleasures and his glory in it—then he is impious, he is tyrannical, he is the scourge of humankind.

"When, on the contrary, a man only wants to govern men according to true rules for their own good, he is less their master than their tutor. He only has the difficulty of it, which is infinite, and he is very distant from wanting to extend his authority further. The shepherd who does not eat the flock, who protects it from wolves in exposing his life, who watches over them night and day to drive them to the best pastures, has no desire to increase the number of his sheep and to steal those of his neighbors. That would be to increase his difficulties.

"Although I may never have governed," added Telemachus, "I have learned, through the laws and through the wise men who made them, how arduous it is to lead cities and kingdoms. I am therefore content with my poor Ithaca. Though it may be small and poor, I will have enough glory, provided I reign there with justice, piety, and courage, even though I may not reign there too soon. Would to the gods that my father, escaped from the fury of the waves, may reign there until the most extreme old age, and may I be able to learn under him for a long time how one must vanquish his own passions in order to know how to moderate those of an entire people!"

Then Telemachus said, "Listen, O princes assembled here, to what I believe must be said to you for your own interest. If you give the Daunians a just king, he will lead them with justice. He will teach them how useful it is to preserve good faith and to never usurp the goods of his neighbors. That is what they have never been able to understand under the impious Adrastus. As long as they are led by a wise and moderate king, you will have nothing to fear from them. They will be obliged to you for this good king whom you will have given them. They will be obliged to you for the peace and prosperity which they enjoy. These peoples, far from attacking you, will bless you unceasingly, not only the king, but also the people; all will be the work of your hands.

"If, on the contrary, you want to divide their country among you, here are the woes that I predict for you: this people, pushed to despair, will restart the war. They will fight justly for their liberty, and the gods, enemies of tyranny, will fight with them. If the gods join them, sooner or later you will be confounded, and your prosperity will dissipate like smoke.

"Counsel and wisdom will be taken away from your chiefs, courage from your armies, abundance from your lands. You will flatter yourselves, you will be brazen in your enterprises, you will silence the good people who want to speak the truth, you will suddenly tumble, and they will say of you, 'Is that those flourishing peoples who were supposed to make the law for all the land and who now flee before their enemies—they are the toy of the nations who trample them underfoot. Voila, this is what the gods have done; this is what unjust, lofty, and inhumane peoples merit.'

"Furthermore, consider that if you undertake to divide among you this conquest, you will reunite against you all the neighboring peoples. Your league, formed to defend the common liberty of Hesperia against the usurper Adrastus, will become odious, and it is you yourselves whom all the peoples will accuse, rightly, of wanting to impose universal tyranny.

"But let us assume that you are victorious not only over the Daunians, but all the other peoples—this victory will destroy you. Here is how. Consider how this enterprise will disunite all of you. As it is not based on justice, you will not have any rules to limit among you the claims of each. Each will desire that his part in the conquest be proportionate to his might. None of you will have enough authority among the others to make this division peacefully. Voila, there you have the source of a war of which your grandchildren will see no end. Is it not worth much more to be just and restrained than to follow one's ambition with so much peril and through so many inevitable misfortunes?

"Profound peace, sweet and innocent pleasures that accompany it, happy abundance, friendliness with your neighbors, glory which is inseparable from justice, authority that a man acquires in becoming—through good faith—the arbiter of all the foreign peoples, are these possessions not more desirable than the mad vanity of an unjust conquest? O princes, O kings, you see that I speak to you selflessly. Listen, then, to the one who loves you enough to contradict you and to displease you in representing the truth to you."

While Telemachus was speaking so, with an authority that had never been seen in any other, and as all the princes, astounded and suspended, were admiring the wisdom of his counsel, a confused noise was heard that spread throughout the camp and came to the spot where the assembly was being held.

"A foreigner," they said, "has come to land on these coasts with a troop of armed men. This stranger is of a high mien. Everything about him appears heroic; one can easily see that he has suffered for a long time and that his great courage has put him above all his sufferings. At first, the peoples of the country who guard the coast wanted to repulse him as an enemy who comes to cause a disturbance. But, after drawing his sword with an intrepid air, he declared that he would know how to defend himself if attacked, but that he was only asking for peace and hospitality. Immediately, he presented an olive branch as suppliant. They listened to him. He asked to be led to those who govern on this coast of Hesperia, and they brought him here to have him speak to the assembled kings."

No sooner had this discourse ended than they saw this stranger enter with a majesty that surprised the entire assembly. One would have easily believed that it was the god Ares, when he assembles on the mountains of Thrace his bloodthirsty troops. He began to speak thus:

"O you shepherds of the peoples, who are no doubt assembled here either to defend the homeland against its enemies or to cause the most just laws to flourish, listen to a man whom Fortune has persecuted. May the gods never have you experience similar misfortunes. I am Diomedes, king of Aetolia, who wounded Aphrodite at the siege of Troy. The vengeance of this goddess pursues me throughout the universe. Poseidon, who can refuse nothing to the divine daughter of the sea, delivered me over to the rage of the winds and the waves, which have shattered my vessels against the reefs many times. The inexorable Aphrodite has taken all hope from me of seeing my kingdom again, my family, and that sweet light of a country where I first beheld the day. No, I will never see again all that was the most dear in the world to me.

"I come, after so many shipwrecks, to seek on these unknown shores a little repose and an assured retreat. If you revere the gods—and above all Zeus, who cares for foreigners—if you are sensitive to compassion, do not refuse me in this vast country some corner of infertile land, some wilderness, some sands, or some steep rock, to found, along with my companions, a city that may be at least a sad image of our lost homeland. We only ask for a little space that may be of no use to you. We will live in peace with you in a close alliance. Your enemies will be ours. We will join in with all your interests. We will only ask for the liberty to live according to our laws."

While Diomedes was speaking so, Telemachus, his eyes fixed on him, displayed all the different passions on his face. When Diomedes began to speak of his long misfortunes, he hoped that this man, so majestic, would be his father. As soon as he had declared that he was Diomedes, Telemachus' face wilted like a beautiful flower that the black Northwinds come to tarnish with their cruel breath. Then Diomedes' speech, complaining of the long anger of a deity, touched him through the memory of the same disgraces suffered by his father and him. Tears mixed with pain and joy streamed down his cheeks, and he suddenly flung himself at Diomedes to embrace him.

"I am," he said, "the son of Odysseus, whom you knew, and who was not useless to you when you took the famous horses of Rhesus. The gods have treated him mercilessly like you. If the oracles of Erebus are not deceivers, he still lives. But alas, he does not live for me. I abandoned Ithaca to seek him. Now, I am unable to see again either Ithaca or him. Judge by my misfortunes the compassion that I have for yours.

"It is the advantage that there is in being unfortunate that one knows how to empathize with the difficulties of others. Though I am only a foreigner here, I can, great Diomedes (for despite the miseries that burdened my homeland during my childhood, I have not been so poorly raised as to be ignorant of your glory in combat),

I can, O most invincible of all the Greeks after Achilles, procure some assistance for you. These princes that you see are humane. They know that there is neither virtue, nor true courage, nor solid glory without humanity. Misfortune adds a new luster to the glory of great men. Something is lacking in men when they have never been unfortunate. They are lacking in their lives examples of patience and steadfastness. Suffering virtue touches all hearts that have some taste for virtue. Allow us, then, the care of consoling you. Since the gods lead you to us, it is a present they are giving us, and we must believe ourselves lucky to be able to ease your pains."

While he was speaking, Diomedes, stunned, was staring at him and felt his heart stirred. They embraced each other as if they had been bonded in a close friendship for a long time. "O worthy son of wise Odysseus," Diomedes said, "I recognize in you the sweetness of his face, the charm of his discourse, the strength of his eloquence, the nobleness of his sentiments, the wisdom of his thoughts."

At the same time, Philoctetes also embraces the great son of Tydeus. They recount their sad adventures to each other. Then Philoctetes said to him, "Undoubtedly, you will be glad to see wise Nestor again. He has just lost Pisistratus, the last of his children. There no longer remains to him in life but a trail of tears leading him to the tomb. Come console him. An unfortunate friend is more suitable than any other to ease his heart."

Straightaway they entered the tent of Nestor, who barely recognized Diomedes, so much had sadness beaten down his spirit and his senses.

BOOK XVI

At first Diomedes wept with him, and their conversation was for the old man a redoubling of pain. But little by little the presence of that friend appeased his heart. One easily recognized that his woes were suspended a bit through the diversion of recounting what he had suffered, and of hearing, in turn, that which had befallen Diomedes.

While they were talking, the kings assembled with Telemachus examined what they should do. Telemachus counseled them to give Diomedes the country of Arpi and to choose, as king of the Daunians, Polydamas, who was of their nation. This Polydamas was a famous captain whom Adrastus, through jealousy, had never wanted to use for fear of someone attributing to this able man the successes for which he hoped to have the glory alone.

Polydamas had often warned, in private, that Adrastus was risking his life and the health of his state too much in this war against so many conspired nations. He had wanted to push him toward more upright and moderate conduct toward his neighbors—but men who hate the truth also hate the people who have the boldness to tell it. They are not touched by their sincerity, by their zeal, or by their selflessness. A deceptive prosperity hardened Adrastus' heart against the most salutary counsels. In not heeding them, he triumphed daily over his enemies. Haughtiness, bad faith, and violence always put victory on his side. All the misfortunes with which Polydamas had so long threatened him did not happen. Adrastus mocked him for such a timid wisdom that always foresaw inconveniences. Polydamas was insufferable to him. He distanced him from all offices. He left him to languish in solitude and poverty.

At first, Polydamas was crushed by this disgrace. But it gave him what he was lacking by opening his eyes to the vanity of great fortunes. He became wise at his expense. He rejoiced in having been unfortunate. He learned little by little to keep quiet, to live on little, to tranquilly nourish himself with the truth, to cultivate hidden virtues that are even more estimable than glaring ones, and lastly, to do without men.

He dwelt at the foot of Mount Garganus in a wilderness, where a half-vaulted rock served him as a roof, a stream that tumbled from the mountain appeased his thirst, some trees gave him their fruits. He had two slaves who cultivated a small field. He worked along with them with his own hands. The land more than paid him for his troubles and never left him lacking for anything. He had not only fruits and vegetables in abundance, but even all kinds of fragrant flowers. There, he deplored the misfortunes of peoples whom the foolish ambition of a king drag along to their ruin. There, he waited each day for the just, yet patient gods to cause Adrastus to fall. The more his prosperity grew, the more Polydamas believed to see the irremediable downfall near—for the lucky imprudence in his errors and the power ascended to the last excesses of absolute authority are the forerunners to the toppling of kings and kingdoms. When he learned of the defeat and death of Adrastus, he showed no joy, not in having foreseen it, nor in being delivered from this tyrant. He only groaned for fear of seeing the Daunians in servitude.

Voila. That is the man whom Telemachus proposed to have reign. He had known of his courage and virtue for some time, for

BOOK XVI

Telemachus, following Mentor's counsel, never ceased to inform himself everywhere of the good and bad qualities of all people who were in some notable post, not only among the allied nations that he served in this war, but even among the enemies. His principal care was to discover and examine men everywhere who had some talent or a particular virtue.

The allied princes had, at first, some repugnance for putting Polydamas in the kingship. "We have experienced," they said, "how much a king of the Daunians, when he loves war and knows how to wage it, is formidable to his neighbors. Polydamas is a great captain, and he can throw us into great perils."

But Telemachus answered them, saying, "Polydamas, it is true, knows warfare, but he loves peace, and, you see, those are the two things that must be wished for. A man who knows the misfortunes, dangers, and difficulties of war is much more capable of avoiding it than another who has no experience of it. He has learned to appreciate the happiness of a tranquil life. He condemned Adrastus' enterprises. He foresaw in them the gruesome aftermath. A weak prince, ignorant and inexperienced, is more to be feared by you than a man who will recognize and decide everything for himself. The weak and ignorant prince will only see through the eyes of an impassioned favorite, or of a flattering, restless, and ambitious minister. In this way the blind prince will commit to war without wanting to wage it. You will never be able to assure yourselves of him, for he can never be sure of himself. He will not keep his word. He will soon reduce you to that extremity, where it will be necessary either that you destroy him or that he crushes you. Is it not more useful, more certain, and at the same time more just and more noble to respond faithfully to the trust of the Daunians and give them a king worthy of commanding?"

The entire assembly was persuaded by this speech. They went to propose Polydamas to the Daunians, who were impatiently awaiting a response. When they heard the name of Polydamas, they responded, "We indeed recognize now that the allied princes want to act in good faith with us and make an everlasting peace, since they want to give us as king a man so virtuous and capable of governing us. If they had proposed to us a cowardly, effeminate, and poorly taught man, we would have believed that they only sought to crush us and to corrupt the form of our government, and we would have secretly preserved a deep resentment for a conduct so harsh and so cunning. But the choice of Polydamas shows us a genuine candor. The allies undoubtedly expect nothing from us but what is just and noble since they grant us a king who is incapable of doing anything against the liberty and the glory of our nation. Therefore, may we profess before the just gods that the rivers will ascend again to their source before we will cease loving peoples so beneficent. May our last descendants remember the beneficence we receive today and renew from generation to generation the peace of the golden age throughout the coast of Hesperia."

Telemachus then proposed to them to give Diomedes the countryside of Arpi to found a colony there. "The new people," he said to them, "will be obliged to you for their establishment in a country that you do not occupy. Remember that all men must love each other, that the land is too vast for them, that they must indeed have neighbors, and that it is worth more to have those that are obliged to you for their establishment. Be touched by the misfortune of a king who cannot return to his country. Polydamas and he, being united together by the bonds of justice and virtue, which alone are lasting, will maintain you in a profound peace and will render you formidable to all the neighboring peoples who would think to extend their border. You see, O Daunians, that we have given to your land and to your nation a king capable of elevating its glory to the skies; give also, since we are asking it of you, a land that is useless to you, to a king who is worthy of all kinds of assistance."

The Daunians responded that they could refuse Telemachus nothing, since it was he who had procured Polydamas for them as their king. Straightaway, they departed to search for him in his wilderness and to have him reign over them. Before departing, they gave the fertile plains of Arpi to Diomedes for him to found a new kingdom there. The allies were delighted by it because this colony of Greeks would be able to provide powerful succor to the allies should the Daunians ever want to renew the usurpations of which Adrastus had given the wicked example. All the princes thought only of splitting up. Telemachus, tears in his eyes, departed with his troop after tenderly embracing the valiant Diomedes, the wise and inconsolable Nestor, and the famous Philoctetes, worthy heir to the arrows of Heracles.

End of Book XVI

THE ADVENTURES OF
TELEMACHUS
SON OF ODYSSEUS

BOOK XVII

The *young son of Odysseus* burned with impatience to find Mentor in Salentum and embark with him to see Ithaca again, where he hoped that his father would have arrived. When he was approaching Salentum he was quite astonished to see all the surrounding countryside, which he had left practically uncultivated and deserted, cultivated like a garden and filled with diligent workmen. He recognized the work of the wisdom of Mentor. Then, entering into the city, he noticed that there were far fewer artisans for the delights of life and much less magnificence. He was shocked by it, for he naturally liked all things that have brilliance and politesse. But other thoughts soon occupied his heart. He saw in the distance Idomeneus coming toward him along with Mentor. Immediately his heart was stirred with joy and tenderness.

Despite all the success he had had in the war against Adrastus, he feared that Mentor would not be content with him, and as he advanced, he searched Mentor's eyes to see if he had anything to reproach himself for.

Straightaway, Idomeneus embraced Telemachus like his own son, then Telemachus flung himself at Mentor's neck and soaked him with his tears.

Mentor said to him, "I am content with you. You made great errors, but they have served you to know yourself and to distrust yourself. Often, one draws more fruit from his errors than from his beautiful deeds. Great deeds swell the heart and inspire a dangerous presumption. Errors make a man reflect and restore the wisdom to him that he had lost in his successes. What remains for you to do, it is to praise the gods and not desire that men praise you. You have done great things. But confess the truth—it is hardly you by whom they were done. Is it not true that they came to you like something foreign which was put in you? Were you not capable of spoiling them through your quick temper and through your imprudence? Do you not feel as if Athena somehow transformed you into another man above yourself in order to do through you what you have done? She held all your faults in suspense, just as Poseidon, when he appeases the tempests suspends the angry waves."

While Idomeneus was curiously interrogating the Cretans who were returning from the war, Telemachus was listening thus to Mentor's wise counsel. Then he gazed in every direction with astonishment and said to Mentor, "This is a change for which I do not quite understand the reason. Has some calamity befallen

Salentum during my absence? How does it come about that one no longer notices that magnificence that burst forth everywhere before my departure? I no longer see gold, or silver, or precious stones; the clothing is plain; the buildings they have built are less vast and less ornate; the arts languish—the city has become a lonely place."

Mentor answered him, smiling, "Have you noticed the state of the countryside around the city?"

"Yes," replied Telemachus. "I saw plowing honored, and the fields cleared everywhere."

"Which is worth more," added Mentor, "a superb city of marble, gold, and silver, with a neglected and unproductive countryside, or a countryside cultivated and productive, with an average city, modest in its mores? A great city heavily populated with artisans busy softening the mores through the delights of life, when it is surrounded by a kingdom, poor and badly cultivated, resembles a monster whose head is of an enormous size and whose entire body, stretched thin and deprived of nourishment, is not proportionate to this head. It is the number of people and the abundance of food that makes up the true strength and the true riches of a kingdom.

"Idomeneus now has an innumerable people, tireless in work, who fill the entire length of his country. All his country is no longer but one single city; Salentum is only the center of it. We have transported from the city to the countryside the men that were lacking in the countryside and that were superfluous in the city. Furthermore, we have attracted into this country many foreign peoples. The more these peoples multiply, the more they multiply the fruits of the land through their work; this proliferation, so gentle and so peaceful, increases a kingdom more than a conquest.

"We have only rejected from this city the superfluous arts which deter the poor from cultivating the land for their true needs and which corrupt the rich by casting them into flamboyance and softness. But we have done no harm to fine arts, nor to the men who have a true genius for cultivating them. In this way, Idomeneus is much mightier than he was when you were marveling at his magnificence. That dazzling brilliance concealed a weakness and a destitution that would soon have toppled his empire. Now he has a much greater number of men, and he feeds them more easily. These men, accustomed to work, to difficulty, and to the scorn of life for the love of good laws, are all ready to fight to defend these lands cultivated by their own hands. Soon this state, which you believe is waning, will be the marvel of Hesperia.

"Remember, O Telemachus, that there are two pernicious things in the government of peoples to which one almost never brings any remedy. The first is an unjust and overly violent authority in kings; the second is luxury, which corrupts mores.

"When kings are accustomed to no longer knowing any laws other than their absolute wills, and they no longer rein in their passions, they can do anything. But, by dint of being almighty, they sap the foundations of their might. They no longer have either fixed rules, or maxims of government. Everyone flatters them over and over. They no longer have people; there only remains to them slaves, of which the number diminishes each day. Who will tell them the truth? Who will set bounds to this torrent? All cede. The wise flee, hide, and groan. There is only a sudden and violent revolution that may bring back to its natural course this overflowing might. Often, the same blow that could restrain it brings it down with no recourse. Nothing threatens a calamitous downfall so much as an authority that one pushes too far. It is like a bow stretched too far that finally breaks suddenly if not released. But who is it who will dare to release it? Idomeneus was spoiled down to the bottom of his heart by that authority so flattering. He had been toppled from his throne, but he had not been set straight. It was necessary for the gods to send us here to disabuse him of that blind and outrageous might that does not suit men. It was even necessary for a kind of miracle to open his eyes.

"The other evil that is almost incurable is luxury. Just as too much authority poisons kings, luxury poisons an entire nation. They say that luxury serves to feed the poor at the expense of the rich, as if the poor could not earn their livelihood more usefully in multiplying the fruits of the land without softening the rich through the refinements of voluptuousness. An entire nation accustoms itself to regarding as necessities of life the most superfluous things. Every day new necessities are invented, and one can no longer do without things that one did not know of thirty years before. This luxury is called 'good taste,' 'perfection of the arts,' and 'politesse of the nation.' This vice, which attracts an infinity of other ones to it, is lauded as a virtue; it spreads its contagion from the king to the last dregs of the people.

"The closest relatives of the king want to imitate his magnificence, the elites that of the king's relatives, the average people want to equal the elites—for who is it who does himself justice? The little people want to pass as average people. Everyone does more than he is able, some through flamboyance and to boast of their riches; others through a false modesty to hide their poverty. Even those who are wise enough to condemn such great disorder are not wise enough to dare to raise their head first and give the opposite example. The entire nation ruins itself. All the stations are blended together.

"The passion for acquiring goods in order to maintain a vain expenditure corrupts the purest souls. It is no longer a question of being rich; poverty is an infamy. Whether you be learned, capable, virtuous, train men, win battles, save the homeland, sacrifice all your interests—you are scorned if your talents are not enhanced through flamboyance. Even those who do not have any goods want to appear to have them. They spend as if they have them, they borrow, they deceive, they use a thousand unworthy artifices to attain them. But who will remedy these evils? The tastes and habits of an entire nation must change. New laws must be given. Who will be able to undertake it, if not a philosopher king, who would know how, through the example of his own moderation, to shame all those who love an ostentatious expenditure and to encourage the wise, who will be very glad to be authorized in a respectable frugality?"

Telemachus, listening to this discourse, was like a man who awakes from a deep sleep. He sensed the truth of these words, and they were engraved on his heart, just as a skillful sculptor impresses the traits that he wants in marble so that he gives it tenderness, life, and movement. Telemachus said nothing, but, passing over

BOOK XVII

all that he had just heard, he ran his eyes over the things that had changed in the city. Then he said to Mentor, "You have made Idomeneus the wisest of all the kings. I no longer recognize him, neither him nor his people. I even avow that what you have done here is infinitely greater than the victories that we just brought home. Luck and military strength are very much a part of the outcome of war. The glory in combat must be shared with our soldiers. But all your work comes from one head alone. You had to work alone against a king and against all his people to correct them. The outcome of war is always gruesome and odious. Here, everything is the work of a celestial wisdom. Everything is sweet, everything is pure, everything is lovable—everything indicates an authority that is beyond man. When men desire glory, why do they not seek it in this diligence to do good? O how they poorly understand glory, to hope for a solid glory in ravaging the land and spreading human blood on it!"

Mentor showed a manifest joy on his face in seeing Telemachus so disabused of victories and conquests, at an age when it was so natural that he would be drunk on the glory that he had acquired.

Then Mentor added, "It is true that all you see here is good and laudable. But know that one can do things still better. Idomeneus moderates his passions and applies himself to governing his people with justice. But he still does not fail to make many errors, which are the unfortunate aftermath of his old errors. When men want to quit evil, evil seems to still pursue them for a long time. There remains with them bad habits, a weak nature, inveterate mistakes, and an almost incurable bias. Fortunate are those who have never strayed!

They can do good more perfectly. The gods, O Telemachus, will demand more of you than of Idomeneus, because you have known truth since your youth, and you have never been delivered over to the seductions of an overly great prosperity.

"Idomeneus," continued Mentor, "is wise and enlightened, but he applies himself too much to details and does not meditate enough on material affairs in order to formulate plans. The capability of a king, who is above other men, does not consist in doing everything by himself. It is a gross vanity to expect to do everything and to persuade the world that one is capable of it. A king must govern in choosing, and in guiding, those who govern under him. He must not handle the details, for that is to perform the function of those who have to work under him. He should only have an account rendered of it, and know enough about it to go into that accounting with discernment. It is to govern marvelously in choosing and in applying, according to their talents, the ones who govern. The supreme and perfect government consists in governing those who govern. They must be observed, tested, restrained, corrected, animated, elevated, lowered, replaced, and always kept in hand.

"To want to examine everything for oneself—it is distrust, it is pettiness, it is jealousy over middling details, which consumes time and the freedom of mind essential for the big things. To form big plans, you must have a free and rested mind. You must think at ease, in complete disengagement from all dispatches of thorny affairs. A mind drained by details is like the dregs of wine that no longer have either strength or delicateness. Those who govern through details are always convicted by the present without extending their sights to a distant future. They are always swept up in the affair of the day, and that affair being the only one occupying them, it makes too strong an impression, it contracts their mind—for one can only judge affairs properly when one compares them all together and places them all in a certain order so that they have the consequences and proportions of them.

"To fail to follow this rule in governing, it is to resemble a musician who is content to find some melodious sounds and who does not go to the trouble of uniting and harmonizing them to compose a sweet and stirring music. It also resembles an architect who believes he has done everything he can, provided he assembles great columns and lots of well-carved stones, without thinking of the order and proportions of the ornamentation of his edifice. In the time that he builds a room, he does not anticipate that he must build a convenient staircase. When he works on the core of the building, he thinks of neither the court, nor the portal. His work is only a confused assembly of magnificent parts, which are not made for one another. This work, far from doing honor to him, is a monument that will eternalize his shame—for the work reveals that the worker did not know how to think broadly enough to conceive at the same time the general design of his entire work. It is a characteristic of short and subordinate intelligence. When a man is born with this predisposition limited to detail, he is only suited to execute under others. Do not doubt it, O my dear Telemachus, the government of a kingdom demands a certain harmony, like music, and just proportions, like architecture.

"If you want me to continue using the comparison to these arts, I will make you understand how mediocre men are who govern through detail. The one who, in a concert, only sings certain things, though he sings them perfectly, is only a singer; the one who conducts the entire concert and who arranges, at the same time, all the parts, is the only master of music. In the same way, the one who carves the columns, or constructs one side of a building, is only a mason, but the one who thought of the entire edifice, and who has all the proportions of it in his head, is the only architect. In this way, those who work, who expedite, who handle the most affairs are those who govern the least; they are only subordinate workers.

"The true genius who leads the state, is the one who, in doing nothing, has everything done; who thinks; who invents; who penetrates into the future; who returns to the past; who arranges; who adjusts; who prepares from a distance; who unceasingly holds firm to fight against Fortune, like a swimmer against the torrent of water; who is attentive night and day to leave nothing to chance.

"Do you think, Telemachus, that a great painter works assiduously from morning until nightfall in order to rush through his works more swiftly? No. That bothersome and servile work would put out all the fires of his imagination. He would no longer work from genius. All must be done sporadically and by sallies, according to where his taste leads him and his mind incites him. Do you think that he spends his time blending colors and preparing pencils? No. Those are the tasks of his students. He reserves himself for the work of thinking; he only thinks of making bold traits that give nobility, life, and passion to his figures; he has in his head the thoughts and the sentiments of the heroes that he wants to represent. He transports himself into their centuries and into all the circumstances where they were. To this kind of enthusiasm, he must combine a wisdom that restrains him, that everything may be true, correct, and in proportion to each other. Do you believe, Telemachus, that any less elevation of genius and expended effort would be needed to make a great king than to make a good painting? Conclude therefore that the occupation of a king must be to think, to form great projects, and to choose the men suitable to execute them under him."

Telemachus answered, "It seems to me that I understand everything you say. But if things work in this way, a king would often be deceived, not entering into the details himself."

"It is you yourself whom you deceive," Mentor rejoined. "What keeps one from being deceived, it is the general knowledge of government. People who do not have principles in their affairs and who do not have true intellectual discernment always go by feel. It is luck when they are not deceived. They do not even know precisely what they seek, nor what they must aim for. They only know how to distrust, and to distrust the upright men who contradict them rather than the deceivers who flatter them.

"On the contrary, those who do have principles with regard to government, and who are knowledgeable about men, know what they must seek in them and the means of attaining it. They recognize, more or less, whether the people whom they use are suitable instruments for their designs and whether they join in their views in order to aim for attaining the goal they propose. Indeed, as they do not throw themselves into burdensome details, they have a clearer mind to see things from a single broad view of the overall work and to observe whether it is advancing toward the main end. If they are deceived, at least they are hardly deceived in the essentials. Indeed, they are above petty jealousies which indicate a narrow mind and a base soul.

"They realize that one cannot avoid being deceived in the great affairs, since one must make use of men, who are so often deceivers. One loses more through irresolution, where distrust casts him, than he would lose in allowing himself to be deceived a little. One is only too happy when he is only deceived in middling things. The big things do not fail to move along, and that is the only thing that a great man must worry about. Deception must be severely repressed when it is discovered; but one must count on some deception if he does not want to be truly deceived. An artisan, in his boutique, sees everything with his own eyes and does everything with his own hands; but a king, in a great state, cannot do everything nor see everything. He must only do the things that no one else under him can do; he must only look at what enters into the decision of important things."

Finally, Mentor said to Telemachus, "The gods love you and are preparing a reign for you filled with wisdom. All that you see here is done less for the glory of Idomeneus than for your instruction. All these wise establishments that you marvel at in Salentum are only the shadow of what you will do one day in Ithaca if you respond through your virtues to your high destiny. It is time that we think of leaving here. Idomeneus keeps a vessel ready for our return."

Immediately, Telemachus opened up his heart to his friend, though somewhat painfully, about an attachment that was making him regret leaving Salentum. "You will fault me perhaps," he said to him, "for falling in love too easily in the places I pass through, but my heart would continually reproach me if I hid from you that I love Antiope, the daughter of Idomeneus. No, my dear Mentor, it is not a blind passion like the one you healed me of on the island of Calypso. I recognized well the depth of the cut that Love had given me alongside Eucharis. I still cannot pronounce her name without being troubled. Time and absence have not been able to blot it out. That calamitous experience teaches me to distrust myself. But as for Antiope, what I feel has nothing resembling it. It is not passionate love; it is tasteful, it is estimable, it is convicting. How happy I would be if I spent my life with her! If ever the gods give my father back to me, and he permits me to choose a wife, Antiope will be my spouse.

"What touches me in her, it is her quietness, her modesty, her reticence, her assiduous work, her skill for wool and embroidery works, her diligence in leading her father's household since her mother died, her scorn for vain jewelry, the obliviousness and even ignorance that appears in her of her beauty. When Idomeneus commands her to lead the dances of the young Cretans to the sound of flutes, one would take her for laughing Aphrodite, who is accompanied by the Graces. When he brings her with him on the hunt in the forests, she looks majestic and adroit at drawing the bow, like Artemis amidst her nymphs. She alone does not know it, and everyone admires her.

"When she enters the temples of the gods and she carries the sacred things in baskets on her head, one would think that she herself is the deity that inhabits the temples. With what reverence and what religion we see her offering sacrifices and diverting the anger of the gods when some wrongdoing must be expiated or some sinister presage averted!

"Lastly, when one sees her, with a troop of women, holding in her hand a golden needle, one would believe that it is Athena herself who took on this earth a human form and who inspires the fine arts in men. She inspires others to work. She eases the work and the boredom of it through the enchantment of her voice when she sings all the marvelous stories of the gods. And she surpasses the most exquisite painting with the delicateness of her embroideries. Lucky the man that a sweet marriage will unite with her. He will have nothing to fear other than losing her and outliving her.

"I take here, my dear Mentor, the gods as my witnesses that I am all ready to depart. I will love Antiope as long as I live, but she will not delay for a moment my return to Ithaca. If another must possess her, I will spend the rest of my days in sadness and bitterness, but in the end, I will forsake her. Although I know the absence may cause me to lose her, I do not want to speak either to her or to her father of my love, for I must only speak of it to you alone, until Odysseus, remounted on his throne, will have declared to me that he consents to it. You can recognize by that, my dear

Mentor, how much this attachment is different from the passion through which you saw me blinded by Eucharis."

Mentor responded to Telemachus, "I am convinced of this difference. Antiope is sweet, natural, and wise. Her hands do not scorn work, she looks far ahead, she foresees all, she knows how to be silent and act accordingly without eagerness, she is busy at all hours and never embarrasses herself because she does each thing properly. The good orderliness of her father's house is her glory. She is more adorned by it than by her beauty. Even though she attends to everything and is charged with correcting, refusing, economizing (things that cause almost all women to be hated), she makes herself lovable to the entire household. One does not find in her the emotion, or hardheadedness, or glibness, or temperament, as in other women. With a single look she makes herself heard, and one fears displeasing her.

"She gives precise orders. She only orders what can be executed. She corrects with kindness, and in correcting she encourages. The heart of her father rests on her, just like a traveler, beaten down by the blaze of the sun, rests in the shade on tender grass. You are right, Telemachus. Antiope is a treasure worthy of being sought after in the most distant lands. Her mind, no more than her body, is never attired with vain ornaments. Her imagination, though lively, is restrained. She only speaks through necessity, and, if she opens her mouth, sweet persuasion and simple charms flow from her lips. As soon as she speaks, everyone falls quiet, and she blushes from it. She comes close to suppressing what she wants to say when she perceives that they are listening to her so attentively. We have barely heard her speak.

"Do you remember, O Telemachus, the day that her father summoned her? She appeared, eyes downcast, covered with a large veil, and she only spoke in order to moderate the anger of Idomeneus, who wanted to have one of his slaves rigorously punished. At first, she entered into his affliction. Then she calmed him. Lastly, she made him understand what could excuse that wretch and, without making the king feel that he was too quick-tempered, she inspired feelings of justice and compassion in him. Thetis, when she flatters old Nereus, does not appease with more gentleness the angry waves. In this way, Antiope, without taking any authority and without prevailing with her charms, will one day manage the heart of her spouse as she now touches her lyre when she wants to draw the most tender chords from it.

"Once again, Telemachus, your love for her is just. The gods destine it for you. You love her with a reasonable love. You must wait until Odysseus gives her to you. I praise you for not having wanted to reveal your feelings to her, but know that, if you had apprised her of your designs indirectly, she would have rejected them and would have ceased esteeming you. She will never promise herself to anyone. She will allow herself to be given by her father; she will only ever take for a spouse a man who reveres the gods and who would fulfill every decorum.

"Have you observed, as I have, that she reveals herself even less and that she lowers her eyes even more since your return? She knows all that befell you of good fortune in the war. She is not ignorant of either your birth or of your adventures or of all that the gods have placed in you. It is what renders her so modest and so reserved. Let us go, Telemachus, let us go to Ithaca. There only remains for me to have you find your father and to put you in a position to obtain a wife worthy of the golden age. Were she a shepherdess in cold Algidus, instead of the daughter of the king of Salentum, you would be only too lucky to possess her."

Idomeneus, who feared the departure of Telemachus and Mentor, only thought of delaying it. He represented to Mentor that without him, he could not rule on a difference of opinion that had arisen between Diophanes, priest of Olympian Zeus, and Helopdorus, priest of Apollo, about the presages that one draws from the flight of birds and the entrails of victims.

"Why," Mentor responded, "would you meddle in sacred things? Leave the decision to the Etruscans, who have the tradition of the most ancient oracles and who are inspired to be the interpreters of the gods. Only use your authority to snuff out those disputes when they emerge. Show neither partiality nor bias. Be content to support the decision when it is made. Remember that a king must be submissive to religion, and he must never undertake to rule it. Religion comes from the gods; it is above kings. If kings meddle in religion, instead of protecting it, they will force it into servitude. Kings are so mighty and other men so weak that all will be in peril of being corrupted at the discretion of kings, should they enter into questions that regard sacred things. Leave the decision, then, in complete liberty to the friends of the gods, and limit yourself to repressing those who will not obey their judgment when it has been pronounced."

Then Idomeneus complained of the predicament he was in concerning a great number of petitions among various individuals who were pressing him to judge.

"Decide," Mentor responded to him, "all the new questions that will establish general maxims of jurisprudence and interpret the laws, but never burden yourself with judging individual cases. They will come all in droves to besiege you. You will be the only judge of your people; all the other judges who are under you will become useless; you will be overwhelmed, and the least affairs will steal you away from the great ones without your being able to sufficiently sort out the details of the least ones. Be very careful, therefore, of casting yourself into this predicament; send the affairs of individuals back to the regular judges; only do that which no one else can do so as to unburden yourself—you will then be doing the true functions of a king."

"They still press me," said Idomeneus, "to do certain marriages. The persons of a distinguished birth who followed me into every war and who lost very great possessions in serving me would like to find some type of compensation in wedding certain rich daughters. I only have to say a word to procure these arrangements for them."

"It is true," responded Mentor, "that it would only cost you a word, but that word itself would be too costly to you. Would you want to take away from fathers and mothers the liberty and the consolation of choosing their sons-in-law, and by consequence, their heirs? That would be to subject every family to the most rigorous enslavement. You would make yourself responsible for all the domestic woes of your citizens. Marriages have enough thorns without also giving that bitterness to them. If you have loyal servants to reward, give them uncultivated land; add ranks and honors to this proportionate to their station and their services; add to that, if you must, some silver taken from your funds intended for your expenditures—but never pay your debts by sacrificing rich daughters, despite their parents."

Idomeneus soon passed from this question to another. "The Sybarites," he said, "are complaining that we usurped lands that belong to them and that we have given those lands, as fields to be cleared, to the foreigners whom we have recently lured here. Should I cede to these people? If I do it, each will think that he only has to make claims against us."

"It is not just," responded Mentor, "to believe the Sybarites in their own cause, but it also is not just to believe you in yours."

"Who do we believe then?" rejoined Idomeneus.

"Neither of the two parties," pursued Mentor, "should be believed. An arbitrator must be chosen from a neighboring people who are not suspect to either side, such as the Sipontines. They have no interests contrary to yours."

"But am I obliged," responded Idomeneus, "to believe some arbitrator? Am I not king? A sovereign, is he obliged to submit himself to foreigners about the extent of his dominion?"

Mentor resumed the discourse thusly:

"Since you want to hold firm, you must have judged that your right is good. On the other hand, the Sybarites yield nothing. They maintain that their right is certain. In this opposition of sentiments, there must be an arbitrator, chosen by the parties, to reconcile you, or may the fate of arms decide. There is not a middle ground. Were you to enter into a republic where there was neither magistrate, nor judges, and where each family believed itself in the right to do justice for itself, through violence, about all its claims against its neighbors, you would deplore the misfortune of such a nation and you would be horrified by that frightful disorder in which every family arms itself against each other.

"Do you believe the gods would regard with any less horror the whole world, which is the universal republic, if each people, who are only like one great family, believe themselves fully in the right to do, through violence, justice themselves with regard to all their claims against the other neighboring peoples? An individual who possesses a field as the inheritance from his ancestors, can only maintain it through the authority of the laws and through the judgment of the magistrate. He would be very severely punished as a seditionist should he want to keep through force what justice has given him. Do you think that kings may immediately use violence to sustain their claims without having attempted all the paths of gentleness and humanity? Justice, is it not even more sacred and more inviolate for kings in relation to entire countries than for families in relation to a few plowed fields? Will one be unjust and a thief when he takes only a few acres of land? Will one be just, will he be heroic, when he takes provinces?

"If he prejudges, if he flatters himself, if he turns a blind eye to the small interests of individuals, must he not fear even more flattering himself and being blind about the great interests of the state? Will he believe himself in a matter where he has so many reasons to distrust himself? Will he not fear being wrong in the cases where the mistake of a single man has frightful consequences? The mistake of a king who flatters himself about his claims often causes devastation, famines, massacres, plagues, deprivations of mores, whose calamitous effects extend into the most distant centuries. A king, who always assembles so many flatterers around him, will he not fear being flattered on those occasions?

"If he agrees to some arbitration to end the difference of opinion, he shows his fairness, his good faith, his moderation. He makes public the solid reasons on which his claim is based. The chosen arbitrator is a friendly mediator and not a rigorous judge. One does not submit blindly to his decisions but has great deference toward him. He does not pronounce a sentence as a sovereign judge; he makes propositions, and something is sacrificed, through his counsels, in order to preserve peace. If war comes despite all the cares that a king takes to preserve peace, he has at least, then, the witness of his conscience, the esteem of his neighbors, and the just protection of the gods."

Idomeneus, touched by this speech, consented that the Sipontines be mediators between him and the Sybarites.

Then the king, seeing that all the means of detaining the two foreigners were eluding him, tried to stop them with a stronger bond. He had noticed that Telemachus was in love with Antiope, and he hoped to get to him through this passion. With this in mind, he had her sing several times during the feasts. She did it so as not to disobey her father, but with so much modesty and sadness that one easily saw the difficulty she suffered in obeying him. Idomeneus went so far as to want her to sing of the victory brought home over the Daunians and Adrastus. But she could not resolve herself to sing the praises of Telemachus. She respectfully demurred, and her father dared not compel her. Her sweet and touching voice penetrated the heart of the young son of Odysseus. He was very moved.

Idomeneus, who had his eyes fixed on him, took pleasure in his distress. But Telemachus pretended not to perceive the designs of the king. He could not keep himself on these occasions from being extremely touched, but reason was above sentiment in him, and it was no longer that same Telemachus whom a tyrannical passion had once captivated on the island of Calypso. While Antiope was singing, he kept a profound silence. As soon as she had finished, he hastened to turn the conversation to some other matter.

The king, unable by this path to succeed in his design, finally resolved to have a great hunt, in which he wanted, against custom, to give for the pleasure of his daughter. Antiope wept, not wanting to go on it, but the absolute order of her father must be executed.

She mounts a horse, lathery, skittish, and resembling those that Castor tamed for combat. She handles him effortlessly. A group of young girls ardently follow her. She appears in the midst of them like Artemis in the forests. The king sees her, and he cannot tire of seeing her. Seeing her, he forgets all his past woes. Telemachus sees her too, and he is even more touched by Antiope's modesty than by her skills and all her charms.

The dogs pursued a wild boar of an enormous size and furious like the one of Calydon. His long bristles were hard and raised like darts. His gleaming eyes were filled with blood and fire. His

BOOK XVII

breathing made itself heard from a distance, like the dull sound of the seditious winds when Aeolus recalls them into his cavern to appease the tempests. His tusks, long and hooked like the sharp scythe of the reaper, gashed the trunks of the trees. All the dogs that dared approach him were ripped apart. The boldest hunters, in pursuit of it, feared reaching it.

Antiope, light in the race like the wind, did not fear attacking it up close. She hurls a shaft piercing it above the shoulder. The blood of the ferocious animal streams, rendering it more furious. It wheels toward the one who wounded it. Immediately, Antiope's horse, despite his pride, shudders and recoils. The monstrous boar lunges against him like the heavy machines that rattle the walls of the most fortified cities. The steed staggers and goes down. Antiope finds herself falling to the ground, in no state to avoid the fatal strike from the tusks of the boar animated against her. But Telemachus, alert to Antiope's danger, has already dismounted. Faster than lightning, he flings himself between the downed horse and the boar, which comes back to avenge its blood; he holds in his hands a long spear and sinks it almost entirely into the flank of the horrible animal that falls filled with rage.

At that instant, Telemachus severs the head that still causes fear seeing it up close and stuns all the hunters. He presents it to Antiope. She blushes. She consults the eyes of her father, who, after having been gripped with fright, is transported with joy to see her out of peril and motions that she should accept the gift. In taking it, she says to Telemachus, "I receive from you with gratitude another gift more grand, for I owe you my life."

No sooner had she spoken than she feared having said too much. She lowered her eyes, and Telemachus, who saw her embarrassment, only dared say these words to her: "Happy is the son of Odysseus to have preserved a life so precious! But happier still if he could spend his alongside you!"

Antiope, without responding, brusquely rejoined the troop of her young companions, where she remounted.

Idomeneus would have, from that moment, promised his daughter to Telemachus. But he hoped to inflame his passion further, by leaving him in uncertainty, and even believed he could still retain him in Salentum through the desire to assure his marriage. Idomeneus reasoned thus to himself, but the gods toy with the wisdom of men. That which should have detained Telemachus was precisely what pressed him to depart. What he was beginning to feel put him in a just distrust of himself.

Mentor redoubled his attentions to inspire in him an impatient desire to return to Ithaca, and he pressed Idomeneus at the same time to allow him to depart. The vessel was already prepared, for Mentor, who ruled every moment of Telemachus' life in order to elevate him to the highest glory, only stopped in each place as long as necessary to train his virtue and to have him gain experience. Mentor had attended to have the vessel readied ever since Telemachus' arrival.

But Idomeneus, who had had much repugnance in seeing it readied, fell into a mortal sadness and into a pitiful desolation when he saw that his two guests, from whom he had drawn so much assistance, were going to abandon him. He shut himself up in the most secret part of his house. There he eased his heart, heaving groans and shedding tears. He forgot the need to eat. Sleep no longer softened his searing pains. He withered, he consumed himself with restlessness like a great tree that covers the ground with the shade of its thick branches and in which a worm begins to gnaw the trunk in the slender channels where the sap flows for its nourishment; this tree, that the winds have never shaken, that fruitful Earth is pleased to nourish at her breast, and that the ax of the plowman has always respected, does not stop languishing without anyone being able to uncover the cause of its malady; it wilts, it despoils itself of its leaves, which are its glory; thereafter, it only reveals a trunk covered with a split bark and dry branches—so appeared Idomeneus in his pain.

Telemachus, touched with tenderness, dared not speak to him. He feared the day of departure. He sought pretexts to delay it, and he would have stayed in this uncertainty for a long time had Mentor not said: "I am glad to see you so changed. You were born harsh and haughty; your heart only allowed itself to be touched by your conveniences and your self-interests, but you have finally become a man, and you are beginning, through the experience of your misfortunes, to empathize with the woes of others. Without this empathy, one has neither goodness, nor virtue, nor the capacity to govern men. But you must not push it too far, nor fall into a feeble friendship. I will gladly speak to Idomeneus to gain his consent to our departure, and I will spare you the embarrassment of a conversation so unpleasant, but I do not want a painful shyness and timidity to dominate your heart. You must accustom yourself to combining courage and firmness with a tender and sensitive friendship. You must fear afflicting men unnecessarily. You must enter into their pain when you cannot avoid causing it to them and soften as much as you can the blow when it is impossible to spare them from it entirely."

"It is in seeking that softening," responded Telemachus, "that I would prefer that Idomeneus learned of our departure from you than from me."

Mentor quickly said to him, "You are mistaken, my dear Telemachus. You were born like the children of kings raised in the royal purple, who only desire that all be done in their fashion and that all nature obeys their will, yet who do not have the fortitude to resist anyone to their face. It is not that they worry about men, nor that they fear, through goodness, afflicting them, but rather that, for their own comfort and convenience, they do not want to see sad and discontented faces around them. The difficulties and desolations of men do not touch them, provided they are not under their eyes. If they hear them spoken of, this discourse importunes and saddens them. In order to please them, one must always say that all is well. While they are in their delights, they do not want either to see or to hear anything that could disrupt their joy. If they must rebuke, correct, set someone straight, resist the pretensions and unjust passions of an importune man, they will always give the commission of it to some other person. Rather than speaking for themselves with a gentle firmness on those occasions, they would rather allow the most unjust favor to be snatched from them. They will spoil their most important affairs for want of knowing how to decide against the sentiment of those with whom they have affairs every day.

"This weakness that one senses in them makes everyone only think of prevailing upon it. They press them, they importune them, they overwhelm them, and they succeed in overwhelming them. At first, they flatter and laud the kings in order to insinuate themselves. But, as soon as they are in their confidence and alongside them in posts of some authority, they lead them far away; they impose the yoke on them. The kings groan under it and often want to shake it off, but they bear it all their life. They are defensive over appearing to be governed, yet they always really are. They cannot even do without being so, for they are like those weak branches of the vine that, not having any support for themselves, always wrap around the trunk of some great tree.

"I will not tolerate, O Telemachus, that you fall into this fault, which renders a man an imbecile in governing. You, who are tender to the point of not daring to speak to Idomeneus, you will no longer be touched by his afflictions as soon as you have left Salentum; it is not his grief that touches you, it is his presence that causes you to feel uncomfortable. Go, speak to Idomeneus yourself. Learn on this occasion to be both tender and firm. Show him your grief in forsaking him, but show him also, in a decisive tone, the necessity of our departure."

Telemachus dared not resist Mentor, nor go find Idomeneus. He was ashamed of his fear, and he did not have the courage to overcome it. He hesitated. He took two steps and came back to Mentor straightaway to allege some new reason to defer.

But Mentor's look alone took his words away and caused all his beautiful pretexts to disappear.

"Is this then," Mentor said, smiling, "that victor over the Daunians, that liberator of great Hesperia, that son of wise Odysseus, who should be, after him, the oracle of Greece? He dares not say to Idomeneus that he can no longer delay his return to his homeland in order to see his father again! O peoples of Ithaca, how unfortunate you will be one day if you have a king whom painful shyness dominates and who, out of weakness, sacrifices the greatest interests for the sake of the least! You see, Telemachus, what difference there is between valor in combat and courage in affairs. You did not fear Adrastus' weapons, yet you fear Idomeneus' sadness. You see, that is what dishonors princes who have done the greatest deeds—after having appeared like heroes in war, they show themselves to be the least of men in everyday matters, where others sustain themselves with vigor."

Telemachus, sensing the truth in these words, and stung by this reproach, brusquely left without heeding his own thoughts. But no sooner had he appeared in the place where Idomeneus was seated, his eyes downcast, languishing and beaten-down with sadness, than they feared one another. They dared not look at one another. They heard each other without saying anything, and each feared that the other would break the silence. They both began to weep.

At last, Idomeneus, pressed by an excess of pain, cried out, "What does it serve to seek virtue if it rewards so poorly those who love it? After having shown me my weakness, they abandon me! O well! I am going to fall back into all my woes. May they no longer speak to me about good governance. No, I cannot do it. I am weary of men.

"Where do you want to go, Telemachus? Your father is no more. You seek him uselessly. Ithaca is the prey of your enemies. They will slay you if you return there. Someone among them will have married your mother. Remain here. You will be my son-in-law and my heir. You will reign after me. Even during my life, you will have an absolute power here. My trust in you will be unlimited. If you are insensitive to all these advantages, at least leave me Mentor, who is my every resource. Speak. Answer me. Do not harden your heart. Have pity on the most unhappy of all men. What! You say nothing? Ah! I understand how cruel the gods are to me. I feel it even more rigorously than in Crete, when I pierced my own son."

Finally, Telemachus responded in a troubled and timid voice, "I am not my own. The destinies call me back to my homeland. Mentor, who has the wisdom of the gods, orders me in their name to depart. What do you want me to do? Will I renounce my father, my mother, my homeland which must be even more dear to me than them? Born to be king, I am not destined to a gentle and tranquil life, nor to follow my own inclinations. Your kingdom is richer and more powerful than that of my father. But I must prefer what the gods destine for me to that which you have the goodness to offer me. I would believe myself happy if I had Antiope for my wife, without hoping for your kingdom. But, to render myself worthy of it, I must go where my duties call me and it would be my father who asks you for her on my behalf.

"Did you not promise to send me back to Ithaca? Is it not on the basis of this promise that I fought for you against Adrastus with the allies? It is time that I think of mending my domestic woes. The gods, who have given Mentor to me, have also given Mentor to the son of Odysseus so as to have him fulfill his destiny. Do you want that I lose Mentor after having lost all the rest? I no longer have possessions, nor retreat, nor father, nor mother, nor assured homeland. There only remains to me a wise and virtuous man, who is the most precious gift of Zeus. Judge yourself if I can renounce him and consent that he abandon me. No, I would rather die. Snatch my life from me. Life is nothing. But do not snatch Mentor from me."

As Telemachus was speaking, his voice grew stronger, and his timidity disappeared. Idomeneus did not know how to respond, but he could not abide what the son of Odysseus said to him. While he could no longer speak, he tried, through his looks and gestures, to at least cause pity. At that moment, he saw Mentor appear, who said these grave words to him:

"Do not grieve. We are forsaking you, but wisdom which presides over the councils of the gods will remain with you. Only think how very fortunate you are that Zeus would have sent us here to save your kingdom and to bring you back from your waywardness. Philocles, whom we have rendered to you, will serve you loyally. The reverential awe for the gods, the taste for virtue, the love of the peoples, the compassion for the destitute will always be in his heart. Listen to him. Use him with confidence and without jealousy. The greatest service that you can draw from him is to oblige him to tell you all your faults without softening. You see, that is what the greatest courage of a good king consists of—that of seeking true friends who point out his errors to him. Provided you have this courage, our absence will not harm you, and you will live happily. But, if flattery, which slithers in like a serpent, finds a path to your heart again so as to cause you to distrust selfless counsel, you are lost.

"Do not allow yourself to be weakly beaten down by pain but strive to follow virtue. I told Philocles all that he should do to unburden you, and to never abuse your trust. I can answer to you for him. The gods have given him to you as they have given me to Telemachus. Each must courageously follow his destiny. It is useless to be aggrieved. If ever you have need of my help, after I have rendered Telemachus to his father and his country, I will come back to see you. What could I do that would give me a more manifest pleasure? I seek neither goods, nor authority on earth. I only want to help those who seek justice and virtue. Would I ever be able to forget the trust and friendship that you have shown me?"

At these words, Idomeneus was suddenly changed. He felt his heart appeased just as Poseidon with his trident appeases the raging waves and the blackest tempests. There only remained in him a gentle and peaceful pain. It was more a sadness and a tender feeling than an acute pain. Courage, trust, virtue, hope for the succor of the gods began to be reborn within him.

"O well, my dear Mentor," he said, "I must then lose everything and not be discouraged. At least remember Idomeneus. When you arrive in Ithaca, where your wisdom will fill you with prosperity, do not forget that Salentum was your work and that you have left an unhappy king there whose only hope is in you. Go, worthy son of Odysseus, I no longer detain you. I am far from resisting the gods who have loaned me so great a treasure. Go also, Mentor, the greatest and the wisest of all men (if, however, humanity can do what I have seen you do, and if you are not a deity beneath a borrowed shape in order to instruct weak and ignorant men), go guide the son of Odysseus, more fortunate in having you than in being the victor over Adrastus. Go, both of you. I no longer dare to speak. Forgive my sighs. Go, live, be happy together. There no longer remains anything in the world for me but the memory of having possessed you here. O beautiful days, such happy days, days of which I did not well know the price, days too swiftly unfolded, you will never come back! Never will my eyes see what they see!"

Mentor took that moment to depart. He embraced Philocles, who soaked him with his tears, unable to speak. Telemachus wanted to take Mentor by the hand so as to pull him away from that of Idomeneus, but Idomeneus, taking the path to the harbor, put himself between Mentor and Telemachus. He looked at them, he groaned, he began choked-up speeches but was unable to complete any of them.

At the same time, they heard confused cries on the shoreline covered with sailors. They tend the ropes. The favorable wind rises. Telemachus and Mentor, tears in their eyes, take their leave of the king, who holds them tightly in his arms for a long time and follows them with his eyes as far as he is able.

End of Book XVII

THE ADVENTURES OF
TELEMACHUS
SON OF ODYSSEUS

BOOK XVIII

Meanwhile, *the sails swell*, the anchors are raised, the land seems to flee. The experienced pilot already spies the Leucata mountain in the distance, whose head hides in a whirl of freezing fog, and the Acroceraunian mountains, which still show a proud face to the skies after having been so often crushed by thunderbolts.

During this voyage, Telemachus said to Mentor, "I believe now to grasp the maxims of governance that you explained to me. At first, they appeared like a dream to me, but little by little, they sort themselves out in my mind and stand out clearly, just as all objects appear murky and confused in the morning, at the first light of Dawn, but then they seem to emerge, as if from chaos, when the light, gradually rising, gives them, so to speak, their figures and natural colors. I am very persuaded that the essential point of governance is to discern the different characteristics of intelligence well in order to choose and apply them according to men's talents. But it remains for me to know how one can be knowledgeable about men."

Then Mentor responded, "You must study men in order to know them, and to know them you must see them often and deal with them. Kings should converse with their subjects, draw them out, consult them, test them through minor posts, of which they have them render an account, to see if they are capable of higher functions.

"How is it, my dear Telemachus, that you learned in Ithaca to be knowledgeable about sculptures? It is through considering them and noting their faults and their perfections with experienced people. In the same way, speak often of the good and bad qualities of men with other wise and virtuous men who have studied their characters for a long time, and you will gradually learn how they are made and what may be expected of them.

"What taught you to know the good and the bad poets? It is frequent reading and reflection with people who have a taste for poetry. How is it that you acquired discernment about music? It is the same diligence of observing various musicians. How can one hope to govern men well if one does not know them? And how will one know them if one never lives with them? It is not living with them to only see them all in public, where one only says, on both sides, things indifferent and artfully prepared; it is a question of seeing them in private, of drawing from the bottom of their hearts all the hidden reserves that are there, of feeling them out from all sides, of sounding them out in order to discover their maxims. But, to judge men well, you must begin by knowing what they should be. You must know what true and solid merit is in order to discern those who have it from those who do not have it.

"Men never cease speaking of virtue and merit without knowing what merit and virtue precisely are. They are only beautiful names, vague terms for most men, who honor themselves in speaking of them at all hours. You must have certain principles of justice, reason, and virtue to recognize those who are reasonable and virtuous. You must know the maxims of a good and wise government to know the men who have those maxims and those who distance themselves from them through a false subtlety. In a word, to measure several things, we must have a fixed measure. To judge, we must, in the same way, have consistent principles to which all our judgments reduce.

"You must know precisely what the goal of human life is, and to what end you should propose to govern men. This sole and essential goal is to never desire authority and greatness for oneself, for that ambitious pursuit will only go toward satisfying a tyrannical pridefulness. Rather, one should sacrifice oneself in the infinite difficulties of government in order to render men good and happy. Otherwise, he tiptoes, haphazardly groping his way along throughout his life. He goes like a ship on the open sea that does not have a pilot, does not consult the heavens, and to whom all the neighboring coasts are unknown. He can only wreck.

"Often, princes, for want of knowing what true virtue consists of, do not know what they should look for in men. True virtue has for them something of harshness; it appears too austere and too autonomous to them, it frightens and embitters them. They turn to flattery. From then on, they can no longer find either sincerity or virtue. From then on, they chase after a vain phantom of false glory, which renders them unworthy of the true. They soon become accustomed to believing that there is no true virtue on earth—for the good know the wicked well, but the wicked do not know the good and cannot believe there are any.

"Such princes only know how to distrust everyone equally; they hide, they shut themselves off, they are defensive about the least things. They fear men and are feared by them. They flee the light; they do not dare to appear in their natural state. Although they do not wish to be known, they do not fail to be, for the malignant curiosity of their subjects penetrates and guesses everything. But they know no one. The self-interested people who obsess over them are delighted to see them inaccessible—a king inaccessible to men is also inaccessible to the truth; it is blackened through vile reports and all that could open his eyes to it is distanced from him. Those kinds of kings spend their lives in a wild and fierce grandeur where, incessantly afraid of being deceived, they inevitably always are and merit being so. As soon as they only speak to a small number of people, they commit themselves to receiving all the passions and prejudices of those people. Even good people have their faults and their biases. Moreover, they are at the mercy of the scandal-mongering rapporteurs, a low and malignant nation, that feed on venom, that poison innocent things, that magnify petty ones, that invent evil rather than ceasing to harm, that play for their own interest off of the distrust and shameful curiosity of a weak and umbrageous prince.

"Know, then, O my dear Telemachus, know men. Examine them, draw them out about one another, test them little by little, and do not deliver yourself over to any. Profit from your experience when you have been deceived in your judgments, for you will be deceived sometimes, and the wicked are too subtle not to dupe the good through their disguises. Learn from that to not judge a person too quickly, neither the good in them nor the bad in them; either is very dangerous. In this way, your past mistakes will instruct you very usefully.

"When you find talents and virtue in a man, make use of them with confidence, the honnête homme wants his uprightness noticed. They prefer esteem and confidence to treasures. But do not spoil them by giving them unlimited power. The one who would have always been virtuous no longer is, because his master gave him too much authority and too many riches. Whomever is loved enough by the gods to find in all his kingdom two or three true friends with wisdom and a constant goodness soon finds through them other persons who resemble them to fill the lesser ranks. Through the good men in whom he confides, he learns what he cannot discern by himself about his other subjects."

"But must I," said Telemachus, "make use of the wicked when they are capable, as I have often heard said?"

"You are often," answered Mentor, "in need of using them. In a nation, agitated and in disorder, you often find unjust and artful men who are already in authority. They have important posts that cannot be taken away from them. They have acquired the confidence of certain powerful people whom you need managed. They must be managed by those men, those scoundrels, because they fear them and they can upset everything. You must indeed make use of them for a time, but you must also have in sight the goal of gradually rendering them unnecessary.

"As for real and intimate trust, be very wary of ever placing it in them, for they can abuse it and then hold your secret against you; a shackle more difficult to break than all iron shackles. Use them for passing negotiations, treat them well, engage them through their very passions to be loyal to you, for you will only hold them in that way. But do not include them in your most secret deliberations. Always have a recourse ready to remove them at your discretion. But never give them the key to your heart, nor to your affairs. When your state becomes peaceful, orderly, led by wise and upright men, of whom you are sure, little by little the wicked, whom you were compelled to use, will become unnecessary. Then you must not stop treating them well, for it is never permitted to be ungrateful, even when it comes to the wicked. But, in treating them well, you must try to render them good. It is necessary to tolerate certain faults in them, for which humanity is forgiven. You must nevertheless, little by little, take away authority and repress the evils that they would do openly if they were allowed to do them. After all, it is a wickedness to do good through the wicked, and even though this wickedness may often be unavoidable, you must aim, nevertheless, little by little, toward making it end.

"A wise prince, who only wants good order and justice, will come, in time, to do without corrupt and deceiving men. He will find enough good men who have an adequate capability. But it is not enough to find good subjects in a nation; it is essential to train new ones."

"That has to be," responded Telemachus, "a great obstacle."

"Not at all," resumed Mentor. "The effort you make in seeking able and virtuous men to promote, excites and animates all the others who have talent and courage. Each makes an effort. How many men are there who idly languish in obscurity, and who would become great men, if emulation and the hope of success animates them to work! How many men are there who, destitute and powerless to elevate themselves through virtue, attempt to elevate themselves through crime! If then, you attach rewards and honors to genius and virtue, how many subjects will train themselves? But how many you will train in having them ascend, by degrees, from the lowest posts to the highest; you will train talents, you will test the breadth of minds and the sincerity of virtue. Those men who attain the highest positions will have been raised under your eyes from the lowest. You will have followed them all their lives, step by step; you will evaluate them, not by their words but by all the results of their deeds."

While Mentor was reasoning in this way, they caught sight of a Phaeacian vessel that had put in at a small deserted and wild island bordered with frightful rocks. At the same time the winds fell silent, and even the gentlest zephyrs seemed to hold their breath. The entire sea became as smooth as glass. The deflated sails could no longer animate the vessel. The efforts of the oarsmen, already tired, were futile. It was necessary to land on that island that was more a reef than land suitable to being inhabited by men. In other weather less calm, one would not have been able to land there without great peril.

The Phaeacians who were waiting for the wind did not appear less impatient than the Salentines to continue their voyage. Telemachus approached them on those steep shores. Straightaway, he asks the first man he meets if he had seen Odysseus, king of Ithaca, in the house of King Alcinous.

The one whom he had addressed was, by chance, not Phaeacian. He was an unknown foreigner who had a majestic air, yet sad and beaten-down. He appeared to be dreaming, and, at first, barely listened to Telemachus' question. But finally, he answered him.

"You are not wrong. Odysseus was received by King Alcinous, as in a place where they revere Zeus and show hospitality. But he is no longer there, and you would seek him uselessly. He departed to see Ithaca again, should the appeased gods finally suffer that he may ever bow before his household gods."

No sooner had this stranger sadly uttered these words than he lunged into a small thick wood on top of a rock from where he sadly gazed at the sea, shunning the men he saw and seeming to be afflicted at being unable to depart. Telemachus stared at him. The more he stared at him, the more he was stirred and stunned.

"That stranger," he said to Mentor, "answered me like a man who barely listens to what is said to him and who is filled with bitterness. I pity unfortunate wretches ever since I have been one, and I sense that my heart takes an interest in this man without knowing why. He received me poorly enough; barely did he deign to listen to me and to answer. Nevertheless, I cannot stop wishing for an end to his woes."

Mentor, smiling, responded, "Voila, that is what the misfortunes of life serve to do—they render princes moderate and sensitive to the difficulties of others. When they have only ever tasted the sweet poison of prosperity, they believe themselves gods, they want mountains flattened to satisfy them, they count men for nothing, they want to toy with all of nature. When they hear suffering spoken of, they do not know what it is. It is a phantasm to them. They have never seen the distance between good and evil. The woes of misfortune alone can give them humaneness and change their hearts of stone into human hearts. Then they feel that they are men and know how they should treat other men like them. If a stranger causes you so much pity because he is, like you, wandering on this shore, how much more compassion should you have for the people of Ithaca when you see them suffering one day. That people whom the gods will have entrusted to you, as a flock is entrusted to a shepherd, will perhaps be unhappy through your ambition, or through your flamboyance, or through your imprudence—for peoples only suffer through the errors of kings who should watch over them to prevent suffering."

While Mentor was speaking in this way, Telemachus was plunged into sadness and grief. He responded at last, a little emotionally.

"If all these things are true, the state of a king is unfortunate indeed. He is a slave to all those whom he appears to command.

He is created for them. He owes his entire being to them; he is burdened with all their needs. He is the man of the people as a whole and of each individual. He must adapt to their weaknesses, which he corrects as father, to render them wise and happy. The authority that he appears to have is not his; it can do nothing, neither for his glory, nor for his pleasure. His authority is that of the laws. He must obey them. Strictly speaking, he is only the defender of the laws in order for the laws to reign. He must keep vigil and work to maintain them. He is the man the least free and the least tranquil in his whole kingdom. He is a slave who sacrifices his repose and his liberty for the liberty and felicity of the public."

"It is true," replied Mentor, "that the king is only king in order to care for his people like a shepherd for his flock, or like a father for his family. But, do you find, my dear Telemachus, that he would be unhappy in having so much good to do for so many people? He redresses the wicked through punishments, he encourages the good through rewards, he represents the gods in leading all humankind to virtue. Has he not enough glory in keeping the laws? That of putting himself above the laws is a false glory that only merits horror and scorn. If he is wicked, he can only be unhappy, for he would not know how to find any peace in his passions and in his vanity. If he is good, he should enjoy the purest and the most solid of all pleasures—to work for virtue and to expect from the gods an eternal reward."

Telemachus, agitated within by a secret pain, seemed to have never understood these maxims even though he had been filled with them and he had taught them to others himself. A black humor was giving him, contrary to his true feelings, a contradictory and subtle mind to reject the truths that Mentor was explaining. Telemachus opposed this reasoning to the ingratitude of men.

"Why take so much trouble," he said, "to make oneself loved by men, who perhaps will never love you, to do good to the wicked, who will use the good you do to harm you?"

Mentor answered him patiently. "You must count on the ingratitude of men and not fail to do good to them. You must serve them less for the love of them than for the love of the gods who command it. The good that one does is never wasted; if men forget it, the gods remember it and reward it. Moreover, if the multitude is ungrateful, there are always virtuous men who are touched by your virtue. Even the multitude, though changing and capricious, do not fail, sooner or later, to do justice, of a sort, to genuine virtue.

"But do you want to stop men from being ungrateful? Do not only work to render them powerful, rich, formidable through arms, happy through pleasures. That glory, that abundance, and those delights corrupt them; they will only serve to make them more wicked, and, consequently, more ungrateful. It is to give them a sinister present. It is to offer them a delicious poison. So, apply yourself to redressing mores, inspiring justice, sincerity, reverential awe of the gods, humaneness, fidelity, moderation, selflessness in them. In rendering them good, you will keep them from being ingrates. You will give them the truly good thing, which is virtue, and virtue, if it is solid, will always attach them to the one who inspired it in them. In this way, by giving them truly good things, you will do good for yourself, and you will not have to fear their ingratitude.

"Should it be surprising that men are ungrateful toward princes who have only ever exercised them in injustice, boundless ambition against their neighbors, inhumanity, haughtiness, bad faith? The prince should only expect from them what he taught them to do. If, on the contrary, he strives through his examples and through his authority to render them good, he would find the fruit of his work in their virtue, or at the least he would find in his virtue and in the friendship of the gods something with which to console himself in all his disappointments."

No sooner had this discourse ended than Telemachus eagerly approached the Phaeacians from the vessel that was stopped on the shore. He addressed himself to an old man among them and asked him where they were coming from, where they were going, and if they had seen Odysseus.

The old man answered, "We are coming from our island, which is that of the Phaeacians. We are going in search of merchandise toward Epirus. Odysseus, as you were already told, spent time in our homeland, but he left there."

"Who is," Telemachus quickly added, "that man so sad who seeks the most deserted places while waiting for your vessel to depart?"

"He is," the old man answered, "a foreigner who is unknown to us. But they say his name is Cleomenes, that he was born in Phrygia, that an oracle had foretold his mother, before his birth, that he would be king, provided he did not stay in his homeland, and that, if he did stay, the anger of the gods would make itself felt to the Phrygians through a cruel plague. As soon as he was born, his parents gave him to sailors who carried him to the island of Lesbos. He was raised there in secret at the expense of his homeland, which had so great an interest in keeping him at a distance.

"Soon he became tall, robust, agreeable, and adroit at all the exercises of the body. He even applied himself, with much enjoyment and genius, to the sciences and fine arts. But he could not be tolerated in any country. The prediction about him made him famous. He was soon recognized wherever he went. Everywhere, kings feared he would relieve them of their diadems. Thus, he has been wandering since his youth, and he can find no place in the world where he would be allowed to stop. He has often stayed with peoples very distant from his own, but no sooner has he arrived in a city than his birth and the oracle that regards it is discovered. He has a fine time hiding himself and choosing in each place some type of obscure life. His talents always shine, they say, in spite of himself, not only in war but in scholarship and in the most important affairs. In each country, there always appears some unforeseen event that drags him in and makes him known to the public.

"It is his merit that causes his misfortune. It causes him to be feared and excluded from every country where he desires to live. His destiny is to be esteemed, loved, marveled at everywhere, yet rejected by all the known lands. He is no longer young, and nevertheless he still has not found any coast, neither in Asia, nor in Greece, where they would want to let him live in repose.

"He seems unambitious, and he seeks no fortune. He would think himself only too happy had the oracle never promised kingship to him. There remains no hope to him of ever seeing his homeland again, for he knows that he could only bring grief and tears to all the families. Even kingship, by which he suffers, does not seem desirable to him. He runs after it, in spite of himself, through a sad fatalism, from kingdom to kingdom, and it seems to flee before him, mocking this poor wretch into his old age. Ill-fated gift of the gods that troubles all his most beautiful days and that will only cause him troubles at an age when infirm men no longer need anything but repose! He is going, he says, to seek in the direction of Thrace some people, uncivilized and lawless, whom he can assemble, establish policies, and govern for several years. After that, the oracle being accomplished, there will no longer be anything to fear from him in the most flourishing kingdoms. He is counting on retiring then in freedom to a village in Carie, where he will devote himself to agriculture, which he loves passionately. He is a wise and moderate man who reveres the gods, knows men well, and knows how to live in peace with them without judging them. Voila, that is what is told of this stranger, of whom you ask me news."

During this conversation, Telemachus often turned his eyes back toward the sea, which was beginning to be choppy. The wind was whipping up the swells, which were going to pound the rocks, whitening them with their foam. At that moment, the old man said to Telemachus, "I must leave. My companions cannot wait for me."

Saying these words, he ran to the shore. They board. Only muddled cries are heard along the shore through the ardor of the sailors impatient to depart.

That stranger, named Cleomenes, had wandered for some time in the middle of the island, ascending to the summit of all the

BOOK XVIII

rocks and considering from there all the vast expanse of the sea with a profound sadness. Telemachus had not lost sight of him, and he did not cease observing his steps. His heart was tender toward this virtuous, wandering, unfortunate man destined for the greatest things and serving as the toy of rigorous Fortune, far from his homeland. *At least,* he said to himself, *I will perhaps see Ithaca again. But this Cleomenes can never hope to see Phrygia again.*

The example of a man even more unfortunate than him eased Telemachus' pain. Finally, this man, seeing that his vessel was ready, descended from those cliffs with as much quickness and agility as Apollo in the forests of Lycia, having knotted his blond hair and crossed over precipices to shoot the deer and wild boar with his arrows.

Already, this stranger is on the vessel that plows the bitter water and distances itself from land. Then, a hidden pressing pain seizes Telemachus' heart; he is afflicted without knowing why, tears stream from his eyes, and nothing is so sweet to him as to weep. At the same time, he spies on the shore all the Salentine sailors, bedded down on the grass and sleeping soundly. They were weary and beaten-down. Sweet Sleep had slipped into their limbs, and all the moist poppies of the night had been spread over them in the middle of the day by the power of Athena. Telemachus is astonished to see this universal sleepiness in the Salentines, while the Phaeacians had been so attentive and in a hurry to take advantage of the favorable wind.

But he is still more preoccupied watching the Phaeacian vessel about to disappear amidst the waves than with walking toward the

Salentines to awaken them. An amazement and a secret distress keep his eyes fixed on that vessel already departed, of which he no longer sees anything but the sails as a bit of white on the azure water. He is not even listening to Mentor who is speaking to him, and he is completely beside himself in a frenzy resembling that of the maenads, when they hold the thyrsus in hand and cause their mad cries to reverberate on the riverbanks of the Hebros, along with the Rhodope and Ismarus mountains.

Finally, he returned from that trance a bit, and tears began to stream again from his eyes. Then Mentor said to him, "I am not surprised, my dear Telemachus, to see you weep. The cause of your pain, unknown to you, is not unknown to Mentor. It is nature that speaks and makes itself felt; it is what touches your heart. The stranger who gave you such a shock is the great Odysseus. What an old Phaeacian recounted to you about him, in the name of Cleomenes, it is only a fiction made up to hide more surely the return of your father to his kingdom. He is going with them straight to Ithaca. He is already very near the harbor, and he is finally seeing those places so long desired. Your eyes saw him, as you had once been foretold, but without knowing him. Soon you will see him and you will know him, and he will know you.

"But now the gods can not permit your recognizing him outside of Ithaca. His heart was no less moved than yours. He is too wise to reveal himself to any mortal in a place where he could be exposed to the betrayals and insults of the cruel suitors of Penelope. Odysseus, your father, is the wisest of all men. His heart is like a deep well; one would not know how to draw his secret from it.

He loves the truth and never says anything that wounds it. But he only says it in need, and wisdom, like a seal, always keeps his lips closed to every unnecessary word. How moved he was in speaking to you, how violently he fought himself not to be revealed! What did he not suffer in seeing you! Voila, that is what renders him sad and beaten-down."

During this discourse, Telemachus, touched and distressed, could not hold back a torrent of tears. His sobs even kept him from responding for a long time. Finally, he exclaimed, "Alas, my dear Mentor, I indeed felt in this stranger a certain something that attracted me to him and left me shaken. But why did you not tell me, before his departure, that it was Odysseus, since you knew him? Why did you allow him to depart without speaking to him and without seeming to know him? What is this mystery, then? Will I always be unfortunate? The angry gods, do they want to hold me like thirsty Tantalus, whom a deceiving water teases, fleeing from his lips? Odysseus, Odysseus, have you escaped me forever? Perhaps I will see him no more. Perhaps the suitors of Penelope will cause him to fall into the ambushes they have prepared for me. At least, if I had followed him, I would die with him. O Odysseus, O Odysseus, if a tempest does not cast you yet again against some reef (for I have everything to fear from enemy Fortune), I tremble with fear that you will only arrive in Ithaca with a fate as gruesome as Agamemnon in Mycenae. But why, dear Mentor, did you envy me my happiness? Now I would be embracing him, I would already be with him in the harbor of Ithaca. We would be fighting to vanquish all our enemies."

Mentor answered, smiling, "You see, my dear Telemachus, how men are made. Here you are completely desolated because you saw your father without recognizing him. What would you not have done yesterday to be assured that he was not dead? Today, you are assured of it with your own eyes, and this assurance, which should fill you with joy, leaves you in bitterness! Thus, the sick heart of mortals always counts for nothing that which it has most desired as soon as it possesses it and is ingenious in tormenting itself about that which it does not yet possess.

"It is to exercise your patience that the gods keep you in suspense like this. You regard this time as wasted but know that it is the most useful of your life—for these difficulties serve to exercise you in the most necessary of all the virtues of those who should command. You must be patient in order to become the master of yourself and other men. Impatience, which appears to be strength and vigor in the soul, is only weakness and impotence in bearing difficulty. The one who does not know how to wait and to suffer is like the one who does not know how to keep quiet about a secret; both lack firmness with regard to self-restraint. He is like a man who races in a chariot, and who does not have a firm enough hand to stop, when he must, his spirited steeds. They no longer obey the bit, they bolt, and the feeble man, from whom they escape, is broken apart in his fall—just as the impatient man is dragged along by his untamed and fierce desires into an abyss of misfortunes. The greater his power, the more calamitous his impatience is to him; he waits for nothing, he does not give himself time to measure anything, he forces everything in order to satisfy himself. He breaks the branches to pick the fruit before it is ripe; he shatters doors rather than wait that they be opened for him; he wants to reap, while the wise plowman sows. All that he does hastily and untimely is done poorly and cannot last, no more than his flighty desires can.

"Such are the foolish projects of a man who believes himself almighty and who delivers himself over to his impatient desires in order to abuse his power. It is to teach you to be patient, my dear Telemachus, that the gods test your patience so and seem to toy with you in a roaming life where they always keep you in uncertainty. The good things that you hope for reveal themselves to you and flee like a light dream that awakening causes to disappear to teach you that the very things one believes he holds in his hands escape in an instant. The wisest lessons of Odysseus will not be as useful to you as his long absence, and the difficulties that you suffered in seeking him.

Then Mentor wanted to put the patience of Telemachus to one last, even harder test. At the moment when the young man was ardently pressing the sailors to hasten the departure, Mentor suddenly stopped him and pushed him to make a great sacrifice to Athena on the shore. Telemachus docilely does what Mentor desires: two altars of grass are erected, the incense smokes, the blood of the victims flows. Telemachus heaves tender sighs to the sky and acknowledges the powerful protection of the goddess.

No sooner was the sacrifice completed than he follows Mentor down the gloomy path of a small neighboring wood. There, he suddenly perceives that the face of his friend is taking on a new shape.

The wrinkles of his brow fade away like shadows disappear when Dawn, with her rose-red fingers, opens the gates of the East and inflames the entire horizon. His deep and austere eyes transform into the blue eyes of a celestial sweetness, filled with a divine flame. His gray and unkempt beard disappears. Noble and proud features, mixed with sweetness and charm, reveal themselves to the dazzled eyes of Telemachus. He recognizes the face of a woman with a complexion smoother than a flower, tender and newly budding in the sun; he sees the whiteness of the lilies mingled with blooming roses. On this face glows an eternal youthfulness with a natural and unadorned majesty. An ambrosial fragrance emanates from her flowing habits. Her habits radiate like the vivid colors with which the sun, rising, paints the somber vaults of the sky and the clouds that it comes to gild.

This deity does not touch the ground. She floats lightly through the air, like a bird parts it with its wings. She holds in her mighty hand a shining lance capable of making the most warlike cities and nations tremble. Even Ares would be frightened by it. Her voice is gentle and restrained, but strong and insinuating. All her words are flaming arrows that pierce young Telemachus' heart and cause him to feel an indescribably delicious sweetness. On her helmet appears the sad bird of Athens, and on her glistening breast the redoubtable aegis. At these signs Telemachus recognizes Athena.

"O goddess," he said, "it is you yourself then who has deigned to guide the son of Odysseus for the love of his father." He wanted to say more, but his voice failed him. His lips tried in vain to express his thoughts that leapt impetuously from the bottom of his heart. The presence of the deity overwhelmed him and he was like a man who, in a dream, is oppressed to the point of losing his breath, and who, through the arduous agitation of his lips, cannot form any speech.

Finally, Athena pronounced these words: "Son of Odysseus, listen to me for the last time. I have instructed no other mortal with as much care as you. I have led you by the hand through shipwrecks, unknown lands, bloody wars, and all the evils that can test the heart of man. I have shown you, through manifest experiences, the true and the false maxims by which one is able to reign. Your errors have been no less useful to you than your misfortunes—for who is the man who can govern wisely, if he has never suffered and if he has never profited from the sufferings his errors have brought him?

"You have filled, like your father, the lands and seas with your sad adventures. Go. You are now worthy of walking in his footsteps. There only remains to you a short and easy crossing to Ithaca, where he is arriving at this moment. Fight along with him; obey him like the least of his subjects. Give thereby the example to others. He will give Antiope to you for a wife, and you will be happy with her for having less sought beauty than wisdom and virtue.

"While you reign, put all your glory in restoring the golden age. Listen to all, believe few people. Be very wary of believing yourself too much. Fear deceiving yourself, but never fear allowing others to see that you have been deceived. Love the peoples. Do your utmost to be loved by them. Fear is necessary when love is lacking, but it must always be used with regret, as the most violent and dangerous remedy. Always consider, from a distance, all the consequences of what you want to undertake. Anticipate the most terrible inconveniences and know that true courage consists of envisioning all perils and scorning them when it becomes necessary. The one who does not want to see them does not have enough courage to tranquilly bear the sight of them. The one who sees them all, who avoids all those that can be avoided, and who aims at the others without emotion, is alone wise and magnanimous.

"Flee softness, splendor, overabundance: show your glory in simplicity. May your virtues and your good deeds be the ornaments of your person and your palace; may they be the guard that surrounds you, and may everyone learn from you what true honor consists of. Never forget that kings do not reign for their own glory but for the good of the peoples. The good that they do multiplies from generation to generation to the most distant posterity. The evils that they do have the same stretch. A poor reign sometimes causes calamity for several centuries.

"Above all, be on guard against your temper. It is an enemy that you will carry with you everywhere until death. It will enter into your counsel and will betray you if you listen to it. Temper causes the most important opportunities to be lost. It brings inclinations and childish aversions, to the detriment of the greatest interests. It causes the greatest affairs to be decided for the smallest reasons. It obscures every talent; lessens courage; renders a man unequal, weak, vile, and insufferable. Fight this enemy.

"Revere the gods, O Telemachus. This reverence is the greatest treasure of the heart of man. With it will come wisdom, justice, peace, joy, pure pleasures, true liberty, sweet abundance, unstained glory.

"I am forsaking you, O son of Odysseus. But my wisdom will not forsake you provided you always feel that you can do nothing without it. It is time that you learned to walk all alone; I only separated from you in Phoenicia and in Salentum to accustom you to being deprived of this sweetness, just as one weans children when it is time to take away milk to give them solid food."

Barely had the goddess finished this speech when she rose into the air and wrapped herself in a cloud of gold and azure, where she disappeared. Telemachus, sighing, stunned, and beside himself, bowed down to the ground, lifting his hands to the sky. Then he went to awaken his companions, hastened to depart, arrived in Ithaca, and recognized his father at the home of loyal Eumaeus.

End of Book XVIII

AFTERWORD

Much *intrigue surrounds* the publication of *Telemachus*- Fénelon may have begun writing the tale as early as 1692, when his charge, the Duc de Bourgogne, was only ten years old. That same year, in recognition of his eloquence and literary excellence, Fénelon was elected to a seat at the prestigious Académie Française with the approval of King Louis XIV. Though forever grateful for the benefices granted him by the king, Fénelon later penned the infamous *Lettre au Louis XIV.* The *Lettre* was an outpouring of criticism and condemnation of the king's absolutist monarchy and his weakness for flattery. In true fénelonian style, the criticism, though stern, was constructive. Discovered after Fénelon's death, there is nothing to indicate that this *Lettre* was ever delivered. There are, however, in the *Lettre* indications of the genesis of Fénelon's teaching objectives with respect to his charge, the young Duke. Many of his aspirations of ideal governance in the *Lettre* are found throughout *Telemachus.*

Fénelon was compelled to leave Versailles in 1695, when he was granted an archbishopric in Cambrai. He nevertheless continued as preceptor to the young Duke as well as his younger brothers. With the publication of his *Maxims of the Saints* in 1698, Fénelon sparked a theological controversy with his former advocate, and the confessor of Louis XIV, Bishop Bossuet. The conflict over the *Maxims* would simmer for almost two years, ultimately boiling over in Rome, with the pope reluctantly condemning twenty-three "unorthodox" maxims in January 1699. Following the papal censure, Louis XIV dismissed Fénelon as preceptor to the royal princes. The illicit publication of *Telemachus* would occur three months later.

As illustrated in Figure 5, *Telemachus* was handwritten and edited by Fénelon. As with all the princes' lessons, scribes would rewrite them. Often the scribes would make clandestine copies and sell them. In this way, many of Fénelon's compositions circulated among the high society of Paris and Versailles. Such was the case with *Telemachus*. Some claimed to have seen a copy of a manuscript as early as 1694. In the fall of 1698, manuscripts of *Telemachus* had begun a "strong run" in Paris due to "a great curiosity." With such a demand, its publication was very tempting, but Fénelon would not consent. The release to the public is generally understood to have happened in this way: a disloyal copyist delivered a copy of the first four books to the widow Barkin, who received a privilege from the king on April 4, 1699 to publish a book entitled *Suite de Odyssey livre de Odyée ou les Avantures de Telemaque, fils de l'Ulysse*. Rumored to be a roman à clef of the French court, it was an overnight sensation in Paris. The printing privilege was quickly revoked and an effort made to acquire all copies. However, copies had already reached Holland and England. By autumn of that year, the Holland bookstore, Moetjens, had reproduced not only the volume originally published by the widow Barkin, but also a four-volume edition. The first English edition appeared in parts, beginning in December 1699.

After being relieved of his preceptorship, Fénelon kept up an informal mentorship of the Duke, who was the hope of all enlightened France. In a marriage arranged by the Treaty of Turin, the Duke wed the Princess of Savoy in 1697. The couple had two sons and were reputedly genuinely affectionate for each other. The Duke became next in line to the throne, upon the death of his father. Six months later, the princess contracted measles. Remaining by her side until she died, the prince caught the disease himself and died six days later at the age of twenty nine. The Duc's oldest son also died from the disease, leaving the younger son, an orphan at the age of two, to be raised by courtiers, first in line to his grandfather, Louis XIV, and the future Louis XV.

Though written for the late Duke, *Telemachus'* popularity across age groups fostered its success for over two centuries. *Telemachus* is said to have been the single most frequently published "children's" book, in the eighteenth century. It has been translated into countless languages. For over three centuries, *Telemachus* has continued to inspire writers, leaders and all lovers of wisdom.

ACKNOWLEDGMENTS

I owe a heartfelt thank you to A. Devlin and D. Hunter for their diligent editing of this translation.

Figure 1 François de Troye, Portrait of the Duc de Bourgogne. Galleria Sabauda.

Figure 2 Bust of François de Salignac de la Mothe-Fénelon. Boston, Museum of Fine Arts.

Figure 3 Bust of King Louis XIV. Washington D.C., National Gallery of Art.

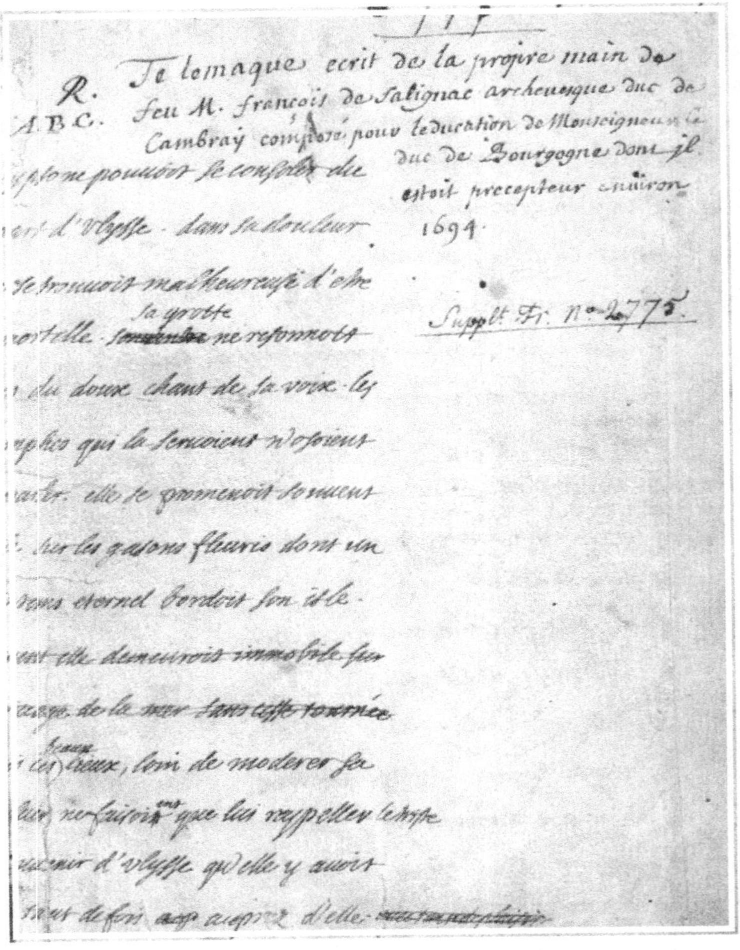

111

R. Telemaque ecrit de la propre main de feu M. françois de Salignac archeuesque duc de Cambray composé pour l'education de Monseigneur le duc de Bourgogne dont il estoit precepteur enuiron 1694.

A.B.C.

Supplt. Fr. N° 2775.

...lypso ne pouuoit se consoler du
...art d'Ulysse dans sa douleur.
...se trouuoit malheureuse d'estre
...ortelle. sa grotte ne resonnoit
...du doux chant de sa voix les
...nphes qui la seruoient n'osoient
...arler. elle se promenoit souuent
...sur les gasons fleuris dont un
...temps eternel bordoit son isle.
...elle demeuroit immobile sur
...riuage de la mer
...ces lieux, loin de moderer sa
...leur, ne faisoient que lui rappeller le triste
...souuenir d'Ulysse qu'elle y auoit
...tant de fois auprès d'elle.

Figure 4 Original manuscript in the hand of Fénelon.

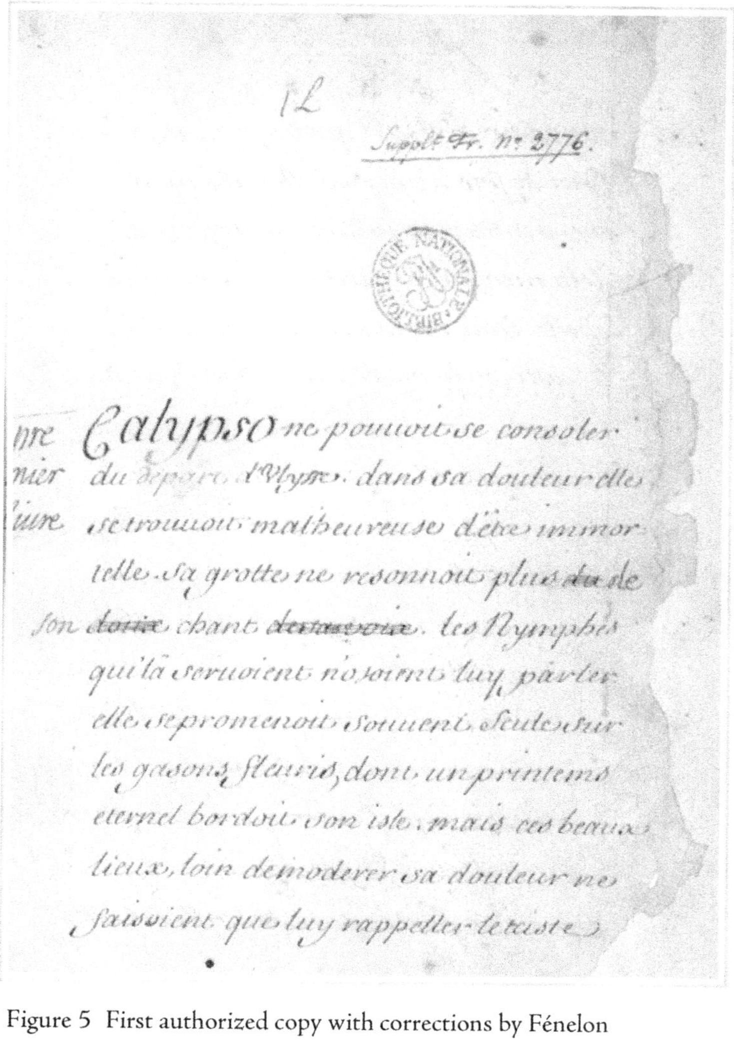
1L

Suppl.t Fr. N.o 2776.

...re Calypso ne pouvoit se consoler
...nier du depart d'Ulysse. dans sa douleur elle
...iure se trouvoit malheureuse d'estre immor-
telle. Sa grotte ne resonnoit plus ~~du~~ de
son ~~doux~~ chant ~~de sa voix~~. les Nymphes
qui la servoient n'osoient luy parler
elle se promenoit souvent seule sur
les gasons fleuris, dont un printems
eternel bordoit son isle. mais ces beaux
lieux, loin de moderer sa douleur ne
faisoient que luy rappeller le triste

Figure 5 First authorized copy with corrections by Fénelon

NOTES ON TRANSLATION

This translation is of Fénelon's handwritten manuscript of *Les Aventures de Télémaque* (*Les Aventures*), penned sometime between 1692 and 1699, which was made available to the public through the Bibliothèque National de France website in January 2021 (Figure 4). This digitized version, along with the first copy, authorized and corrected by Fénelon in 1700 (Figure 5) were used as primary resources. In addition, two twentieth-century French publications of *Les Aventures*, one by Albert Cahen in 1927, and the other by Jacques LeBrun in 1995, provided critical insight into the history of the work, as well as the classical sources on which Fénelon based the education of the prince. With these foundational documents in hand, the primary goals for this translation were threefold: to respect Fénelon's pedagogical lessons in leadership, to preserve the fénelonian style of writing, and to produce a translation as enjoyable to modern readers around the world as it was to the young prince for whom it was written.

More than forty thousand English words derive from French roots. This is in large measure due to the eleventh-century King of England, William the Conqueror, and the consequent influence of the French clergy and noblemen for more than two hundred years. With this in mind, Fénelon's original word choice is respected in this translation when English equivalents exist, and they have aged well. Aged well? Even words lose their vitality over time. For example, the French verb *charmer* (to charm) was used in reference to "casting a magic spell" from the Middle Ages throughout the seventeenth century. Its meaning has weakened over time and may be better translated today as "to enchant," or "to bewitch."

Another area where the word choice will differ from Fénelon is in the names of certain characters from Greco-Roman antiquity. This novel is a spin-off of the Greek poet Homer's epic, *The Odyssey*, and includes over four hundred characters and places, some borrowed, some invented by Fénelon. Writing for his young charge, who had been born and raised within the gates of Versailles, Fénelon sometimes used the Franco-Latin names that would have been familiar to the prince, e.g. Le Bassin de Neptune, Le Bassin de Céres, Le Bassin de Bacchus. In this translation, however, for the sake of clarity and to render *Les Aventures* more harmonious for the modern reader, the original Greek names, e.g. Poseidon for Neptune, are used for all characters, an approach of which Fénelon would have approved:

NOTES ON TRANSLATION

Prenons de tous côtés tout ce qu'il nous faut pour rendre notre langue plus claire, plus précise, plus courte et plus harmonieuse; toute circonlucution affaiblit le discours.

—François Fénelon, *Lettre à L'Academie*, (1714)

"Let us take from all directions all that we must in order to render our language more clear, more precise, more concise, and more harmonious; all circumlocution weakens discourse."

For readers interested in the instances where Fénelon uses Franco-Latin appellations, they are noted with an asterisk in the index to the Provenances of Names.

Syntax. It is well known that syntax (sentence structure) in French varies from that of English. In the interest of preserving the tone, style, and cadence of Fénelon's writing style, his syntax is preserved whenever possible, as long as the meaning is clear. This may require an extra effort on the part of the modern reader, in deference to maintaining the original cadence and tone.

The original text, as illustrated in Figures 4 and 5, did not include the many pagination, punctuation, and paragraphing standards practiced today. For ease of reading, an overlay of modern techniques has been applied when useful to the reading and understanding of the text.

SELECTIVE BIBLIOGRAPHY

Primary Sources—Fénelon manuscripts and period dictionaries

Fénelon, François. *Les Aventures de Télémaque*, c. 1694–1699. Bibliothèque National, Gallica, manuscript 14944, Jan. 24, 2021, Accessed Feb. 12, 2023. *https://gallica.bnf.fr/ark:/12148/btv1b10077186m*

Fénelon, François. *Les Aventures de Télémaque*, c. 1700. Bibliothèque National, Gallica, manuscript 14945 Copy, with corrections in the hand of Fénelon, Oct. 1, 2012, Accessed Feb. 12, 2023. *https://gallica.bnf.fr/ark:/12148/btv1b9064573t/f11.item*

Dictionnaire de L'Académie française 4th Edition. *https://www.cnrtl.fr/definition/academie4/*

Johnson, Samuel. *A Dictionary of the English Language*. 1755, 1773. Edited by Beth Rapp Young, Jack Lynch, William Dorner, Amy Larner Giroux, Carmen Faye Mathes, and Abigail Moreshead. 2021. *https://johnsonsdictionaryonline.com/*

Secondary Sources—French Publications

Fénelon, François, *Les Aventures de Télémaque*, 2 vols. Edited by Albert Cahen. Second ed., Libraries Hachette Boulevard Saint-Germain, 79, 1927. Accessed Feb. 12, 2023. *https://gallica.bnf.fr/ark:/12148/bpt6k51377*

Fénelon, François *Oeuvres*. Edited by Jacques Le Brun. 2 vols. Paris: Gallimard (Pleiade). 1983–97.

——*Les Aventures de Télémaque*, François Fénelon, (1995)., Edited by J. LeBrun. Gallimard (Folio). Original work published in the seventeenth century).

Société d'étude du XVIIe siècle (France). Pierre Sipriot. "XVIIe Siècle : Bulletin de La Société d'étude Du XVIIe Siècle." Gallica, Jan. 1, 1970, Bulletin N°s 12–13-14, pp. 343–366. https://gallica.bnf.fr/ark:/12148/bpt6k9737324z

English Translations of Greek and Latin Classics

Homer, *The Iliad* (c. 800–c. 700 BC) Translated by R. Fagles. Viking, Penguin Classics, NY 1990.

Homer, *The Odyssey* (c. 800–c. 700 BC) Translated by R. Fagles. Penguin Classics, NY 1997.

Hesiod, (c. 800) *Theogony, Works and Days, The Shield of Heracles*, Translated by H. G. Evelyn-White. Alicia Editions, Kindle Edition.

Sappho, (c. 630–c. 570 BC) Translated by A. Poochigian. Penguin Classics, NY 2009.

Sophocles (c. 496–c. 405 BC). *The Complete Sophocles, Vol. II*. Edited by Peter Burian and Alan Shapiro. Oxford University Press, NY 2010.

——*Philoctetes* (409 BC) Translated by Carl Phillips. 2003.

—*The Women of Trachis* (c. 496–405 BC) Translated by C.K. Williams and Gregory W. Dickerson. 1978.

Herodotus. *The Histories* (c. 484–c. 425 BC) Translated by Tom Holland and edited by Paul Cartledge. Penguin Classics Deluxe Edition, NY 2014.

Horace, *The Works of Horace (Odes)* (c. 35 BC) Translated by Christopher Smart. Kindle Edition. 2020.

Virgil, *Aeneid* (c. 29–c. 19 BC) Translated by R. Fagles. Penguin Classics. NY 2008.

Ovid, *Metamorphoses* (c. 43 BC–c. 17 AD) Translated by David Raeburn. Penguin 2004. Kindle Edition.

Pliny the Elder. *Complete Works* (c. 23–c. 79 AD) Translated by John Bostock and Henry Thomas Riley. Delphi Classics, 2015. Kindle Edition.

Pausanias. *Guide to Greece* (c. 110AD–c. 180 AD). Translated by Peter Levi. Penguin Books. NY 1985.

Apollodorus. *The Library* (c. 1 or 2 AD). Translated by James G. Frazier. Loeb Classical Library Volumes 121 & 122. Cambridge, MA, Harvard University Press; London, William Heinemann ltd. 1921.

Modern Translation of The Adventures of Telemachus, including a survey of other British translations

Fénelon, François de Salignac de La Mothe, *The Adventures of Telemachus*, Translated by A. J. B. Cremer. Anastasis Books, London, England, 2023.

Biographies and Commentaries

Little, Katharine Day, *François de Fénelon: Study of a Personality*. Harper & Brothers, NY 1951.

Hillenaar, Henk, *Le secret de Télémaque*. Presses Universitaires de France, Kindle Edition. 1951.

Edmonson, Robert J. and Hal M. Helms (Translators and Editors), *The Complete Fénelon*. Paraclete Press, MA 2008.

Hayes, Kevin J., *The Road to Monticello, The Life and Mind of Thomas Jefferson*. Oxford University Press, NY 2008.

Devillairs, Laurence, *Fénelon Ou Le Génie Méconnu*. Pocket, 12, avenue d'Italie, 75627 Paris 2012.

Hanley, Ryan Patrick, *Fénelon: Moral and Political Writings*, Oxford University Press, NY 2020.

"The ancients had only the books which they themselves wrote, but we have all their books and moreover all those which have been written from the beginning until our time ... Hence, we are like a dwarf perched on the shoulders of a giant. The former sees further than the giant, not because of his own stature but because of the stature of his bearer."

> William of Conches, 1123 Glosses on Priscian's
> Institutiones grammaticae

PROVENANCES OF NAMES

Greek (*Latin equivalents)
Invented ~ *Inspiration
from Ancient Classics*

Acamas, *Iliad, Aeneid*
Acanthus, Invented
Acestes, *Aeneid*
Achelous River, *Iliad, Metamorphoses*
Acheron River, *Odyssey, Philoctetes, Aeneid*
Acherontia, Invented
Achilles, *Iliad, Odyssey, Philoctetes, Aeneid, Metamorphoses*
Achinoe, *Apollodorus*
Achitoas, Invented
Acragas, *Aeneid*
Acroceraunian mountains, *Odes*
Admetus, *Iliad*
Adoam, Invented
Adonis, *Sappho, Metamorphoses*
Adrastus, *Iliad, Aeneid*
Aegis, *Iliad, Aeneid*
Aeneas, *Iliad, Aeneid, Metamorphoses*
Aeolus, *Iliad, Odyssey, Aeneid*
Aetolia, *Iliad, Odyssey,*
Agamemnon, *Iliad, Odyssey, Aeneid, Metamorphoses*
Ajax, *Iliad, Odyssey, Philoctetes, Aeneid, Metamorphoses*
Alcaeus, Invented ~ *Sappho, Odes*
Alcides, *Aeneid*
Alcinous, *Odyssey*
Alcmena, *Iliad, Odyssey, Metamorphoses*
Algidus Mountain, *Odes*
Alpheus River, *Iliad, Odyssey, Theogony*
Amathus, *Aeneid*
Amphimachus, Invented ~ *Iliad*
Amphitrite, *Odyssey*
Anchises, *Iliad, Aeneid*
Antilochus, *Iliad, Odyssey*
Antiope, Invented ~ *Odyssey*
Antiphates, *Iliad, Odyssey, Aeneid*
Apennines, *Aeneid*
Aphrodite (*Venus), *Odyssey, Aeneid, Metamorphoses*

Apollo, *Iliad, Odyssey, Aeneid, Metamorphoses*
Apulia, Apulians, *Aeneid*
Arabs, *Aeneid*
Arachne, *Metamorphoses*
Arcesius, *Odyssey*
Archidamus, *Pausanias*
Ares (*Mars), *Iliad, Odyssey, Aeneid, Metamorphoses*
Argonauts, *Odyssey, Aeneid*
Argos, *Iliad, Odyssey, Aeneid*
Ariadne, *Iliad, Odyssey*
Arion, Invented ~ *Iliad*
Aristodemus, Invented ~ *Pausanias*
Aristogiton, Invented ~ *Pausanias*
Arpi, *Aeneid*
Artemis (*Diana), *Iliad, Odyssey, Aeneid*
Asclepius, *Iliad, Philoctetes, Aeneid, Metamorphoses*
Astarbe, Invented
Astraea, *Hesiod, Eclogues*
Atalanta, *Metamorphoses*
Athena (*Minerva), *Iliad, Odyssey, Aeneid, Metamorphoses*
Athens, *Iliad, Odyssey*
Atlas, *Odyssey, Aeneid, Metamorphoses*
Atreidae, *Iliad, Odyssey, Aeneid*
Atreus, *Iliad, Odyssey, Aeneid*
Attica, *Pausanias*
Atys, *Aeneid*
Aufidus River, *Aeneid*
Aulon Mountain, *Odes*
Avernus Lake, *Aeneid*
Babylonians, *Pausanias*
Baetica, *Pausanias*
Baetis River, *Pausanias*
Baleazar, Invented
Barbarians, Invented
Bellerophon, *Iliad*
Belus, *Aeneid*
Bocchoris, Invented
Brindisi, *Strabo*
Bruttii, Bruttians, *Diodorus*
Butis, Invented
Cacus, *Aeneid*
Callimachus, Invented
Caledonian boar, *Hesiod, Metamorphoses*
Calypso, *Odyssey*
Caphereus, promontory of, *Aeneid*
Caria, Carians, *Iliad, Aeneid*
Carpathus, Carpathians, *Aeneid*
Carthage, *Aeneid*
Castor, *Iliad, Odyssey, Aeneid, Metamorphoses*
Cayster River, *Iliad*
Cecrops, *Strabo, Metamorphoses*
Centaur, *Iliad, Odyssey, Philoctetes, Aeneid*
Cerberus, *Aeneid*
Charon, *Euripides, Aeneid*
Charybdis, *Odyssey, Aeneid, Metamorphoses*

PROVENANCES OF NAMES

Chimera, *Iliad, Aeneid*
Cilicia, *Iliad*
Circe, *Odyssey, Aeneid, Metamorphoses*
Cleanthes, Invented
Cleomenes, Invented ~ king of Sparta
Clytemnestra, *Iliad, Odyssey, Philoctetes*
Cocytus, *Aeneid*
Colchis, *Herodotus*
Crantor, Invented ~ *Metamorphoses*
Crete, Cretans, *Iliad, Odyssey, Aeneid*
Crotona, Crotoniates, *Pausanias*
Ctesilas, Invented
Cyclops, *Odyssey, Theogony Aeneid*
Cyprus, Cypriots, *Iliad, Odyssey, Aeneid*
Cythera, *Iliad, Odyssey, Aeneid*
Daedalus, *Iliad, Aeneid, Metamorphoses*
Daunians of Apulia—*Strabo*
Danaids, *Metamorphoses*
Danaus, *Iliad*
Dawn (*Aurora), *Iliad, Odyssey Aeneid, Metamorphoses*
Death, *Iliad, Odyssey, Aeneid*
Deianira (*Daïanira), *Philoctetes, Metamorphoses*
Demeter (*Ceres), *Iliad, Odyssey, Aeneid Metamorphoses*
Demoleon, *Iliad*
Demophantes, Invented
Desert of Oasis, *Herodotus*
Deucalion, *Iliad, Odyssey, Metamorphoses*,
Dido, *Aeneid*
Dioclides, Invented
Diomedes, *Iliad, Odyssey, Philoctetes, Aeneid, Metamorphoses*
Dionysus (*Bacchus), *Iliad, Odyssey Euripides, Aeneid, Metamorphoses*
Diophanes, Invented
Dioscore, Invented
Discord, *Aeneid*
Dog Star, *Iliad, Aeneid*
Dolopia, Dolopes, *Iliad, Aeneid*
Dreams, *Iliad*
Dulichium Island of, *Iliad, Odyssey, Aeneid*
Earth, Mother of the Gods, *Odyssey, Philoctetes, Aeneid*
Echinades, *Iliad*
Echo, *Metamorphoses*
Egypt, Egyptians, *Odyssey, Aeneid*
Egyptius, *Apollodorus*
Elysian Fields, *Odyssey, Aeneid*
Enna, *Cicero*

Enyo (*Bellona), *Iliad*, *Aeneid*
Epirus, Epirotes, *Aeneid*
Erebus, *Odyssey*, *Aeneid*
Erichthonius (*Erysichthon), *Iliad*, *Metamorphoses*
Eros (*Love, Cupid), *Aeneid*, *Metamorphoses*
Eryx, Invented ~ *Aeneid*,
Ethiopia, Ethiopians, *Odyssey*, *Aeneid*
Etruria, Etruscans, *Aeneid*
Euboea, *Iliad*, *Odyssey*, *Philoctetes*, *Aeneid*
Eucharis, Invented
Eumaeus, *Odyssey*
Eunesimus, Invented
Euphorion, Invented
Europa, *Iliad*, *Aeneid*, *Metamorphoses*
Eurotas River, *Aeneid*
Eurydice, *Odyssey*, *Metamorphoses*
Eurymachus, Invented ~ *Odyssey*
Eurymedes, Invented
Fates, *Iliad*, *Odyssey*, *Aeneid*
Fauni, *Aeneid*
Fortune, *Aeneid*
Furies, *Iliad*, *Odyssey*, *Aeneid*
Galesus River, *Odes*
Ganymede, *Iliad*, *Aeneid*, *Metamorphoses*
Garganus Mountain, *Aeneid*
Gibraltar, Isle of, *Pausanias*
Gibraltar, Strait of, *Pausanias*
Golden Age, *Theogony*
Graces, *Iliad*, *Odyssey*
Great Bear, *Iliad*, *Odyssey*, *Aeneid*
Greece, *Aeneid*
Hades (*Pluto), *Iliad*, *Odyssey*, *Philoctetes*, *Aeneid*
Hazael, Invented
Hebe, *Iliad*, *Odyssey*
Hebros River (*Hebrus), *Aeneid*
Hecate or Artemis (*Hecate, *Diana) *Iliad*, *Aeneid* *Metamorphoses*
Hector, *Iliad*, *Philoctetes*, *Aeneid*
Hegesippe, Invented
Helen, *Iliad*, *Odyssey*, *Aeneid*
Helenus, *Iliad*, *Philoctetes*, *Aeneid*
Helopdorus, Invented
Hephaestus (*Vulcan), *Iliad*, *Odyssey*, *Philoctetes*, *Aeneid*,*Metamorphoses*
Heracles (*Hercules), *Iliad*, *Odyssey*, *Philoctetes*, *Aeneid*,*Metamorphoses*
Hermes (*Mercury), *Iliad*, *Odyssey*, *Philoctetes*, *Aeneid*, *Metamorphoses*
Hesperia, Hesperian, *Aeneid*
Hesperides, *Aeneid*, *Metamorphoses*
Hileus, Invented

PROVENANCES OF NAMES

Himera, Himerans, *Pausanias*
Hippias, *Pausanias*
Hippocoon, *Iliad, Aeneid*
Hippolytus, Invented ~ *Aeneid, Metamorphoses*
Hippomachus, Invented ~ *Iliad*
Hippomenes, *Metamorphoses*
Hydra of Lerna, *Philoctetes, Aeneid*
Hylas, *Theocritus*
Icarius, *Odyssey*
Idalium, *Aeneid*
Idomeneus, *Iliad, Odyssey, Aeneid*
Ilium, *Iliad, Odyssey, Aeneid*
Inachus, *Aeneid, Metamorphoses*
Iole, *The Women of Trachis*
Iphicles, Invented
Iris, *Iliad, Aeneid, Metamorphoses*
Ismarus Mountain, *Odyssey, Aeneid*
Italy, *Aeneid*
Ithaca, Ithacans, *Iliad, Odyssey, Aeneid*
Ixion, *Iliad, Philoctetes, Aeneid*
Joazar, Invented
Lacedaemon, Lacedaemonians, *Iliad, Odyssey*
Laconia, Laconians, Invented
Laertes, *Iliad, Odyssey, Philoctetes, Aeneid*
Laestrygonians, *Odyssey*
Laomedon, *Iliad, Philoctetes, Aeneid, Metamorphoses*
Lapiths, *Iliad, Odyssey, Aeneid*
Lemnos, *Iliad, Odyssey, Philoctetes, Aeneid*
Lesbos, Lesbians, *Iliad, Odyssey*
Leto (*Latona), *Iliad, Odyssey, Theogony, Aeneid, Metamorphoses*
Leucata, *Aeneid*
Leucothea, Invented ~ *Odyssey, Metamorphoses*
Lichas (*Lychas), *The Women of Trachis, Aeneid, Metamorphoses*
Linus, *Theogony*
Liris, *Aeneid*
Locrian, *Iliad, Aeneid*
Lucanian, Invented
Lycia, Lycians, *Iliad, Aeneid*
Lycomedes, *Iliad, Philoctetes*
Lydia, Lydians, *Aeneid*
Machaon, Invented ~ *Iliad, Aeneid*
Maenads (*Bacchantes), *Aeneid*
Malachon, Invented
Mandurians, *Pliny II*
Memphis, *Pausanias*
Menecrates, Invented

Menelaus, *Iliad*, *Odyssey*,
Philoctetes, *Aeneid*
Mentor, Invented ~ *Iliad*,
Odyssey
Meriones, Invented ~ *Iliad*
Messapia of Apulia,
Messapians, *Aeneid*
Metapontum, Invented
Metophis, Invented
Metrodorus, Invented
Minos, *Iliad*, *Odyssey*,
Aeneid, *Metamorphoses*
Morpheus, *Metamorphoses*
Mount Etna, *Aeneid*
Mount Ida, *Iliad*, *Aeneid*
Mount Lebanon, Invented
Mount Oeta, *Philoctetes*
Muse, *Iliad*, *Odyssey*,
Aeneid
Mycenae, *Iliad*, *Odyssey*,
Philoctetes, *Aeneid*
Nabopharsan, Invented
Naiads, *Odyssey*
Narbal, Invented
Narcissus, *Metamorphoses*
Nauplius, *Apollodorus*
Nausicrates, Invented
Naxos, *Aeneid*
Nebrodes, *Livy*
Nemean Lion, *Theogony*,
Aeneid
Nemesis, *Theogony*
Neoptolemus, *Iliad*, *Odyssey*,
Philoctetes, *Aeneid*
Nereids, *Iliad*
Nereus, *Iliad*, *Aeneid*

Nessus, *Philoctetes*,
Metamorphoses
Nestor, *Iliad*, *Odyssey*,
Philoctetes, *Metamorphoses*
Nicostrates, *Pausanias*
Nile the River god,
Apollodorus
Nile the River, *Odyssey*,
Aeneid
Nilus, Invented
Nireus, *Iliad*
No, Invented
Nosophugus, Invented
Ocean, *Iliad*, *Odyssey*,
Aeneid
Odysseus (*Ulysses), *Iliad*,
Odyssey, *Philoctetes*,
Aeneid *Metamorphoses*
Oebalians, Invented
Olympus, *Iliad*, *Odyssey*,
Philoctetes, *Aeneid*
Omphale, *The Women of
Trachis*
Orestes, *Iliad*, *Odyssey*,
Aeneid
Orpheus, *Aeneid*,
Metamorphoses
Paean, *Pausanias*
Palaemon, *Pausanias*
Pallas, *Iliad*, *Odyssey*,
Aeneid
Pan, *Aeneid*,
Metamorphoses
Pandora, Pandora's Box,
Theogony
Paphos, *Odyssey*, *Aeneid*,
Metamorphoses

Paris, *Iliad, Philoctetes, Aeneid, Metamorphoses*
Patroclus, *Iliad, Odyssey*
Peleus, *Iliad, Odyssey, Philoctetes, Metamorphoses*
Peloponnese, *Pausanias*
Pelusium Invented
Penelope, *Odyssey*
Periander, Invented ~ *Pausanias*
Persephone (*Proserpina), *Iliad, Odyssey, Aeneid, Metamorphoses*
Petilia, *Aeneid*
Peucetians of Apulia, *Pausanias*
Phadael, Invented
Phaeacians, *Odyssey, Aeneid*
Phalantus, *Pausanias*
Pharos, *Odyssey*
Pherecides, *Pausanias*
Philocles, *Pausanias*
Philoctetes, *Iliad, Odyssey, Philoctetes, Aeneid*
Phlegethon River, *Iliad*
Phocis, *Iliad*
Phoebus Apollo, *Iliad, Odyssey, Aeneid*
Phoenicians, *Iliad, Odyssey, Aeneid*
Phoenix, *Iliad, Philoctetes, Aeneid*
Pholoe, Invented ~ *Aeneid*
Phrygia, Phrygians, *Iliad, Aeneid*
Phthians, *Iliad, Odyssey*

Pillars of Heracles, *Pausanias*
Pisistratus, *Odyssey*
Plowman, *Odyssey*
Podalirius, Invented ~ *Iliad, Aeneid*
Poias, *Odyssey, Philoctetes*
Polycletes, Invented
Polydamas, *Iliad*
Polydeuces (*Pollux), *Iliad, Odyssey, Aeneid*
Polymenes, Invented
Polyphemus, Iliad, *Odyssey, Aeneid, Metamorphoses*
Polytropus, Invented
Poseidon (*Neptune), *Iliad, Odyssey, Aeneid, Metamorphoses*
Priam, *Iliad, Odyssey, Philoctetes, Aeneid, Metamorphoses*
Protesilas, Invented ~ *Iliad*
Pterelas, Invented
Pygmalion, Invented ~ *Aeneid, Metamorphoses*
Pylos, Pylian, *Iliad, Odyssey*
Rhesus, *Iliad*
Rhodes, Rhodians, *Iliad*
Rhodope Mountains, *Metamorphoses*
Ruin, *Iliad*
Rumor, *Odyssey, Aeneid*
Salapian, Invented
Salentum, Salentines, (*Sallentine, Salentino, Sallentini), *Aeneid*

Samos, Samian, *Iliad*, *Aeneid*
Saturn (*Saturnus), *Aeneid*, *Metamorphoses*
Satyr, *Pausanias*
Scylla, *Odyssey*, *Aeneid*, *Metamorphoses*
Scyros, *Iliad*, *Odyssey*, *Philoctetes*, *Aeneid*
Scythians, *Pausanias*
Semele, *Iliad*, *Metamorphoses*
Sesostris, Invented ~ *Pausanias*
Sicily, Sicilians, *Odyssey*, *Aeneid*
Sigeum, *Philoctetes*, *Aeneid*
Silenus, *Metamorphoses*
Simois, *Iliad*, *Aeneid*
Siponto, Sipontines, *Pausanias*
Sirens, *Odyssey*, *Aeneid*
Sisyphus, *Iliad*, *Odyssey*
Sleep, *Iliad*, *Aeneid*
Sophronymus, Invented
Sparta, *Iliad*, *Odyssey*, *Philoctetes*, *Aeneid*
Spercheios River, *Iliad*, *Philoctetes*
Stygian Marsh, *Aeneid*
Styx, *Iliad*, *Odyssey*, *Aeneid*
Sun (*Sol), *Aeneid*, *Metamorphoses*
Sybarites, *Aeneid*
Sychaeus, *Aeneid*
Syria, Syrians, *Odyssey*
Tantalus, *Odyssey*

Tarentum, Tarentins, *Aeneid*
Tartarus, *Iliad*, *Aeneid*
Telamon, *Iliad*, *Odyssey*, *Metamorphoses*
Telemachus, *Iliad*, *Odyssey*
Termosiris, Invented
Termutis, Invented
Thebes, *Iliad*, *Odyssey*, *Aeneid*
Theophanes, Invented
Thersites, *Iliad*, *Philoctetes*
Theseus, *Iliad*, *Odyssey*, *Philoctetes*, *Aeneid*, *Metamorphoses*
Thessaly, *Theogony*
Thetis, *Iliad*, *Odyssey*, *Aeneid*, *Metamorphoses*
Thrace, Thracians, *Iliad*, *Odyssey*, *Aeneid*
Thyestes, *Iliad*, *Odyssey*
Timocrates, Invented
Tiphys, *Pausanias*
Tityus, *Odyssey*, *Aeneid*
Topha, Invented
Trachis, *Iliad*, *The Women of Trachis*
Traumaphilus, Invented
Triptolemus, *Pausanias*
Triton, *Aeneid*, *Metamorphoses*
Troy, Trojans, *Iliad*, *Odyssey*, *Philoctetes*, *Aeneid*
Tydeus, *Iliad*, *Odyssey*, *Philoctetes*, *Aeneid*

PROVENANCES OF NAMES

Tyre, Tyrians, *Herodotus, Aeneid*
Underworld, *Iliad, Odyssey, Aeneid*
Venuse, *Pliny the Elder III*
Xanthus River, *Iliad, Aeneid*
Zachynthus, Island of, *Iliad, Odyssey, Aeneid*
Zeus (*Jupiter), Olympian Zeus, *Iliad, Odyssey, Philoctetes, Aeneid, Metamorphoses*

ABOUT THE AUTHOR

François de Salignac de la Mothe-Fénelon

Fénelon was born August 6, 1651, at the chateau de Fénelon, the next oldest of four children from the second marriage of a minor nobleman in the Perigord region of France. He lived in the ancestral home until the age of twelve, where he was initiated into the study of ancient classical scholars. He continued his education at the University of Cahors, then the Collège du Plessis, in Paris. Having lost his father early in his childhood, his uncle, the Marquis de Fénelon, convinced him to enter into the seminary of Saint Sulpice. Ordained a priest at the age of twenty-four, he devoted the next fourteen years to religious studies and pedagogical theories where he distinguished himself as an advocate for the education of girls. His *Traité de L'Éducation des Filles (Treaty on the Education of Girls)* was published when he was thirty-six years old. Sometime afterward, the Duc de Beauvilliers was named governor of the royal Children of France. The Duke convinced King Louis XIV to nominate Fénelon as preceptor to the oldest grandchild, the Duc de Bourgogne along with his two brothers.

For his young charges, Fénelon directed and prepared curriculum, including the *Fables*, followed by the *Dialogues des Morts (Dialogues of the Dead)*, and ultimately *Les Aventures de Telemaque (The Adventures of Telemachus)*.

Admitted to the prestigious Académie Français in 1693, he received from the king in 1694 the abbey of Saint-Valery, followed by the archbishopric of Cambrai in 1695. As archbishop he was compelled to spend nine months of the year in his parish at Cambrai and, continuing as preceptor to the young princes, three at Versailles.

In 1697, Fénelon published another masterpiece, *l'Explication des Maximes des Saints sur la vie intérieure (Explication of the maxims of the saints on the interior life)*. His advocate-cum-adversary, Bishop Bossuet challenged them as unorthodox and, with King Louis XIV's approval, convinced the pope to condemn several of the maxims.

Despite the considerable income afforded Fénelon by his responsibilities as abbot and archbishop, he died penniless in Cambrai following a carriage accident in 1715. He had expended all his resources in attending to his parish. His legacy of spiritual growth, selflessness and ideals of leadership live on in his writings and his admirers.

Made in the USA
Monee, IL
15 October 2025